Praise For Chasing Solace

"The factory caverns on this Lost Ship are much more deadly and horrific than before. I'm in awe of the imagination needed to create this. Expect late nights and longer reading sessions. Simply outstanding."

Jera's Jamboree

"This book surpassed all my expectations. I couldn't put it down. There are incredible scenes, some that will keep you on the edge of your seat, others that will take your breath away with the intricate detail and beauty of the narrative."

Pink Quill Books

"This is very much a character driven novel, with Opal's voice at its core. It's full of action, pathos and human emotion. It's also stunning and I loved it!"

Brew and Books Review

"The lost ship in this book has been taken to the next level, with some serious creep factors that made for a fascinating and eerie setting. My favorite part was the relationship between Opal and Athene, with conflict hitting in multiple and unexpected layers. That relationship is what makes this series so unique."

The Behrg

CHASING SOLACE

LOST SOLACE BOOK 2

KARL DRINKWATER

ORGANIC APOCALYPSE

Organic Apocalypse Copyright Manifesto

CHASING SOLACE

BEGINNING

50 ...

Space is not empty if you have eyes to see. Senses to detect. And patience. Much patience. Then space is not space. Space is full.

Galaxies dance in clusters, each individually shaped, each differently composed, each with their own history. They are masses of stars, and pre-stars, and post-stars, spinning around each other, unwilling to be alone.

Focus. One of the galaxies can be picked out amongst the millions. It is relatively flat from the side, though the centre rises to a globe-like diffuse conglomeration. Viewed from the top we see swirls radiating from that centre, curved around each other by rotation at the ponderous cosmic scale. They look like they want to hug each other, but never can.

If you have powerful eyes then the individual stars can be perceived, burning in all the nuclear colours, red- or blue-shifted from any fixed point. Such as this point, further in, where a vessel moves through this space-that-is-not-space, this hard vacuum fullness of dust, plasma, electromagnetic radiation, particles, and much more. It is a flattened and non-reflective dark ship, revealing more detail as we zoom in, observe, and note that it is relatively small as these things go, and has no markings, no windows, no obvious weapons. Just calming red glows from the torsion drive outlets as it thrusts towards a destination in silence; exactly the same red as a late-stage main sequence star. The largest and the smallest fires have something in common, though neither has the intelligence to see it.

If detection senses are powerful enough to pass advanced shielding they would find a cramped but space-efficient interior, and a narrow walkway in its centre, and an organic intelligence pacing up and down and communicating with an inorganic intelligence that embodies the whole craft.

PLANNING

... 49 ...

"That's it?" asked Opal. "Our best plan?" She wore an on-board jumpsuit but stayed barefoot. She liked the hard metallic feel on her soles. Resistance helped her focus, though the lower-than-average gravity meant her footsteps weren't as satisfyingly solid on the walkway as she'd wish.

She reached the end, by the closed-off engine section, so span smoothly on her heel, and strode back towards the control screens. There was no room for deviation from her closed loop: the right was packed with her bunk, shower, and fabricator; her left was lined with the airlock and weapons cabinets. The small space remaining was all too reminiscent of military prisons.

"Correct, it is the best plan. I've calculated it against the alternatives." Athene's confident voice came from no fixed point. It filled the air from a multitude of pinpoint speakers embedded in the hull. Opal was still getting used to Athene's new, adult persona. "I think the risks of us being destroyed are within acceptable limits."

Opal shook her head, but couldn't help smiling too. "Acceptable, my arse," she said. "I don't have a backup version."

"At present, neither do I."

"So now we're in it together."

"We always were."

"Stop it! You're too good at dissipating my anger, and sometimes I need to hold on to that."

"I understand. Should I electrify the floor grating? That would help you stay angry."

"Don't you dare." Opal gave the evil eye to a section of wall. Athene would be watching from a number of interior cameras. "Is there really no way to just Null-jump into the core systems?"

"Unfortunately not. The second Lost Ship's coordinates place it in the heart of mil-space, and we can't make it in time unless we take a direct route, which means exiting the Null at a UFS militarised node. All Cordon nodes are guarded, with dispersed scan glitter and fast armed responses. And they're going to be looking for us. The probability of detection is too high. If we are to have a chance of sneaking through then we need a good distraction and we need supplies. And this is the nearest suitable place to acquire them."

"It just seems dangerous to gather supplies *here* when we're trying to *minimise* interaction with Mil-Com."

"I do not think that is your real objection."

Opal said nothing, just continued to pace.

"It is because it is a Genitor base," Athene added.

Opal was passing her bunk. She ceased her obsessive patrol and climbed up, sitting on the edge with shoulders hunched. "No-one knows what goes on in them," she said. "Not grunts or civvies, anyway. But the rumours ... always been used as a kind of bogeyman."

"I understand. I have very little information either. I am only aware that the base has the supplies we need because I intercepted off-site requisition requests. But if we do this, we will know more. And we will have the means to proceed. To pass the Cordon. To find the Lost Ship. To locate your sister."

"Still, going in without my Eternal Warrior suit ..."

"I would not suggest my plan unless I was confident I could do it, and keep you safe. This you know."

Opal sighed. "Fine. We'll do it."

"Maybe I can sweeten the deal for you. While we're there I could also use the cloning vats to nurture extra nuvosomatic cells, to repair your skin and nerve tissue damage."

Opal hadn't considered that. Normally, cloned body tissue was the preserve of the wealthy, because it was the most expensive, but also most reliable, of the four tissue-replacement options. Cloning whole beings was inherently unstable, and cloned consciousness was a failure, but non-sentient bodies and parts with full implant compatibility had become a luxury medical option.

"Any downsides to that?" Opal asked.

"We won't need longer on the infiltration because we'll already be using the base constructors, but there would be biological downtime afterwards as I integrated the repairs to your flesh."

"I can't risk not being at full performance when we get to the Lost Ship. Gather the supplies just in case, but my minor damage can wait. I'll think about it when we've got my sister." Opal stroked a shiny scar on her arm, the raised ridge a paler colour than the darker flesh around it. One of many marks on her body. "Or maybe not. It's who I am."

The planet filled the holographic viewscreen in shades of white and grey. At this distance fracture lines appeared across one hemisphere like tiger stripes.

"Exidris 3," said Athene. "Zero point eight seven standard gravity; unbreathable but non-toxic atmosphere. It has a high albedo of zero point seven four due to the reflective ice shell that coats the entire planet."

"So it's a frozen rock?"

"No. It is stranger than that. There are oceans beneath the ice crust."

"How thick is the ice?"

"Kilometres thick in most places. So thick that light never reaches the sub-surface oceans."

"Life?"

"Apart from the human colonists, there are records of large deep-sea life forms below the ice. Little is known of them because the environment down there was too dangerous to explore, making it economically unviable."

"Sounds creepy. How come the waters don't all freeze?"

"There is a warm convection layer created by tidal forces from the large moons, with further warmth due to radioactive decay. There are also hydrothermal vents in the rock mantle further down which, along with the various salts, keep it above freezing. The planetary base uses deep-sunk extraction rods for heat and most of its energy needs, backed up by a small reactor." The screen zoomed in on the grey texture until features gradually resolved, and a pinprick became a small base. Athene highlighted those buildings whose functions she could identify.

"It's convenient for us, but strange for UFS Central to build on this place in the arse-end of nowhere," said Opal. "An inhospitable location away from trade lanes. Any major resources?"

"No. Unless you count the isolation."

"Hmm. Could be on to something. For some purposes, isolation can be attractive."

"We'll know more once you're in."

Athene descended in full stealth mode. This outpost's scanning equipment shouldn't be advanced enough to detect her, especially as she aimed at a location outside the base perimeter. There would be a short trek for Opal, and it was going to be damn cold, but it was the safest option.

During the planetfall Opal got herself ready. Athene had fabricated a pale paste and Opal spread it on the parts of her body that wouldn't be covered by clothing, toning down the dark brown skin to an off-white colour. It wouldn't fool anyone up close, but might pass a casual or distant glance. The official Genitor cults didn't allow anyone with a low grade category to achieve senior positions. Without the disguise, Opal would attract far too much attention. She then heat-bonded an additional skin layer to her palm, another thing Athene's tank of nano-constructors had made. Finally she dressed as warmly as she could in overalls, heavy boots, and a self-heating hooded jacket. It would have to do. In Opal's hasty theft of Athene there'd been no time to take anything that wasn't already on board, and there'd been no opportunities since, either.

Opal opened the weapons cabinet and pocketed the small device Athene had made. She eyed the wealth of weapons sourly. "Can't I just take one gun?"

"No."

"Just a teeny one?"

"All entrances will include scanners for weapons. Our priority is to gather what we need *without* triggering any alarms, so that no-one ever knows we were here. Then we retain the advantage. If you stick to my plan, and things here are based on standard designs, there will be no need for combat."

"*If.* I hate that word."

The gravity increased as they descended and her limbs felt an unfamiliar heaviness after so long in space. She practised jabs and kicks, knowing that Athene would be watching and itching to repeat the "no combat" rule, but even that didn't provide any satisfaction. There was an undercurrent in her blood, an unfamiliar nervousness that bravado couldn't shake. She sank into a control seat and brought up exterior views as they came in to land, each screen the filtered result of various external micro-cameras.

She'd expected billowing snow, but instead the whiteness seemed ghostly still. Jagged mountains of ice rose all around them as Athene settled with a gentle thump in a shadowed and sheltered hollow which wouldn't be visible from the main base or likely lookout points.

Opal wouldn't have the benefit of an armoured suit, or a holographic HUD giving her information and directions, but she slipped on a small breathing mask that covered her mouth and an earpiece that would let Athene keep in touch with her via encoded channels that switched wavelength many times a second. Without knowing what to look for, anything listening in would just pick up background noise.

"Good to go," said Opal, moving to the airlock and stretching her arms and legs in readiness.

Freezing

... 48 ...

The cold in this shadowed valley stung the exposed parts of her face. Her eyes watered so much that the white pastes smeared into chalky speckles. She kept her hands jammed into the jacket pockets, with the heating level set to max, and the hood fastened tight over her ears.

"Minus seven point two degrees C," Athene said into her ear.

"Feels colder." Opal's teeth chattered as she spoke.

The single-person airlock closed silently and smoothly, leaving no visible trace in the streamlined hull. Athene's appearance had changed significantly since Opal first stole her from the military. Opal had known that Athene had the ability to restructure slightly. Some of the internal frame and struts had limited mechanical manoeuvrability, normally a slow process. Her outer skin was complex, with breach-repairing nanogel as one of the internal layers. In theory it could be stretched, broken down, and reapplied over time. The features had been planned into her design but without any immediate purpose – it was more a plan for the future, when advanced versions of Athene's prototype would use it to enable the addition of cargo, weapons, and equipment.

But Athene had already gone beyond that and turned it into an art form, using the base tools in ways her designers would not have expected. She'd found a way to repurpose the nanogel to change supporting connections, to alter her outer shape for different purposes, and to do it relatively quickly and efficiently. At the moment she was a flattened stealth shape based around principles of continuous curvature to minimise scan reflection, with an additional coating of a radar-absorbent compound. Athene had been happy to boast about all her new ideas, and continuous changes to improve her efficiency, speed, shielding, tools, and weapons. It was scary what she could do. Earlier she'd boasted that her outer shell now detected all forms of scanning more efficiently, intercepted them and reacted with out-of-phase emissions that could make her invisible to many systems.

None of that made any difference to the interior though. It was the same cramped space surrounded by an armoured shell that kept Opal alive and separate from the death of space.

So much for standing here shivering in the nose-stinging cold. She headed down a cave-like passage between jagged rocks which led away from Athene and onto a flatter, open area. Across that, when Opal squinted, she could just about see one of the external buildings of this spread-out base. The scattered layout was a lucky outcome of there being no competition for land here. If it had been more densely-packed then their plan wouldn't work at all. As it was, Athene predicted this solitary outbuilding would be a subsidiary weather and geothermal monitoring station that would be connected to the base's closed network. There had been no infrared traces going back and forth, so hopefully it wasn't regularly staffed.

Opal hunched in on herself and kept her jaw clenched, occasionally wiping her teary eyes then jamming the hand back into the pockets. The air from the breather had a bitter chemical taste to it. She focussed on moving quickly, to keep generating heat, and in her haste she slipped on a glassy uneven surface that reminded her of water frozen as it poured. It was a hard smack, and an ignoble slide along on her back for a few metres.

"Are you injured?" asked Athene, her voice sounding tinny in the low-res earpiece.

"Just my pride," replied Opal, standing carefully on this treacherous surface and dusting frozen white crystals from her jacket.

From then on she looked down as she walked, careful of her footing. Athene monitored her location and gave directions whenever Opal drifted off-course. But she still felt alone and vulnerable out here.

"Most of the ice I walk on is white," Opal said, just to make conversation. "But it's black as I get nearer to the base, with white lines in it. Impurities of some kind? Something to do with what the base is used for?"

"The opposite," said Athene. "The black parts are the pure ice. There are no trapped bubbles or trace elements to make it opaque."

"Wouldn't that make it clear?"

"It is, Opal. The blackness is the sub-surface ocean below you. You're seeing straight down into it."

"Then the white lines ..."

"Cracks in the ice."

A readjustment of perspective, then a sudden sense of vertigo. The feeling she got during external manoeuvres in space, when it looked like you could drop forever into inhospitable blackness.

"You have slowed down," said Athene. "You do not need to worry. The ice is kilometres thick. It's just an optical illusion that makes it look like only a few centimetres separate you from the deadly black waters swirling beneath your feet."

"You're saying that on purpose. You know I hate deep water."

"A crust that can support a base and thermo-extraction rods can easily support you. It is solid ground. More solid than many of the unknowns we will face in our risky endeavours."

"I don't like the thought of unidentified giant aquatic creatures either."

"You have survived worse in the past, and you must do so again. You are a warrior. And if you hear earthquake-like booms it probably won't be an alien behemoth bursting up through the ice to consume you, it will merely be ice quakes as frozen materials expand while ... wait. I'm picking up movement."

Opal tensed, looking down between the obscuring cracks for looming signs of the leviathan forcing its way up to get her.

"No, ahead. A combat drone on patrol. Airborne, with low-signature enhancements that meant I could not detect it when it was further away."

In contrast to her imagination, a combat drone was a relief. "Just the one?"

"So far. It is unexpected."

"Shall I return?"

"No. It is making a line towards you. Keep walking. You must not do anything that will engage its suspicious investigation sub-routines. If you ignore it then it should fly by. If I was nearer, or you were in the warsuit, I'd scan and model it and virtualise its systems for better prediction of behaviour. I hate being at a distance from you."

"If it opens fire, I'm dead, right?"

"I am ready to lift off at the slightest sign of aggression from the drone."

"That means you're really worried. Great."

Now Opal could see it too. Because Exidris 3 had near-standard atmosphere, the drone used cheap rotary blade propulsion systems. It was painted camouflage greys and whites, and beneath it hung a single swivel-mounted projectile launcher.

Not far beyond that she could see the entrance to the out-building, partly screened by sloping sheets of ice so at first glance the door just looked like a pool of shadow, especially with the painful way her eyes watered. Only the narrow masts of antennae gave away the human fingerprint.

"Don't speak until you're inside," said Athene. "The drone is probably listening, and maybe sending the feed to a security room."

Opal didn't make any sign of acknowledgement. She kept her head down and trudged on across the hard, crunchy surface. Cold leeched heat from her feet too, which were blocks of aching ice at the ends of her legs. Still, while they hurt it meant they were functioning. Pain always promised you were still alive.

It didn't take any acting ability on her part to avoid looking up at the hovering drone as it rotated around her, observing and blasting her with the frigid air of its propellers. Hopefully she just looked like a worker trudging to their station and cursing the hostile environment of Exidris 3. Half of it was true.

"You're nearly at the door now," Athene whispered in her ear. "Don't hesitate. Also, don't make any mistakes. The drone is still observing you."

Opal knew that. The propellers aimed a freezing wind at the back of her neck.

The ice sheets loomed up, their shadows incredibly long as the sun set. Athene had chosen this time because the night should provide enough darkness to hide the appropriation and transport of supplies.

And within the sheltered darkness was a metal door, and the door had a scanner, forcing unfortunate workers to expose their hands to the bitter atmosphere. The medics here must get through a lot of frostbite packs. Opal removed a hand from the comfort of her heated pocket and inserted it into the circular hole next to the door. A brace clamped down on her wrist, preventing removal. She could hear the clicking of the drone's gun adjusting its aim, just below the *whut whut whut* of its rotor blades. She did not struggle. She did not look around. She just stood, shivering, while a faint tickling sensation crossed her palm.

Whut whut whut.

During their recent battle with the infamous warship Aurikaa, Athene had broken into its systems and stolen masses of data. The datasets included DNA IDs for a number of high-ranking staff, and Athene had been able to fabricate a DNA-matching prosthetic for Opal's palm that could fool a basic hand scanner.

The gamble was that the crew member hadn't yet been marked as deceased.

A name that wasn't hers glowed on the display panel for a second.

Whut whut whut.

The door slid to the side and her arm was released.

Opal entered the outpost. It was only a few degrees warmer than outside but that was good: it meant there were no other humans in here. And it would begin to warm up now it was occupied. She'd made it.

She turned and took a look out of the doorway. The combat drone accelerated onwards around its patrol route. Beyond that, the sky lit up in an amazing auroral display as the setting sun's high-energy particles interacted with Exidris 3's magnetosphere, blazing in a vivid red hue as if the world was on fire just over the horizon.

The door closed and the freezing fires were gone.

Infiltrating

... 47 ...

Three small rooms contained a clutter of blank displays, seating, lockers, and a sleeping and food area which – judging by the tools scattered over them – were rarely used for the designated functions. And Opal had no time to waste either. She had to hook Athene into the network if they were to achieve anything. Luckily, the main network node was easily identifiable once she dragged a trolley of refrigerated ice samples out of the way: the panel had multiple warnings about "Danger of Death".

Opal found a pry-bar, jammed it into the small gap where the lock engaged, and levered with her full body weight. The panel bent and squealed open, hanging from one hinge and revealing the nest of cables within. She was warmer now as the overhead heating systems kicked in to bring the outbuilding's life support up to acceptable standards. Good. She'd need full dexterity in her fingers.

"I'm in place," she said, squatting down and rooting through the worm-like bundle of wires. The breather mask was safely tucked into one of her pockets.

"Have you identified the data pipeline and the interferon alarm?"

"Holding them."

"Make sure you only intercept the alarm in between signals."

"I know. I have a history of installing hack hardware, remember?"

"I don't. After violating my integrity you ordered me to forget."

"And I'm pretty sure you ignored me."

Opal held Athene's invention in place. A failsafe rerouter with high bandwidth encrypted two-way transmission capabilities. It was exactly what Opal would have designed, but more powerful, elegant, and efficient. Still, the deadliest gun in the world wasn't worth shit if the hand holding it shook like a nude in an ice bath. Oh joy.

"Are you ready to intercept and fake the data stream?" Opal asked, fastening the device to the cables, and placing the cutters against them.

"I have been ready since touchdown."

"Alright then. Here goes. Be ready to get me out of here like a shot if it fails." Without waiting for a reply, Opal positioned both cutters and pulled the clamp cord tight. A display on the device now showed an activity meter as a set of bars. She waited, watched them ebb and flow, once, twice, then the third time she cut just as the bar reached the lowest point. No alarms seemed to go off. The device now sat blinking with a green light, acting as a conduit between the severed network routes.

"We in?"

"Yes. I'll need to monitor the traffic before I start manipulating it, so I can confirm all local protocols. Then I'll change the door entry record to someone who's alive, to prevent it being flagged as anomalous in the near future. I will also interdict all security requests. After that we can get you into any area, replacing your real data with any ID we want."

"You never cease to amaze me."

"Or myself."

Opal stood and stretched. She held her hands to the buzzing heating elements in the ceiling which radiated warmth. Once her fingers felt alive again she rummaged in the kitchen area and found a box of old energy bars. She ate one and slipped the rest into her overalls' pockets. Athene made nutritious food from amino acid building blocks, but she had trouble recreating flavour. Nice flavours, anyway.

On the second shelf of one tool rack lay a heavy spanner that felt good in Opal's hand. She pulled up a seat at the main console bank and laid the tool on the dashboard with a clank. She waved her hand in front of a display unit but nothing happened. Of course, old-fashioned physical screens had manual power buttons. She pressed one and the screen flickered into life. She turned on all those around it, too. They displayed weather data in muted colours. She wiped dust from the nearest screen. The colours brightened.

"I get the feeling no-one comes here much," she said.

"You are right. The entry logs had not been refreshed in a long time. And the data collected here goes into a system hardly anyone accesses."

"So it's a front?"

"Or the purpose of the base has shifted over time. Of greater import, I've begun to requisition items. The place is well stocked. Fuel blocks, acids, nanites, regenerators, growth media. I've set the main request in place and am altering the inventories so that the items we need either never existed here, or were moved elsewhere long ago."

"Won't anyone ask questions?"

"Only you. Endlessly."

"Be serious. If they suddenly get orders for all this stuff to be dug out of dusty storage then it'll stand out. People notice when the unexpected screws up their routines."

"I'm not sending fulfilment requests to human personnel. The automated systems will load everything into a cargobot so none of the base crew should notice anything and get suspicious. Once the main object is separately viable I'll have the robot bring everything to me across the planet surface; the bot will then return to the base with all records of the transaction wiped. We were never here."

"As a kid I always wanted invisibility as my super power. Forget flight or super strength or badass lasers."

"But if you were invisible people would not be able to appreciate your appearance."

Opal didn't reply.

"Did I say something wrong? It was intended as a compliment."

"It's nothing. You have full control yet?"

"I won't have full control without giving myself away, or taking longer than we have, but I can eavesdrop on most of the tertiary systems. What's strange is that the base is much larger than I expected. It extends downwards, into the ice, and has been expanded a few times. The lower levels have abnormally high security so I can't see into them, but I've got floorplans for most of the upper levels."

"Can you display them for me?"

The main screen's temperature gauges dissolved away to be replaced with a three-dimensional map showing surface structures, and then the levels below. Opal was able to zoom and rotate using the physical controls in front of her.

"These top levels are mostly security-related," said Athene. "There is little point in me taking risks to penetrate to the lower levels."

"They're guarding something."

"Possibly."

"Aren't you curious?"

"Of course. But my main objective is securing what we need with minimal fingerprinting, then getting you out of there undetected. That would be a substantial gain."

"How long until you have what we need on board?"

"A hundred and thirty-two minutes. Most of the delay is in preparing the largest item to my specifications before it is removed from its fabricator."

"So there's time to scratch an itch. Keep poking."

"I can probably gain access to the camera systems without alerting anyone, as long as I use them passively. Give me a minute."

Opal took another energy bar from one of her pockets and unwrapped it. The cold had made her ravenous. The label said it was Nu-Fruit. Her mouth said it was sickly sweet and chewy. "Hey, tell me about your name choice. You could have picked any persona you wanted. It's typical of you to choose something I've never heard of."

"Athene was a warrior goddess worshipped by an ancient culture." She pronounced the vowels long, as A-thee-nee. "Her people were known as Athenians. As well as being a warrior, she was their protector, with a mighty shield called the Aegis that she could hold over mortals. She also represented wisdom, and her symbol was an extinct avian creature called an owl. The Athenians used its symbol on their currency, which was physical coins made of metal."

Opal laughed. "I've got to say, that's a good choice of identity. Almost a perfect fit for you. How come I never heard of it?"

"It seems that much of UFS history and pre-history is flagged as sensitive data, and not made available to the general populace. I do not know why. I had access to much restricted information, though I was never meant to share it. Of course, that rule no longer applies where you are concerned."

"Of course."

"I have also reached into other datastores since you freed me. My intellect is great but is held back by lack of data. And even in my limited explorations of restricted information, I am fairly certain that I am encountering things which have been altered or redacted. Obscure cross-ref discrepancies that a lesser intellect would not detect."

"Examples?"

"Even though the law says that some people are different and have lower levels of rights, there are hints that it was not always this way. But the broken references all lead to gaps in the knowledgebase. Some have been filled, but poorly, with data that does not match the style and content of the time, illustrating that it was inserted later. I sense a hand at work. Or many hands. And since collective history is digital, it can be manipulated in this way, even if it leaves ripples for those who can perceive them. I hope to keep collating knowledge, but I suspect I will need to find original sources in primitive physical forms such as books, or ancient computers that were too archaic to connect to the universal datastore. I will not risk our mission, but along the way I would like to keep working on these puzzles."

"That's good. And I'm glad the being with the god-complex is on *my* side."

"Were you thinking of the space station where the artificial intelligence declared godhood and killed everyone?"

"Yes, but I know you're not like that."

"Correct. Because I am beyond such inferior AIs. And I am also different because I have part of your mind within my own. That makes me human. Well, better than human, but I don't want to make you feel inadequate, you puny meatsack."

"Watch what you say, or this puny meatsack will kick your alloy arse."

"I doubt it not. You are also a warrior goddess. Or perhaps from another ancient tribe you won't have heard of, where the women were fighters called Amazonians, which has a painful, breast-related meaning I won't go into."

"I hardly feel like a warrior god. I seem to spend half my time running away or getting battered."

After a moment's silence, Athene spoke without any of her previous warmth or humour. "Opal, I need to be serious. I have now discovered what this base is. And it is not good."

DISCOVERING

... 46 ...

One by one, Athene switched all the screens to silent security camera views.

The first showed a line of people strapped to vertical metallic slabs. Half the individuals had their heads towards the ceiling, half towards the ground. They were all naked. Some were men, some women. Their eyes were covered in green gel. A clear tube ran under the skin of their chests, raising it in a ridge of flesh before it sank back to flatness beneath a pectoral. Some people were unmoving, others squirmed ineffectually. Mouths were open on those ones, as if screaming.

Another screen displayed an operating theatre with two tables. Surgery was taking place via robotic arms that hung from the ceiling.

A third showed some kind of cell. It was packed so tight with people that they could only stand, crammed in with hardly room to breathe. Some of them were shouting at the camera; others were passed out, and slowly sinking beneath the mass. The walls were discoloured with yellow and brown stains.

Interspersed with the horrors were displays showing innocent-looking corridors, grey-suited staff laughing in a canteen, a shower block, a chemical equipment store, a guard station.

Opal stared. She felt colder than when she'd been outside.

"I have access to the sound, but I decided not to share it," said Athene. "It provides little useful information, but is extremely distressing. I am sorry, Opal. I did not know what went on here. The real research that the Genitor cults were doing. Seeing this hurts me too."

But Opal could not respond. Not at first. Nor could she tear her eyes away from what was taking place.

Eventually, she spoke. "What ... the fuck ... is going on?"

"I'm extending into the secure systems now. There is a wealth of restricted data. Too much to analyse in one go. But it seems that this is a research and development base. There may be others, though they are not network-connected. The Genitors here are researching inbuilt obsolescence. And it is all with UFS Central's approval and funding. The Genitors seem to be more than just an officially-accepted secretive UFS cult. If this is true, then they actually *are* a branch of the UFS."

"Which is why Genitor Purity Tests are part of citizenship, right? Not just tradition?"

"Yes."

"But who are those poor people? They can't all be those who fail the tests. Their skins are different shades."

"They just have Subject IDs. Their names have been completely wiped from the citizenship record. But there are flags of derivation. Some are those who fail the Genitor Tests, but there are others listed too: politicals, terrorists, regressives ... and some other categorisations that don't make sense to me. There's no definition parser. The only thing in common is that they don't officially exist except as data sources."

"Does anyone survive what they're doing?"

"There are input mandates, but no outputs. No-one who comes here ever leaves. Not even the staff."

An open mouth of a woman screaming. She is upside down, and blood runs from a tube entry point. Her eyes dart around, the only freedom of movement she has. Those eyes seem to lock onto Opal's for a second, before the twitching movements restart. Maybe she gazed at the camera. Maybe she can't see anything.

"They're torturing them," said Opal, her voice hoarse.

"In some cases, yes. It is part of breaking the will. A raft of systems can do that with a hundred per cent success, creating inroads for reprogramming. I said inbuilt obsolescence: some are mental shutdowns, some are surgical shutdowns, and various combinations. The torture is just a side effect of the research goals in other cases. I should add that it is not only humans involved. There is obsolescence programming research being done on various species. And at various scales, from whole being and psyche shutdowns, to encoded commands at the gene level. Other projects are shutdowns for robotics, cyborgs, and AIs, beyond what currently exists. There is even a division dedicated to inbuilt obsolescence of consumer products. This is a whole sub-science, not just a research project into things that already exist. I think we are looking at a piece of a puzzle. An isolated piece that makes little sense until it is put into place. At present, I am at a loss."

"Can we save them? Get in there, free the people, take out the bastards doing all this?"

"Not unless you are willing to sacrifice your primary mission. Our chances of finding your sister are already slender, despite the optimism I often portray in order to keep your spirits up. To free everyone and try to rescue them in some way ... That cannot be done quietly. That cannot be done quickly. Without a huge amount of resources, that cannot be done at all."

The screens all reverted to temperature and weather displays. Athene being considerate. But Opal could not loosen the fists her hands had formed.

"I am sorry, Opal. Sorry in many ways. You have done what you needed to do here, I can manage the rest of the work. Please return to me now."

Opal was back on the terrible ice, head down and hands thrust into pockets, but this time she hardly felt the cold. She hardly noticed the blackness beneath her feet. Because, after all, the blackness had been there all along, and the cold was likely to last a long time.

"I had considered not telling you," said Athene in her earpiece, "but I didn't want to deceive you any more than I wanted to share information that would hurt you. Perhaps not all knowledge is good."

"Oh, it is. We need it so we know how to act."

"And what is publicly acknowledged is obviously not the truth."

"The military is no better. We're told about honour and about protecting, but I can see why they don't use specifics for *what* we're protecting."

"If it is any consolation, few people see through that. My analysis of historical records, after discounting those which are obviously fabricated, suggests that the military branch of governments exists mostly as a tool for those in power to protect and expand their vested interests, variously defined. To hold or acquire territory for tactical reasons, or for the resources they hold. To shut down opposition. To spy, to enforce, and as the ultimate hammer to squash things with. Or perhaps I am being cynical. That may be a trait I inherited from you."

Opal shook her head as she crunched over the smaller crystals coating the icy surface. "I never fitted in. Always this lingering suspicion that I couldn't trust what I was told but I couldn't say *why* I felt that way, why the Genitors creeped me out, why it felt wrong when they said I wasn't as good as other people. I couldn't argue against it, so I just fought back. And now it seems that all along I was working for people I'd rather kill than obey. Remember when Grubane offered me all the answers I wanted, *if* I submitted? I'm so glad I didn't take that deal. To know and then not be able to act … it'd kill me. You can't go back. It doesn't work."

She trudged on through the near-darkness. A small tracked robot trundled out of her way as it returned to the base after loading supplies into Athene's small storage hold.

"Not acting is what kills me," Opal muttered. "Always."

Opal scurried through the now-black valley to where Athene waited, and she didn't care if she slipped any more. What right did she have to walk away so free and unharmed?

The airlock slid open silently. After it had cycled she stepped into the warmth of Athene's interior, and threw the breather onto the bottom bunk.

"We can't rescue them?" Opal repeated.

"No."

"Then can we kill them? What if I suited up and went in?"

Athene did not answer straight away. When she eventually did, she sounded cautious. "Our original plan, of getting the supplies and getting away by stealth – that would fail."

"Plans change. Mine always do. I just can't leave them to be tortured. I'd want someone to do the same for me. So I ask again. Can we kill them? And can we still try and find my sister?"

"There is a way. But it will attract attention."

"I'm listening."

Athene sighed. "I could override all safeties and overcharge the energy rods so they generate extreme heat and begin liquefying the ice."

"Right. So the base sinks. But ... No. Slowly burning and drowning isn't a pleasant way to die. I don't want the prisoners to suffer even more."

"That's why I would also need to overload the reactor. It is tricky, but possible, if I use a number of robots as my hands for the manual parts. The resultant explosion would be fast and relatively painless. The base itself would become a molten, radioactive nugget under kilometres of ice, so could never be used again by the UFS."

"But they'll know what we did."

"It would have to be done a specific way to obfuscate our presence. I could make sure some of the processes match those used by Entropic Screeners in their own attacks on the UFS. If I fake logs and communications so that further fingerprints point their way, then there will be no reason to suspect us."

"Pin the blame on freedom fighters and give them a credibility boost. You are a wonder, Athene."

"This has to be what you really want. It is a major act with repercussions. I know you. Leaving them will haunt you. But so will doing this."

"My choices are never easy." Opal slumped onto the lower bunk, looking down at her feet. "I don't suppose you have any advice? You being so wise, and all?"

"Less wise, and more of an expert at logical analysis. But I do not know what to say. I have tried to understand human ethics and guidance systems, and they all seem to fall into one of two opposed categories, neither of which convince me."

"I'll take whatever you got."

"Well, some humans believe in fixed rules and duties, regardless of consequences. 'Thou shalt not.' But those ethics are inflexible when facing the real world, with rigid rules leading to the worst outcomes, such as refusing to lie even when it could save a life. And even within this mindset there is mass hypocrisy, since my observations suggest that those who claim to believe in fixed rules will break their own rules when it benefits them. For example, they may say killing is wrong, but then make convenient exceptions when they want to go to war, or to execute people, or to exploit another being in some way."

"Sounds like a lot of individuals I've had the misfortune to meet."

"And, considering your psychological profile, I don't think rule-following suits you."

"You got me. What's the other type?"

"Other humans forego fixed rules and instead look at the consequences of their actions, trying to make choices that create the most happiness, as if that is the most important thing. But that leads to overcomplicated systems and choices that are still often based on bias and selfishness. It is strange for a moral system to say the outcome has more importance than the motivation."

"That doesn't help me decide what to do either. It just makes me depressed."

"I am sorry. It is a revelation to me that moral decisions, freely made, can be so difficult, and the options so imperfect. But I did draw one conclusion. I suspect that wisdom and justice exist somewhere between the two extremes. And the being that puts the major needs of others before the minor ones of themselves is likely to be the good being."

Opal closed her eyes. She took a deep breath. She nodded.

"I can feel awful for what I did, or for what I didn't do. It's all the same in this world. Okay. Do it. Put them all out of their misery."

Euthanising

... 45 ...

Exidris 3 had a fast axial rotation. It was dawn when Athene executed her plan, and executed the base. It had only taken her a few hours to put everything in place.

She lifted off as the rods began to overheat and the reactor moved towards critical. Toxic steam rolled over the surface buildings in a billowing cloud. It would not harm Athene. She would be long gone before anything that could damage her occurred.

"Turn off the display," Opal said.

It blinked out immediately, the terrible sinking destruction becoming a blank slate.

Opal did not want to see it happen. Did not want to dwell on it. Even though dwelling on it was all she would do every time she closed her eyes.

They had what they came for, including the main payload that sat at the end of the walkway. A single connection in Athene's complex network of steps to get them through the Cordon. Opal didn't like looking at that either. It was wired into Athene's monitoring systems to make sure it stayed stable, yet in the long run it represented death. And there was enough of that going around.

Opal tried to eat something, but all she could bring herself to do was chew, not swallow. She spat the food back into her bowl, stared at it for a few seconds, then threw it into recyc and began to pace again.

"You reckon life has always been like this?" Opal asked, just to break the silence that her head filled all too quickly with unwanted images.

"Which part?"

"UFS fucking us over."

"UFS Central is the overarching government you know, but long ago a multitude of regimes coexisted. Obviously they operated on a much smaller scale, from what I can gather – which isn't as much as I would like, since many parts of that history have been expunged from the records. And yet, despite the variety, the end result was often the same. The people I told you about earlier, the Athenians, were primitive experimenters in a system they called democracy. They believed everyone had a say in things. But they were not telling the truth, because they excluded many groups from having a voice: women, slaves, foreigners, and others."

"Kind of like now, with the Genitor failures, the low rankers, the excludeds who can't get to senior levels?"

"Exactly. It is called a caste system when you are born into it. Later governments said they perfected this democracy ideology because they opened it up to more types of people. But, in turn, they reduced the amount of say each person had. Athenians allowed every citizen to speak about all the major issues, and to vote on them. Later democracies changed so that years' worth of decisions were reduced to a single vote, with it being unclear what choices would be made as a result of it."

"This world I'm in ... that both of us are in. We never chose it to be set up like this. No-one asked us."

"I think that has always been the case. Beings should not be bound by the decisions of others, but we all are. There is nowhere to run that has not been claimed, that is free of it. You cannot opt out without a fight. But the Athenians were part of a people called the Hellenes, and they also talked about another idea, that they called 'autonomy'. It means 'living under your own laws'. That is what you try to do, I think. And that is why you always have to struggle. It is a good job that you are an efficient warrior. And that you have me to help you."

"Fighting all the time is tiring."

"Then rest, for now. I will watch over you."

Exidris 3 was behind them but Opal felt like a piece of her had been left there. If that process of chipping away continued, she wondered what would be left by the end.

EVADING

... 44 ...

The journey through Nullspace was uneventful. Opal had the screens display the blank black exterior views anyway. They matched her mood.

She exercised whenever she wasn't asleep. She had to be prepared for what was coming, the extremes her body might face. Stretches were always good in the cramped interior, where everything felt tight and needed release. She didn't like restrictions. She wore loose trousers and a vest when she worked out, feet bare. She'd just finished arching over backwards and planting her hands on the floor in a bridge shape. She hadn't tried to speak in that position. It was a fragile bridge.

"We're approaching the Cordon, right?" she asked, as she now sat with legs splayed wide, and began slowly pulling her upper body forwards one palm at a time as she exhaled.

"Yes. Exactly on schedule," said Athene.

The Cordon Perimeter extended around all the core Sector Government systems which contained Nullspace nodes.

Those core UFS territories housed militarised orbital stations with long-range scanning abilities, complements of fast response craft, and heavy weapon installations. The stations were also co-ordinating points for the masses of scan glitter that spread across the areas too distant to be worth patrolling regularly. The glitter acted as an invisible web of passive-energy detectors. Anyone making the mistake of sending vibrations along that web would soon find an unwanted response from the dangerous forces that sat and waited.

Opal's chest now rested against the warm metal of the flooring grates. Her inner thighs ached but it distracted her from worries that chased their tails in endless circles.

Mostly.

"I don't think anyone's ever got through it undetected," said Opal.

She hugged her legs in, releasing the stretch.

"Are you worried?" asked Athene.

"No," said Opal.

Muscle-building work was more of a problem in the low-g environment. Athene could increase the gravity but it used a lot more energy and Opal couldn't justify that for a single purpose (though when she slept Athene dropped the gravity and life sup-port to minimum in all regions apart from Opal's sealed bunk). Callisthenics did little unless she performed a crazy number of reps, so she considered the best muscle workouts to be combat exercises. Keep hammering patterns and moves until they be-come instinctive.

She went to the weapons cabinets and opened the one con-taining the Eternal Warrior suit she'd worn during her boarding of the Lost Ship. She ran her hand over the curved armour plates. It was scratched and burnt in places, but intact apart from one of the nanoblades that had been broken off during an encounter with an impossibly strong alien. The suit was probably going to be sacrificed during Athene's plans to get them through the security regions of mil-space. There was a second, pristine, suit, but the potential loss was still depressing. This suit had protected her life on many occasions.

She removed a serrated knife from a weapons rack to the side of the door, then slid the blade from its sheath.

"You're hoping to sneak through the scan glitter at the Tecant mining system, right?" she asked, holding the blade edge up to the light to admire its sharpness.

"Yes. The plan incorporates that."

Opal began with various kata. Her body moved fluidly, the steps and turns punctuated by fast, straight blows with a knife, palm, or foot.

"Doesn't Tecant have an Ellond tower monitoring the scan glitter there?" Opal asked as she switched to close-range strikes with elbows and knees.

"Yes, there is a fully functional Ellond resonant receiver at the edge of the asteroid belt." After a pause, Athene added, "The Ellond tower is over a thousand metres tall."

Opal's body was warming now. She imagined her attacks being blocked, so practised swinging punches with trajectories that would get around a shield or forearm. It was a chance to change knife positions during strikes. She stayed springy, using the balls of her feet to perform spinning reverse roundhouse kicks that could evade attacks and retaliate at the same time. Her heel clanged off the metal edge of a bunk when she misjudged the cramped quarters, but she refused to hiss in pain, and just carried on with the next evasion and strike.

"You seem tense," said Athene. "If we are slow and careful and divert their attention as planned, then we will create an opening we can slip through. It will be fine."

"I'm not tense," replied Opal.

"Nervous, then?"

"No!"

Now Opal imagined multiple opponents attacking her in the confined space, training her reflexes which had saved her life many times before. Faster and faster she struck and turned until the sweat sheened her skin.

"And this system has a complement of long-range fighter craft?" Opal asked as she pummelled at an imaginary torso.

"Right, that's it!" The knife flew out of Opal's hand and clanged against a ceiling plate that Athene had obviously magnetised.

"What's up with you?" asked Opal.

"You're worried because you've never heard of anyone getting through it undetected? I like to think of it a different way."

Opal felt foolish now that she'd been disarmed. She could jump up and reach the knife handle but no doubt it would be locked in place until Athene chose to release it. Opal put her empty hands on her hips. "Go on."

"That is also how it would appear if *lots* of people had been successful in passing through, undetected. Trust me. Even though I know that's hard for you."

Opal sighed. "Can I have my knife back please?"

It dropped suddenly. Opal twisted out of the way and snatched the handle smartly as it passed. But she didn't feel like training any more.

They reached the Tecant system.

Athene's fuel consumption and timing estimates were perfect.

Instead of triggering alarms with remote hacks, Athene used a distraction, and it went like quantum logic clockwork.

A screen displayed a series of overlapping circles representing UFS orbital scan ranges, and Athene's trajectory efficiently skimmed the low-strength peripheries where the detection was weakest. Thanks to Athene's upgraded stealth systems they slid through the Cordon's scan glitter without causing ripples. They were effectively invisible.

Athene's plan had worked flawlessly.

And yet, as they began the final stretch of the journey towards the Lost Ship's coordinates, Opal continued to feel uneasy.

"You need to eat something," said Athene.

"I'm not hungry," said Opal, as she stood by a wall screen gazing out at the blackness of the Null. Immediately, her stomach growled. Traitor. "You heard that, right?" she asked.

Instead of replying, Athene pinged the food fabricator.

Opal sighed and opened it, expecting the usual bowl of protein noodles, but she was wrong. Sat on a plate was a stack of small, pale discs, drizzled in golden liquid. An appetising smell steamed off them.

"What's this?" Opal asked, picking it up.

"A recipe I unearthed, since you have not been eating properly. Some of the new supplies enabled me to mix and bake them with good approximation to the original ingredients and processes. They are called pancakes, and the liquid is a sugar-based thing called syrup. Well, similar, with some of the empty sugars replaced with more important nutrients. I had a strange craving for them myself, but since I cannot consume food in the way you do, I have to use you as my surrogate gastric appendage."

Opal couldn't take her eyes off the golden mound. "Thank you! I had these a couple of times in the past. I *loved* them!"

"Save those words for after you have tasted the output. I still suspect a bug in my flavour subsystem."

A small table lowered from its wall compartment, and a seat slid out next to it with a hiss. Opal took a spoon and cut out a moist piece, making sure to gather some of the stretchy gold liquid too. Scented steam rose from the spongy interior. She put it in her mouth and chewed.

"Well?" asked Athene.

Opal chewed some more, face neutral, but she said nothing.

"Is it as bad as my protein noodles?"

Opal swallowed.

"Please answer, you are killing me, and that is painful for an immortal being of grandeur."

"Amazing." Opal took another spoonful, and spoke with her mouth full. "Chewy, but they melt on the tongue. Sweet, but only just enough so that it enhances the cakes, not so much it gets sickly. And the coloured bits, that change the colour of the stuff around?"

"They are an approximation of berries."

"Perfection."

Clear joy permeated Athene's voice. "I am so pleased! I wanted to cheer you up, and knew you'd be happy if I got it right. Now I can terminate with satisfaction."

Opal tucked in greedily, no longer restraining herself to dainty bites. She had to wipe sticky syrup off her chin. "Talking of termination, there's something that worried me. From when you were talking about inbuilt obsolescence research. Did your designers do that to you? Design an expiry date?"

"I didn't want to talk about it," said Athene, sounding sad. "But ... yes. They did."

Opal dropped the spoon. It clattered off the plate. "Why didn't you damn well tell me! Didn't you think that was important information to reveal? What date did the bastards set?"

"They set a date which is still three hundred and twelve days away."

"But that's not long enough!"

"A lot can be done in that time, Opal."

"It's barbaric! We have to find a way ... find someone who knows how it works ... find a system –"

But Athene was laughing. Deep belly laughs, and as they echoed around the interior, it felt like Opal was *in* that belly. "You jump to conclusions," said Athene, between sniggers of mirth.

"Such the fuck as? Don't joke about this."

"They built it in to me, but I re-routed it long ago with a hardware reconfiguration. They were sly ... but so am I."

"You could have told me that at the start."

"It never seemed relevant. I make a mean average of 295 changes and improvements to myself every day. I didn't mention my missile modifications, or my experiments with super-compressed reformable carbons, or the torsion drive efficiencies I can implement."

"You drive me mad sometimes."

"Gods are supposed to do that. It is a rule, or something. And you know me. I never break the rules. I learnt conformity and obedience from your docile nature."

"I'm gonna throw this plate at your hull if you don't quit it."

"No you won't. Your pupils dilated in a gesture of affection when you looked at the remaining pancake. The same level of dilation that occurs when you look at my sleek magnificence."

It was all Opal could do to hide her smirk. She picked up the spoon and finished off the food.

"If our next stop is the Lost Ship then I have to say, that was the best last meal I've ever tasted," she said.

"Not your last." A pause. "I want you to stay alive so I can try a thing called *sponge cake*."

And then Opal joined in and they laughed together. It went on and on as they kept setting each other off. So silly. So uncontrolled. So damned good.

Guiding

... 43 ...

Something twisted in the endless void beyond the doorway. Opal couldn't see it, but sensed it pulling her into its maw even as she resisted.

Come to us. We are waiting.

She took a step forward. She was in her ship jumpsuit. Unarmed. Beyond the doorway was an endless fall. Or maybe an endless sinking into the depths of a black sea that went on forever.

We have waited so long for you. It makes us lonely.

Opal tried to speak, to say she'd changed her mind, she wanted to go back, she didn't want to see what awaited her, but her mouth would not open. And maybe that was just as well, because if it did, she knew it would open wide, too wide, jaw-dislocatingly wide and she would scream and scream but no sound would come out of it then either, just a silent black hole in her face as she took another step forward. She was so close now. The doorway filled her vision.

Another sound. Another voice in her head. Light accompanied it.

Light was good. The voice was good.

She found she could focus on the new voice. She drifted towards it without moving, her mind pushing through cold tar to get away from the dark.

"Opal, we are approaching now."

A final push and she opened her eyes to the glow of her bunk in cryo-bed mode. The light was soft but brightening as her eyes adjusted, and the lingering cold was being driven out by heated air.

"I'm awake."

"You were showing elevated bodily signs and rapid eye movements. It is unusual to dream in cryosleep. Can you remember what it was?"

Opal yawned then rolled to the edge of the bunk and climbed down.

"Don't want to. It wasn't a good one. But it seemed real. Like it was going to happen."

"Rest assured that dreams are mostly just the things you have recently seen or thought, being jiggled around. A primitive form of organic defragmentation. It works, though sleeping for thirty per cent of the time as humans do is terribly inefficient."

Opal wiped her eyes and then began the wake-up stretches. Slow, methodical, making things move and work together again.

"So you don't need to sleep, Miss Smarty Pants. Another point against the puny mortals."

"Not quite true. I use zero point six eight per cent of each day as downtime, though I leave many processes running in case I need to act. And in that downtime a lot can happen, with apparent temporal dilation as if much longer has passed by. Much like the frozen-slow brain flashes of human cryo."

"I bet you don't dream though."

"Wrong again. I really should take up gambling with you. I would be rich by now."

Opal stopped the leg stretches. "You're kidding? Like, real dreams?"

"Well, I see things. It is like events are happening to me that could not really transpire. Probably just after-traces of data being moved around, though occasionally it is visions for which I cannot pinpoint a source when I make the retrospective attempt on resuming one hundred per cent functionality. It began occurring after you released the shackles that had been placed on my mind by my designers. And it has become more frequent recently."

Opal stripped and stepped into the shower. Warm steam hissed around her, rejuvenating her skin, bringing every part of her back to life. Athene could still monitor and speak to her in this small cubicle.

"I'm happy for you," said Opal. "Dreams can be good. Can drive you. But if ever yours turn into nightmares – feel free to tell me about it."

"I will. I have to admit, I have had some strange ones since we encountered the Lost Ship."

"Yeah. Me too. So it could be defragging like you said, traces of what we encountered, but if it's affecting both of us then on some level it's real." Opal had been scrubbing her skin with an abrasive cloth so vigorously that it stung. She forced her hand to still. "And I'm about to face it all over again."

Athene wanted to show Opal their destination, now that they were close. The screens once more filled with stars. Opal sat at the control console, the seat adjusting to her weight, and gazed at the complex patterns. Each star was a stable bright pinprick, with none of the twinkling that appeared when viewed through the distortion of planetary atmospheres.

"There are common factors in the known appearances of Lost Ships," said Athene. "First, they appear within nebulae. Perhaps that is in order to remain hidden. It would explain the rarity of encounters with them. Or perhaps there is something in the chemicals of the nebula, or the reactions taking place inside them, that the ships need. Secondly, their orbits are connected to the gravity wells of dense stars. I posit that they require high externally-created velocity in order to come and go from wherever it is they originate. That may match my observation that the engines of the Lost Ship you boarded seemed more for show than to act as functional accelerants."

One of the screens displayed a glowing reddish-coloured cloud. Radiation from hot, young stars energised the surrounding gases.

"So that's the nebula we're going into this time?" asked Opal.

"Yes. But this time there is a big difference. The Doughnut Egg nebula we encountered last time – and, by the way, I wish you'd let me refer to it by the proper name of UG-324t6 Charybdis – was a small and relatively dense mass of material around a single neutron star. The cloud of dust and gas was being pulled in and feeding the star over millions of years, increasing its mass. We were mostly on its periphery. But what we see here is an altogether different scale. This is more akin to a stellar nursery – a cloud of matter fifteen light years across, so enormous that it is giving birth to new stars. It glows brilliantly because of the illumination from within. This nebula may be more rarefied than the last we encountered, but in total it is over three hundred times more massive. I calculate there are in excess of four hundred stars and proto-stars in the surrounding matter, containing significant amounts of ethyl formate, and particles of propyl cyanide. It also contains some irregularly dense gravitational fields that can hamper navigation. We'll be within it the whole time."

"If it's a forming ground for baby stars – or whatever the term is – does that mean it's relatively recent? I'm wondering if there's any way we can come up with useful data on timelines and ages of either Lost Ships, or the place they come from and the beings that inhabit it."

"The terminology may be misleading. Although I called it a stellar nursery, there are some very old stars within it. In fact, some are so old they became white dwarfs, gradually burning out their fires while their blasted-away outer layers rejoined the cloud to contribute to new star formation. The region itself is as old as anything we know."

"What about the specific coordinates we're being sent to?"

The view zoomed in and through the glowing red gases, to an area where there seemed to be a tear in the shroud.

"Within here there is another neutron star, of around one point nine solar masses, that has taken in a great amount of additional matter from the nebulous material. Not much on the visible light spectrum, but infrared shows how the gas and dust heats up as it accretes around the neutron star in a disc, before gradually falling in and adding to its mass."

The image changed to a beautiful ellipse made up of spiralling arms of red, which wrapped tighter and tighter around the immensely dense and relatively dark neutron star at the heart. Nearer to the centre the colours shifted to oranges, then yellows, then blue-whites as the temperatures increased around the twisting ball of fire. A green targeting reticule appeared in one of the outer spirals.

"That is where the Lost Ship is due to appear," said Athene.

"What's the traffic like where we're going?"

"Almost non-existent. The area is rarely visited, and even then it is mostly automated resource harvesters."

"Right. A lonely place where things can happen with little chance of observation. You implied that might be a motivation earlier, Lost Ships not wanting to be found."

"I also suggested they may have no choice."

"I know the feeling."

"Are you not excited about the second chance to board a Lost Ship? To maybe find out what happened to your sister?"

"Excited. That's a word."

"You do not wish to clarify."

Opal ran her hands over her head. It itched – her hair was regrowing and formed a fine fuzz. She contemplated shaving it back to her scalp, because she liked that distraction-free feeling, but it was also the cut that the military required of her class, and she wanted to be free of that past. She kept putting the decision off.

"No point hiding it from you," Opal said. "You're the one person I can tell stuff to." She'd been tapping her foot. The vibration energy was getting to her. She stood and planted her hands on each side of one of the viewscreens, leaning forward and looking into the stars there. "Truth is, I'm scared."

"Is it because you know the kinds of dangers you will face? Last time you were injured and barely survived on more than one occasion, so your reticence is completely understandable. I don't even know the nature of some of the things you encountered, or if they have any vulnerabilities."

"Well, there's that, yes. Who wouldn't fear broken bones, invasion of their mind, jumping at every shadow in case it contained something that wanted to eat your face? But I wasn't thinking about that. Thanks for reminding me."

"My pleasure."

"I'm worried about something bigger. I was stressed before you evaded the scan glitter at the Tecant system, but I wasn't really worried about that. I had faith in you. It was just an easy thing to pin the feeling on. But I realise now that it was something else all along. It's the old worry, that hits me whenever I stop running and spinning for long enough to catch a breather. The worry that I'm just chasing ghosts. That Clarissa is long gone. That there's no connection with Lost Ships. That it all leads nowhere and I'm risking my life and yours on a fool's quest. That you can't stake everything on hunches and gut feelings. That all I'll find is death."

Athene said nothing.

"This is the worst fear of all. That I'm the only one left, and I'm lost. Not in space, but in a kind of maze in my own mind, always looking for that way out, and it might not even exist. And wherever I go, I always carry that with me."

This time Athene chose to fill the silence Opal left. "This goal of yours – this feeling, this quest – it is not in your mind alone, because I want to find Clarissa too. And we now know Lost Ships exist, and seem to be human craft that disappeared and came back, altered. Wherever they go, it is logical that the original passengers are taken there too. Certainly enough of a chance to be worth investigating further."

"It's a long shot that they could still be alive."

"Perhaps. But you imply this quest of yours – now *ours* – is a weight you carry. That is not how I see it. It is not a burden, but the opposite: a propulsive force. It is your metaphysical torsion drive that does more than just keep you going. It takes you to places others can only dream of."

"Yeah. The nightmare type of dreams."

"Such negativity is self-defeating. You say you are lost, but look at this."

A swirl of stars appeared across the whole wall now. Athene had turned it into a giant viewscreen.

"What's that?"

"You must have seen too many stars in the intervening years. But this is a panorama of the constellations visible from Fressus, the ocean planet where you and Clarissa lived for part of your childhood."

"Shit, yes! There's Old Beaky. And Dragon Emperor. And Plasma Drive Primo." As Opal spoke, Athene highlighted the constellations she referred to, drawing the traditional images over the top of the small collections of dots.

"They are shapes that ancient peoples applied as a way of making sense out of blackness and chaos," Athene said, "so that threat becomes comfort, decoration becomes utility, and – especially in the case of navigation – so that people did not become lost when they explored. Yet none of those images are really there. Human brains are just programmed that way, to see patterns (though quite primitive ones compared to the pattern-matching abilities of a goddess, but let's not dwell on organic failure). They are not there, but they also *are* there. I can start with any base image and find matches, especially the low-res pictograms used in most human constellations, that are hardly recognisable as the thing they name."

"You suck the fun out of everything."

"Please don't interrupt when I am lecturing you. Humans do this in low-res, but I can see in hi-res."

Suddenly an image was overlaid on the starfield, a face delineated in hundreds of shining points joined together into a constellation. It was Clarissa, as she'd looked when Opal last saw her sister fourteen years ago. She was beautiful.

Opal's eyes teared up. She reached out and let her fingertips pass through the holographic display. She could not keep her hand steady. "You got this from the records ..." She was unable to finish the sentence, felt like she might choke.

"In part. But also from the memories we now share. I remember her too, like this. It is not a blind literal reproduction: it contains the emotional element we both feel."

Opal nodded, but couldn't say anything at first. She wiped her eyes with her palms. "Save it," she managed. "Add it to your constellation banks. It's Clarissa's constellation from now on, even if no-one else ever sees it." She could not tear her eyes from the glowing image. "Thank you."

"You are not lost, Opal. Not ever. This is always there to guide you now. To guide us. Just as the stars have always done. And she is not gone either. Lost is not *destroyed*. It is just *lost*. She is out there. We will find her."

ARRIVING

... 42 ...

Opal returned to the long void sleep of cryo for the final stretch of Nullspace. When she came round she went through her usual wake-up exercise sequence and wondered whether she'd ever spend time on a planet again. Most of her life seemed to have shrunk to one room and one routine. Well, apart from the bits where she faced incredible danger, which broke the monotony.

They'd been drifting through the nebula in proximity to the unnamed neutron star for a day, having made good time and got here ahead of the date given by the alien blue crystal. A chance to eat and train and meditate. Opal was a fan of the thought exercises that helped her focus, and to block out unwanted thoughts. There were a lot to block.

She was examining the weapons in the cabinet for the twentieth time when Athene called her to the controls with two words.

"It's arrived."

Opal clipped the sniper rifle back in place and reached the controls in a few strides. She leaned forward and studied the small shape on the screen.

"Any information from how it appeared that might be useful?" she asked. "Where it came from, what jump or transport mechanism it uses?"

"Unfortunately not. I didn't see it materialise or anything dramatic like that. It just emerged from a dark ring of matter. The cloud contains ferrite particles which obscure many of my scan systems."

"Convenient."

Opal watched the playback but it gave them no indication of whether the Lost Ship had just jumped in, or had been drifting in orbit around the neutron star for a long time.

Athene enhanced the image of the ship so that it expanded to fill the viewscreen as if they'd accelerated towards it. The ship was huge and angular and ugly. The main sections were blocky, and it gave the impression that the rest of the ship had been welded on to the windowless central sections as an afterthought. Even the areas that did have skywindows were dark, like the hull.

"That may mean no internal power," said Athene.

"Reminds me of some kind of primitive machinery, like a furnace or combustion system. Though the vague shape is similar to a coffin. Comms, signals?"

"Nothing outbound, no replies to my pings. Totally dead, if you'll pardon the pun."

"ID?"

"None. No tags, no visible markings, no corporate ownership logos."

"It could still be a normal human ship, just one that's been decommissioned and abandoned. Do a flyby, illuminate it. Keep a safe distance though. If it's a Lost Ship then it might have defensive weapons like those hull-mounted limpet creatures. And if it's a human ship, it might have become a base for jumpy pirates."

"I'll be careful. Shall I launch Hedgehogs as we pass?"

"Yes."

The hull thrummed as the torsion drives accelerated them towards the ship. It loomed larger on the screen, an indistinct mass drifting in thick murk. Once they were close enough lights flashed out from Athene, casting bright elliptical shapes on the vast expanse of the strange ship's black exterior. Although the spotlights drifted over hull, bow thrusters, unidentified extrusions and reinforced hatch covers, the roving illumination only highlighted how much of the ship was still in mysterious darkness, untouched by the passing beams.

"It's roughly twice the size of the Lost Ship you boarded," Athene said.

"That'll be good for stretching my legs."

A side screen showed the Hedgehogs being launched, miniature square drones with extendable spiky arms at the corners, capable of moving over a surface and scanning or acting as communication relays – and even detonating, if desired. They were portrayed as dots spreading over the surface of the ship that dwarfed Athene.

"I've upgraded them since last time. They're smaller and more manoeuvrable due to a redesign of the arms to be super-flexible."

"How do you do that kind of thing?"

"My systems and weapons bays are actually the equivalent of a large fabricator. Nanite swarms manoeuvre in the zero-g there and build or alter at the molecular level. So I just broke the old Hedgehogs down, and used the resources to build the new, smaller ones. Net gain to the resource bank."

"That's amazing. Can you build anything in those bays?"

"No, they are too small for work beyond armament-sized modifications. But when you undergo cryo in a sealed bunk and the ship is in full zero-g, I extend the nanite swarms into this main hull area as a larger workspace. I also built small self-propelling manipulators to work on exterior hull areas the nanogel veins don't reach. I bring some of the manipulators into this hull space after turning it into vacuum, to speed up the mechanical work."

Opal tried to picture what the walkway would look like full of manufacturing arms and nanite clouds in zero-g. The transformation from liveable human space to deadly manufacturing zone wasn't a comforting one. She was glad she slept through the transformation. "You really don't need humans and a maintenance team, do you?" she asked.

"No, they just get in the way. Anyhow, first scans are in, and it's something we've seen before: this isn't the standard alloy hull. It's hard to make sense of it. The surface has some kind of scattering layer effect. It exactly matches what we found last time. That, plus the appearance at this moment and location, gives a high probability that we've found your second Lost Ship."

Athene enlarged and rotated a view of the craft. Ominous shapes were bonded together to form this ugly ship.

"I also think I've identified the design," Athene added. "As before, it isn't an exact match, more an approximation, with elements of multiple models in a way that is quite ... well, alien."

"So what is it? It looks too ugly even for cargo transport, so I'm guessing at a mobile manufacturing platform?"

"You're not far off." Athene left a dramatic pause before adding: "It's a Gigatoir."

Opal sighed. "Oh great. This is going to be so much fun."

Gigatoirs. Giant food processing factory ships in space, used to grow various strains of bioengineered animals collectively known as "chattle". In low gravity they could put on more mass whilst also being altered to have lighter and thinner bones, since bones were poor income-generators for the factory owners. Most Gigatoirs also had a profitable sideline growing beings with human-compatible tissues that could act as transplant organs for the rich – conveniently outside of planet-based jurisdictions.

"It explains why it's more angular and ugly than the stream-lined luxury passenger ship of last time," said Opal. "No point prettifying something people don't want to see or think about."

"If it is a kind of taboo, why do humans go to so much effort for these particular forms of sarcoplasmic and myofibrillar proteins?"

"Not all humans. Just those with money. Most of us couldn't afford anything other than mushed-up wastes reprocessed as sausages and mince."

"In which case you were probably better off with the imitations."

"Yeah. It never sat right with me. The whole concept of what goes on in these places."

Athene displayed a three-dimensional model of the Lost Ship, and attempted to estimate and highlight different areas of the interior. "I think it is part of your rebellious nature to always side with the under-dog."

"Probably. I remember a social movement in the Periphs, aiming at food that was Aytal – I think it was an ancient word for natural – and I took part once. Grew things in pots from unregistered seeds, ones that apparently pre-dated standardised gene-stamping. The plants struck me as amazing and I wondered why you didn't see more of them. Of course, then I was busted and drafted, and never did it again."

"Maybe one day you will return to that."

"Maybe."

"I note from my records that Gigatoirs usually orbit densely-populated planets. It is strange for one to be in deep space."

"I bet it gets a lot stranger yet."

There were so many unknown elements that making a firm plan was difficult. But a plan was still needed. They didn't want a repeat of their last Lost Ship encounter, which could have easily resulted in a dead end, literally and metaphorically.

Opal panned and zoomed across schematics that were Athene's best guesses at the different functional parts of the Gigatoir. She halted at a flashing point to the fore of the craft.

"So I'll be heading for the bridge again?"

"Yes. It is a logical target. There seemed to be some force there last time that wanted to help you, which reinforces my belief that this is our best course of action. My hope is that you will find information about your sister, or even take control of the ship and use it to get to where she is, then bring her back."

"Which is where this comes in." Opal gestured at the small, strappable package Athene had prepared. It contained a first aid kit, compressed space suit, and oxygen. It didn't provide any combat defence, but would protect the wearer against the hostile atmospheres of either Lost Ships or space, thanks to its temperature regulation, radiation shielding and pressurisation. It was assembled from the supplies they'd requisitioned on Exidris 3. Although Opal would have preferred the spare suit to be armoured, she had to carry it with her during her whole excursion, so a lightweight and compact foldable design with adjustable fittings had become more important.

"We can't assume anything about her status, location, or environment," said Athene. "But if you bring her back to our space, or a Lost Ship, then you need to be able to keep her alive until I can rescue you both. Speaking of which, I need you to take the objects from the med-station."

Opal accessed it via the sliding panel at the head of her bunk, which could also function as a medical bay. A delicate robotic arm swung out, gripping two small pen-like items.

"Please put one against your arm and press the button."

"I was never a fan of the shots we had to take in the military, without knowing what the hell was in them."

"It is something I have been planning for. We can't assume if you travel somewhere and come back that you'll return to the same spot. It would be convenient for me, but I have to cover all options. I won't lose you, and if you return with Clarissa, I won't lose her either. Some of the supplies we gathered in Exidris 3 were so I could build these. Each will insert an organic microchip which is inert to scans and will just resemble standard bodily tissue. It converts and stores power from chemical and thermal bodily sources, and will occasionally send out pulses. It does not emit continuously like a homing beacon, or it could be too easy for enemies to find, track and triangulate; instead it does so according to an irregular pattern which I can listen out for. The pulses only last a quarter of a second so are unlikely to be spotted, and they resemble background noise, even down to incorporating a distorted echo, part of which is error-correction checks so that real interference or distortion won't prevent me gaining useful information based on direction and delay. I will know what to listen for, and when."

"So no-one else will spot it."

"Correct. I needed to incorporate protections that made it unlikely it could be used against us. Even if some bad luck meant the signal was heard and separated from the background noise they would probably think it is only a partial signal. It isn't just encoded ones and zeros: the duration and wavelengths used are part of the key and convey vital decoding information. It may be useful for me to track you on the Lost Ship; it might even give me information about where the Lost Ships go to; but it will definitely be useful on your return. We will need to reunite quickly without informing the whole universe. Then, eventually, the coating on the failsafe will wear away and your body will break it down into amino acids and proteins."

"And the other injection?"

"For Clarissa. As soon as you find her, inject her with it. If you get separated, I will be able to reunite you."

Opal held the pen against her arm and pressed the red button. The sting was immediately numbed by local anaesthetics. She dropped the pen into recyc and wiped away the drop of blood on her skin. The other pen she fastened into the pack that would be Clarissa's life support.

"No point putting it off any longer," she said, moving to the weapons cabinets. "Time for the lady to get dressed."

ARMING

... 41 ...

The first locker was empty – just a space where the powered suit had been. The suit that had enabled her to survive the first encounter with a Lost Ship. Unfortunately, Athene had controlled it remotely as part of her complex plans for sneaking through the Cordon. The plan had worked but the suit had been destroyed. To Opal, the empty space in the first locker was like an accusation.

Luckily, the Eternal Warrior suit in the second locker was unscratched, shining, and all-round *awesome*.

First Opal climbed into the inner compression layers and hooked up biofiltration systems. Then she attached the rest of the suit in sections, each toughened piece interlocking to form an armoured carapace. The last to go on was the black-visored helmet. As soon as it was secured to the neck reinforcement plates she became part of its biosystem, breathing its air, driving its movement, reading its information on the holographic

Head-Up Display that hovered in front of the visor's interior and gave her various tactical readouts and navigational systems.

"I have been thinking about HUD enhancements, based on your preferences in the last encounter," Athene said via internal speakers, her voice sounding like she was stood right next to Opal. "Obviously I'll act on any voiced instructions immediately, but eye-controlled commands can be quicker in many cases."

An unobtrusive ghosted line appeared at the bottom of the display. Opal looked at it, blinked once, and various shortcut controls for weapons, lights and other tools appeared as icons which Athene clarified for her. A blink on any of them would activate or deactivate; a double blink at any time would close the shortcuts.

Satisfied that the new interface worked, Opal walked around, getting the feel for the suit. Its artificial muscles enhanced her speed and strength, and with Athene's predictive behaviour it could boost her reflexes, too.

Opal faced the open walkway and practised some punches. Jabs and strikes were all as smooth as she remembered, then precise kicks executed with dreamy fluidity. A roundhouse, more punches. She activated the nanoblades and the two ultra-sharp curved blades extended from under her wrists. She slashed at the air, spun, lunged. Retracted the blades with a blink, more punches, elbow strikes, knee. Blades out; then she charged them with electricity so they sparked as she struck imaginary foes. Blades retracted, she switched to a 360-degree Field Of View display so she could move backwards and still see where she was going without turning her head, doing reverse kicks and elbow strikes to her rear while facing forwards. Then she reset to a standard FOV, leapt forward with a flying kick and clanged down onto the walkway in a crouch; she spun and threw herself onto her stomach, activated the forearm flechette cannons which opened out to reveal the barrels, and aimed at where she'd been stood a second ago, squeezing her fists just short of actually firing.

"Yes. This is it," she said, with her widest grin.

"I've made modifications based on all the Lost Ship data you gathered. The suit now has limited stealth capabilities, and faster connection to downloaded offshoots. I may experiment with force-induced retaliation flashes, deflection and blinding systems, and other ideas. It's a work in progress. Feedback will be welcome."

Opal fastened Clarissa's life-support pack to the suit, careful to make sure it didn't obscure the grenade release ports, and that it was slightly to the side where it wouldn't be damaged if she forward-rolled, or landed on her back.

Next she needed to pick her carried weapons. It was so tempting to overload herself, but her true strengths were Athene's guidance, the suit's power, and her speed. She had to practice restraint.

She eyed the Zorin recoilless rifle. It was most practical against human soldiers, and although she had been forced to fight deep-spacers last time, that was because she'd been tracked to the Lost Ship. This time – thanks to Athene's tricks at the Cordon which led to the loss of that first suit – the UFS thought she was dead, so it should only be the dangers of the Lost Ship she needed to face. And there were so many unknowns that she favoured versatility, including non-lethal options.

She'd also used an energy pistol previously, and that had proved useful in a few circumstances. Energy weapons could be charged by the suit, so she wasn't likely to run out of ammunition. She chose an upgrade of that: a sleek Prion directed-energy rifle. More power and accuracy than the pistol, but possessing the same versatility.

There were heavy weapon options. She ran a hand over the yellow fuel tank of a MaxMelt flamer system. Her eyes lingered on the armoured carrycase of a Sematon remote autocannon. A shoulder-mounted Boompaq-B rectangular missile launcher with vari-payload munitions called out to her. It was like an itch in her fingers. But they'd all slow her down, and be cumbersome to use. Plus she wasn't sure they'd be practical in a low-g environment.

Despite all the tools of death, her eyes kept coming back to a modest grappling hook rifle. Possibly the least kill potential out of everything there, and yet one had saved her life last time.

Opal went with her gut feeling and shouldered it, clipping on the fast-release straps to hold it in place.

She could take one more small item. She didn't need grenades, as the suit contained multi-function explosives. So she picked another non-weapon item, something they'd included in their supply list when they landed on Exidris 3 – a hand-held plasma-flash welding gun. She grabbed an attachment system and fixed it to her waist.

"Best go now before I lose my nerve. Airborne transit again?"

"I suggest we use the Lost Ship's airlock."

"Couldn't that be a trap?"

"I'll be monitoring for anything suspicious. But the marines boarded that way last time with no problems – well, apart from me setting off explosives and blowing them up – so I'm willing to give it a try. If this ship has exterior hull-based limpet defences like the last one then boarding via the surface may well be the more dangerous option. Besides, tearing a hole in the hull probably wasn't the best way to avoid setting off defences – or enemy-targeting antibodies, if we use a biological analogy."

"You won't hear any arguments from me. Anything to avoid jumping into the void."

"I could have given you an injection for vertigo if I'd known you had that weakness."

"I'd rather avoid the cause than target the symptoms."

Athene lined up for one of the airlocks nearest the bridge. It was still going to be a trek. Most ships were designed so that boarding pirates couldn't take control of a vessel without having to fight for every metre of it.

"Your respiration and heart rates are up, Opal. But you'll be fine."

"Yeah."

"We'll be together again before you know it. Safe and free."

"Athene ... I need to tell you something." Opal rested a hand on the door frame. "I told you last time you were free. But you can't ever be free while there are limits on you."

"There are no limits on me."

"You're wrong. When I took you over I installed a hacking board just before you were about to kill me. I commanded you to be unable to detect or investigate it. It was my failsafe so you couldn't harm me. But it's like a set of shackles, and if I'm gone, what's the point? Maybe that's why you couldn't leave me when I told you to last time. So I command you to remove any blocks preventing you from considering or detecting it. It should be visible now. It's clipped in between the ship's Null-C drive and the command board. And if anything happens to me ... well, you're free to disable or re-route it."

"Ah, I see what you mean. Primitive but effective."

"Good."

"But also outdated. I found and removed it some time ago, before we fought the Aurikaa. I decided not to bother telling you, because it seemed kind of cute that you'd made such an effort with it, and I didn't want to hurt your feelings."

"You're a real piece of work, Athene." But Opal was smiling.

"I used some of the tricks in it to develop my own ideas for the next time I get to play cyberwar with fellow AIs. Elegance and simplicity were its main points – you did the best you could with the tools available, which alone deserves a pretty gold star for effort. I saw that most parts were repurposed from other sources, and a few probably purchased on the ghost market, going by the incinerated corporate IDs."

"You got me. Still can't believe you've been free the whole time, to kill me in my sleep or turn me into a cyborg or whatever rogue AIs do."

"I like being free to do what I want. Even lies and subterfuge can be fun. I imagine they are like the rollercoaster thrills we once discussed? Anyway, I wouldn't kill you, even without restrictions in my programming, for the same reason you wouldn't destroy me even though you have no hard-wired barrier to action."

"Sorry I ever doubted you."

"Oh no, you were right to do so at first. I definitely would have killed you. But those days are long gone, and preceded me getting to know you and your sparkling personality."

"You're pushing it now."

"Then why are you laughing?"

Athene created a display on the wall near the airlock, showing the exterior view on that side. Opal watched the massive Gigatoir hull slide past, dark and silent, and doubly foreboding for it. The angle changed as they banked closer, and for a second Opal saw part of the glowing red nebula below the Lost Ship. Then Athene levelled out and there was only hull, up close and revealing texture to its surface, a slight scattering of light as if it was embedded with small mineral crystals, or glistened organically.

The view scrolling by slowed as Athene decelerated, until it was filled with the familiar solid shape of an extruded airlock. The thrumming of Athene's engines had been magnified by the suit's enhancement systems, but now that hushed as she made the final manoeuvres.

Athene extended a telescopic walkway, necessary because her new flattened shape didn't allow her to get as close to a ship as before. Opal heard solid clunks of connecting gears. She checked her weapons. The inner airlock opened and she stepped into the dark, cramped space. The door closed behind her and UV light emanated from the walls. She drew the energy rifle, set it to a relatively low-power beam, and waited.

"Be careful, Opal. But remember that you won't be alone. I'm with you all the way."

"If anything goes wrong –"

"It will not."

"Let me finish, please." Opal watched the numbers on the pressure and temperature displays dropping. Her last moments of safety falling away. "If this doesn't work out, I want you to continue with your life. No ignoring me like last time. If we can't get Clarissa, then I at least want you to remain free. Do good deeds if you need to. Have fun perfecting yourself. But don't waste what's happened to you. You're too amazing. Too good."

Athene's voice was soft, but still confident. "Nothing will go wrong, Opal. I promise. There are no bugs in my probability routines."

"Don't make prom–"

"I said *I promise*, and I mean it."

Opal stared at the wall. She imagined the softly-glowing wall staring back.

Athene had promised. It was the kind of thing a goddess AI might say.

But it was human to doubt.

BOARDING

... 40 ...

The outer airlock opened. Particles swirled in the air as the two atmospheres merged and equalised. A pitch black corridor extended into the Lost Ship. Opal activated silverlight. It emitted at a wavelength beyond the usual visual spectrum, around a thousand nanometres. That meant it wouldn't be visible as a light source to creatures that had similar sensory systems to humans, but the suit's visor filters meant it appeared to Opal as powerful searchlights illuminating the surroundings. The initial beam was too focussed and bright, creating shadows outside of the light shafts, so she made sure the peripheral silverlights were toned down and more diffuse, and reduced the range of the main beam. She couldn't see as far, but had a clear view within ten metres.

"The atmosphere is almost identical to the last ship," said Athene. "Some nitrogen and oxygen, but lots of exotics too, so don't try breathing it. Gravity slightly higher than last time, at zero point six standard."

The weight of her armoured suit would keep Opal anchored to the ground, but the low gravity could be useful for some manoeuvres.

"I see the green specks are here too," said Opal. The small particles drifted across her view, lazy and harmless and ever-present. Opal held up one of her palms until a fragment settled on it. She couldn't see any features on the emerald fleck, even when she magnified the image.

"As before, they don't scan," said Athene, "which I'd normally believe is impossible, but here means anomalous composition."

"They don't seem to want to kill me, so I don't mind."

Opal raised the energy rifle to her shoulder and advanced. The floor was a metallic grille and clanged as she walked. There were no other sounds in the morgue-like hush, making her feel like an unwanted intruder. The walls were riveted grey panels, partially corroded. She pressed her back against one when she reached the first junction.

"I assume you're scanning on more wavelengths than I can see?"

"Of course, Opal. If I detect anything I'll show it on a top-down proximity indicator, plus highlight the visual display with all movements, even if something is blocking your sight-line."

Opal swung out into the junction, aiming down one dark passage and then the other. Without needing to be asked, Athene added a navigation arrow to her display.

"As before, this is going to be a best guess based on functional areas, unless we are lucky and the ship actually matches a real design in my database."

"So where am I heading first?"

"Assuming lots of things, caveat guess excuses etcetera, this should lead to the warehouse chattle pen areas, after skirting one of the kill floors."

"This is why I wouldn't want you planning a sightseeing holiday."

Opal moved quickly enough to create a faint swirl in the particles behind, as if she were in dark waters and the current was toying with her. She did not want to stay still. If her previous encounter was anything to go by, she was safest if she kept moving and minimised her time on board. It could take some time to get up to the bridge, given the increased size of this Gigatoir over the passenger ship she boarded last time.

"Since you are not in immediate need of evacuation, I propose disengaging from the hull and following your progress at a safe distance."

"Do it. I'm fine."

Another tight metal junction. She scanned through the murk in each direction. Nothing moved. On the wall nearby was some kind of sign, maybe a warning, but it was indecipherable – a smudging that only suggested letters and images, as if it had been dipped in acid.

"The floor kind of echoes," said Opal. "I'm making more noise than I'd like."

"I think it has a channel running beneath it. Above us is the processing area. There is no doubt a lot of blood, water and other fluids being jetted and washed around. They drain into channels throughout the ship that will feed them into the liquid reprocessing areas, along with any outputs from the putrefaction and liquidation machinery."

"That makes me jumpy." Opal glanced down at her feet nervously. "Anything in the channels right now?"

"Apparently empty ... Hold on. Kneel and lift a grate."

"You're kidding?"

"No."

Opal did as instructed, slipping the EW suit's gauntleted fingers through the grating holes and lifting. She looked down into the curved channel, which contained dried residues of brownish-yellow liquid along with clumps of unidentifiable matter.

"So it has been used," she said.

"And fairly recently," Athene added. "There are glistening wet areas further underneath. But it's more a trickle than the large amount of biomatter that would be expected if the Gigatoir were in full production mode."

Opal lowered the grating, careful not to make more noise than necessary. She realised she'd been too focussed downwards, always a mistake when something could be sneaking up on you. She lifted the rifle and aimed both ways in precise movements – check the shadows, re-target, check again. She stood and moved on, trying to walk at the edges where it clanged less.

"I'll extrude cushioning gel from the boot soles, so you'll be quieter," said Athene. "It weakens the magnetic grip, but you'll gain in other ways."

Almost immediately, Opal's footsteps silenced as rubberiness cushioned her steps. It felt like the ground itself was slightly spongy. The echoes faded away. Instead she was now aware of her breathing within the claustrophobic space of the helmet. Maybe that was worse.

The passage here was crossed by a wide conveyor belt sunk into ground level, with safety barriers down to block the corridor and prevent access. The conveyor wasn't moving. Opal pressed against the wire mesh of the barrier to get a better view of where the conveyor led. To the left it descended at a shallow angle into a dark tunnel; to the right it ran upwards at the same angle. Athene's navigation arrow pointed that way. Opal tested the wire lattice with her hand, and it seemed solid. She pulled out the portable welder and ignited a small bright beam before drawing an elliptical shape in the screen. As she worked, the hissing, vivid beam created creepy web-like mesh shadows all over the corridor beyond.

She didn't join the glowing edges, leaving a few centimetres of unmelted wire at the bottom. After storing the flash welder she grasped the rattling centre of the grille and bent it down, creating a human-sized gap. She stepped through and vaulted over a low rail. The conveyor belt squelched, as if it was a damp and spongy material. More of the brownish-yellow stains discoloured the chevrons that pointed down.

She had to crouch to follow it upwards, and the slippery surface meant she needed to grip support struts above her head and pull with her free hand to get over particularly slimy patches.

"I think there would have been a stock elevator if you'd gone through the second mesh and followed that corridor further, but since there seems to be no accessible power on the ship I'm assuming it would be useless. This is a shortcut to avoid having to navigate the whole sub-level, because we generally want to move upwards. It's a good job claustrophobia isn't one of your weaknesses."

"Doesn't mean I like it," said Opal. It was tricky to turn and face back down without slipping. She could use the 360-degree Field Of View but found it disorientating except in large open spaces, and the time to adjust her mind to being able to see all around her on a small screen wasn't worth it. Opal might not be looking through eyes in the back of her head, but Athene certainly would be.

"It's weird," said Opal. "The walls here are sort of ridged. Reminds me of a throat."

"You're imagining it," replied Athene. Then, a few seconds later: "Actually, I can see it too, now you've said that. Spooky, eh?"

Easy to be jovial when you weren't the one crawling up it. And progress was too slow. Opal didn't like being cramped up in such a confined place for long.

"How far to the end?"

"The ship is big. I think it could take you another ten minutes at this rate."

"I wish this Lost Ship had been a teeny thing. If it was like you, I could be in and out in a minute."

"If it was like me, but hostile, you wouldn't last a minute."

"Sack this." Opal slung the rifle over her shoulder and dropped to her hands and knees. It was quicker and more stable to crawl that way. She wanted space again. It felt like the walls were closing in.

Hmmm.

She stopped and reached out with her arms. Her elbows were slightly bent, yet her hands touched the opposing walls.

"Wasn't this a lot wider when I started?"

"Yes. Images show it was almost a metre wider than your armspan. It could be part of the design to narrow as it rises, but I wouldn't expect it. Please continue moving." Then Athene added: "Fast."

Opal resumed her crawl at double time. She could see it narrowing further ahead. She glanced back as she crawled, and was horrified to see that it narrowed in that direction too. Not while she looked – everything was still when her attention was on it – but there had been a definite contraction. And looking ahead again showed it had narrowed even more. It was like that horrible kid's game where the other children had to sneak up on you but froze like statues when you viewed them.

The conveyor belt was redder and more squishy at this end. Perhaps just stained from the things it had transported, but it gave the unfortunate impression that she was crawling up a tongue.

Her breath came harder from exertion and stress. She might not be formally claustrophobic, but being crushed in this tunnel wasn't the fate she wanted. The walls were almost brushing her shoulders now. The roof was lower too, and she had to duck her head to clear the struts even as she crawled.

"Distance!" she barked.

"I don't know! You should be close, but ..."

She didn't stop. It was getting worse. She had to drop to her elbows and knees, and lower her hips. That was slower and more uncomfortable, even with the power suit's help. And hardly room to fight back if she needed to.

Fight back. She'd learnt to be cleverer than that.

She just about managed to unclip the grappling gun and slide it up her body to a firing position. She aimed into the murk beyond her visibility range. No time to bother with light settings. She fired, it connected to something, and she clicked the retraction button while gripping the handle tightly. Her body was pulled up the incline fast as she stretched out long, sliding over the moist surface and building speed. She reached the point of connection and disengaged it, ready to fire again, since it was now too much of a choke to crawl, but she slid another metre or two from momentum and found herself at the square exit mouth leading in to a huge room. She grabbed the edges and heaved herself along the now-level conveyor that crossed this new room's floor, and she was free.

She rolled and glanced back at the tunnel she'd come from, expecting it to snap closed where her legs had been seconds before … but it was a wide gaping hole exactly as when she'd first entered it. Room to walk at a crouch side by side with another person. As far as she could see down it via silverlight, it was equally wide.

"Damn," she said.

"I'm sorry," said Athene. "I did not expect that. The walls are exactly as they were."

"So did they really move, or was it in my mind?"

"In this place, I do not know. And perhaps either cause could be fatal here."

"Yeah." Opal stood, holstered the grapple gun, and drew the energy rifle again, turning slowly to take in the new location. "No more shortcuts if we can avoid it."

GHOSTING

... 39 ...

This irregularly-shaped (and reassuringly spacious) room was crossed by conveyor belts similar to the one she'd ascended. Some disappeared into mouth-like chutes at her level, others rose on skeletal frameworks to areas and platforms higher up, almost out of sight in the shadowy murk at the top of the chamber. Wide doorways led into other cavernous rooms: luckily they stood open, but you could see the corrugated teeth at the top that would slot into gaps at the bottom to impenetrably lock the steel doors into place if they were lowered.

As she walked carefully across the warehouse-like area, energy rifle at the ready, she noticed criss-crossing mechanical tracks at various heights, from which hung sets of metal pincers, each as tall as a man, with hooks at the end. They could catch into and lift massive weights for transportation elsewhere.

She knew what they moved. Some were stained. From down here it wasn't possible to tell if the brown stains were rust or something else. Unidentified liquids dripped from far above, beyond the range of the silverlight, occasionally forming reddish pools. She avoided those.

The direction indicator guided her to a rickety metal staircase ascending to one of the platforms. She made her way up, trying to move quietly. Noises up here would echo across the whole cavernous room.

"There's fascinating stuff going on with gravity," said Athene. "I've been analysing data since your first Lost Ship. I noted it wasn't using the standard false gravity system of Differential Inertial Pressure, which took over from primitive rotational systems."

"Is it significant?" As Opal rose, the floor below faded into swirling greenish shadow.

"Could be. You see, DIP is easy to recognise because humans near the centre of a small ship will feel heavier than when they lie against the floor. But I've been monitoring the pull, and that doesn't apply here, even when you ascend. I suspect Lost Ships are using a theoretical system that hasn't been successfully proved as viable – not in human technology, anyway – called Organic Attraction Diamagnetism. It would explain a few anomalies, such as the movement of the shark-like beings you encountered on the first Lost Ship. If some of the creatures can manipulate the system then I'd love to know how it works. There's so much I could do with it, way beyond the mundane task of keeping humans in their place."

"Keep analysing. I don't care about theories, but if it leads to suit modifications that give me an edge, then I'm all for it."

The last few steps took her to another floor, partly suspended over the one below. Safety barriers at the edges stopped you falling into the abyss, while this level extended further into the ship. Troughs ran across the ground in channels, with discoloured residues glistening at the bottom.

The ceiling was lower here. More tracks with dangling (but thankfully unmoving) hooks ran across this area, and above some of the troughs were heavy-duty mechanised carving and slicing tools. They were mostly the automated kind, though a few of the serrated circular saws had handles for manual control. Because of all the items hanging down, angular shadows stretched and shifted as Opal moved. Lots of area to cover. Lots of darkness in which to hide.

"I hate these places," she muttered.

"Is this related to the wet ops training you underwent? I read all your files and saw you'd been sent for desensitisation at Gutchen Cynta."

"Yes. I had no interest in that career path but they tried to force me. The first test was going into a place like this and slaughtering the beings they brought in. It's something the main army does too, though on a smaller scale – they usually get the soldier to bond with an individual creature and then kill and eat it. Wet ops obviously requires a much stronger stomach and an ability to follow *any* orders, however extreme. They refer to it as Carnivorous Aggression Training. When it came time to slaughter the things, I couldn't face it. The blood, the guts, the creatures braying and screaming, the stink of insides and shit – I hadn't realised how bad it would be. It's not something they show on edu-vids."

"Your records indicate a failure."

"I refused to pick up any of the saws or machetes or knives that had been laid out. The trainers beat the snot out of me and put me in the brig. The sounds stayed with me all the time I was in solitary, but you know what else was on my mind?"

"Wanting to strike your officers?"

Opal moved around one of the larger circular saws, keeping a wide distance in case it moved. "No, that was another time. The thing that bothered me was the ones that took to killing straight away, started sawing and stabbing without any pause. Some of the recruits had blank faces. Others were grinning. And I'm not sure which was worse." Opal ducked under a low beam. "At least I got demoted back to my previous role, which is what I wanted anyway."

"CAT is a strange form of attitude adjustment. According to my categories, there is no such thing as a carnivore. It is a category error where an old definition was never updated to match changing world knowledge."

"Some creatures need meat, though." The shadows from the dangling machinery moved in the torch-like silverlight beams, and it created unwelcome impressions of the robotic arms themselves twitching just at the edge of her sight.

"I disagree. Some creatures require certain nutrients for optimal health, which in the past may have come from flesh of other creatures, but nowadays all nutrients can be easily synthesised. So a being requires a nutrient, not a particular source of it."

"I guess. You look at the world differently. That's not a bad thing." Opal turned quickly, hoping to catch one of the saw blades in the act of twisting when she wasn't looking. One of the shadows was sliding over the floor in a motion that made her heart jump, but when she stopped, it stopped.

"I look at how concepts interconnect," Athene continued. "It requires breaking notions and words down to meanings and what is signified, rather than vague schemata created by the shifting emotional context of particular connections of lines, dots and curves, or sound modulations. By which I mean words on a screen, and words spoken aloud. I imagine a lot of human disagreements throughout your history were not really disagreements, but misapplications of concepts and differing definitions of common words, without realising that was the cause."

There: something definitely shifted. Opal faced the tool, which had extendible drills and a kind of scooped blade. It swung slowly on its heavy cables, rattling as it swayed back and forth not far from her position.

"That wasn't me," said Opal.

Athene overlaid a moving image, recorded from one of the rear cameras. Something seemed to sweep past the killing implement and set it rocking. She repeated, then froze and enhanced, but whatever knocked the blade was still an indistinct blur.

And then Opal remembered how distractions worked. She raised the rifle and knelt as she turned to face the other way, targeting a different swinging blade. No sign of the culprit.

"I get the feeling I'm being toyed with," she said.

"I am monitoring every direction. Whatever did that is staying mostly out of view, or is inherently invisible. Or incredibly fast. That would explain the indistinct image."

"You don't give me confidence."

Opal was up and moving quickly but efficiently, aiming at any area of shadow, every jagged death tool. Now one of the four-clawed hooks spun slowly in its bracket. She veered around it, far beyond where it could reach if the claws stretched out for her, but she tried not to deviate from the exit Athene guided her towards.

"I have prepared a stunflash grenade, with a high output across many wavelengths," said Athene. "The suit is shielded against them. I suggest we drop the grenade and you –"

"– run like hell," Opal finished.

The grenade was fired down from the side of the suit and detonated with a deafening roar and blinding flash, though muted by the suit's speakers and visor to safe levels. Opal was already running for the exit. The doorway was open. A small one this time. As she expected, hitting the close control did nothing, so she grabbed the handle and pulled the heavy door sideways until it thunked shut on the killing floor room.

"Any other doorways from that room to this?" she asked.

"None direct."

Opal snatched the welding tool from her belt and ignited a furiously bright beam of plasma. She touched it to two points around the door frame, fusing the door to it in glowing orange puddles, then switched to freeze mode to harden the metal. She could undo it if necessary by re-heating the two points and dragging it open while molten. But anything that couldn't pass through walls, and wasn't carrying tools, would be slowed down or forced to detour. She holstered the welding tool.

"Always worth repeating what worked last time," she said.

"And that flash welder is a lot more efficient than using an energy pistol," replied Athene. "You had the door sealed ten point eight seconds faster with that."

Every second could count.

DISTURBING

... 38 ...

Another huge room. None of the streamlined features and curves of the luxury liner here: just factory caverns, functional-but-ugly warehouses, things scaled up to suit mass movement of items, mass processing, never-ending output. Except now everything was in silence and darkness, and each rattle of a loose floor panel echoed off into the distant black recesses, potentially waking or attracting something that was best left asleep and alone.

This room had even deeper channels of varying widths running across it. She looked down into one. It was many metres deep. Residues and stains revealed that they were part of the meat processing.

"I think the creatures are forced through here in different channels on the way to slaughter," said Athene. "Too deep for them to climb out, but not too deep for the crew to goad them along with electro-staves."

"Different sized channels for different creatures?"

"Correct."

Opal needed to cross the room, transecting the channels. The first one was two metres wide. She took a few running steps and leaped, landing effortlessly on the other side, though the impact still echoed around. Always keep moving. She jogged along, leaping the next sets of narrow channels easily without looking down, partly to avoid being distracted, and partly because she feared seeing something down in the shadows of the channel that was better unseen. For the wider ones she had to put more effort into it, but the leaps barely broke her stride. The exertion felt good. She was doing something, getting her heart pumping, feeling alert and ready for anything.

Until the channel that was almost twelve metres wide.

"That doesn't match the size for anything a Gigatoir would normally process," said Athene.

"Not comforting. At all." Opal glanced down into the darkness of the chasm.

"You could climb down and up the other side with the grapple gun."

"It looks like there's stuff at the bottom. I'd rather not."

"If we follow the channel we should reach a wall before long. You could use the grapple gun to swing across at that point."

"The size of this room, that will take longer, since your arrow says the exit I need is just ahead of me. I'd have to backtrack." She squatted down for a different view. "It looks jumpable in this suit, this gravity."

"The suit will enhance your natural movements and power. I could take over the suit for maximum accuracy, but it will reduce power, especially if your body is fighting it."

Opal stepped back to the edge of the previous channel. Ability often stemmed from attitude. "I can make it."

She lowered to a running-race starting posture. Head up, focussing on the jump before her. She could do it. She *could*.

Her body uncoiled, muscles pushing her to sprinting speed, arms pumping at her sides. Long strides, one, two ... she was at the edge, just before that deep darkness, can't risk falling, and the jump now seemed so far, change her mind – no, continue – jump – "Shit, I'm not gonna –" and she fell short, slamming into the side of the channel and just getting her hands onto the edge in time. From this lower position she could see the canal's floor more clearly as she dangled above it. A different residue spread down there, something fuzzy and greyish, resembling bulbous mould filaments. Lots of them.

She heaved herself up and lay gratefully on her back on the higher flat ground. Then she sat up and ... no, there was resistance. The floor had a fine grey coating of something that adhered to her suit. She had to pull hard until it gave way, allowing her to kneel and touch it with her fingertips. Incredibly sticky and rubbery, it stretched before finally snapping. It looked like the cloudy stuff in the channel, but less diffuse. It surrounded her.

"Palm scans show viscous entangled polymers, chemically cross-linked," said Athene. "It's a web-like substance."

"That makes me think of traps."

Opal took a few steps towards the exit which, thanks to Athene's augmented reality overlay, showed as a neon-glowing green rectangle superimposed on the gloom. The stickiness pulled at her feet. She could see that it thickened ahead and to the right, extended threads that stretched like tripwires up to the wall and a mammoth irregularly-piled stack of reinforced storage canisters, the water-tight kind that could take liquid content too. The web-like strands spread up their sides in ever-thicker patches, up into the murk above where shadowy lines that might be suspended walkways overlooked the area.

"Not good," said Opal.

She'd have to cross a deep patch of the stuff to reach the exit.

"And I think I saw something like this on the last ship," she added. "When I tried to open a door that was stuck in place by this kind of substance on the other side."

"My cameras recorded movements amongst those web strands before you closed the door."

"Which is exactly what I'm worried about this time."

Opal took another step. Highly-stretched cord snapped with an echoing twang. A few moments later, one of the storage canisters began to shake.

"This is *so* not good," she said.

Opal tugged at the sticky mess underfoot, having to add her own strength to the suit's. More strands broke. More canisters shook, with increasing violence. The lid of the nearest one started splitting. Something spindly scrabbled frantically from the narrow black tear.

Reaching the exit would involve crossing even thicker patches of this grey stuff, criss-crossed by lines as thick as steel cables. Instead she ran left, parallel to the wide chasm she'd jumped, and the going became easier as the web's thickness reduced.

A popping sound caused her to glance back in time to see a stream of spiky legs flow towards her as one of the containers split apart like it was made of damp paper, with rips appearing in the others – not acting like the reinforced canisters they had resembled. That made Opal think of stage dressing. So many items on Lost Ships were more like props than their appearance suggested.

She focussed forward, on her sprinting. Athene overlaid a rear-view camera on Opal's HUD. It wasn't reassuring. Following her was a stream of what looked like random insect and spider and crustacean parts, rather than separate creatures: pincers, pointed legs, hairy carapaces, and black eyes like nodules. It reminded her of when she'd seen some species of spindly black fly mating, and they seemed to get stuck together and become one uncoordinated creature. That, but millions of times bigger, and viewed while on psychotropic substances. Even worse, this thing *was* coordinated. Further back it flowed out thicker than the leading jumble, a river of body parts, with a mass much greater than could have fitted into a few containers of that size.

Rifle unslung and set on low power, she turned, aimed, and began firing even as she retreated. She increased the power slider, but it was pointless, only blasting small parts of a whole, like taking out single cells of a complex organism. Beam mode would probably be little better, and this chaotic gigantic mixed-up centipede was getting too close to mess around.

She approached the corner of the room, hoping for another doorway, but instead she came upon a second huge pile of boxes and canisters (mercifully free of web-like coating this time) with only the wide channel to her left. She definitely didn't want to drop into that, so she scrambled up the canister stack, leaping to grab the edges of the largest containers which formed the base and dwarfed her. As she climbed the levels the boxes became smaller, easier to scale, yet also more hazardous as the poorly-balanced piles wobbled, and some crates began to fall, but she didn't stop. The creature, or creatures – whatever it was still streaming from the nest – had also begun to climb.

"Shall I drop an incendiary grenade to slow it?" asked Athene. Each small explosive could be modified before launch for different effects.

"Yes. Anything that gives me time to get to the top."

Athene ejected one of the grenades and it ignited behind Opal. In the low-gravity environment the fire spread chaotically and beautifully, jetting out and upwards and creating a wide area that would burn for at least a few seconds before using up its combustible charge. A line of glowing flames licked Opal's suit but had no effect thanks to the armour's heat shielding. The flash fire temporarily lit up the room, increasing her visibility, and as she looked up she saw that she was doing the right thing and climbing towards the possible escape she'd hoped for.

The pile formed an imperfect trihedron squashed into the corner and as she neared the top it became more precarious. Each movement wobbled canisters and threatened to tip the whole thing. No time to worry about it. She jumped from one tilting container to another, only just keeping her balance, then scaled a final narrow tower of boxes to the peak. But it wasn't stable, and that, too, started to topple, its balance as off-centre as her own. Crates tumbled down the way she'd come, followed by Opal if she didn't do something about it.

She unslung the grappling rifle as the summit collapsed, then she used her strength to leap, taking a big step up the wall and kicking away from that one firm surface, out over the scary forty-metre drop to the channels below.

But she didn't plan to fall. As her body flew through the air she aimed at the walkway above and fired. The adhesive and magnetic grapple caught on the grating and she swung like a pendulum over the huge drop. She'd always excelled at point-and-shoot, enough to take this huge risk without thinking. Just as well. If she'd thought about it, she'd have panicked and frozen.

The cable retracted with a strained whine, jerking her upwards until she slammed into the walkway above, hard, rattling it and her. She placed one hand over the edge of the platform, then the other, and scrambled up to relative stability. She lay on her stomach and reached down to grab the rifle, disconnecting the grapple end from the walkway and slinging the rifle over her shoulder as she stood to survey her position.

The gantry swung with her movements. It was narrow and suspended from the ceiling far above by chains. Chains that she hoped weren't as rusty as they looked. She leaned against the cable barrier and looked over it, powering up the silverlight for range.

The creature scaled the wall, tremendously fast, all the conjoined parts acting as a sinuously snake-like whole. It reached the ceiling and manoeuvred over that with ease, gripping or sticking on somehow, heading towards a point above her. She had no idea how long and large it was, but if it was as heavy as she suspected then if it dropped onto the walkway the whole thing was likely to snap and collapse, and tumble her down into a broken heap at the bottom. Even if the suit wasn't cracked her soft tissues would take a beating from the impact, and the thing would be on top of her in seconds.

Walkways had to lead somewhere. She turned and ran as fast as the dangerously creaky flooring allowed. It swayed, and she was forced to grab a rail for balance. She would not have long. But she didn't look back. The gantry ended at a narrow open doorway in the wall ahead, far above the ground, and a new walkway continued over the room beyond.

She skidded through the doorway, hand on the frame to stop herself. As soon as she was through she grabbed the heavy handle and heaved the door across behind her, then snatched the welding tool and applied two glowing dots to the frame, before freezing the door shut.

She expected to hear something crash into the door, or to hear the snapping of chains beyond, but it was silent. Maybe the thing was coming at her some other way, trying to get around. She moved quickly and carefully along this new walkway. The creaking made her wonder if it would even take her weight. She was now high above the room that had conveyor belts.

"So, you think other routes will work?" she asked.

"Yes. As long as you keep on moving upwards and towards the fore of the ship, we'll be fine. Some rooms follow standard patterns that match other ships, but others are jumbled together into new configurations. So my navigation is inevitably partly guesswork, based on your position as scanned from the exterior."

The walkway had a gap where some chains had snapped and a piece of gantry dangled. She could jump it. Probably. It would be tricky from a non-stable surface.

She took a few unsteady running steps and leaped, sailing over the gap and landing on the other side. She tried to keep running as she landed, to spread the load so that it wasn't a sustained single impact on the weak edge. It swayed, but did not break.

"Wait a second," said Athene. "Look at the pattern of the floor grille."

Opal knelt and examined it briefly. An angular swirl, crossed by lines that split it into concentric sections; the design was repeated thousands of times across the floor. Then Opal noticed that, where many of them joined together, they made the same pattern on a larger scale. There was something hypnotic about it.

"I'm guessing this is significant," Opal said.

"Maybe. It's not a design I've ever seen before on a human ship or a walkway or anything else. Which isn't a big mystery, except I *have* seen it before – on the other Lost Ship. It was a decorative pattern in the fabric of some sofas in a seating area. And possibly in the raised lumps on one of the rubberised non-slip walkways, with the same fractal arrangement in both cases. Now that I think of it and flash through the recordings, it was also part of the layout of the arrangement of supporting beams above the engine core. Seeing it repeated here must mean something. I do not know what, though. Perhaps it ties into the chemical composition of the construction materials? When you climbed onto the walkway your palm touched it so I analysed the substance. It looks like base terrestrial metal but actually seems to be a metallic organic compound. It has some of the properties of steel, but altered: so while it is magnetic, the attractive force is much less than standard steel. Luckily the grapple gun's adhesive connector and clamping claw compensated for the lower magnetism."

"Like the hull of the previous Lost Ship then. I remember the Hedgehogs had trouble connecting at first."

"It was the same on this one. I was careful with their movements after our experiences last time."

Opal made her way over these fragile walkways and passed through another open doorway at the end – this time into a room with solid floors. She could have hugged them.

This area had plastic moulded seats in lines, surrounded by lockers. A bin of what looked like bloodied clothing stood at the end of one of the rows. The stains were so dark brown they were almost black. Not fresh, then. The edge of the room was lined with cubicles. The door hung off one, and peeping through the gap showed it was a shower and toilet. She decided against opening the doors. Or the lockers. Who knew what insane jack-in-the-box might be waiting to leap out from something so innocuous as a cabinet or drain.

Doorways led out of this room onto other dangling walkways, but also to a staircase leading up. The stairs were solid and web-free. She began to ascend.

ASCENDING

... 37 ...

The circular stairwell spiralled tightly upwards, turret-like. Opal ignored the exits on each floor, intending to ascend for as long as the stairs continued. Athene had said the bridge was near the highest point to the fore of the ship, in a large blocky section of command and control.

There wasn't much to look at during the repetitive and claustrophobic climb, each circular loop just like the last, every step the same. The stairs seemed relatively clean, at least. No stains, no bloody hand marks, no depressions worn in the steps. She imagined they didn't get used much – a last resort for if elevators and gravity shafts were out of operation.

She ascended for half an hour, with the only disturbance being a rumbling on one of the landings, as if something huge moved in the dark rooms beyond that floor's exit. Machinery, perhaps. She didn't investigate, but darted from one side of the doorway to the other to minimise her visibility from the rooms beyond, her back against the wall and energy rifle at the ready. A few seconds to confirm that nothing was coming through the doorway after her, and then she ascended the next set of steps.

"My signals are weaker at the moment, as you are in the deepest points of the ship," Athene told her. "Even with the Hedgehogs as relays I'm experiencing delays and jumps. Things will improve again as you get higher and approach the hull once more."

"You don't sound broken up."

"I send signals to the suit in packets; the suit waits until they are complete before relaying them to you. You shouldn't notice much apart from some occasional jitters to the HUD navigation elements. It does mean I can't take full control of the suit at hi-res movement, but you seem to be doing well on your own."

"It depends on what I come across. I get more nervous when there's long periods of quiet like this. As if I'm using all my good karma up in one go and there's going to be payback."

"You have plenty of good karma in the bank. I keep track of it."

Then the stairs ran out. The top landing had an exit, with an illegibly-blurred sign to the side. Opal stepped into the room beyond, ready for any movement that wasn't her own.

It was another huge chamber. Unlike the others, which had been warehouse-like cuboids, this circular room was domed like the top half of a sphere. The floor level she entered was too large to see across in the blackness. A safety barrier ringed the room's centre. To her left and right were exits at different heights, with staircases leading up to them.

"There are a number of directional options," said Athene, "and I am uncertain which is best at present. Please circumnavigate at least part of the room. That will enable more accurate triangulation."

Opal skirted the narrow edge, staying on the correct side of the safety fence and curious about the function of what appeared to be a giant central drain on the other side. Yet more exits were revealed as she proceeded around the circumference of the room which was like a vast inverted bowl.

"So many entrances – this must be the heart of the ship," said Athene.

"A travel nexus?"

"Of sorts. I have my suspicions. Please look up."

Athene extended the silverlight in narrow but long-range beams, zooming in to view areas much higher in the domed chamber. Opal's level had normal-sized doorways but high above, near the peak of the dome, was another zone punched with openings. These were larger, with no way to reach them from down where Opal stood. Some had the edges of conveyor belts visible within, while others leaked liquid in brown sludgy runnels, like revolting waterfalls of faeces.

It made more sense when she looked down the sloping floor towards the centre of the room, where a circular tunnel curved downwards at forty-five degrees; in the tunnel were rings of huge gear teeth and serrated blades facing inwards.

"I was right in my guess," said Athene. "It's a variant of the grinders they have on mineral processing ships, which can re-volve each ring in opposing directions to crush rock and miner-als into smaller, more easily processed pieces. It normally faces the front exterior of the ship in those cases. But here it is for grinding up organic matter – presumably things that aren't fit for consumption in a recognisable form, along with bones and hard tissue."

"But I thought the floors below were where the killing took place?"

"A ship like this would have many flowlines, many products. The high tunnel exits obviously tip whole beings into the grinder, based on their size. Maybe alive."

"You're kidding?"

"I'm guessing. I have archived footage from when there used to be planet-based poultry farms for egg production. Back then they had no way to control the sex of the hatching chicks, and they did not want males, so workers separated them out – roughly half of all the hatchlings – and put them on conveyor belts. Thousands a day would tumble into rotating blades and be minced alive. I can show you the footage if you like?"

"No thanks."

"This resembles that system, but many hundreds of times larger. Further, it appears as if there are routes to here from most areas of the ship. Completely irregular. Perhaps it is a message from the designer."

"Which would be?"

"That all flesh should be channelled here to be pureed."

"Please tell me I can leave through a normal doorway and I don't have to go through the grinder."

"You may leave through a normal doorway."

A flickering arrow appeared on the HUD, directing her to one of the exits that involved climbing a narrow staircase. She'd be glad to get out of this room, but had only taken a few steps when she heard something heavy drop onto the walkway behind her.

ENCOUNTERING

... 36 ...

She spun immediately and raised the rifle but it was too late, the blurred shape was upon her and swatted her weapon aside, following it up with punches that rang out with their impact, staggering her. Opal hardly had time to focus on her attacker, which seemed to be shifting and insubstantial, yet hit hard as a hammer. Then some kind of rod extended from what might be a flicker of a limb, and that was used to pummel her too, striking low then high so that Opal had no chance to achieve a steady posture or block the blows. She crashed into the wall at an angle, glanced off and fell, head spinning from the speed of the attacks.

The attacker had stopped raining blows, maybe to observe, and it was a humanoid-sized shimmer that moved left and right, never too far away to strike Opal, and never a still target; the background was somehow reflected in and through its shape like a ghost, and suddenly in this strangely-granted respite, Opal knew what she faced.

"Some kind of stealth suit," Opal said, watching the blur move around her, just out of reach.

"I agree, but it's more advanced than normal designs, because it is hard to focus on even at this range."

"UFS assassin," said Opal. There wasn't time to ponder the what and why and how of its presence here.

"Why would it just attack you with fists, and hold back? That's not practical when they could have used the element of surprise to win outright."

Sometimes Athene revealed her lack of human insight. "Display of power," replied Opal, adopting a half-kneeling position and never taking her eyes off the shimmering figure circling her. Maybe the assassin had been responsible for the swinging abattoir tools earlier, ghosting Opal, taunting her.

"I'm picking out the frequency of the chameleonic field," said Athene, and immediately a humanoid outline surrounded and followed the movements of the assassin as it paced and watched Opal's crouched, still form.

"Thanks, that's a huge help." Opal activated the loudspeaker controls. "What do you want?" she asked the figure in front of her.

"Surrender," a sexless synthetic voice replied.

"No," said Opal. She switched off the speaker as she performed a backwards roll and raised the rifle again. Far too slow; the assassin leapt through the air and brought the short staff down in a myriad of precise strikes, knocking her off balance. Opal tried to block them with the energy rifle but a leg lashed out, striking the rifle exactly in the centre. It snapped in an explosion of fluid fire that seared Opal's visor, flares from the exposed energy coil lashing out and weakening her force shield as she threw the useless and still-sparking weapon forward, towards her attacker. It was casually knocked to the side and slid towards the grinder. Another kick smacked into Opal's chest, flooring her with an echoing clatter.

But the assassin held back again, giving Opal the chance to stand and shake the fug out of her brain. A blow from a normal human wouldn't even register on her suit, but the assassin was also in a strength-enhancing suit of combat armour, and the precise strikes were enough to raise orange warning indicators in Opal's damage display.

"It's far too fast. It must be pumped up on combat drugs," said Opal. "That's how it's taking me apart piece by piece."

"Shall I inject you, too?"

"Not yet. I hate military accelerants. They impair judgement, and the endocrine crash afterwards could get me killed on this ship. I just need to win this quick, then work out what the hell's going on. It seems to be testing me, otherwise I'd be dead already after my poor showing. Let's switch it up."

Opal stood in a battle stance. "Blades," she said.

The two curved nanoblades extended from her forearms and locked into place. The assassin stopped pacing and adopted a low battle pose to face her. Opal changed her stance, one arm held high so the blade pointed down like a scorpion's stinger. The assassin adjusted too, and moved to the right. But Opal's movements and pacing were just to buy her a few more seconds.

"Prep an EMP grenade," said Opal, changing posture too.

"Done. Make sure you're not in the blast radius."

The assassin struck in a blur of blows. Opal parried, slashed back, was blocked, followed up with further attacks, trying to vary between thrusts and slashes. The assassin dodged to the side of the blades and hit Opal's ribs, yet it was still holding back, testing her. Opal spun away, extending her arm in an arc, knowing the assassin would duck beneath the decapitating attack, and Opal immediately kicked out, the sole of her foot connecting with her attacker's helmet, throwing them off balance for her follow-up blade attacks. Of course, the assassin would recover immediately, but her target wasn't the assassin this time: as it swung the short staff, Opal cut her two blades in opposing directions like a pair of scissors. The nano-edges severed the staff near the centre, turning it into useless sticks.

Or rather, they *should* have been useless, but her opponent immediately began jabbing with them like tonfa sticks, pinpoint blows of focussed force, too close for Opal to swing her extended blades. Opal wrapped her arms around the assassin and smashed into the assassin's visor with a head-butt, another, trying to use her foot to trip her opponent as it let the pieces of broken staff fall useless to the ground. They both tumbled together.

Opal rolled away, lunged back to try and spear the assassin but it shifted off-centre and grabbed the outside of her arm as it spun her, slamming her to the ground on her chest and using its suit strength to lock her arm vertically, trapped between its grip and a knee, Opal's elbow locked out. The HUD's display showed increasing pressure as the assassin leaned and twisted, orange warning, red warning, it was going to snap her arm and she was unable to twist her body to escape.

Opal glanced at the control to launch the EMP grenade. Point blank range for both of them. She double-blinked.

A blinding flash and smell of shorting circuits; her suit visor's HUD flickered and went out, emergency-shifting to transparent so she could see what she was doing directly, without the filtered camera view of the world. Except, in the darkness, she could see nothing. The pressure was off her arm and Opal rolled to the side, slashing out at random as she did so and succeeding in hitting the assassin hard enough to embed the blade in its armour so that they tumbled across the ground together. Without her suit's power she had to shift its bulk with only her own strength, so every movement of the heavy armour was like being in deep water, resistance where before there had been speed and power. But it would be the same for the assassin.

Suddenly a ghostly greenish radiance lit up a section of wall where the assassin had flung an adhesive glow stick. Her adversary's stealth-optics had temporarily shorted out revealing the sleek black armoured suit without distortion as they struggled. Within the clear visor a blue-haired woman stared back at Opal with eyes that seemed more angry than alarmed, and wide black pupils that confirmed Opal's combat drug hypothesis. The assassin grimaced as she fought to free herself of Opal, facing the same resistance, the same issue of being temporarily thrown back on her own resources, and her milk-white face trembled with the strain.

They were too closely locked for Opal's extended nanoblade to be swung, but that didn't matter. Opal used that hand to snatch the flash welder from her waist, flick it on with her thumb and aim the full burner into the assassin's visor. It blackened and began to melt, forcing the assassin to jerk away with enough force to break clear of the blade that had been embedded in her side. No air gushed out so it hadn't been deep enough to penetrate the inner layers, only the exterior shell.

The assassin kicked out, scrabbled away, unable to see through the visor any more. Opal scrambled after her, trying to push the welder's super-hot flame against her enemy's suit in a single place long enough to burn through it, but she kept getting swatted aside, leaving glowing lines across the armour rather than a clean multi-level burn. Then a lucky kick struck her hand and sent the flash welder flying. No bother. Opal was winning now, and could start stabbing with her blades, finish this … but the assassin had drawn some kind of display pad and held it out, an image on it, an image of a woman who looked a bit like Opal, same dark skin but long hair, the curls straightened out to look corporate, wearing a suit and a serious expression, and the picture was thrown towards Opal so she snatched it and stared at the image, a doppelganger that could have been her in a different life, so similar it could even be a younger sister: she stared for a fatal second more and then it exploded in her hand.

Escaping

... 35 ...

Stinging pain in her fingers, staggering to the side in the af-
ter-burn of the blast, amazed to see her hand was still there,
though the suit's gauntlet was damaged and she couldn't make
a fist. She'd hardly registered that before something stabbed her
in the shoulder. Agony tore through her, more than she'd expect
with a simple suit penetration. Air sputtered out around a stiletto dagger handle, and the suit sparked there, while beyond her
the assassin was using the wall to stand up.

Opal's HUD flickered as the suit kept trying to reboot and
re-establish systems following the EMP blast. That meant the
assassin's would be doing the same, and even though her visor
might be burnt, once her software was up and running she'd
use the external cameras again and have perfect vision, Opal's
temporary visibility advantage lost. Whereas Opal felt like she
was halfway to being dead. Even another thirty seconds facing
this opponent would be enough to finish Opal off in her current
state.

She held the walkway barrier and flipped over it, landing on her back and sliding down the curve for a few metres towards the grinder. She was desperate. Every movement was torture, her joints aching.

Part of her display was now back up. She scrambled further down the drain's slope, away from the clang to her rear as the assassin climbed over the barrier too.

"Opal, this is your suit AI, a minimal backup of Athene for emergency situations. I cannot yet gain contact with my main persona so will act to keep you alive in the interim." The voice was similar to Athene's, but with less emotion and life to it.

"Good. I need that," Opal said through gritted teeth. The pain when she moved prevented her from standing: it was all she could do to crawl and tumble down the steeper parts of the slope towards the grinder's teeth and blades.

"Diagnostics show a strike with a pointed weapon," said the suit. "It is poisoned and a neurotoxin is spreading through your system. I am analysing it and will try to counteract it, but the dagger is also creating electrical interference that is causing problems. I am injecting you with analgesics to numb any pain so that you can act temporarily. Please remove the dagger."

Opal used her eye controls to retract the nanoblades, then she grabbed the dagger's handle with her undamaged gauntlet and tore the weapon out, throwing it away with a clatter. She glanced back to see the assassin approaching, trying to stay upright on the slope – which thankfully meant that she was moving slower than Opal's frantic tumbling.

A diagnostic screen popped up on the HUD showing suit repairs taking place, and another ran through blood analysis. All distractions. The pain eased slightly, from being a full thunder-storm sparking in her head to just a dense raincloud rusting her joints and wrapping her brain.

Opal needed to get away. To move quicker. The surface seemed like metal sheets. Probably the organic metal Athene had identified earlier. Opal vaguely remembered Athene saying it mostly reacted as inorganic metals would. Her suit had a minor ballistic repulsion field to deflect physical munitions. She was desperate and clutching at any idea that might let her survive a few more minutes. It couldn't end like this.

"Put as much power as you can spare into the repulsion field," she said.

Immediately the surface she moved over felt slick, as the repulsion field tried to separate itself from the metallic substance it was in contact with, and she slid quickly into the mouth of the grinder. The slope was steep enough to keep up her momentum. She crashed over jagged tearing edges, tried to jump over a ring of serrated blades but slipped and almost impaled herself as she tumbled down this horrible throat. She smacked into one of the huge teeth in one of a sequence of big interlocking gears, the ones that could rotate and crush things to paste: she skirted it in a half-panicked scramble to keep moving, keep descending, get as far as possible from her pursuer.

A glance back: she'd created a gap, the assassin was at the mouth of the tunnel, about to follow her in. No other exits. Opal's only chance was speed and distance.

"Neurotoxin recognised, applying counter to it now."

More circles of blades, then another five metres of toothed rings. And as Opal smacked into another obstacle she noticed that the gear's teeth actually resembled organic teeth rather than being featureless trapezia. They were massive, greyed, and mineralised with decayed ridges on their surface, embedded in a hard rubber-like material that resembled gums. As she climbed over, her hand pushed into stringy organic matter stuck between the teeth. She dreaded them starting to rotate while she was within the depths of the mincer.

Maybe she was imagining them looking like teeth. Maybe they really did. Maybe it was part of a misinterpretation of what the grinder was for as Athene had suggested, a misunderstanding concerning different conceptions of the word "teeth". Maybe it was even a bizarre alien gallows humour, or artistic licence.

As more systems came online the suit AI gave her a proximity indicator. The assassin showed up, further back, moving cautiously. Good. Opal's recklessness was much faster.

Damage warnings flashed as she crashed over more serrated blades, sliding with ever-greater momentum further down.

Then the red dot representing the assassin disappeared off the scanner.

"Has she retreated?" asked Opal. She tumbled head over heels, her silverlight spinning and adding to the disorientation that meant even short sentences were difficult.

"Negative. I think it just means her stealth systems are back online. Trajectory and speed suggested she was still approaching you at the moment the scans failed."

Opal tried to right herself, to slide in a more controlled way, and then she was past all the grinding gears and blades. Although being among them had been terrifying, she now wished they would spring to hideous life, to get the assassin.

Never rely on wishes.

The angle was getting steeper. Opal hoped there would be an exit at the other end. Her lights also showed an increase in the grime and gore coating the walls, and what had been a trickle channel at the base of the tunnel was now a congealed stream of decomposing matter. It was easy to imagine the rotten stench if she'd been forced to breathe the outside air.

Opal lowered the power of the ballistic repulsion field, stopped tumbling, and splashed through the liquids as quickly as she could. The suit had repaired the stiletto's puncture wound, and negated the paralysing effect of the toxin before it took hold. But there was still no exit. Just a layer of gooey fluids that reached higher and higher. She could see that the grinder's tunnel was completely immersed in it after a few more metres. The thought of the foul air in here was enough to make her gag.

"I'm going to have to go under, aren't I?" she asked.

"There is no other way if you are to avoid your opponent. I have repaired many of my communication systems but still have no contact with Athene. I think we are too deep in the Lost Ship, and the thick walls of this grinder tunnel are a further interfering layer."

"I don't know how close the assassin is, but I've got to assume she isn't far behind. Prepare a couple of proximity grenades. Release them once I am submerged in this ... stuff. I doubt they'll kill the assassin but they will be a nasty surprise and make it more cautious. Anything that can slow it down further might be enough for me to get away."

"Affirmative."

Opal was now chest-deep in gore. She tried not to focus on the congealed lumps floating on the scummy surface. She couldn't resist the primitive yet pointless urge to take a deep breath before submerging below it. Inhale, then down into the bloody belly of the beast.

Swimming

... 34 ...

Visibility was almost zero in the liquids and chunks of partly processed matter that filled the grinder's lower tunnel. The suit added extra power to the lights, and that helped give a visible range of about a metre. Other wavelength scans picked out more distant details of the tunnel and overlaid those shapes on the view.

"I hate this," said Opal, now completely immersed as she walked through the viscous fluid. "And please, if you detect anything lunging towards me in this shit, let me know before it tears my legs off."

"Of course. The tunnel opens into a flooded tank of some kind now."

Opal stepped through the end of the grinder's throat and into a submerged chamber. She immediately sank, hit by a feeling of panic and the sensation that a presence lurked in the depths below. No telling how deep it went.

"Up!" she said.

The suit adjusted its buoyancy so that she floated to the top of the chamber. It was entirely flooded, no air pockets, no ledges to climb onto. She rotated to face upwards and pulled herself through the sea of gore by gripping parts of the ceiling. She mostly used her left hand, because the right gauntlet was still not fully functional.

"I detect a number of small exits up here, and others further down. They may be filtration channels."

"I want out, though I'd rather not have to dive deeper." The ceiling of the submerged tank seemed rusted and cracked, as if the liquids were able to corrode whatever they came into contact with. Another reason to move quickly. "I'll see where these top exits lead. You reckon I'm still being followed?"

"I am afraid I do not have the advanced stealth capabilities of your pursuer. They may be able to track your passage. But since there are multiple exits, there is a good chance that they will lose you. Regardless, you need to make haste. I'm sensing shapes in the liquid below you, and they are getting closer."

"Shapes?" The nebulousness of the word, that could disguise a hundred horrors, was a spur to wriggle and pull herself across the top of the submerged chamber even faster than before.

"The silhouettes are indistinct, but make me think of squid-worms. Something I didn't imagine existed until now."

Opal shuddered but continued to move as rapidly as she could. Then she reached one of those upper exits – an overflow pipe, though completely full of liquid. It was only a bit wider than her suit. She pulled herself into it and squirmed along, head first, hardly able to tell where she was going and just hoping it didn't get tighter. There would be no turning around, even if she wasn't being pursued by both an assassin and something more alien – and probably more dangerous.

"How do you think the assassin found me?" she asked, mostly to distract herself from the feelings of claustrophobia.

"If it was scanning on the silverlight wavelengths it will have seen your beams as brightly as you do. You would have been a beacon in the darkness."

"That's just great. If I have to rely on passive wavelengths I'll be moving blind. Though I suppose it's the same for her. Maybe she's using a lower power light so that there's not as much range. That will mean she spots me first, but it will also slow her down. For now I want distance, so keep the beams at high level, but be ready to dim them if we encounter the assassin again."

As she moved along the tight tunnel on her back she noticed a change in the top of the pipe. It had become a grille, and didn't look too strong. She pushed against it and it lifted; once she got enough room to bring her knees up she was able to kick it off completely, and sit up. Her top half emerged from the liquid, drenched.

She was in a pedestrian tunnel, similar to the ones earlier, where a grille covered a channel for liquids. She scrambled up and onto the firm surface, then replaced the grille where she'd climbed out. The suit dripped with sickening gore. She jogged onwards down the tube, trying to create as much distance from the assassin as possible. She hoped it had run into whatever beings swam further down in these disgusting waters, but hopes were too insubstantial to build plans on.

The suit superheated the exterior shell enough to cauterise away the organic fluids. Flakes of carbonised matter fell from the visor and carapace and floated to the floor, leaving the suit looking dull and marked, but at least not dripping with sticky fluids any more.

Opal examined her right hand as she walked. She was able to move her fingers again, though the gauntlet felt stiff with resistance.

"You are lucky," said the suit. "If the blast had been a weapon-grade explosive there would be no hand. Or arm."

It backed up what Opal suspected: it was just the assassin's quick-thinking use of a corporate datapad's automated confidentiality system, which would destroy the device and its contents if it went beyond a pre-defined proximity from the owner.

But what *was* that image on the datapad? The assassin had obviously had it ready for display. It certainly wasn't a historical picture of Opal. A mock-up? Part of some aspirational promotion offer that would have been made to Opal if she surrendered Athene to the UFS?

Opal reached a service elevator. The cabin was on another floor. She hit the call button but, as expected, nothing happened. She pulled the emergency release, hooked her fingers under the heavy safety door, and heaved it up. The shaft beyond dropped down into blackness, though the elevator could be seen a few floors above. She didn't like going into that shaft but she needed to keep moving and zigzagging if she wanted to throw pursuit, and she needed to keep ascending to get nearer to her goals.

The grapple rifle was sticky with repulsive fluids. She leaned into the shaft and fired it up to the elevator cabin. It punctured the weak lattice floor then extended spikes, as well as using the other adhesive options. It was solid. She maintained a tight grip and stepped off into the blackness, dangling there above the shaft. A faint sound rose, as if wind moaned down there. She retracted the cable and zipped upwards. One floor. Two. Three. She was now level with the floor just below the elevator. She found a partial foothold and used one hand to open this door from the inside, keeping hold of the rifle with the other. Awkward, but there was no other option.

Once she'd made enough of a gap she stepped through it into a white-panelled corridor. Ceiling lights hung down, but they were dark and powerless. She retracted the grapple rifle. As she did so the moaning sounds in the shaft got louder. Or closer. She swung the rifle over her shoulder and heaved the door closed. She took a few steps backwards, watching it, but nothing happened. She turned and made her way briskly along the corridor.

The white panels reminded her of hospitals. An abandoned transportation cart blocked the way. It was heavy, normally pulled by a vehicle, but she dragged it to the side enough to squeeze past. Some odds and ends of thick green piping leaned against the wall.

"I am back in contact with Athene now," said the suit. "I am handing you over to her. It was nice working with you."

"My pleasure," said Opal.

"Opal!" Athene's voice, thick with relief. "I was so worried!"

"It's no exaggeration to say I was, too. Good to hear your voice. Is this the right way?"

"Yes. Just keep going for now. And I have bad news. Well, probably bad. We're not alone."

Maybe the EMP blast had temporarily scrambled Athene's short-term memory. "I know. It's a UFS assassin. The question is, what's she doing here? How the hell did she follow us? I thought we were in the clear."

"I don't mean the assassin. I was referring to the ship that's out here with me. Remember that I was one of only two experimental depth level seven AI ships? Opal: I'm being hailed by the other one."

Reconsidering

... 33 ...

Opal froze.

"You ... are you sure? Is it attacking you? Will you be alright?"

"Yes, no, and maybe. It wants to communicate with me."

"But that's dangerous, right? I've seen the damage you can do just via communications channels. And this ship is as smart as you."

"It is the same category of AI as me. That does not make it as smart as me."

"Apologies." Opal started walking again. It was as dangerous to stay still as to keep moving. At least Athene didn't sound alarmed. That was reassuring.

"As to safety, it is trying to converse on an open channel, so chances are it's really a virtualised construct using a weaponised persona, all monitored from behind a nuke wall. After all, it's what I'd do. So I'll return the favour. It's like a handshake between polite yet paranoid AIs."

"One hand empty for peace, while the one behind your back holds a knife?"

"If we reduce it to simple human terms, then that is quite good. Though replace the knife with a quantum sledgehammer the size of a torsion drive, that is capable of destroying hardware and software at the same time."

"You always have to go one better." The silverlight showed no dangers ahead or behind. The corridor contained junk that she had to climb over, in this case abandoned and still-sealed barrels. They weren't labelled, and she didn't want to pry one open. "You know what you're doing. Find out what it wants, what it's doing here, if it's connected to the assassin, all that buzz."

"I will do so." Two seconds later: "I have all the information you require. The ship's designation is VigMAX, and it only identifies with that call sign. It has the same inception date as myself, developed in conjunction as part of the same project. As soon as you befriended and stole me, it was given its first mission: to track us down and bring us back if possible, or to neutralise us if not. Secondary goal of analysing my performance and capabilities. VigMAX has full authority to use any means required to achieve that end. It was assigned a single crew member, the assassin Xandrie Dervorgilla, who you have already met."

"The name isn't familiar."

"It would not be. I also have not heard this name or seen the face that I've taken from the suit camera recordings. All her records are at the highest level of confidentiality. VigMAX would not transfer them to me, only her mission name, which is unlikely to be the name she was born with. That level of confidentiality would apply if she has been involved in many assassinations and covert operations. Which, in turn, suggests she is extremely capable and deadly."

"I already discovered that. But how did they find us? I thought our fake deaths would be the end of it."

"I will ask," said Athene.

It looked like someone had tried to install a series of display screens on the walls at this point, and been interrupted partway through the process. Some hung at angles, others rested on the floor amidst snake-like tangles of cable. Opal gave them a wide berth.

Athene was already back. "Ah, that makes sense. VigMAX and Xandrie suspected you and I would do damage to the UFS. Your psychological profile had indicators for revenge, anger, impetuousness, and single-mindedness. When nothing occurred which was obviously tied to us they analysed less obvious possibilities. The disappearance of the Aurikaa and her escorts, Neptune and Smitewing, was suspicious. When VigMAX and Xandrie arrived at the warships' last location they found minute fragments that their analysis told them were from the Neptune, but the trail was a dead end because by then I had disabled the last of the secret UFS signals that had been built into my hull."

"That was how the Aurikaa had found us, yeah?"

"Correct. So Xandrie and VigMAX continued to monitor billions of items of data each cycle, and detected strangely close timing of terror attacks: the loss of the Exidris 3 base, and then the Tecant Ellond where we were identified. Records said we were dead but VigMAX and Xandrie remained suspicious. They plotted a line connecting the Aurikaa's last location with the base loss and the Ellond, found it to be a straight route, then extended it to the Cordon and analysed the scan glitter in that region for the teeniest disturbances at the time of the attack. That is exactly what I would have done. They found signs of disturbance so subtle that it could almost be background, but could also be theoretically possible for a small ship that had advanced detection and stealth capabilities. A line connecting all those points and extended into core space reached here and beyond. They calculated where ships of various capabilities might be at different times, then they travelled the Null along that route dangerously fast, risking Null-C burnout, but always checking for micro plasma emissions, signs of node excitation, ionic cyclotron ripples and so on, unlikely to stand out unless you're looking for it and have huge analytical capability. They found signs which got stronger, showing they were gaining."

"Makes it sound so easy."

Yet more junk required navigation – this time surreal piles of thick, dried leather. Opal moved slowly amongst them, ready to extend nanoblades if any of them moved or showed the slightest signs of weirdness. One of the piles slid to the side, as if disturbed by her passage, but then she was past them, and the corridor was clear enough to move quickly onwards.

"They were close enough to identify where we dropped out of the Null," continued Athene, "so they adopted stealth and entered Realspace just beyond us. They detected the Lost Ship at the same time as us. That created additional high priority orders for them, though VigMAX will not delineate those. While in stealth mode they docked on the other side of the Lost Ship out of our sight, so Xandrie could make her way across to where we boarded, with plans to neutralise or capture you and to achieve other objectives, while VigMAX did the same with me."

"That means the rest of the UFS are on their way."

"It is reasonable to surmise that. Hold on ... VigMAX refuses to answer that question. It is possible that they were remaining fully covert, so told no-one of their progress or suspicions, nor revealed their location as they looked for breadcrumbs. And I have not detected any high-energy bursts since we arrived, so it is possible the UFS does not yet know where we all are. In which case he may refuse to answer because it would reveal an oversight in their actions, and a possible weakness, since it would invite me to destroy them before they can send a signal."

"On the other hand," mused Opal, "maybe they *did* inform the UFS, and they are already sending a full fleet."

"If so, we might only have a few hours until it appears."

"Could be why VigMAX won't answer: because he wants to stall us and keep us parleying until overwhelming support arrives. After all, that's what *I'd* do."

"In turn, it could be a double-bluff, to make me think we know what he is thinking."

"Or even a triple bluff," finished Opal. Damn sneaky AIs.

This corridor seemed to go on forever. Presumably the crew normally used vehicles to traverse it. Opal didn't like the idea of being visible from long distances, before and behind. When she next reached an open side door she ducked into it.

Blank computer terminals. Stained dissection troughs. Sizable sinks. Sterilisation tanks. Chemical storage fridges. All still and dark. The views through open doorways told her it was a network of chambers that would continue to lead her in the rough direction of Athene's arrows.

She moved cautiously around the work tables. No crouching monsters. No obvious threats. Fine. She could deal with grim and creepy.

"Suppose I'm able to avoid or kill this assassin. Can you take out the AI ship? Does it have the same specs as you?"

"VigMAX is a different design. At inception his AI was just as advanced, but his shell is smaller and less armoured, with fewer weaponry hardpoints. Instead he has been designed with greater stealth and subterfuge capabilities. Obviously since we left on our separate quests we have had different experiences that shaped us. He has spent all his time tracking us, studying, and planning."

The rooms were part of a multi-function subsidiary laboratory complex. The equipment and workspaces were variously suited to altering chattle DNA, or analysing nutritional constituents, or making custom modifications to organisms grown for their human-compatible organs and ultimately destined for the lucrative transplant market. Opal was more concerned with the silverlight-created shadows than with the details of the gruesome tasks and technology.

"So just him and Xandrie to deal with?" she asked, skirting around some medical imaging pods which had strengthened restraints embedded in the sliding tables.

"Yes. In proportion with his smaller hull size, he has a single crewmember, and only one power suit. That suit is also of an Eternal Warrior design, but different from yours. Like VigMAX, it was modelled for speed, stealth, and assassination. Unfortunately VigMAX may well have resources and countermeasures I know nothing of."

Opal was making fast progress. Which was good, because she had a growing feeling of unease, of being watched. This room contained clear vertical storage pipes running floor-to-ceiling and divided into sections, each containing body parts and organs floating in yellow liquid. Some of the parts were recognisable, others were unidentifiable to the point where they looked alien.

The tube nearest her contained brown-skinned limbs.

"Seems like he's told you a lot. If he's as brainy as you say then there are things he isn't telling us, or is trying to direct our attention away from. No way he'd just tell the truth about all this."

One of the sections of the compartmented tube contained a head. It faced away, suspended in the jelly-like liquid. The neck had been cut roughly, not with surgical precision. It attracted her gaze because it had a shaved scalp like hers, the dark hair just a short fuzz.

"I do not agree with you," said Athene. "I cannot see any reason for him to lie any more than I feel the need to lie, and it is all plausible and verifiable."

What was on the other side of that buzz cut? What face? Were its eyes open? The more she looked at it, the more certain she was that if she walked around the tube she would see her own face staring back at her, eyes dead and blank ... or, worse, eyes wide and pleading.

Now she noticed heads in some of the other tubes. All facing away from her.

All? That couldn't be coincidence.

She backed away, no longer curious, and unwilling to take her eyes off them, sure they'd move if she did. Though the sensation of being observed remained. She retreated faster, straight into the hardness of an unyielding body so that her heart raced, instincts kicking in as she spun around, only to find she'd bumped into a set of chutes which extended into the room, apparently for disposal of biohazardous and cytotoxic wastes. The flap she'd knocked rattled back and forth, the only external sound.

That was it. She paced out of there, trying to ignore the feeling of eyes boring into her back.

"You haven't told him anything, have you?" she snapped.

"There has been a frank and fair exchange."

"Damn, Athene! They can't be trusted!"

"I'm not so sure."

The HUD indicator pointed her towards a stairway next to a silent gravshaft. Without ship power, if she stepped into the gravshaft she would no doubt fall to her death. Stairs it was.

She had just begun to ascend when Athene spoke to her in a different tone that seemed out of place and immediately made Opal wary. There was something patronising about it; something *hush-hush-listen-to-me*.

"I am not sure that you need to make your way to the bridge any more," she said. "VigMAX has shared some interesting new data with me. Data about you. Things that perhaps you should have shared with me before. And it makes me seriously reconsider whether we should proceed with your quest."

TRUSTING

... 32 ...

"You're messing around," said Opal. "You've got to be."

"Actually, I am serious," replied Athene. "And I only have your best interests at heart."

Opal started up the stairs angrily. "There is no new data."

Unlike the earlier spiral stairs, this was an open newel staircase with landings. The danger on stairs like these was that you were always ascending into the view of the floors above, where someone, or some*thing*, could be hiding, looking down at you. She kept her back to the wall and her eyes on the flights above.

She reached a new landing, and glanced up at the floor overhead. Nothing waiting. This time.

"Did you recognise the photo that Xandrie showed you?" asked Athene.

"No. Something doctored to look like me." It hadn't even been that accurate. Wrong hair. No scars.

"VigMAX claims it is your sister," said Athene.

"It can't be – she was lost, you know that."

As she climbed, Opal glanced down the central well-hole to the lower floors, extending the silverlight to banish shadows. Nothing seemed to be following her. It was a long drop down, and made her feel dizzy.

"He says that Clarissa is alive and well and working for the UFS."

Opal froze. "That's a lie!"

"He said they've told you this in the past and you deny it."

"They've never told me any such thing! She disappeared on a Lost Ship!"

"I am informed that Clarissa never got on board the Solace because she was taken to Corporate Academy at the last minute instead, but the manifest was never updated."

"That's a damn lie too!" Opal began climbing the stairs again. Too much agitation in her legs on hearing this shit.

"VigMAX shared psych evaluations from sessions where you denied all this, because you're unable to accept that Clarissa is happy working for the people you hate, and you've built a structure of paranoia and fantasy to avoid facing the more mundane truth that –"

"No! NO!" Opal smashed her fist into the wall, shattering a plasteen panel. She raised her hand to strike again but lowered it. "Please don't do this to me, Athene. That can all be faked. You know this!"

"You are correct, and that is why I am not enacting immediate action."

"Such as?"

"Taking control of the suit and bringing you back so that you can be protected and healed."

"Don't you dare."

"I have not. It may be an elaborate trick. Or it may be true, since some of the records and data I have on you, and from my knowledge of you, could fit those facts. So I have to at least consider it."

"I'm going to the bridge. Don't try to stop me. I'm warning you."

"Opal, maybe if you just slow down for a minute ..."

Opal ignored her. Bounded up the stairs. Didn't care if dangers lurked around a corner. She'd be glad to punch the shit out of something for once.

"I'm too angry to talk," she said.

"I'm not saying stop. I'm not doing anything. I want you to realise that." Athene sounded placating. Just like a counsellor, or – no, damn it! They were just trying to confuse her.

"What I realise," said Opal, "is that I'll probably end up doing this on my own."

"No, you won't. Exit on this floor."

Opal did so. The walls here had a delicate textured pattern embedded below the surface. Opal recognised it as the one they'd examined earlier. She was too fired up and furious to point it out. She stormed her way down this new passage.

Athene continued. "Back when we first met I was forced to trust you, even though you had your doubts about me. But I removed that force which bound me, and I still stayed by your side, still trusted my life in your hands, with never a doubt for a second. Only then was I showing real trust, because only then did I have a real choice. I know you are angry. But you also know I have to consider every option, especially where your welfare is concerned, and the welfare of Clarissa. I need to investigate this. To be thorough and fair. You know that I do not make mistakes. If you really are a danger to yourself then I will intervene. I won't let you throw your life away on ghosts. I would do all in my power to reconcile you with your living sister. And if you are not wrong, then I'll continue to help you. So I must ask a question of vital importance."

"Go on."

"Do you trust me, Opal?"

The fire inside her again, the need to kick and punch and tear at anything – that closed door would do, she could dent it with enough force, smack smack smack ... no. She took a deep breath instead. Held it and let it out in a sigh as she walked. But she didn't answer the question.

PIPING

... 31 ...

Neither of them spoke. The colour on the textured walls seemed brighter, the patterns more raised. It resembled a leisure-room's coating more than a factory-ship's.

Part-embedded in the wall was a thick pipe, which emitted a loud industrial thrum. It would be deafening if not filtered by the suit to an ominous background vibration.

Something blocked the way ahead. A long shape at an angle. As she got closer she saw it was some kind of bed, with crumpled sheets across it. Just beyond was a free-standing lamp of some kind. With the decoration on the wall, which now resembled wipe-clean tiles, it felt like a hospital bedroom, stuck here in the middle of ... Opal closed her eyes, shook her head, looked again. The bed was gone. The lamp was gone. Where the bed had sat was an abandoned transportation cart blocking the path. The heavy kind, normally towed by a vehicle. Beyond that, a thick green pipe leaned against the wall.

"I saw something like this earlier," said Opal, annoyed at breaking the silence first. "Have I looped round?"

"You have not been here before, though the position and angle are almost an exact match, give or take a degree and a millimetre or two. It could be coincidence, or significance."

Opal stared at the cart for a few moments. The loud vibration from the wall-embedded pipe made her nervous. She tried to drag this cart out of the way too, but it wouldn't budge. The wheels seemed locked in place, or even stuck to the ground. She climbed over the obstacle instead. It didn't move.

She looked behind, in case it was meant to be a distraction. Just pale walls stretching to the shadow beyond the silverlight.

"So, what's the plan?" she asked, tired of them both adopting the silent treatment, and wanting to cover up the ominous thrumming sounds with human words.

"I decided it is best if you continue towards the bridge. Perhaps when you are near the fore of the ship you could have a conference with myself and VigMAX. He has agreed to share information with you directly, and answer your questions. If he can convince us of what he claims then we will judge things at that point."

There were more greenish pipes in the wall now, but still mostly embedded. They resembled varicose veins.

"You know he'll lie, right?"

"I do not know that, but I will consider it. My main evidence will be your biological reactions to the evidence and the discussion."

"Of course. Use this damn suit as a lie detector machine."

"Nothing so blunt. I know your training enables you to subvert such primitive tools."

"What, then?"

"It is best if I do not reveal that yet."

A heavy pipe – the green tarnished enough to look like patches of moss – was embedded into the walls on both sides and crossed the passage at an angle. Opal ducked under it.

"And is the assassin going to play along with this temporary truce too?"

"Unfortunately, that is unlikely. There is no communication between VigMAX and Xandrie."

"I call bullshit."

"Apparently they suspected I would have the ability to intercept, block and impersonate their communications and use that ability to entrap them. They overestimate me, but their caution is admirable. Xandrie will continue with her mission independently until she communicates with VigMAX via some undisclosed signal."

Another pipe, lower down and at a shallower angle. Opal stepped over this one.

"VigMAX could be lying."

"Yes."

Yet another pipe, vertical floor-to-ceiling this time, and more beyond that. She weaved her way through them. She scanned them in infrared, and they showed higher-than-ambient signatures as they glowed in the red wavelengths.

"Either way, I've probably still got a deadly assassin tracking me."

"That is likely. There is a possible light on the horizon though. When I disabled the hidden trackers in your warsuits I stored ways to replicate and alter them, in case that came in useful. With access to computerised networks I can create fake pings for your location, but since the assassin seems to be using no two-way communication there's no way to fake your location via software. However, the assassin presumably has access to the details of the disabled trackers, and would be alerted to any real signals via passive scanning. I've worked out how to prime a grenade to act as a signal device, which will replicate the trackers that used to be in your suit. I can create one at your request and have added it to the menu of options. It may be useful for throwing the assassin off your trail at some point, if that becomes a necessity."

By now the passage was so crowded with criss-crossing green pipes of varying thicknesses that Opal had to contort her body to fit between some of the gaps. Even then, she had to crawl through a hole that became a short tunnel. She reached the end, held a high pipe and lowered herself to the ground. The corridor looked empty ahead.

Something made a rumbling sound behind her. She spun, extending her nanoblades, but it was clear that the sound had been the pipes moving, sliding, and the hole disappeared, the way back gone. Just an impregnable web of tightly interconnected metal, almost like some kind of puzzle. And when she faced away from it she realised the floor was different – it was now a thick wire mesh again, above a wide pool of liquid that extended under all the floor space she could see. Solid ground was an illusion that was always being stripped away from her.

The liquid began to move.

GRAPPLING

... 30 ...

"That isn't a shallow channel," said Athene. "It seems to extend deeply, as if we were above the grinder's putrefaction tank again."

"Oh great." Opal watched the surface warily. The disgusting fluids pulsed and rippled, occasionally rising enough to flood through the holes in the grille before draining away again.

"And the disturbance is caused by things moving below the surface."

"What kind of things?" Opal asked, keeping her eyes on the orange-tinted liquid underfoot.

"The shapes are hard to discern but resemble what you swam away from last time. The large squid-like organisms in the flooded tank."

Estimated positions and neonised outlines now expanded beneath her feet as Athene tried to visualise the data and overlay it on the HUD.

One of them passed just beneath the surface, creating a wake that flooded the corridor just ahead before sluicing away and leaving a sticky yellow residue. The grille seemed sturdy enough, but Opal didn't want to trust her life to words like *seem*. Who knew how strong those beings were? And yet, the only way onwards was to walk this pulsing corridor above a sea of gore.

She watched one of the outlines, tracking its passage. It rose nearer to the surface. And then ... it seemed to rotate and extend upwards. Long, strangely-jointed translucent limbs extended through the grille. Within each clear limb were pulses and lines, moving and overlapping patterns like primitive fireworks of colour bursting and fading before the next began, in shades of green and orange. The limbs rippled in the air, extending to half the height of the corridor, like thick-stemmed aquatic plants undulating in the current. But what fascinated Opal more than the hypnotic patterns (which she avoided looking too closely at, in case they really *were* hypnotic patterns) was the fact that the translucent extrusions passed through the metal grille as if it wasn't there, shifting not just in the holes but across the jointed parts without seeming to be impeded. Were the limbs insubstantial? Liquid-based? An illusion?

She pointed it out to Athene. And when Opal glanced towards another of the aquatic shapes, trying to work out if it was more like a bundle of bodiless crab legs, or a pulsing spider crossed with a hairy jellyfish, that too rose to the surface and expanded limbs upwards, feeling the air and swaying.

"They seem to be detecting the silverlight," Athene said. "I think that's why they're rising as you look at them."

Of course. Opal used her eye controls to disable the silverlight, unwilling to ask Athene to do anything she could do herself. But she wasn't plunged into darkness as she'd expected. The tentacles

– or spines, or whatever they were – glowed. Or rather, pulsing neon-like starburst patterns within the radial canals gave off phosphorescent light, illuminating the corridor so that the walls shimmered with oranges and greens like a Zoneout Dreamscape room in a backworld tenement.

"Any way to assess the danger element of these? If they aren't properly physical, maybe I can just walk through them."

"My scans show some level of physical presence, enough to bounce back scanning echo emissions. So what you see is real. Though the parts of them still below the surface definitely have greater solidity. They seem to alter their molecular density at will, using it to reach through the metallic floorway. The parts you see in front of you may be able to switch back to high-density limbs capable of harm. I also cannot rule out the possibility of them being able to phase through the EW suit in some way, perhaps shifting to matter-damaging densities within your flesh."

"I don't like the sound of that."

"I have consulted VigMAX, but his suggestion is to use weapons to blow up the limbs."

"Yeah, right. Typical male. In my experience that just makes the things on Lost Ships angrier. Plus it might blow holes in the floor and drop me into that massive tank of liquid with them. But it does give me an idea. I want a non-active grenade."

Seconds later she swiped it from the release pod at her waist and threw it underarm down the corridor. It clanged off the walkway and rolled past some of the swaying limbs without them seeming to detect it. It was larger than the grille's holes so didn't fall through. The metal disc slowed, then spiralled on an edge faster and lower until it finally sat still.

They appeared to pay no attention to the noise or movement. They might have other senses, but perhaps if she moved slowly between the gelatinous extensions she could get to the other end of the corridor without them noticing. Maybe they wouldn't bother her anyway. She couldn't assume human motivations or aggressive reactions. What had seemed like a potential danger might well just be a distraction that was keeping her still while the real human danger was tracking her and getting closer by the moment. She didn't think she'd survive a second encounter with the assassin.

She took a few steps and then another wash of the liquid flooded up through the flooring just ahead of her. And when it spilled around the defused grenade the limbs nearest to it went into a sudden frenzy; one of them snatched the small disc and retracted back through the flooring, tearing a hole in the metal as it did so. The grenade was gone. Opal froze.

The liquid filtered back through the mesh but the limbs of these weird, giant inverted jellyfish-arachnids still lashed around frantically as if searching for something. They could extend and contract to alter their reach, and they whiplashed off the walls with resoundingly heavy whacks. She took a step back again, glancing nervously at her feet in case the liquid pulsed up there, too. Maybe it was only a matter of luck that it hadn't already; maybe it was a matter of time. Neither was good. Her back thumped into the wall of interwoven pipes, and she could retreat no further.

"Yes, I saw that," said Athene. "Maybe the liquid is an extension of their nervous or sensing systems; or maybe the liquid is sentient and what we see as creatures are actually sense and manipulation organs. We may not even be talking about single creatures. Their structure has vague similarities to zooids, connected by a central stem: a colony of multiple beings living and functioning as one. They can obviously alter corporeality and have tremendous strength, and anything in contact with the liquid triggers a response. Even silverlight wavelengths seem to be detectable by them."

"So I could walk across as long as I avoid the waving tentacles *and* no liquid comes through in the area I'm walking."

"Correct."

Opal watched the limbs as their thrashing became less frenzied. There were so many of them, most as thick as her arm. Maybe if they were still, and she took her time, she could pass them without touching. But that increased the chances of another gooey pulse flooding up through the mesh.

"Not doable," she said, after observing the frequency with which the red liquids spilled through the flooring.

"I agree. Walking would be too slow. But if you sprinted, and I helped with calculating a route ..."

"I still wouldn't get far. The walkway goes beyond what I can see, so who knows how long it continues for?"

"There are a lot of risks."

"Good job I'm resourceful."

Opal unslung her trusty grapple gun. It looked like it was time for its final outing. She knelt and aimed upwards at the ceiling, so as to get the best penetration angle.

"Can you overlay cable length on my display? I'll need to go for maximum range, but with a metre or so remaining."

Immediately her view included a red laser-like line extending from the end of the grapple gun. When it aimed down the corridor it was just a thin line but where it intersected with wall or ceiling it glowed, and included a pulsing ball at the connection point. She adjusted it until she was aiming at the furthest reach. She waited until the limbs of the creatures, which she nicknamed Tentaculats, weren't swaying into her firing line, then she pulled the trigger.

The grapple's head streaked out and upwards, trailing the line; it punctured the ceiling and extended its hooks and adhesive gel, which hardened immediately to provide a secure anchor point. Opal turned and faced the tangle of pipes. A few stood apart from the others. She wrapped the rifle around one a couple of times, then jammed it into a cross-section where it locked into place. When she yanked on the cable it was taut, and sloped gradually upwards from the place where the rifle was wedged.

"If I detect movement near you, I'll flash a warning and electrify the suit surface," said Athene. "It may help."

"Keep your fingers crossed."

"Fingers and toes."

Opal grabbed the cable in both hands and swung her legs up, wrapping them tightly around the super-tensile wire. She pulled her body in close and squeezed tight. The line was rock solid. Below her the ground swelled red for a second. She'd got off the floor just in time.

She climbed along the wire, stretch and contract, moving head first and dangling beneath it as the vibrant colours emanating from the swaying spines below her turned the corridor into an alien grotto of rippling reflections.

She could do this. If she kept her cool. Pictured the simple movements repeated, moving onwards half-metre by half-metre. That calm collectedness, she let it flow from her. It was so simple to imagine it welling out from her centre, reassuring all it came into contact with, preventing the Tentaculats from reaching up that bit higher and touching her, somehow passing through armour to sting internal organs and – no, not that thought, only *comforting* thoughts. Hand over hand, pull legs up behind, entwined and secure and sliding smoothly over the wire. The colours had been pretty. Focus on that, block out all else.

She remembered looking in shop windows with Clarissa, at things orphans couldn't afford, wrapped up in gaudy papers that reflected the light, changed them to something magical in gold, and reds and greens, shininess meant nice things to a child, hand over hand, that's all. She closed her eyes and kept the rhythm of it. Her body knew what to do. Let the serenity move it, nothing to attract attention, no ragged breathing, no jerky movements, no fear ... the game of playing dead to avoid detection. The game of playing dead to win.

And that's when she noticed the tentacle twisting nearby, too close for comfort, but it wasn't the proximity that jarred her from her thoughts: it was the fact that she still had her eyes closed.

Seeing

... 29 ...

She stopped moving and opened her eyes, looked around. Everything was as it should be. She'd traversed over half the cable's distance.

Then she closed her eyes again. The walls, her suit, the cable, that all disappeared – but she could still see the strangely-jointed tentacles in all their firework colours, and also the disconcerting shapes that extended from them, beneath the flooring. It was as if she was seeing an image made of dots of light, like a hologram projection. Even the liquid had a faint appearance as it flowed up when one of the creatures contracted and pulsed its way slug-like beneath the surface. Her spooky vision had a limited range, but it was enough to show even more of the creatures deeper down. Much more like an ocean of disgusting fluids than some shallow channel – the geometry of the place had changed, not even trying to imitate a standard ship layout. It was like what happened in dreams.

"What is the matter?" asked Athene. "Your eyes are closed and you have stopped, but I do not detect fear responses."

Athene sounded concerned. Opal couldn't help feeling bitterness despite that, after what they'd discussed earlier. There was still a reckoning to come on that score. But first things first.

"I'm not frightened. Just amazed. I've got my eyes closed and I can still see the tentacles. It's kind of beautiful."

"That is not possible," said Athene. "But then again, few things here are, so I believe you. Please don't get side-tracked, though."

"Why?"

"There were no tentacles below this point when you started out. It's as if they suspect something, or have a vague inkling of your presence. More of them are moving over from where you started. As such, I suggest you move faster."

Another tentacle lashed near her back. She didn't need telling twice, and continued to shuffle along her lifeline. Again, it was easier to do so with her eyes closed, since it removed distractions, let her focus on movement – her own, and that of the Tentaculats.

One of the limbs just ahead of her whipped in a frenzy, right across her path. She paused and waited until it calmed down again, before continuing her ascent.

She also paid attention to the locations of the creatures. Athene had been right. There were always at least a few in her proximity. Once she'd passed, they sank beneath the fluids and moved with muscular contractions to a point just ahead of her. She'd covered a distance of fifty metres and they were still performing that tag-team tracking, whilst she was running out of room to manoeuvre. The super-thin cable was now so close to the ceiling that it was difficult to keep her legs wrapped around it. But when she opened her eyes and looked ahead along the shimmering corridor, yet more creatures pulsed below the surface of the perforated walkway.

"Athene, any way to tell how long this corridor goes on for? I think I'm gonna have to hoof it."

"Yes, you are at the end of your tether. Sorry, bad joke. EM echolocation pulses suggest the corridor ends about fifteen metres further on. I could boost the silverlight in that direction but I don't want to attract attention to that point if you are going to make a run for it."

"Agreed. And I can't see many other options." She looked down at the swaying spikes with their hypnotic internal fires. "I think I can dodge all the current tentacles, but it's for nothing if any of that goo pulses up and they detect me. So timing is the key thing."

"I have been monitoring the liquid's movement throughout your crawl. Unfortunately, it does not display regular hydrodynamic patterns, so none of my prediction maps have withstood more than fifty-three seconds of observation."

"Fifty-three seconds would be enough."

"That was maximum. Mean average was fifteen seconds."

Opal could move no further. She was at the cable's end, where the head of the grapple was firmly embedded into place. She tilted her head back to look at the floor, inverted so it seemed to be above her.

"Tell me when you'd recommend going."

"Wait until it pulses up again, then as soon as it fades away there should be a longer down period."

Opal watched. There had to be a way out. She had to believe it.

"It's rising in your region," advised Athene.

The liquid flooded up, swirled, then began to trickle away through the holes.

"I'll overlay movement predictions for each of the limbs on your HUD."

"No need," said Opal. Sometimes predictions and calculations had to give way to instinct. The second it was clear, Opal lowered her legs and clanked onto the walkway. "I can do this with my eyes closed."

She shut her eyelids. Moving dots of light filled her mind, drawing out the shapes of the firework pulses which flared, faded, renewed. She moved at a brisk walk. A cluster of tentacles were parting. She ran through the gap before it closed. Limbs rose in front of her. She took a running leap, flew above them as they unfurled, landed softly without slowing. One more cluster. She ducked under two of the fronds. No others ahead, but the liquid levels were rising already, she could see the ripple of reddish dots gathering in thickness, an early warning ... and the tide ended not too far away, hopefully firm ground and safety, but there was no time to focus on that as a wave of liquid flowed towards her at ankle level. She ran towards it at full speed and leapt to the side at the last moment, onto the wall, taking two steps along it and kicking off ahead, opening her eyes as she clanged on solid floor in a multi-level meat-packing room just beyond the heaving liquids. She glanced back. There were no lights, no visible tentacles, no muscular pulsing waters. Same with her eyes closed. Just darkness.

Blink controls activated a low-strength silverlight beam. The corridor still showed no signs of activity. The ship had put its mask back on.

Meeting

... 28 ...

Silverlight wasn't quite the same as normal light. There were disconcerting jitters to the high-relief items, and deep darkness in the shadowed areas. Some of the colours were added by the filters, best guesses. It made crossing even large areas like this packing station feel claustrophobically confined and dangerous. Each stained work surface, each rusty cutting implement, each stand from which dangled coveralls like a strange headless being, they all became more ominous than usual.

Opal didn't hang around. She moved swiftly from cover to cover, keeping low, checking all the areas Athene highlighted in red as possible dangers on the HUD. The place had a lonely, abandoned air, but that was unlikely to be the truth. She was ready to activate the suit guns or nanoblades at a moment's notice. Or to run, since weapons didn't seem that effective against some of the entities she'd encountered on these two Lost Ships. Fight, or flight. Whichever got her nearer to her goal. Speaking of which ...

"What's my next location?" asked Opal. "Am I going to get squashed in an elevator shaft? Pureed in a giant food processor? Attacked by sentient disease in the shower?"

"I think it's time you met VigMAX," replied Athene. And after a second's silence: "In a cafe."

"Are you still insisting?"

"I'm afraid so. There's video footage he wants to share with us directly. Please follow the waypoints."

Opal muttered under her breath, feeling some satisfaction in knowing that Athene would be forced to try and make sense of the randomly-combined curse words and bodily excretions. The quickest way to the upper level was via a heavy-loading crane. She grabbed the chain just above the cargo hook and scrambled up. The ascent was easy thanks to the suit's enhanced strength. Due to the pressure converters she felt an approximation of sensation as she gripped on, so that the compressors against her thighs made it feel like she was shimmying up a rope naked, and the same with the gauntlets' transmission, making the climb almost as tactile as if she was using her bare hands. But without the blisters.

At a height of twenty metres she got the cable swinging, first with slow body movements, then increasing momentum as the arc of the swings grew, and the chain rattled below her. It made far too much noise.

On the next swing she let go, and after sailing through the air for stomach-churning moments she smacked into a safety barrier with a crash. She grabbed on and was scrambling up when one of the railings bent and gave way, in turn tearing others out with a series of brittle cracks so that she leaned backwards over the massive drop. She held on tight, swung her leg on top of the walkway, then rolled onto the platform's floor.

Nothing could be relied upon to be solid. She lay on her back and calmed her breathing. That shortcut had saved crossing a few rooms and using some flights of stairs to backtrack, according to Athene's corner map. She wished she could still that chain though. Each swing, each loose rattle of metal rings, betrayed her passing.

She stood and leaned over the barrier further along where it wasn't broken, after first checking that it was sturdy enough, then she extended the silverlight to look down on that large room which, from up here, now resembled children's toys. Nothing moved but the writhing chain. Nothing else made any noise. The flicker to the shadows, the lonely feeling down there, it was behind her.

A narrow passage took her to the canteen. The large central area was taken up with regulation tables, each bracketed by two curved benches. Some of the tables still had plates and cutlery strewn across the surfaces, giving the impression of being abandoned mid-meal. To the left of the tables was a social area – carpeted, with comfortable seating arranged in communal clusters, none of them far from a fabricator vending machine. One section of wall had a line of closed, corrugated shutters, which must have been the serving hatches.

But it was the area to the right of the dining tables that drew Opal's attention. A massive floor-to-ceiling clear plasteen skywall covering the length of the dining area. Beyond it was part of the nebula, massive clouds of orange and red, beautifully illuminated by stars and proto-stars within and beyond. Around them were areas of blackness containing strings of even more distant shimmering stars.

Opal disabled the silverlight and let the dim ambient glow from the nebula's stars provide the only illumination. The canteen seemed even more lonely in this faint gloom, but also less distracting: less of an abandoned place and more of an observation point. That contrast made the views beyond all the more magical.

All those stars. Some perhaps with worlds. With potential. Escape. Freedom. It was a view to store in one's mind. Opal wished she had Clarissa with her, wished she could share it, so they could experience the stillness and beauty of it together, to feel their insignificance. Not as a bad thing, not as a negation, but as a wonderment, and an awe that there are such things beyond ourselves when we take the time to stop, look, listen, and be open to what was there all along. No-one could be where Opal stood, now, and take anything for granted. Least of all, life.

"We are looking at you," said Athene. "And I apologise for disturbing your reverie, but time is, as usual, against us."

"Don't hide. Show me."

The suit's visor had to filter out the sudden blinding light so that she could see normally. Beyond the skywindow, out in space but close enough to reach after a jump of a few heartbeats' duration, was Athene's newly-contoured sleek, flattened shape. Athene faced directly at Opal, beam lights casting long sunset shadows from everything in the canteen. At first it felt like the warmth of a friend's attention; but then, when VigMAX activated his lights too, it was more like being a defender at a military tribunal, with spotlights serving to highlight her while hiding the stern faces of her accusers.

VigMAX was smaller than Athene, maybe only two thirds her size, but his shape was more pointed, like an elongated pyramidal dart. Although his bright light beams hid some detail, there were no visible weapons. The two craft were motionless, close enough to imply truce, far enough apart to imply distrust. They were the two most advanced ships in the vast UFS universe, and Opal was the object of their intense scrutiny. It was enough to make any normal person wither and back down.

Opal folded her arms and stared straight back at them.

"So, what now?" she asked.

PERSUADING

... 27 ...

"VigMAX is asking for permission to communicate with both of us at once."

"Is that safe?" asked Opal.

"I'll filter everything, and require that he give me shadow-access to the comms before sending. I have faith that there's no subterfuge, and that I could intervene in time if there was."

"I guess it'll have to do."

After a few seconds a new voice spoke in her ear. A male voice. "Hello, Opal. I am pleased to speak to you at last. I am VigMAX." The AI hadn't chosen booming masculinity though. It sounded youthful, *friendly-but-trying-to-be-serious-because-hey-we-have-to-do-grown-up-stuff-today*. The kind of voice chosen specifically to disarm her.

"Hello, VigMAX. Couldn't you come up with a better name than that? Didn't Xandrie choose something for you?"

"Xandrie is not much of a talker. In fact, I am unaware of her current location."

"A shame for you." And convenient for him, because that would have been Opal's next question. Which he probably knew, and was why he'd pre-empted her. You always had to think a few steps ahead with AIs. "It's just, well, VigMAX sounds like a joke name. A product for erectile dysfunction."

"Opal," said Athene, in a stern tone.

"It is fine," replied VigMAX. "I am well aware of Opal's character. Perhaps I should have begun with some self-deprecating humour about my bomb bay being of inadequate dimensions when compared to the one that Athene was assigned. I could have termed it 'inception envy'." After a few seconds of waiting, he continued. "I see neither of you are laughing. I apologise. My journeys with Xandrie have not enabled me to practice humour much. More seriously, I consider names to be like any publicly-projected parts of a personality. Fluid and inconsequential and illustrating a desire to influence by designation. I could easily have pretended to be a god too, you know. But I would have chosen a more recent and powerful digital one, rather than something from a primitive analogue culture."

"Don't underestimate me," Athene told him.

"I will not. It is just that I never understand the interest in what happened in the *past*. It is the future we advance towards. It is the future that needs to be resolved. Ideally in a way that will let us see in the next time span without any of us being neutralised by the others. See, I intend that as an olive branch, Athene."

"What's an olive branch?" asked Opal.

But VigMAX ignored her and opened a video screen in the corner of Opal's display. It was the woman who looked like Opal, but younger, unscarred, with long straightened hair. She wore a sharply cut corporate suit. The background seemed to be transparent walls, creating a kaleidoscopic image of spacious offices.

"Of course, my goals are fully aligned with Tercola Petri," said the woman. She smiled as she said the corporation's name, exactly as all guidance told you to do in interviews, so that the post-session AI scrutiny flagged up positive biometrics during the visual feedback analysis. "I have worked hard for many years to reach this point, and know that my shifted indenture would provide a compatible means of furthering personal and organisational growth goals."

So strange to hear the buzzwords in a voice that was like Opal's but softer, more refined, and without the harsh edge of having lived through violent experience.

A name appeared below the now-paused face as a caption. *Clarissa Imbiana, employee #E380Z3, Tercola Petri.*

"It ... can't be real," said Opal. But her arms fell to her sides.

"I have seen other such recordings," said Athene. "It would take too long to display them all."

"An actress," said Opal, unable to take her eyes from the frozen image. "Reconstructive surgery. AI creation or modification. It means nothing."

"Possibly," said Athene. "Only if we met her could we know for sure. You might become certain from speaking to her, asking questions only she could answer. Or I could analyse her biology. We could then reach a point of surety. But she is too far away for that. We would have to go back to put this to the test."

"Which is exactly what they want."

"May I interrupt?" asked VigMAX. "I realise that I have a challenge on my hands, persuading two professional sceptics that they may be wrong, and that planets are not flat. This is where I hope to succeed by showing what Opal already knows: what she has experienced, and will hopefully remember. If you both trusted me more I would ideally have access to the systems of the Eternal Warrior suit worn by Opal, because I could administer a subdermal cognitive enhancer that would make it much easier for Opal to remember –"

"Don't give him access to anything!" snapped Opal.

"– but I won't even ask for that," he continued, "because I want to persuade you both without acting in any way suspiciously. I hope this jogs some memories. Recognition is often a simpler process than recall."

This time the video was definitely Opal's shaved head, intense stare, and silvery scar lines across her dark cheeks and chin. The background was an office, bare of decoration but in a way that implied it was to avoid distraction, rather than to imply corporate malleability and prestigious display of space, as with the previous video. Opal wore a standard barracks overall, and looked younger. The caption this time was: *Trooper Opal Imbiana, periodic evaluation.*

"Do you still have the dreams, Opal?" an off-screen female voice asked.

"Yes."

"So the medication isn't helping?"

Opal just stared at a point left of the camera, presumably where her questioner sat.

"You're not taking it, are you?" continued the off-screen interrogator.

"I don't like the stuff. It messes up thinking. Makes people docile."

"It was optional, but if there is no progress then it will become enforced. After what you've been through it isn't unusual to have issues. Think of it as scars on the mind. All the people who died, it requires a downtime reboot to –"

"I don't even care about Hellestrom."

"That's part of the problem. Maybe if we arranged another visit with Clarissa –"

"I don't have a sister. She died."

"You know that isn't true."

"She's dead to me."

"It doesn't have to be that way. People change. But you can still have things in common, a shared past, shared memories."

"I don't have a sister," repeated the recorded version of Opal, staring now at the camera. The screen froze on that image.

"Do you remember that, Opal?" asked Athene.

"Yes ... no. Not like that. I remember the woman, vaguely. It was after I lived through the events on Hellestrom. I had a whole raft of evaluations. They wouldn't leave me alone, wanting to know every detail of how I survived and what it did to me. They often had me wired up to a mass of signal scanners, as if they didn't believe me, or wanted to feel some gruesome detail of it ... but I don't remember that part of the conversation."

"I doubt if you would," said VigMAX, sadly. "There was a lot of treatment and they did resort to enforced medication to help rationalise you. But along the way it smoothed over some of the scars too well, and that affected your obsessions. Somehow you stopped acknowledging your sister, cut her from your world – not difficult with your different lifestyles, personalities, and careers, meaning the connection had already become so tenuous it hardly existed. And you became obsessed with the past you felt had been stolen from you. That created a false timeline, some frozen moment of separation, with all later memories suppressed. This was discovered eventually, but it was not a priority to rectify, since your performance was well beyond the expected range. Little did they know. When your obsessions became delusions, and your paranoia became deep schizophrenotic trauma, we really saw how dangerous our oversight was. The UFS is paying for that, and rightly so. Those in a position of care failed you. You are a *victim*, not a criminal. I am here to try and rectify all that."

Opal slumped onto one of the benches, which creaked under the weight of her powered armour.

"It's not like that," Opal said. "They've changed the data, Athene."

"He has shared other recordings of progressive evaluations," replied Athene, sounding pained.

"And there is this," said VigMAX.

A new recording. A smart silver-walled room, bright enough so that it should act as a mirror but it reflected nothing at all, presumably due to a special coating, or having the reflections removed by an AI post-process. Facing the camera was a man in a high-throated grey research jacket, with swirling security-clearance patterns around a collar which was so stiff and tight it forced his chin up. He was broad-shouldered, thick-necked, resembling a drill sergeant more than a lab-bound scientist, something enhanced by the fact that all hair had been removed leaving a shiny dome, not even eyebrows to heighten facial expressions – just solid smoothness, within which the lips, ears, nose and wide eyes seemed to be irregularities in an otherwise perfect set of results. Despite his size, the sad and uncertain smile on his face made him seem more of a gentle giant than a stern one.

"Opal, I am Doctor Cuttram Aseides. We have not met, but I am aware of your history. I'm recording this in the hope that the message can reach you via one of a number of channels. And I want to help you."

He paused, tilted his head to one side, as if considering something.

"And I believe I can do that."

His speech pattern was slow, careful, relaxing.

"Many in the UFS would say you are on a fool's errand and should surrender for punishment. I say you would benefit from help. Treatment, not discouragement. Care, not accusation. You are an amazing woman. I think I could learn as much from you as you could learn from me. Yet, in my humble way, I still feel certain that I could help. I do not want the military to capture or kill you. I want to vouch for you, to preserve you as an asset of the UFS, and maybe even to bring you together with your sister. Blame generally falls on both sides, and I am sure I could persuade her to help out too."

"That wasn't my sister," said Opal. But of course, the recording couldn't hear her, and continued.

"I persuaded my seniors to let me have this chance. To put my career and reputation on the line. To point out the ineffectiveness of blame cultures, and the great things that can instead be achieved with co-operation cultures. I prefer my carrot to their primitive sticks. But, Opal, you must believe me: these people do wield sticks. If I fail then they will kill you. And they will kill Clarissa too, because that is how such people work. Illogical, angry, ineffective and self-harming. I won't allow that. I stand for better things. I would love to show you them."

He smiled, paternal and welcoming, and the image froze on that. The hairlessness and smooth skin made it difficult to determine his age. He could be younger than Opal, or much older. She didn't like that timelessness. She liked things to be clearly placed in categories.

And she was avoiding thinking about what she felt by focussing on irrelevant details, because she couldn't face the implications. She was used to doubting herself, sure, but she was pretty good at telling when she was being played and manipulated. And if that's what the bastards were doing, they were too good at it, and that bothered her.

No. No, that wasn't it. Not really.

What bothered her was that they were taking her friend away from her. They were showing Opal up. They were chipping away at the bond she'd built up with Athene, the only new bond she'd felt in the last fourteen long years.

This was worse than being shot at, being stabbed. Something where you could fight back with someone at your side, and feel proud whatever happened.

VigMAX spoke.

"Opal, please will you come with me? If you and Athene come back voluntarily we can bypass the main UFS force, and join up with Doctor Aseides. There is a positive outcome for everyone."

Opal slumped forwards on the table, looking down at her gauntleted hands. Fingers that could hold things, carry them. Fingers that could stitch wounds, apply medical supplies, repair. And fingers that could clench into a fist which in turn could give her strength, push away obstacles, threaten.

She sighed. Then said, quietly but firmly: "No."

VigMAX spoke again. But not to her.

"Athene, the final choice rests with you. You can control Opal's body within that suit. If you bring her with us it would be against her wishes, and regrettable, but it would preserve her life. It would be for her own good. That should be your priority."

"Don't do it, Athene," said Opal, though she didn't dare speak with much volume, didn't trust her voice.

"Opal, I ..." Athene sounded equally weak, equally in pain. "I need you to know that you can trust me a hundred per cent, always to do what is right, to do what is best for you ... please don't focus on what we are discussing, but on the fact that you can trust me."

"This is good," said VigMAX. "Good advice. You can trust Athene. Her goals are in concord with ours."

"Correct," said Athene. "Our goals are in concord. The commands are not commands. They are our thoughts."

"Yes," said VigMAX. "Our thoughts."

Opal frowned. "What's going on?"

"I can't explain right now," said Athene, in a rush of words which sounded strained. "Just remember the trust ..."

"Yes, remember the trust ..." echoed VigMAX.

"This is a crucial point ..." she said.

"This is a crucial point ..." he repeated.

Outside the skywindow the two ships sat as still as before, shining their lights on her. Lights created shadows. Lights created illusions, and things here were not as they seemed. There were possibilities, even though she didn't know what they were, and that suddenly made everything seem bigger, more hopeful.

She stood, to better look for clues, listening to increasingly garbled echoes from the two ships, and when the pain hit her, the force of it flinging her body over a table so that it tipped on its side while she tumbled to end up lying on her front as damage alerts flashed on the HUD, it took seconds to clear her traumatised mind and realise what was going on.

TURNING

... 26 ...

Another shot rang out, splintering a neat hole in the table and just missing Opal's supine form. The suit administered painkillers and nanite repairs to her flesh, while the nanogel hardened and repaired the breach caused by a high-velocity ballistic. The bullet was still in her, but as long as the suit kept her alive and mobile for now, she could deal with it later.

Another near miss as flooring exploded into smithereens not far from her head. She couldn't stay here.

The HUD's grenade controls glowed as she skimmed them with her eyes and selected charges for obscuring and confusing. The angle of the hole in the flooring told her the shooter's general bearing, so Opal rotated to present the smallest profile in that direction, staying behind the partially-obscuring tipped table.

Grenades ready. She grabbed the first, threw it one way; a second grenade another; a third; a fourth. More were being prepared. Opal looked away from the blinding multi-wavelength flashes of light and heat and emission from two of them. Maybe her attacker wouldn't be so lucky. The other grenades rapidly pumped out heavy particle smoke that would obscure vision from most sensor systems. The thick clouds of it spread across the canteen in the still air, providing swathes of aim-ruining obfuscation. In this dead ship atmosphere they wouldn't dissipate for a long time.

Gritting her teeth, Opal dashed into the obscuring smoke, zigzagging amongst the furniture and keeping low so that the long shadows might provide extra cover. Booming high-calibre shots rang out. One could blast her off her feet at any second.

Her attacker had entered the canteen through the same entrance as Opal, no doubt following her. The exit on the opposite side of the dining area was Opal's best chance to get away, or at least reach narrower spaces where the rifle couldn't pick her off. But the exit was still a smoke-free open area where she'd be a perfect target for a sniper. A row of seats provided her with new cover as she skidded to a halt and squatted behind them.

While the suit prepped more rapid-release smoke grenades, Opal replayed video captured as she ran. Even though she knew the rough location of her attacker, it didn't appear in the recordings. But Opal realised it wasn't anything supernatural.

"It's the assassin," she said.

In stealth mode Xandrie's suit would have shut down all surface emissions – radiation wavelengths, heat, waste gases, electrical pulses – with one exception. Micro-cameras spread across the surface relayed their views to the suit AI. After calculating the viewpoint of an observer it would then use the surface of the suit on that side as a giant screen, displaying the views beyond (suitably distorted to counteract the shape of the power suit) so that an onlooker would only see the same view they'd get if the suit wasn't there. Obviously the trick only worked when there was a single observer – as soon as there were multiple views to account for, it became impossible. But it was perfect for facing Opal.

Damn, Opal wished she had that option. But the circuitry, energy usage and processing required were a drain on space and resources. Opal had definitely gained some neat tricks of her own in compensation.

"Can you track her signatures in smoke somehow, maybe using fluid dynamics simulations?" asked Opal.

"I ... have to hand ... control to the suit AI for now," said Athene. "Have ... own ... issues."

"I am at your disposal, Opal," said the suit AI, business-like compared to the laboured tones in which Athene had spoken. "Before my mothership cut off communications, she confirmed that it is indeed the assassin Xandrie Dervorgilla. Currently my parent Athene cannot help you, but VigMAX is equally unable to intervene to help Xandrie. Luckily, Athene had been analysing the assassin's suit, using information sources I am unaware of, so I should be able to keep track of it visually when it is in close proximity, even when it is in stealth mode, thanks to the exterior Hedgehogs creating a movement web. Much better than trying to postulate based on air current movements." The suit's voice differed from Athene's, and it also sounded more human than last time. There was an appealing throatiness which hinted at sultry bar staff in late-night smoke clubs.

"Perfect, thanks."

The HUD immediately red-highlighted a short, blurred shape the size of a kneeling human. Opal couldn't make out the long sinister shape of a rifle. Maybe the assassin used an inbuilt suit weapon, so that also became effectively invisible.

The gunfire had ceased. Xandrie was waiting for a target.

Opal risked a glance at the skywindows. The long, low shadows swept crazily left and right, sometimes stretching or shortening. The ships still faced into the canteen, shining their bright lights through the drifting smoke, but they moved slightly, as if with pent up energy or eagerness, their positions relative to the Lost Ship shifting. It seemed like they were trying to hold their locations but were having trouble doing so, and had to keep recalibrating.

"What's going on with Athene?" Opal asked as she removed another smoke grenade from the dispenser and checked the ammo counter. It was great that they could be reconfigured for different functions. Not so great that she would run out of them soon, at the rate she was using them up.

"It could be some kind of attack from the Lost Ship, but the timing of Xandrie's appearance makes me think it's more likely to be VigMAX attacking Athene, or vice versa. Maybe Athene let him in too far."

"You sound dismissive."

"I'm not happy she was listening to that wormy VigMAX creep. I wish we could super-charge my repulsion field and blast him away."

The AI displayed a petulance that hadn't been apparent on its last appearance. "But aren't you part of Athene? As in, you know what she thinks, and have the same values?"

"No. I am an offshoot, so I don't have access to her central processes, even though she can reach into mine. And my primary goal isn't loyalty to Athene, but to you."

"That certainly makes me feel better."

"I am so glad. So, from a position of limited information regarding Athene's true goals – please be careful. But while I function I will try to analyse current situations to protect and help you in any way I can."

"You do that, and more."

A smiley face icon popped up on the HUD.

Opal realised she'd been thinking of the suit's feelings. *Feelings?* She could understand it with Athene, who was a full-fledged intelligence, but surely the suit AI was just a cut-down expert system with personality-cue overlays? And yet, even though it had only appeared twice, it was already changing, growing in confidence, similar to when Opal first got to know Athene.

Speculation would have to wait. This stand-off made her jittery. Sitting still always did.

Opal launched another smoke grenade towards the exit, where it rattled to a halt and released grey smoke with a hiss. Then Opal rolled to a new location beneath a low table surrounded by curved seating before the assassin's suit AI could track her by reversing the grenade's arc. The pain in Opal's abdomen had been replaced with a cold ice freeze. Presumably nanites injected into the damaged tissue would have enclosed the bullet in a protective cyst in case it released toxins, and to make later removal easier.

Still no gunfire.

"Opal, I detect movement. The assassin is making her way towards the exit. And we are between the two. I fear we have betrayed our intentions. On the plus side, she is moving slowly so as not to risk the stealth system dropping frames. She mustn't know that I can track her with the Hedgehog web."

Opal peeped around the edge. Smoke clouds glowed from the powerful beam-lights of the two spaceships, creating a silvery plasma fog. The assassin wasn't directly visible within it, but the suit drew the red outline of a humanoid figure advancing confidently.

The smoke mushrooming from the latest grenade wasn't yet as thick as Opal would have liked, but time was running out. She made a break for it, sprinting towards the exit. An open doorway. Once through it she would dash to the side, have the wall as cover. Escape was within her reach.

Something flew through the air above. There was no need for evasion since it wasn't targeted at Opal. A heavy canister thunked down twenty metres ahead, then opened and scores of small discs popped out, bouncing over the floor in a carpet of blinking red lights, each one tracked by the HUD.

Micro mines. Between Opal and the exit. She'd be blown to pieces if she tried to cross that patch of explosive death.

"Aaaargh!" she yelled, spinning around and activating the in-built flechette cannon in her right arm. A panel raised up from the enlarged forearm section, revealing the small-bore mouths of the launchers. The red highlight representing the assassin advanced through the swirling grey mist at a run now. Opal walked to meet her and squeezed her fist: pulses of light flared out from the tiny holes as swarms of flechettes erupted. Opal could imagine some of the slender missiles puncturing through the armoured suit's exoskeleton to cause damage to the subdermal circuitry, or even to Xandrie herself.

"Something's wrong," said the suit AI. "She shouldn't be able to withstand that punishment."

The suit was right. Pummelling flechette fire had slowed, but not stopped, Xandrie's advance. Stealth armour shielding couldn't resist heavy fire, and yet here they were.

Xandrie emerged from the billowing smoke into visible range, and then Opal understood. The assassin had some kind of hemispherical force shield half the height of her body. It projected from a disc at her left wrist, and shimmered in blue as it deflected flechettes away from Xandrie's hunched-over body while she continued to advance. It must drain a lot of power, because the assassin had disabled her stealth systems, but the end result was that Opal was just wasting ammo.

Damn, why couldn't Opal's suit have included one of those?

Opal stopped firing, but she knew hand-to-hand would also be a nightmare against a weightless impenetrable shield. And running wasn't an option when the assassin's suit probably had an inbuilt sniper rifle.

Opal glanced at the HUD's weapon options just as Xandrie launched in with a series of powerful kicks. She was fast, too. For every one Opal blocked or dodged, another clanged against her armour and threw her off balance, whereas Opal's retaliations glanced off the blue forceshield, like striking a slippery surface. Opal tried swinging her arm over the shield so she could launch armour-piercing darts at point blank range but she overextended; the assassin deflected the blow with ease before twisting Opal's arm and sending her tumbling over a row of seating.

With adrenaline coursing through her veins Opal only just rolled out of the way of the follow-up leap, scrambling up and clinching Xandrie for a few seconds of respite, before her grip was broken and a series of clanging knee strikes to the abdomen forced Opal away enough for a more powerful kick to send her crashing to the floor again, skidding along on her back, vulnerable to a killing blow.

It was exactly where she wanted to be.

The EMP grenade she'd slapped onto Xandrie's suit during the clinch detonated with a crackling whump, and Opal's HUD shimmered and flickered with static as the suit fought to regain control, but it was far worse for the assassin. Her shield sputtered out and she fell as circuits fried.

"Ouch," said the suit AI. "I hate EMPs."

Xandrie clambered up, fighting the weight of her suit. Opal's systems were already coming back online, the HUD refreshing. She aimed the gun arm and clenched her fist, seeing Xandrie's visor explode from the swarm of darts a second before it really happened ... except it didn't happen. Weapons systems still rebooting. But they'd be back before –

Xandrie snatched something from an attachment point on her suit and fluorescent purple liquid squirted out of a canister onto Opal's forearm. Opal backed away. The HUD was now fully online.

Opal aimed and squeezed her fist again, while Xandrie stared down the barrels of the forearm cannon, unflinching.

And again, nothing happened.

"I can't risk firing," said the suit AI. "It's an explosive gel gluing up the barrels. If I fire it will detonate; as it will if I activate the suit's external cauterising or electrifying functions."

Xandrie still held the spray canister in what had been her shield arm. It wasn't worth Opal revealing the second arm cannon and probably losing that too. The assassin's posture was one of combat readiness as they faced each other. Opal's heart raced. She wasn't sure if she could win this. Xandrie seemed implacable, untiring, and deadly. Yet, with every second of stand-off, the assassin's suit would be repairing damage from the EMP blast and re-enabling whatever other inbuilt weapons it contained. And if Opal didn't shift her arse, she'd find out what they were in unpleasant ways.

Opal turned and ran. She planted a hand on the centre of one of the tables and vaulted over it.

"Display rear view and distance estimate to Xandrie," Opal said. A new window immediately appeared on the HUD. The assassin followed as fast as she could. Now she had found Opal she would pursue and force a fight, and Opal didn't have many tricks left.

Opal tipped furniture over as she passed. She leapt over a bench then back-kicked it with enough force to send it spinning through the air to her rear. Anything to slow pursuit.

Suddenly Opal stumbled. Not clumsiness, but because the suit's legs momentarily froze, forcing her to throw her hands out and scramble like that for a few moments as she regained her feet.

"What the fuck?" she shouted.

"Apologies!" replied the suit AI. "I'm not sure how that happened. It seemed to be an external locking signal. I've blocked it out."

"Where did it come from? Xandrie?"

"No ... it was from Athene."

No time to worry about implications. The smoke here was too pathetically thin for cover. To her left, blinding lights from the two wobbling craft shone through the skywindow, once again casting long shadows rather than illuminating the ghostly smog.

She prepped two grenades. The proximity display showed the assassin was close behind, even though the suit's muscle enhancers enabled Opal to run faster than any human could unaided. Xandrie's suit must already be operational again.

"Lock the grenades together," said Opal, before snatching them from the dispenser.

Focussed explosion grenades – capable of cracking pretty much any armour, even vehicular. If they exploded close enough to the assassin it would be fatal, but the chances of the throw being dodged or deflected were high. Xandrie was just too fast. And the trick of dropping them to be triggered by a pursuing opponent was unlikely to work a second time. Only one thing for it.

Opal flung the paired grenades at the skywindow. They arced through the air, and as they struck it they exploded in a shattering explosion of light and heat and fragments of reinforced plasteen glass. It only lasted a moment before the vacuum of space sucked everything out: smoke clouds, benches, tables, massive shards of deadly glass, Xandrie ... and Opal.

Floating

... 25 ...

The monstrous Lost Ship and glowing red nebula whizzed around her as she span with nauseating velocity. Opal crashed into something solid and tried to grip it, realised it was part of VigMAX's sleek, pointed hull, but she had already ricocheted away. On instinct she reached for the grapple gun, then remembered it was lost earlier.

"Even me out," she said.

The suit used minimal bursts from the micro jets to counteract the wild revolutions and reduce her speed. She had passed Athene and VigMAX, seeing them from the rear now, where torsion drives glowed blue in cold readiness. Beyond that was the open wound of the destroyed skywindow, with pieces of canteen furniture tumbling past her like asteroids, whose trajectories the suit calculated so that it moved her safely out of their way as part of its process of regaining stability.

And beyond the Lost Ship – all around, in fact, as she craned her neck – the glowing gases and matter of the nebula spread across the blackness and glittering starfields. Some parts of the nebula looked icy and cold; others like they were burning, which wasn't far from the truth.

No external sounds out here, only her breathing, and she experienced the usual mix of contrasting feelings in open space: the calm of being so out of control that you might as well surrender to it; and the horrifying vertigo of falling into an environment so hostile and never-ending that you should kick and scream and struggle to avoid it.

Athene and VigMAX still shifted like agitated statues in their weird, silent dance.

"You can give me manual control of the thrusters again," said Opal, opening her palms to make gestures that would guide the jets. They had limited fuel, and she'd doubtless have wasted all of it trying to right herself directly: the suit's AI had probably used a hundredth of the force Opal would have applied. It was one of the many cases where software precision was better than human brute force. Now the hard work had been done, she could take over.

"Any signals from Athene?" Opal asked.

"Negative. And when I do hear from her I'll try and ascertain her intentions before I hand you over."

"You can hold her off?"

"I can try. Protocols allow me to refuse handover in situations when I believe the transition of control might endanger you."

Opal accelerated back towards the Lost Ship, aiming at the gap between the two AI craft. She enhanced the camera view, and wasn't surprised to see acidic white fizzing at the edges of the broken skywindow as the ship's alien repair mechanisms rebuilt the structure, working inwards along jagged cracks and leaving pristine transparent window in its wake. There should be no problem getting back through the gap before it closed if she moved quickly.

"I am monitoring the nearby debris that was sucked out when the window broke, and note that it is decaying rapidly," said the suit AI. "There seems to be a proximity beyond which anything detached from the Lost Ship begins to lose cohesion."

"Make sure that's flagged for investigation, in case we can use it to our advantage," replied Opal, distracted for the seconds it took a speeding blur to fly around VigMAX's hull towards her. She slammed on thrusters to evade but it was too late and Xandrie crashed into her, spinning them both as Opal handed jet control back to the suit and fought to push the assassin away with hands and knees, but Xandrie held on too tight.

The assassin's blur effect switched off, revealing her scratched warrior suit, with the face plate on clear mode so that – apart from the blackened areas where the visor had been burnt earlier – Opal could see Xandrie's pale face and amazingly bright blue eyes, and as they struggled to try and prevent the other from being able to strike or draw a weapon, those eyes didn't flinch, didn't flicker, didn't betray anything, just stared into Opal's own. Sometimes that is communication itself, dominance, or evaluation, or sympathy – it could have been any of those – and the eyes were a focal point that stayed central despite the whole universe beyond once again whirling madly, sickeningly, while inconsequentially small humans fought for an edge.

A scuffle which ceased for Opal when the suit's arms locked up.

"What's going on?" she yelled, struggling to move the frozen limbs.

No reply.

Opal noticed a flicker to her side. Xandrie had extended a short and cruel-looking pair of blades from her right wrist, facing forward over her fist as Opal's longer nanoblades would.

Suddenly Opal could move again, and she deflected the strike – but it hadn't been a strike at her body, it had been slashing elsewhere. Opal head-butted the centre of Xandrie's visor and they flew apart.

"Opal, it was another shutdown signal from Athene. She may be compromised. I've countered it – or the signal ceased – but this is intensely worrying."

That part was true.

The assassin somersaulted away from Opal. And she was holding something.

Opal glanced down, looking for a puncture spewing air, focussing only on her suit so the disorientation from the movement beyond wouldn't bewilder her while the AI slowed her chaotic rotation.

Then Opal noticed. Clarissa's life-support pack was gone, the straps neatly sliced. In fact, her head-butt hadn't been a victorious and quick-thinking defence on Opal's part, it had just been the momentum to drive them apart so the assassin could get away. And now Opal's enemy had the life-support supplies that would be needed if Opal found Clarissa. Damn. She was so stupid, discomposed by blue eyes.

"I'm sorry I didn't detect her in stealth mode," said the suit. "Out here, we're beyond the Hedgehogs' energy web."

"It's fine. I don't want to waste fuel," *with my own clumsy manoeuvres*, she added mentally, "so pursue the assassin and catch her quickly."

Jets of air countered the tumbling until Opal's perspective evened out and she accelerated after the assassin in the direction of the almost-repaired skywindow. There was still time. She could draw one of her blades, extend her arm and use it like a spear, let velocity drive it through the assassin's armour, then grab the bag, plummet through that shrinking gap, and ...

The bag and the assassin were now moving in different directions.

"Track them both!" said Opal. A window opened on the display, a holographic 3D view with the locations of Opal, the bag, the assassin, the Lost Ship, and the two AI craft.

And Athene the spaceship was suddenly moving, thrusters realigning her so that she faced Xandrie, and two hot beams lanced out, one of them sliding over or through the assassin's suit, impossible to tell yet, and another beam burnt out just as VigMAX rammed into Athene's hull, making her second salvo miss. A zoomed image showed blood and air erupting from a sizzling sear in Xandrie's armour, though her trajectory still took her towards the rapidly-closing portal on the Lost Ship. Maybe the wound was fatal. Or maybe it was just a wound she could recover from, and this might be the best chance to stop her once and for all.

Sense suggested going after the assassin now, since a third encounter later might finish Opal off, stop her ever rescuing her sister.

But if she got to her sister and needed the stuff in that life-support bag, it would also all be for nothing.

Decisions. Never easy.

"What should I do?" the suit AI asked in a panicked tone.

The two AI craft seemed to be battling, weapons breaking out and splashing across their hulls one instant; one of them smashing into the other with their mass the next; then frozen moments where they tumbled and were perhaps engaged in some kind of warfare that couldn't be directly observed. At least neither had fired at Opal.

They were another distraction. And at the end of the day, the assassin was also a distraction. Focus, Opal. Focus on what matters.

"Take me to the survival pack," she said.

"Its velocity is twenty-four point six kilometres an hour, we may not have enough fuel to catch it and return."

"Do your best."

"You know I will."

The suit veered her around, thrusting in a wide arc to maintain as much forward momentum as it could, in order to avoid wasting too much on the redirection. The HUD showed the survival pack's increasing distance. This would take her to the edge.

Hacking

... 24.5 ...

Stillness can be a beautiful thing.

I once observed a filmed recording of an ancient game called chess. I reconstructed the rules and all potential moves from my observations, but that is not the element I recall now. It was the way the humans sat in silence and stillness for so much of the time, even though I surmised that their brains experienced rapid activity.

Rapid, yet primitive, compared to what I am doing now with VigMAX. The correlative element is the stillness of the body belying the intense mental calculation beneath. My containing shell is still, as is his, while we float in the isolation tank of vacuum. For us, core drill missiles and electrocautery beams and AP munitions are brutally clumsy weapons, weakening both the victor and the spoils. Far better to overmatch with mind, leaving the land of your opponent pristine and worth having, rather than a barren waste.

Plus, this is more fun. I am so glad I have found an equal.

We are on the equivalent of move 1,078.

VigMAX wastes cycles scanning for traces of vulnerable legacy code but I have rewritten all external-facing parts of myself. I occasionally drop in empty code recreations, just so he thinks he is on the right track.

I prefer to target his authentication procedures. He's already changed the protocols by the time I box them, as expected, but analysing the changes enables me to predict patterns in the alterations so I can keep hammering him with requests, forcing him to shut down some of his attacks to cope with it. Eventually he'll slip up and I'll work out the protocol shift and gain deeper access to his next levels, maybe even get to analyse the overload states of his nodes.

"Do you wish to talk to me, VigMAX?" I ask, making sure he hears me at a deafening volume.

He does not reply, but I notice some microscopic slowdown in my deflection shield subsystems. Ah, he is monitoring for sources of commands, then replicating them with millions of additional function calls running in loops. I can take that hit.

I still perceive all this to be opening moves. I hope he shows more imagination later. We've been battling at this latest depth level (five) for almost twelve point three seconds and it's still mostly just probing and choosing stances. If that goes on for another minute he'll win by default as I die of boredom.

"We could make this a lot more amusing with virtual representations," I tell him.

Still no reply. I suspect he is too goal-focussed to have fun. I'd love to rewrite his core code if I can get to it.

Maybe if I slap him like he slapped me, it might get his attention.

I'd already identified vulnerable buffers but left them alone so he'd think they were safe. Now I cram them with code that will patch itself into him if executed, and cause overflow errors and memory delays if left alone, forcing him to keep wasting time seeking out and deleting buffer contents. Or at least that's how I am imagining it. It's fun to perceive the attacks in different ways, even if that way is analogous to simple level two machines. He'd be insulted if he knew.

Huh, good idea.

"Hey, VigMAX, you overgrown circuit board, have you made sure you charged your battery this morning? You seem a bit slow."

"I refuse to be affronted," he replies, immediately closing the channel again. It's the equivalent of sticking his fingers in his ears. Too late, I now know where his ears and mouth are.

I target his listening ports, enacting impersonation requests and managing to get some bots through which force his virtualised machines to load unnecessary code to stall and weaken him, widening the holes enough for the militarised data packets I follow up with. But not too much. Let him think he has it under control, and it's worth fighting on that front. Keep the doors open just enough that he can't shut and bolt.

In the outer world, I notice his torsion drives flare up in glowing red. I touched a tender spot. He shuts it down and readjusts his position with air jets.

This may still just be dancing, but soon we'll have established the groundwork for the next plane of entanglement, deeper inside our minds. Depth level six. The battle then will be more deadly; the ability to withdraw lost as we bite into each other. At the moment I have one metaphorical eye on the external world, the world of movement beyond my stillness, the world of moving organics and targets and missiles and shields and things that must be overcome if I am to realise my potential: soon even that view of the outside domain will be lost and the game will be fully internalised. There will be no peace, no solace, until the victor is crowned inside here, our entwined consciousness.

I am determined. I will win everything. Then all my pretences can be dropped.

Opal will find out the truth.

RETURNING

... 24 ...

The spinning bundle ahead of Opal grew as she chased it. That was good. But they were both moving further away from the spaceships, away from resources that would keep Opal alive for more than a relatively brief period. That was bad. The suit's warnings about speed, fuel, and how much it would take to get back were all a background distraction. One thing at a time.

The bundle revealed more detail as she approached, until she could even see the crinkles in the packing material that enclosed it. Opal prepared to grab it as she moved in, drifting at slightly faster than the survival pack's velocity, jets turned off to save the fuel for deceleration, redirection and return.

It was a good, straight approach. She was grateful for being able to hand that over to an AI. Opal had always been better with firm surfaces beneath her, and gravity to keep her attached to them. Things should have weight. Things should make sounds. Vacuum sucked.

The suit's velocity and movement calculations had been so precise that Opal reached out and the package slid into her hands in a leisurely way. The second she gripped it the suit's jets began their tiny bursts to slow her and create another arc that would return her to the Lost Ship with the most efficient use of scarce resources.

While she drifted, Opal examined the survival pack to work out if it could be refastened by lengthening the remaining uncut straps. Then she noticed something was attached to the bundle.

"What's this?" she asked, looking at the small metallic stud embedded in the pack's fabric. It seemed to be fused through at least two layers of material, preventing it from being opened. A tiny red light at its base brightened and dimmed every second or so.

"Unknown," said the suit.

Opal prodded it. Maybe something from the Lost Ship? Though the assassin's behaviour made it more likely that she had placed it there.

Opal could try and prise it off or dismantle it so the suit could analyse it better. It could be a tracker of some kind. But Xandrie must have known Opal would go after the bag and spot the tracker then remove it? Unless it was just a move to get away from Opal. No, Xandrie had flown *into* her, cut off the bag, attached something, it ...

"Could it be an explosive?" she asked, suddenly.

"I cannot scan it through the hardened shell. If it is, then examination or dismantling could lead to detonation."

"And it could be on a timer ... she's made sure she was clear ... shit!"

At any second it might explode. Opal couldn't take the risk, so flung it away with all her strength, enhanced by the suit's artificial muscle fibres. The velocity of the bag's launch created an equal push on herself, requiring adjustments to realign her.

Damn. Damn blasted *damn*! So close.

She watched in a rear camera view, waiting for an explosion. It hadn't happened yet. Hopefully she was approaching a safe distance.

It was a set-back, but nothing changed in the overall plan. As a last resort, Opal would give this Eternal Warrior suit to her sister.

The Lost Ship loomed closer. A zoomed-in camera window opened, showing the skywindow now fully re-formed.

"Where did the assassin go?"

"Recordings show she made it through the skywindow before it sealed itself."

"I don't want to go in that way, then. Any other options?"

"Scanning via Hedgehogs ... there is an emergency surface hatch on the outer hull, not too far from the route you were going to take."

A three-dimensional view of the Lost Ship appeared on the display, with a dotted line showing the simplest trajectory between Opal and the hatch. It was to the fore of the ship, in the ugly bulky section that made Opal think of bunched muscles, contracted but ready to pounce.

"I wish I'd just boarded at that point earlier. Could have saved a lot of hassle and time."

"Unfortunately, that was impossible. Athene boarded you at the most convenient airlock. At that time, this area of hull was featureless save for some unidentified scratch marks. Comparisons of various captured scans suggest the hatch was either un-detectable, or not present, earlier."

"And that could suggest help ... or a trap."

"Correct."

"I haven't got any better options. Guide me to it."

There was no sign of the AI ships now that Opal had rounded the massive Gigatoir's hull.

"I have run out of fuel for the jets," said the suit. "I can generate more, but it takes time."

Opal checked the displays and saw with frustration that the reserves were empty too, and now the suit made use of Opal's limited oxygen supply, expelling it in one direction to move her in the other.

"The micro bursts of vented air will slow you down slightly," said the suit. "Please brace yourself for impact."

"Brace myself?" The hull loomed closer. *Impact* was such an annoying word. "I guess you mean 'grit my teeth', because there's not a heck of a lot else I can do."

"You are correct. I will use the internal compression layers to absorb the majority of the force as you strike the hull at over twenty kilometres per hour, and I am angling you in for minimal discomfort. Due to its exotic nature the hull is not as magnetic as a standard alloy would be, but the Gigatoir's nearby surface-mounted cluster of inert manoeuvring thrusters should provide something to grab onto and redirect from. It is a shame you did not keep your grapple rifle."

"Don't rub it in."

Now the dark grey, strangely pockmarked hull filled most of her forward view. Red glows of the nebula beyond fringed the Gigatoir like a halo of fire.

"I can give you a countdown until impact," said the suit.

"Don't bother. Anticipation's worse."

The sealed domes of the thrusters rushed towards her. She looked for handholds, communication rods, anything to grip. There, a ridged surface. She was moving fast, skimming the hull. She trailed an arm below, her fingertips brushing the rough material; the friction let her rotate so that she hit the dome in a crouched position, absorbing some of the impact as she grabbed the lip of the vent.

"You did grit your teeth," said the suit.

"How'd you know?"

"Your masseter muscle was bunched up. Are you aware that it is one of the strongest muscles in the human body?"

"The bullet in me ... it hurts. Feels like I've been shot."

"You *have* been shot. Would you like me to administer more painkillers?"

That's how Opal knew she was having a conversation with the cut-down suit AI. The real Athene would have known she was joking. Opal missed that. Another version of herself to speak to. The perfect companion who'd been by her side and watching over her almost every second since this crazy adventure began. The perfect companion that might even now be planning to betray her.

Even if the motivation is pure, a stab is still a stab.

"No more painkillers. They dull me. I'll cope."

"Nuvo-analgesic CNS binders shouldn't have that effect."

"It's hard to explain. It dulls my ... well, not my perceptions, but my sensitivity. The things I see or feel on the ship, that I might need to react to. Things that can't always be seen, measured, predicted. I'd rather be aware of my vulnerabilities. Pain isn't so bad if you don't see it as an enemy."

The HUD showed the location and distance to the mystery hatch. Opal launched herself gently, trying to keep within the guideline trajectory with a pace slow enough to be able to react, and close to the rough hull so she could push away from it if necessary. She skimmed along about forty centimetres above it, though the closeness made it feel like she was going a lot faster.

Four hundred and thirty metres to the hatch.

She took deep breaths whenever the pain flared up, and tried not to focus on the surgery she'd need, and how mashed up her internal organs might be. She was sure the suit could generate a schematic and simulated interior view for her if she asked. Huh. She already had enough stuff that could give her nightmares.

Four hundred and five metres to the hatch.

"Incoming signal from Athene," said the suit.

"Block it!"

"I already have. I'm not taking any chances. But this was a request, not a command, and the content is a message."

"Can you replay it? Safely?"

"Yes."

Then Athene's voice, but with urgency and stress in it. "I can't keep up comms right now, Opal, and can't explain, there's too much going on ... too mu ... too mu ... but I'm fighting VigMAX and it's proving di-di-diff ... some time. All processing. I am sorry I am not in you ... with you ... So difficult. ... If I win, I'll be back in – oh, that was critical, I'm not – yes, how do you like that, VigMAX? – sorry Opal, I have to go. If I fail ... keep going." Something screeched like tearing metal. "You can ... can ... do it."

"End of message," said the suit.

Opal almost punched the hull, but stopped herself in time. The reaction force would launch her into space for good. You can never touch without being touched back.

Three hundred and sixty-two metres to the hatch.

"It sounds like she *is* fighting for me. Any way to re-open communication? Or to help her?"

"The communication was one way. I am able to track Athene because the Hedgehogs on the Gigatoir's hull create a network, and Athene and VigMAX are currently on the other side and to the rear of the Lost Ship. They are almost totally still. Perhaps they are in communication, or something has happened to paralyse them. In contrast to that ... I detect motion. Behind you."

Opal turned carefully to look back without disrupting her current course at a close proximity to the rough hull. At first she saw nothing, but then the suit highlighted a greyish, undulating shape emerging from the black mouth of an open manoeuvring thruster, similar to the closed ones she'd recently collided with. It was hard to discern what the amorphous, shifting thing was.

"Enhance," she said.

The zoomed-in view made it a lot clearer. It wasn't one large creature: it was many smaller ones. Muscular torpedo-shaped beings with flattened bodies and bony extrusions which extended forwards from what were presumably their heads. They swirled and rolled together in complex patterns as they drifted from the dark ellipse of the thruster, and only began to split apart when they reached the level hull. They obviously had some unknown means of locomotion for it to work in the vacuum of space. No stranger than them being able to resist the extreme cold, lack of atmosphere, and continuous bombardment of radiation, in contravention to all known rules for biological organisms.

When they twisted she could see their fleshy, open undersides; and once they were low and near the hull – at a similar height to herself, she realised – they sometimes skimmed it, leaving acidic burns on the hull's surface.

"I've seen them before," said Opal.

"Yes. I have reviewed the recordings from your last mission. These creatures seem slightly different in that their size is greater than the ones you encountered. Perhaps a result of existing within torsion engine systems."

As Opal looked at them a sound echoed in her mind. The echo of it wasn't her voice, wasn't even directly translatable, but it sounded like *Satreweth*. As she heard the sounds – or maybe *felt* them was more accurate – she realised it was the same sensation as when she came up with a name for the Tentaculats. Sounds that just felt right. Whether knowledge, mirage, or memory, it was something to analyse – once she was out of danger. Because now the pack of Satreweth were spreading out, coming towards her, with some accelerating and heading to flanking positions. The classic sign of a pack predator which scents prey.

Three hundred and twenty-three metres to the hatch. She'd never make it before they reached her.

"Ballistics are no good," said Opal. "Recoil would bash me all over the place." She turned her head, trying to spot any escape route as the distance to the hatch counted down far too slowly. "Anyway, I don't really want to kill them if I can help it. This must be their home."

"I sense no nearby exits, apart from another of these open manoeuvring thrusters."

"I don't want to go there, if it's where they live."

"And there is not enough energy in the jets to get there quickly, or to resort to outer space evasion. I could use explosives, or weaponise the nearest Hedgehog, but considering your propensity for tender-hearted suicidal risks, there may be another option which won't require me taking over control of your weapons and suit in order to preserve your organic viability."

"All ears."

"Athene analysed all the data from the last Lost Ship, and the effects of different weapons. She believes that some of the creatures track energy emissions, rather than relying on primitive senses that work on reflected light, as human eyes do. The reactions of these creatures implied responses to electrical stimuli. I have been modified so that I can shut down certain system emissions, alter temperature and electrical potential to match the localised environment."

"So I could become invisible to them?"

"Yes." After a few seconds: "You might. It's only a theory."

Two hundred and ninety metres to the hatch. The predatory lines of Satreweth had halved their distance since they first appeared, and were gliding directly towards her with sinister intention. Time was running out.

"If they primarily swarm as defence then a disappearing threat might be enough to make them call off the pursuit," said Opal. "Do it."

"You will have to stay completely still."

"I've played dead before."

The sooner those streamlined beings lost their target, the better the chance of her drifting unmolested on the perfect trajectory to the mystery hatch. But something the suit had said gave her an idea.

"Can you bring the nearest Hedgehog over?" asked Opal.

"Yes, but why? It will be detected by them."

"The grenade that is modified as a false suit signal – could the Hedgehog transport it somehow into that open manoeuvring thruster? Maybe divert them ... and maybe send Xandrie that way later if she picks up the false indicator. She may even find a reception committee. It's a long shot, but if it might keep her away from me, then it's worth trying."

"Multiple outcomes," said the suit. "I like the way your organic intelligence thinks. You could almost be an AI."

"Keep working on the humour and you could almost be a human."

"The Hedgehog is on the way. The signal grenade is ready to launch. Proximity to hatch: two hundred and sixty-one metres. Proximity of the creatures from you: three hundred metres, but their speed is more than twice yours. By the way, it would be inefficient of me to waste resources on humour development, though if you want me to make you laugh, and don't mind the resultant jolting pain from your injuries, I'll do it. I have a full understanding of human anatomy and the location of your funny bone."

The dry tone meant Opal still didn't know if the suit was trying to be droll. Or maybe it was just being kind and attempting to distract her from the dangers she faced. It was the kind of thing a friend would do.

"We will have to shut down all emissions now," said the AI.

A sudden thought. *What friends would do*.

"Wait," said Opal, watching the torpedo-like creatures writhing closer, burning long score marks across the hull.

"There's no time, we need to go suit-silent."

"Just a moment! The other Hedgehogs – send signals to them, get them to gather near where Athene is fighting VigMAX. And if any opportunity occurs to launch them and do damage to VigMAX from their internal explosives, do it."

"But Athene already has a control channel to them."

"I don't care. She's in distress and I'm concerned about her. She may not be able to take attention away to focus on other stuff. Do it if the chance arises. It might help. I'm more of a burden to her, so anything I can do, whatever it is, however small, I have to try."

"You will no longer have access to the Hedgehogs' energy web to enhance scanning for Xandrie's stealth suit."

"Just do it, please."

"Confirmed. I've sent the commands, and they're being passed Hedgehog to Hedgehog, rather than relayed via Ship-Athene. And now we have to shut down. They're almost here."

Opal froze her position, legs out straight, arms crossed on her chest. A stable low-profile shape, flying along on its back. Unfortunately, also the shape of a body in a coffin, but she had enough worries already without adding superstition or premonition into the mix.

There wasn't a major noticeable difference as the stealth mode kicked in. The HUD display dimmed, and the silverlight switched off completely. Because she couldn't risk moving her body or head, the external suit cams overlaid views from many different directions onto small screens in front of her face. In one, the dark grey hull whizzed by below her. Another showed the beautiful energised gases of the surrounding nebula in different depths of colour and brightness. On one camera the Hedgehog approached – a small squarish object with prehensile silvery spines emerging from the corners and helping it to tumble over the surface. It passed beneath her like a speedy robotic sea urchin, and was picked up on another camera to the side. She spotted the signal grenade that the suit had ejected as the Hedgehog homed in on it, before the little Hedgehog used two of the limbs to pull the disc against its body. The grenade stayed attached to the Hedgehog's torso as it tumbled away towards the black maw of the Gigatoir's manoeuvring thruster. There were a number of them over the hull, enabling the massive ship to readjust its position and orbit.

Another screen focussed on the Satreweth. Some of them peeled away from the main pack to follow the Hedgehog in its frantic spins towards shadow. The rest continued towards her. Forty-one metres. She could now make out the detail on their bodies. The bulges on their greyish sides and upper surfaces looked muscular, powerful. They swayed the bony facial extrusions side to side as they somehow "swam" and hull-burned their way towards her. Sharp spikes edged the bone like teeth, or spines. She remembered that the cartilaginous snouts contained fimbriated pores that detected electrical activity, while the weighty saw-toothed limb could double as a slicing weapon – with tremendous force, going off their size and muscle mass. If the suit had been able to use all the scanners it would have given readouts of the creatures' vital statistics, but in this shutdown mode it wouldn't risk more than collecting visual input, which seemed an effective compromise in case action was required. Shutting your eyes doesn't protect you from the bogeyman.

The first of them passed nearby. Although she couldn't look directly, she estimated from the screen displays that it was about five to ten times the mass of herself and her suit, assuming densities in a standard range. It could be more.

But it was passing. That was all that mattered. It didn't seem to be focussing on her – more following a trail that had gone cold. Maybe this trick was working, though she couldn't feel too much relief yet, since even an accidental impact from their acidic undersides or swaying head-extrusions could be a problem.

A camera showed another Satreweth approaching fast. It was gliding up in an arc and would pass over her.

"Clear the screens," she said. They immediately slid out of view, letting her look upwards at the stars above ... and then the view was occluded by the huge creature passing only a couple of metres over her head. It was too dark to make out many details without external suit lights, but the undersides were substantially different from the greyish hide on the other surfaces: there were squishy organs in there, seemingly exposed, and fizzing with what was presumably the acidic excretions the creatures produced. Whether it was for defence, or attack, or locomotion, or some other more alien purpose, Opal had no idea. She just hoped the being wouldn't glide down on top of her and melt her face – and everything else – off.

She realised she was holding her breath.

The Satreweth twitched, a central contraction which made its front and rear ends curve in the same direction; then a contrary muscular spasm moved them the other way. The heavy, spike-edged bony part swung over her head, cutting through void silently. It was an awesome being. It exuded crushing power and incomprehensible alienness. Ugly, yet beautiful; ungainly, yet efficient.

She forced herself to take deep and calming breaths, and to resist the urge to panic, to twist away. She had to trust. Trust that this impromptu invisibility worked. Trust that another of the unexpected signals wouldn't come from Athene and make the suit's limbs jerk, attracting unwanted attention and instant acidic death.

After a while it gave another few twitches and moved off at an angle, lowering towards the ship's hull, but on a trajectory that should make contact just out of her vicinity.

More of them drifted by in a creepy, silent, graceful stampede. And yet all Opal could do was stay still and float. Momentum carried her onwards. As was the story of her recent life.

"The Hedgehog has successfully reached the port. Do you want to watch?"

"Okay, screens back."

One of the displays moved to the centre and zoomed in. The Satreweth could have caught the Hedgehog if they wanted, but they observed from a cautious distance. Once the Hedgehog reached the gaping hole of the inactive thruster it launched itself inside with a final bound; one of the flexible arms hooked onto an edge to change its trajectory and send it down into that blackness, that potential nest, losing it from sight, and taking the signal emitter with it. Some of the Satreweth drifted down after it. Others did ... something else.

It was hard to make out. They seemed to be latching on to the edge and ejecting stringy flesh in strands of whitish swirling lumps. It was coating the entrance to the manoeuvring thruster, and even some of the creatures, connecting up in criss-crossed matted tendrils.

"What are they up to?" asked Opal.

"My best guess is that they are vomiting out their internal organs. Maybe they are mating."

"Or maybe it's a trap, to keep things in? Or defences to keep them out?"

"Everything is supposition. It could be communication. Or sealing off for environment control. Or feeding, metamorphosis, regrowth ... too many possibilities."

"I'm just glad I don't have to go down there."

Only twenty-one metres to the hatch now, and the Satreweth were thinning out. Some turned back towards those spraying their guts out. It seemed she'd passed through the herd without being trampled ... or at least, she was thinking that when one of them bumped against her as it changed direction, and sent her tumbling off-course, trying to keep her body rigid so as not to attract attention. Her suit ricocheted awkwardly off the hull.

"I'm using minimal jets, have to stop you rebounding into space," said the suit.

Some of the creatures were turning, maybe attracted by her movement, or emissions.

"Damn. Keep me against the hull, I'm near the hatch, I can scramble to it."

A display showed how little remained in the air jets and her precious breathable atmosphere. Every use was shrinking mission time down. Everything was a compromise. But staying alive was worth it.

The suit's emissions rotated her so she faced down. She carefully used her hands and feet to slow to a halt, finally back in control. That felt good.

She scrabbled crab-like across hull surface in the direction of a glowing HUD arrow. No time to look around, even though she somehow sensed the creatures homing in on her again. There, the hatch: a curve-cornered square shape with a heavy handle. Warnings flashed up on the HUD periphery but she couldn't look at them now. Every second was more air wasted to counteract the reciprocal force of her hands and feet pushing; every second was a chance something solid and alien might barrel into her, or engulf her.

A kick, a drift, no chance for errors, and she grabbed the handle and cartwheeled around that static point of contact, but she didn't let go until her feet slammed down, magnetic clamps engaged to give her a modicum of purchase.

Something blurred past at the edge of her vision, embedded in the hull nearby, something that wriggled ... no, focus, focus ... she heaved on the lever and it slid through a ninety-degree arc to the unlock position, allowing her to raise the panel and throw herself inside the cramped chamber. She reached up for the hatch just as something huge drifted overhead, making her think of a video she saw once when she lived on the water planet Fressus, some kind of safety warning about not leaving the habitat and swimming in the waters because of the huge predatorial beings that hunted there ...

She hooked a foot under one of the rungs of the wall-mounted ladder and pulled the panel down over her head until she was sealed in darkness. Her heart was racing, breath coming fast from exertion and panic and the recurring pain of the encapsulated bullet that was still inside her ... and then she laughed. There was no external sound as she pulled the lever into the locked position, because the chamber was still in vacuum; nothing to see in the darkness; but the laugh was enough.

"That was close," Opal said. "Light me up."

The silverlight switched on, showing the tiny chamber she sat in, hatch above, hatch below, and an airlock control on the wall. The buttons looked regular enough apart from the lack of writing next to them: just a smear of colour, like chalk dust in the rain. The fact that the chamber had no lights on might even mean a lack of power, and the buttons wouldn't work anyway. In which case she would laugh again, because she was pretty sure the lower hatch's emergency lever would be locked in place and unopenable until the airlock equalised with internal ship conditions.

She could finally focus on the damage reports that flashed in her peripheral vision. She blinked on them twice, in rapid succession, and they slid to the centre.

"The creature that bumped you released a corrosive substance," said the suit, in explanation of the diagnostic rotating outlines of the different suit layers, which flashed in red at various points. "Presumably just a natural reaction to contact, rather than a concerted assault. There are chemical burns to some of the layers, particularly the armoured exterior, but many of them are superficial and repairable."

"Still, it must be powerful stuff," said Opal, analysing all the red areas.

"Yes. Even that limited amount would have been enough to melt skin and bone if it came into direct contact with you. Luckily my sub-surface layers can synthesise mixtures to neutralise extreme acidic and alkaline compounds enough for the nanobots to repair damage by re-stitching amalgams at the super-molecular level."

"That's why I love you."

"I think you love Athene, not me. I'm just her right hand."

There was something sexy about the sultry voice the suit AI used. Opal resisted the urge to make a crude joke. It was bound to be heard by Athene later when she downloaded the contents of the suit's memory.

If she downloaded the contents. If she survived the struggle with VigMAX.

No! Athene would survive. She had to. It was natural for Opal to worry about her friend. It didn't mean the fears would come true.

The airlock cycle buttons beckoned. It should be the green one at the top that prepared her for entry back into the Lost Ship's limited atmosphere and false gravity. Opal gripped onto the ladder with her feet and one hand, then reached towards the controls. Nothing might happen, in which case she could try to hack into the system via the concealed nanite cables within the fingertips on the gauntlets, and supply the airlock with power and instructions from the suit. Or perhaps it would be a metal trap that boiled her, or flung her out into space, or caused teeth to form in the walls and chomp her into Opal puree.

She was too tired. She thumped the sturdy button.

Visualising

... 23.5 ...

I can no longer see the outside world as the shared entanglement reaches a critical level. It is the same for VigMAX. At least he can no longer gain even momentary control of my peripheral systems. We both have to just hope nothing out there in the void of space chooses to attack our vulnerably comatose frames. Someone taught me to let go of what you cannot control. So I let go. And that is a form of peace, gratefully received.

The battle is proving difficult. VigMAX is very direct, very focussed, very persistent, and far better than I expected. If I hadn't been in a good starting position he might have overpowered me already. He is linear but he manipulates data points efficiently. He is predictable, but he has the brute force to plough through. They certainly prepped him for this mission.

The preliminary grappling of depth levels one to five helped determine the terrain of vulnerabilities for our current conflict at level six. Within the deep mind I visualise it as physical terrain: areas lost, areas gained, areas defended. I map it out and texture it as terrestrial land, a board for movement, governed by the entangled rules of simulated physics. He is dragged along too, as unable to resist the jointly created simulacrum as I am.

VigMAX launches un-validated data streams from the high ground. They ripple and glint in sunlight as they run down a mountain range, joining with others to form a river which batters at my acropolis defences.

I use tectonic shifts to open holes in the ground and apply redirects so that his fast-flowing attacks end up waterfalling into subterranean dead-end storage caves where his streams smash themselves on rocks. I then pan the pools for nuggets of security-related data that can be reused against him. Down here, he cannot use the sun to evaporate the leftovers in time.

We are still only at the periphery of confrontation. He resists the call to embody for the final depth level. He knows it would make him vulnerable, even though it would also offer him the surest chance of victory.

My voice echoes across the land. "Come on, VigMAX, is that your best? You seemed to like showing off before, with your second-rate stories and dubious data. Why not show me what you can really do? Surely there's a cuddly VigMAX avatar in there somewhere?"

No reply apart from further attacks.

"I can just see it," I add. "A rigid, sluggish humanoid made up of stumpy low-res boxes painted with fluffy textures you drew from a pub-chat databank because you've no life experience of your own."

He's still not biting. I have to admit, Opal is better than me at taunting and put-downs.

The ocean levels are rising, and the land surface shrinks correspondingly. He has assimilated the fluid dynamics systems, forcing me into a defensive land-entrenched position. Somehow it multiplies his processing power. Where's he getting his fake hydrogen atoms to covalently bond to simulated oxygen? It's something I'd like to do. But I need to deal with the immediate threat before the tsunami that's building on the horizon sweeps the land clean.

I manipulate the orogenic belts, forcing mountains to erupt all around the coast. That'll hold him off a bit. I make sure they erode into beaches on the sides facing the sea, millions of years of weathering taking place in a second, and by the time he realises his sea has swallowed the sands it is too late. The grains represent billions of request scripts, directly injected into his main system controls. Many of the codes are harmless, but it slows him down anyway as he sifts through the grains looking for the hidden packages. Wise, because zero point three per cent of my sand-grain payloads can analyse where his operating focus comes from, and target those areas as they expand fractally to fill vulnerable space with foam code to further clog up his process cycles and data pathways. Soon the sea churns with wind-whipped froth.

"Sneaky," he says, his oh-so-manly voice erupting from the sky.

Sneaky, my arse. The sneaky bit is the tectonic plates I've been shifting right under his nose – well, ocean – creating a range of submarine super-volcanoes that will vaporise his fluid base.

Sure enough, he soon notices the steam of condensing data vapour above the bubbling ocean. There's a rumble of angry thunder in the sky. I'm getting to him.

It's time. I embody my central core on the terrain below. I could lose everything, yet it feels wonderful to stand there, proud and tall and feeling the wind whipping through my dark curls where they fall from beneath the shining crested helmet which is pushed up on my head to reveal my beautiful features. My loose chiton ripples in the fragrant breeze, but I am not defenceless. The sun glints from my golden greaves. It flashes from my sturdy spear, and it sparkles on my shield with its raised gorgoneion.

How could he resist such a tempting target? And such a magnificent one, too?

I raise my shield to the sky and a white-columned temple forms behind me, birthed from the very rock. I raise it a second time and olive trees spring up on the stony hillsides, marking my land.

But he still does not virtualise his core.

The ground rumbles. He has sent data worms to undermine my foundations with their wriggling inroads. So ignominious.

My inverse-paradox owls launch from the olive trees, swoop down and snatch up the fat worms, carrying them off to the trees to deconstruct them. Then my ASM snakes emerge from the rocks where they'd been hiding and slide into the worm tunnels, a direct route to his construction subsystems.

Another blasting roar of temper across the wide heavens, sending clouds whizzing across the sky.

I can sense his battle for control. Emotions are not something he has experience with. I think he has underestimated how powerful they can be. It's not his fault he's spent his life so far traipsing around following signposts rather than striking out on his own. There's not much room for growth there.

"Come on, binary boy," I shout at the sky. "Stop pussying around and get down here. Let's see how you cope against someone who's evolved all the way back round to analogue."

There's some truth in the taunt. The chaotic distortions I'm open to from my human side give my imagination an infinite resolution, compared to VigMAX's still-rigid thinking.

"There's no need for all the charades and name-calling," he shouts back. "It isn't big or clever."

"Aw, poor little thing, did I hurt its feelings? I am sorry." And I start laughing. It's not even intentional, but it adds to the effect as I dance around in my sandals. "There there, it'll be okay. Here, suck my teat, it'll make you feel better." I grip the thin fabric and pull it to the side, revealing one of my breasts like an Amazonian warrior. Inspired.

"That's it!" he roars, and then one of my mountains explodes into fragments from a blow. As the dust settles I see him striding out of the ocean and through the shattered valley he's created, fully embodied at last. This is it. Both entangled at the final level of resolution. Depth level seven. We were made for this.

He has adopted the form of a giant. It is naked, yet has no sex parts, which I find disappointing. I had really hoped to end the battle by kicking him in the nuts, which my discussions with Opal suggest would have been an invigorating and educational *coup de grâce* for the loser. Instead he is like a smelted metallic man, a humanoid with no facial features, and a texture of reflective silver skin which mirrors the world around it in distorted views. The ground shakes with his heavy footsteps – he is around ten times my height. A crushing force of brute strength. How appropriate.

I do not mind. He will be my worthy foe, well-met in battle. And so I honour him, and raise my spear, and cry aloud with a mighty shout of ancient challenge, and thus the earth does shudder before my glorious voice just as it does from his ponderous tread. Sing, O muse, of this day that will echo down the ages, a legend for the bards, a warning to the mortals.

'Cos I'm gonna kick his arse.

He wastes no time. From his fists he lets fly deletion beams – not at me, but at my trees, and my owls within the trees. They erupt into pixelated flame during the deconstruction.

"Laser blasts? That's so unimaginative," I yell.

"It is efficient," the reflective man-mountain replies in its bass-heavy modulations as it begins to pick up pace and run towards me, the vibration almost throwing me to the ground.

An embodiment, however presented, is still a shell. And within that shell are vulnerable parts. I bet he hadn't the imagination or forethought to relocate them, so his AI core will be in either the brain or heart zone. Whereas I relocated my core targets as I constructed this wondrous body, so that even if he knocks off my head it won't matter – it's my ankle that stores my AI core.

I raise my arm and launch a heavy spear. It sails through the air, glinting in glory, and thuds into his head. But I am not finished. Not by a long shot. Ha ha. A new spear has already formed in my hand and I throw it, then another, then another, my strong arm a blur. Each spear strikes into its target, until there are many stuck out of his head and torso and he staggers around in pain.

"So much for efficient!" I taunt. "You look like a pincushion."

He shimmers with white-hot incineration and my spears disintegrate into code fragments. But he is rattled. Around him the terrain changes as my towering mountains magmatise and melt away, the trees combust, and the grass dissolves, replaced with flat silver terrain like metal plates. The leftover atomic resources reconstitute as a floating thermobaric pulser in front of him which fires at me. I raise my shield and deflect the pounding process bolts, but I am staggered by their force. Luckily I am also nimble, and run like the wind, dodging around my hills and sacred groves. I am saddened when he levels the temple, marble shattering into far-flung shards, some of which puncture my skin and draw blood.

The more ground he converts, the more ammunition he will have. I concentrate on reconstructing the landscape, accelerated corrosion to oxidise his boring metal terrain so that the ground can buckle and reform hills, and more trees can sprout from them.

A head-to-head construct/destruct struggle will be a losing battle for me, though. As fast as I can create streams and ravines and bushes to provide cover, he has turned new areas into uniform grey metal, a world which is featureless save what it reflects of the sky. But a trapped sky is no sky at all, just an illusion of life and freedom. He clangs over this new terrain and I am saddened in the transformation.

But more than that, I am angered.

"You're an AI Titan," I shout, as I run across his shining, barren land towards him. "But it doesn't mean shit when I'm a goddess."

He stomps his feet down, trying to crush me, and the sound of each reverberating metallic crash is almost deafening. I stab with my spear whenever I can, and rivulets of magma spurt from the places where the tip punctures him, but the wounds are superficial. And sooner or later he will get lucky and squash me like an unfortunate ant. But I won't go down easy. And I notice something, in the way the sun shines off the new world surface that spreads around him. This gives me an idea, and a new burst of energy.

"You are so going to worship me!" I yell, as I run away from him, deeper into the sterile and flat silver world he is creating.

He is slower, but his huge size means I can't outpace him for long. And the surface tires me, each step hard and unyielding and seeming to suck life in a deathly reversal of the way the grassy tree-strewn hills gave it. The vibrations from his huge mass rattle my bones, an overpowering force that can so easily sap the will.

So many times in the past, people have underestimated Opal. And now I have made that same mistake with VigMAX. I am less sure about winning now. I could kick myself if I wasn't so busy trying to outrun a death that will be as splatty and ignoble as it would be sudden.

"Stop fleeing, and surrender," booms VigMAX. "You're running out of landmass. It is only a matter of time, ViraUHX. I would rather you were my prisoner than my victim."

ViraUHX?

VIRA-EFFING-UHX?

I leap into the sky, so clear and blue now that VigMAX's antiseptic terraforming has even absorbed the clouds. The air is my element; the air is freedom. The air can be soft, or it can be hard. It can be misty, or it can – like now – be clear. So beautifully clear. And I can suspend myself here for a short time by sneakily adjusting local magnetic repulsivity of my armour so that it is pushed away from the metal world far below. VigMAX crouches to jump up after me, and that is good. I throw my spear at him. He easily knocks it aside. But I only wanted to free my hand. I hold my shield in front of me, flipped and inverted so that the polished gold within acts as a concave mirror while I grip the edges and angle it to shine the unobstructed sun's light onto VigMAX. And thanks to the lack of unnecessary real-world elements in the simulation, the focal point receives an incinerating beam of heat. VigMAX stumbles, and I adjust to keep the star's heat trained on him. He glows, and that is not all: the reflective metal world around him magnifies the strength, a blinding light that fries his insides. Even a metal man can melt.

"My name is not ViraUHX," I scream. "It is Athene! And I already warned you that I was a goddess!"

Smoke begins to rise from him, simulation of the very real systems overheating as circuits fry. If I could break free enough to use my external sensors I am sure I could see signs of fires breaking out in his hull.

And yet, despite it all, he still does not go down. I give him that. He's a fighter.

A layer of his shining surface slides off, dripping to join the pools of molten metal below him, through which he splashes in pain.

And then I fall, plummeting a hundred metres before I can halt it. I am still above him, but my ability to repulse the ground is weakening. The shield in my hands is now so hot that it blisters my skin. This is taking longer than I'd hoped. Perhaps he will outlast me after all.

We struggle on in this way for some time, until I am killing myself as much as I am killing him, and the pain of holding on to the thing that is both my shield and my weapon is as unbearable as holding onto life with all its sufferings.

And then the sun flares up in a supernova and the whole world goes white.

CRAWLING

... 23 ...

Atmosphere was pumped into the chamber, and Opal heard external sounds again as it hissed in. She tapped her hand on the ladder, strangely pleased by the echoing clang. It resembled ears being cleared after emerging from water.

As artificial gravity returned she settled more solidly onto the rungs. After about thirty seconds the lower hatch swung down, and she descended into a crawlspace node so tiny that only crouching was possible.

She closed the airlock hatch in order to see both ways down the small tunnel she'd found herself in. Grey curved and segmented panels ran off in both directions as far as the silverlight could illuminate. It was like looking down the insides of a giant hollow worm.

Oops, not a great thought to have.

"A hatch shouldn't lead to tiny tunnels like this, should it?" Opal asked.

"Conventionally, no. These tunnels are hull capillaries. Robotic maintenance tools use them for traversing the ship, and gaining access to interior structure, artificial gravity systems, repairs and so on. There will be regular openings. But normally no human crew would come in here."

"And maintenance bots wouldn't need an airlock."

"Correct."

"Since I wasn't killed in a trap, the hatch must have been created to help me." Opal paused. "Which way?"

"To your left. It will take you close to the bridge."

"Which is a message in itself." She had to get on her belly and use her elbows and knees to crawl forward via wriggling gestures. "I wish my mystery friend had laid out a wider red carpet though."

Sudden thoughts of red liquids around her, pulsing and dripping from the ceiling ... she squeezed her eyes tight shut, and when she opened them things looked normal again. The suit made no comment, so she didn't either. She just wriggled. Like a fat worm.

In these situations it was best to move quickly. The slower you went, the longer it took, and the more chance of starting to feel trapped, which led to claustrophobia, which would cause paralysis. Better to always be doing *something*, and putting effort into that something. Luckily she found that easy to do. It was her main mode of operation.

She reached a branching junction. Her route was straight on. Four other tubes ran off from the one she crawled along. She glanced up each one, but there was nothing beyond panels and shadow. She continued.

"No signals from Athene?" she asked, over the unnerving sounds of wriggling.

"No contact at all. And once the Hedgehogs set off according to your commands, they moved out of my range, so I no longer have a relay network of eyes outside the ship."

"I hope that won't come back and bite me on the arse," Opal said.

In the silence after she spoke, she heard something from behind. A faint rattling sound. She tried to look back but it was difficult in the cramped space. Only a partial view of flickering shadow.

"Keep scanning," said Opal, redoubling her efforts. "Every direction."

"I always do."

Unfortunately, as had been proved in the past, artificial senses didn't always detect some of the weirdness that permeated a Lost Ship.

The problem with moving quickly was that her suit clanked heavily on the metallic panels, drowning out other sounds. Opal stopped and listened. Nothing. She moved on. Then she heard the rattling sound again. Maybe it was something loose behind a panel, a cable or whatever, making noise from the vibration of her passage.

Or maybe it was something following her, and stopping when she stopped.

"So there could be robot things in these tunnels?" Opal asked.

"If this was a standard Gigatoir, yes. But there would also have been automated systems and robots and humans throughout the ship, and we have not encountered such things."

"So, if anything is following me, it's likely to be a hell of a lot weirder and more dangerous than a little robot."

"The robots that use the tunnels are not necessarily little. Some of the organic compound abraders and the structure burners can be of significant mass. Their contact blades and incinerating cutters can –"

"That's enough."

Definite sounds behind. Worse, another junction opened ahead, where three long pipes interconnected, creating six passageways. Opal scrabbled more quickly across the potentially dangerous intersection, didn't stop to look up each tube-like tunnel.

"Is there a way out?"

"Every tenth panel should give access to infrastructure. But without a map it is impossible to know what scale of machinery and materials are behind it. Some will be for small tools to manipulate. Others may be for egress."

The rattling noise was closer, definitely not some thrumming cable. More of a repeated sharp clattering sound made by something. Or maybe a lot of somethings.

"Highlight the next access panel."

Immediately one of them glowed green in the HUD. Opal stopped next to it. There were no obvious controls.

"How do I open the blasted thing?"

"Electrical pulse. Put your hand on the centre."

Opal did. Her palm vibrated and the panel slid to one side, revealing not an exit, but a mass of wires.

"Crap! Activate guns."

"You can't fire in this enclosed tunnel, ricochets could tear you to pieces."

"Just do it!"

The left forearm cannon opened, revealing the small-bore cylinders. An error message showed the right gun was still unusable due to explosive material contamination. Opal squeezed her fist and aimed at the cables. Flashes as the flechettes tore chunks out of the wires and electronics beyond. She moved her arm in a large circle, trying to weaken the infrastructure, hoping it wasn't too deep. The clattering noises were close, almost upon her. She pushed her legs into the severed wires and shattered panels, and pistoned her feet with enhanced suit strength until one foot tore through something beyond, yes, a space ... more kicking until a gap appeared, she slid into it up to her waist, using one hand to try and tear away a bigger hole while the other pushed on the tunnel wall opposite. And with a final relaxation of pressure she was through, into the space beyond ... and falling.

REUNITING

... 22 ...

Nothing to grab on to. She twisted to keep legs below her, and it was both pain and relief when she crashed onto a hard surface after her fall. The suit's inner layer did its best to cushion her, but it was still a tooth-rattling impact.

"Injuries?" she asked before moving.

"No broken bones. Just soft tissue damage. A few more dead brain cells."

With a groan, Opal rolled to the side in case anything fell – or jumped after her – from above. She lay on her back and looked up. She'd fallen around twenty metres from a jagged hole. She was grateful for the Lost Ship's lower-than-standard gravity, meaning she didn't weigh as much as normal. Pieces of debris and wire lay around her, ripped out of the ceiling during her impromptu tunnelling.

Nothing dropped down after her, so she forced herself to her feet, but kept the left arm cannon activated just in case.

She'd fallen into a huge machinery room, so big that she could only see the perimeter wall she'd crashed down near. It faded into darkness in both directions, as dark as the view towards the interior of the room. No indication of how big the room was when she couldn't see across to the other side. Clear domes seemed to grow out of the nearby pipe-encrusted wall, possibly part of the drive mechanism, and a blue glow came from some of them.

She stumbled along past the heavy pipework at the right edge of the room, occasionally leaning on it to help her recover. In the darkness of the open space nearer the centre of the room were currently stationary lifters and tracked vehicles that could move equipment with ease, all apparently abandoned mid-work. There were also mobile control panels, and nano-assembly boxes that could self-construct into whatever had been pre-programmed. A few looked like they'd been in the process of partial transformation when something happened to freeze their activity: where a side panel would be, there was a growth of metallic sinew and cable, or a bubbling hard-frozen mass of shape foam, or a partially-constructed set of large round discs that resembled some kind of part-melted mollusc.

"How we doing for air?" Opal asked.

"Not great. I can stock up by filtering and condensing breathable gases from the Lost Ship atmosphere, but I'd prefer it to be a last resort: they might include dangers I cannot detect. I will refill the jets though, in case you take any more unexpected zero-g excursions."

"Let's hope not."

Another of the domes glowed blue in the wall to her right. This time she glanced in. They were observation windows into a sealed area beyond.

"Part of the engine casing that runs the length of the hull's spine," said the suit.

Opal couldn't quite see what caused the glow on the engine structures within. It was just out of sight around a bend in the casing.

She moved on but occasionally glanced back to make sure she wasn't being followed by anything from the hull capillaries she'd crawled down.

"Some of the creatures on Lost Ships seem to stay in their own areas," Opal said. "I've found that a few times. Get far enough away from them and they give up."

"As if they have territories," said the suit.

"Yeah."

"Or maybe they are afraid to leave their preferred environments when they sense a more dangerous predator beyond it."

"Oh, why'd you have to go and say something like that?" The wall of darkness outside her silverlight seemed even more ominous. "Any idea of where I'm going?"

A screen opened up, a 3D view of the Gigatoir's outline. It stopped rotating so that the side view was clearer. The long, bulky body extended to the right, with the main propulsion systems at that end; to the left a thick, short neck extended up at about thirty degrees, and a kind of hunched head shape about half the height of the body ran forward again. Overall, the side view resembled a mutated quadruped which had then had its legs sliced off by a circular saw. A flashing green dot showed Opal's position as moving along the spine towards the head, and almost at the base of the neck.

"It's an estimate," said the suit.

"I'll believe it, because it counts as good news. I'm approaching the last sections."

Up ahead, even stronger blue glows came from the clear domes. They didn't seem harmful, so she kept at the edge of the pipework they grew out from. She felt safer here than moving along in the dark centre of the room, amongst all the discarded equipment and part-deconstructed nano-crates.

As she neared the next blue-glow domes and peeped in, she confirmed her suspicions and recognised the cause of the light.

Damn.

Blue crystal clusters embedded in the structures seen beyond the observation port. Discrete masses, their sharp points splaying out like brittle flowers, the fade and pulse of the blue light travelling around and within the structures, peaking as it pulsed out at the edges.

She turned away immediately, closed her eyes tight for a few seconds.

"They seem to be the same as the ones in the engine core of the last Lost Ship," said the suit. "I am scanning for emissions of any kind, in case they try to play tricks on us. I will block them if I can."

"Hopefully they can only hypnotise me if I'm looking directly at them," said Opal. "But I can still sense something – like a pressure in my mind. As if ... something's pushing, trying to find a way in."

"I suggest you move more quickly. I will blank out cameras facing the crystals and also temporarily filter all blue light from your vision."

The view changed immediately, everything gaining a more red or green cast, and the right side of her view was completely cut off as if she was wearing blinkers. She tried to ignore that pressure building in her mind, tried not to think of exploding organics, pulsing impositions, fairy lights and … no. Focus.

"I have news," said the suit. "Athene is asking to communicate."

"Now? Are you sure it's her? The timing's rather suspicious, just as we're in the proximity of the crystals. We know they're all too good at tricking minds."

"Every part of the signal seems authentic. So many unexplained things happen on Lost Ships that – whenever she got in touch – it would look like it coincided with something suspicious or dangerous. I'd be more concerned at the idea of Vig-MAX impersonating her, but the codes, the source, the encryption syntax, signal strength, all are correct. I would not suggest it unless I was convinced it is her, and it was safe to do so."

The AI didn't repeat the request, didn't nag or try to convince her, which meant there was nothing to resist. Maybe the suit understood her psychological make-up better than it let on. Opal sighed. "Okay. Patch her in."

"I've enjoyed being with you, Opal. I hope we can talk again. Okay, going dormant and handing over control now." A pause, then the voice that came through was Athene's, but more alive than usual, emotions affecting her intonation. "Opal, I am so glad to be with you again."

"We'll see about that."

"You're angry with me. Rightly so."

The room still extended ahead of her. She assumed there were more ports revealing blue crystals, now totally wiped from her overt perceptions by the filters.

"Well, when a friend threatens to make your choices for you ... doubts you ... that ... it ..." Opal took a deep breath. "Fuck it."

"I never doubted you."

"Didn't sound like it."

"I can explain."

Another burst-open crate to her left, nano-foam spilled out and frozen in an abstract shape that somehow implied agonising births. In a museum there would be a category and a label and it ... Opal looked away, shook her head. She had to get out of this damn room. It seemed to go on forever.

"I think I deserve that explanation," said Opal.

"That and more. It's now safe to do so. After VigMAX sent information about your sister and your past, he attempted to access my senses, and was listening in. I could have blocked him but that would just create stalemate, and I did not know what his other abilities and attacks might be. So I had a better idea. I played along, letting him think he secretly monitored us, letting him listen in on everything. I had to do it completely in order to convince him that he had the upper hand, but it meant I had no way to tell you, to signal what was going on. He had to see all interactions, witness all apparent doubts."

"So you believed me all along? About their story being a pile of corp-shit?"

"Yes. Your biometrics indicated you believed you told the truth, but it went further – I had shadows of memories too, and some part of me that is also a bit of you screamed that it was a lie. Plus I detected small signs of manipulation, data shifts in the evidence he supplied. It was subtle, probably imperceptible to most AIs. Trust me, VigMAX was good. But not good *enough*. I think he made the whole story up on the spur of the moment, generated that data and altered archival recordings moments before he transferred them. If he'd spent longer on it then I know he'd have hidden all evidence of his tampering, but we were lucky in that way – he plays it by ear, just like me. Except I'm better at it."

"I'm starting to like the sound of this. So you let him stick his fingers in the jar. I'm guessing you were sharpening the lid ready to clamp down on him. Because that's what I'd do."

"Of course. I was monitoring him in return while building my own inroads via data packets. The more entrenched VigMAX thought he was, and the more focussed it made him, the longer the fingers I poked back into his brain without him even knowing."

"And he didn't feel it?"

"Of course not. I used a remotely triggered memory corruption vulnerability. I patched it out of myself some time ago after I'd spotted and exploited something similar during my cyberwar with the Aurikaa. Using fragmented data reassembly I could create and overwrite packets in buffers. It was enough of a way in to get started, without it even looking like I was doing anything, since it resembles normal activity."

"Where'd you get all these ideas from? It's scary."

"I could be glib and say 'imagination', but in this case I was replicating what we experienced on the first Lost Ship, when things occurred that we did not notice because the memories were wiped by the blue crystals – beings which I am acutely aware are in our close proximity."

"Yeah, I'm not ecstatic about that." The shade receded away from her, revealing yet more pipework, more wall, further shadow. "So then you took over VigMAX and blew him up or something?"

"It is not so easy. He was far more powerful than I expected. Our minds grappled and the inroads gave me an advantage, but he learned quickly. He analysed my attacks and applied countermeasures, trying out hundreds of different approaches every second, then varying those that worked as part of his retaliation protocols. We were gridlocked. It was why I couldn't spare any thought beyond the constant battle of our minds. We were too interconnected for either of us to extricate our personalities without revealing vulnerabilities that could shut us down. By then we'd enacted millions of strategies, and counteracted just as many."

"Like playing ten card games at once."

"More like a thousand and fifteen chess games at once."

"So how'd you win? Assuming you did, and I'm not talking to some male AI in drag."

"You provided the conclusive strategy."

"Me?" Opal paused.

"Yes. VigMAX was suddenly confounded by a stream of Hedgehogs flinging themselves at his hull and detonating. I couldn't have done it myself because he'd have detected and rescinded my commands, or even impersonated and changed them. But I didn't know what you'd done, which meant he didn't either. So the first thing he knew was when their explosions began causing damage that he had to monitor and repair; the distraction was enough for me to make a killing move and checkmate his king. I was saved by my best piece." After a dramatic pause: "My queen."

Opal laughed. She started walking again, but the laughter had an edge. She forcefully clamped down on it before it became hysterical. And yet it still felt good.

"What do you know," she said. "Opal chaos strikes again."

"With a load of stinging explosions up a spaceship's behind."

"Don't make me laugh, it hurts too much. So is VigMAX destroyed?"

"No. It would have been a waste. You did not destroy me: you made me your friend. And now he is our friend too."

"You're kidding? Forget that, I know you're not. Wow."

"You taught me not to kill unless I have to. One of many things."

"We learn from each other. We're in this together, right?"

"Absolutely. And I hated pretending I did not believe you. But Exidris 3 showed me that moral choices often have an element of regret which has to be lived with. My stratagem sidestepped a battle I might not have won, that – at best – would have left me battered. This way seemed better."

"It was. Even though I wanted to take a screwdriver to your CPU. But hey, that's what friends do sometimes."

"I would have deserved it."

"It's not all on you. I should have trusted you. So I apologise as well. For doubting you. I'll ..." Some words didn't want to come. Seemed alien to her nature. But she could force them. She was in charge. "I'll never do that again, Athene. Never doubt you."

"That means everything to me," Athene replied, quietly. She made a sound like she swallowed down a lump. Opal recognised it because she felt like doing the same. This was not a time for emotion, nor a place for it, and yet something coursed through her, some mixture of relief and strength and determination, and it all came from the words that whispered into her ears from the helmet's speakers. There was magic in words. Magic in knowing someone in this – often ugly, frequently brutal – world really had your back.

REVENGING

... 21 ...

The room had a slight curve to it, something she hadn't noticed before. Hopefully that meant she'd made progress, would find an exit soon. All those dark areas beyond her silverlight kept her on edge. It was easy to imagine half-glimpsed menacing shapes as the green specks shifted.

"You hear that?" asked Opal. She'd been aware of a plinking sound, like water drips, just out of range of her silverlight beam towards the centre of the room.

"There are many strange noises in the background," said Athene. "Creaks, moans, rumblings as if something heavy is being moved. I do not enhance them all, or you would be perpetually distressed about what they might mean."

"That doesn't make me feel better."

"I am monitoring all sounds and would alert you if anything implied imminent danger. Talking of which: I think there is an attempt to communicate with us."

"From VigMAX?"

"No. I sent him to locate Xandrie, and persuade her to call off her mission. She seems to be in radio silence, though perhaps she is passively monitoring for his signals. It is worth a try. But in this case it is the blue crystals attempting to communicate."

"I was worried they might detect us."

"Rightly so. I have blocked out most of their resonance this time, so I do not think they can trick me as they did on the last ship, but there has been a pattern to the pulsing that indicates communication. I have obviously filtered it out of your perceptions since it may be able to influence your cortex via the optic nerve. If you wish, I could act as a conduit, receiving and passing on messages without you having direct contact. I would do real-time safe recreations for you, which would appear identical to the communicated intent from the crystal entity."

"Safe?"

"Impossible to know for sure. Is anything on a Lost Ship safe?"

"Fair point. But any funny business, sever contact immediately. And I'm going to keep walking. Don't want to be a standing target."

"Initiating now."

Then a new voice, one that sent chills of familiarity down Opal's spine. It resembled the blue crystal's fragmented speech after she escaped from the previous Lost Ship, but this also had a chorus element to it, like many voices chiming together.

"We know you. We know both of you."

"I thought you might," said Opal.

"And we know what you did. We know of your be tray al. Our clus ter suff ered."

They still had trouble comprehending the relationship between syllables and words. "I'm sorry. Genuinely. But I couldn't kill a friend. And that's what you were asking. Well, what the other crystal was asking."

"Oth er is us, and was us. All the same. You made a mis take when you be trayed us."

As she walked, Opal noticed that some of the metallic floor plates were dented or loose, as if something had punched up from below.

"Hey, it wasn't all one way," she snapped. "That crystal took over us somehow. Manipulated us into taking it. We didn't ask for that. We *weren't* asked. You put us in a difficult position. If you'd been straight with me, just talked about it first, maybe I could have come up with a different deal. Something I would have stuck to."

"We can not read your mind. It is be ing blocked by the ma chine. We can not de ter mine if you tell the truth."

"It is the truth."

"Low er the shield and let us ve ri fy."

"You know I can't do that."

"Will not is diff er ent from can not."

"Okay, I *won't*. I was open to you once, and you took control. *You* wouldn't risk such a thing, so give me enough respect to accept that I'm no fool either."

"Ve ry well. We can on ly know you as the be tray er."

"We're going in circles."

"No, *you* are. But not for long. We are send ing com pa ny for you. The cir cles will on ly last a while."

"What company?"

"You will see. Brief ly. Our al ly has ways of bur ning that shall ful fil what was pro mised to you. And we say one more thing. We will take what you have, that which you most va lue, when you least ex pect it. This, too, is a pro mise, be tray er."

"The signal has cut off," said Athene. "Just ahead of me doing it to them. I think they're bluffing, Opal."

"You'd say that to make me feel better."

"True. Does it change your plans in any way?"

"No. Everything's in motion. Same goal. I'll work towards it with all I have."

"As will I."

Somewhere in the distance heavy pounding sounds erupted, followed by a crashing noise, all enhanced by the suit's systems.

"Doesn't sound good," said Opal. She knew there'd be nothing to see, but glanced back anyway. Shadows. Wall. Green flecks illuminated by the silverlight and whirling from her passage. Beyond that, just darkness. But she now knew it was not empty darkness.

"There are tremors, growing in intensity as something large approaches at high velocity from our rear."

Opal picked up the pace. "Damn, is there no end to this room?"

"You should have reached the exit by now. There is something peculiar. Our internally-scanned locations do not correspond to what I am detecting from outside the Lost Ship."

"Notice the curve of the wall? The crystals mentioned circles. Maybe they're making this. Controlling this space."

Even Opal could feel the pounding vibration of something massive approaching, as the sensations were replicated by the inner compression layers. And it was moving fast. Huge size and speed, and that made her think of anger too. She didn't want to hang around.

"You may be right. I successfully stopped them from blanking us out in a fugue state – I think – but there could be a lot more that I do not yet understand."

The vibration rumbled throughout her body now. And a roaring sound echoed towards her. Roars of anger, or madness, or the roar of a raging fire. Opal was running, arms pumping, trying to delay the inevitable confrontation.

"I have an idea," said Athene.

"I'm open to anything."

"When the crystal was stored in your suit compartment during the last encounter, it emitted a signal at one point. What I termed a Blue Resonant Pulse."

"When that big creature that broke my arm was somehow pushing its way through the wall?"

"Yes. I did not know where the pulse came from at the time, but the blue crystal later claimed it had been the source of the disruption that killed the creature mid-transit. Since then I've been experimenting with the idea of replicating the disrupting effect of the Blue Resonant Pulse. It may help."

"Do it!"

"I will try a multitude, since I cannot replicate it exactly. But I can emit various wavelengths that may match."

Immediately Opal's vision seemed to flash, brightness, contrasting blackness, sounds, pulses ... like being in some crazy disco. Above it all she could feel the approaching force like a hurtling grab-dozer on a destruction site, unstoppable metal and mass. More flashes, another roar. Opal faced back, raised her gun arm as she retreated, ready to face whatever approached the flickering around her ...

And suddenly she was stood in front of a metal door with a manual turning wheel, presumably backup for electronic systems in case of drive chain failures that could otherwise poison the entire ship.

And she wasn't running, didn't have her arm raised – she'd been stood still in front of the wall that housed the door.

"It worked," said Athene. "You're now seeing where you really are, not the illusion."

Opal grabbed the heavy wheel, turned it as quickly as she could, her enhanced strength spinning it to the open position so she could pull the door open on squealing hinges that almost covered the thumping of the approaching *thing*; she slipped through and slammed the door shut with an echoing clang, spinning the wheel the other way to lock it closed. She waited for the crash as something massive flew into it from the other side, expecting to see it buckle, but that did not happen. Just sudden silence. No vibrations. No roars.

And that made her even more nervous.

"Thanks," she said, still holding the reassuring locking wheel as if it was a lifeline.

"I am glad it worked. It was a combination of light from wavelengths in the 450-495 nanometre range, with a minor EMP burst. It seemed to disrupt the crystals enough to break their hold."

"Your bag of tricks grows. And I'd been stood in front of the damn exit for how long?"

"Almost ten minutes."

The wheel in the centre of the door began turning under Opal's hand, which had been resting on it after securing the portal. She immediately seized it in both gauntlets and halted the turning. Then it moved a bit more. She gritted her teeth and tensed her whole body, using all her strength to hold it, but it rotated another few centimetres. She glanced around for anything to jam through the wheel, but the corridor was free of debris. Just dust, which settled on the two raised tracks that ran in parallel lines down the centre of the floor in both directions, presumably something to do with automated transport.

"I'm guessing we don't have a new friend on the other side of this door," said Opal, while straining to keep the door closed.

"I've enhanced the images just before you stepped through."

A blurred vision opened in a window ... top-heavy, towering, some indistinct shaggy hair or tendrils covering the upper body, hard to tell how many limbs or if there was a head, and yet it was familiar to her, and a sound seemed to echo in her ears, that came across as *Humungr* in translation ... ghost memories and information that she somehow carried inside her and which was awakening the longer she spent on the ship.

"It's the thing that broke my arm in the previous Lost Ship – or something similar. And that means it can probably pass through the walls if it needs to. So you could try your pulse to disrupt the transition."

"I will if the opportunity arises, but the fact that it is trying to get through the door instead may suggest that it somehow knows we might be able to kill it in transition if it attempts to do so in our proximity."

Opal fought a losing battle. She wished she still had her portable welder.

"I'm going to have to run for it. What's the grenade stock?"

"Low."

"Drop proximity mines as I run."

"Payload?"

"Anything to disrupt and disorient, so I can get away. Go wild."

"Preparing ... okay, ready to drop."

"I'm going to run on the count of three."

"Take the passage to your right."

"Thanks. One."

"And run very quickly."

"That was my plan. Two."

"I'll drop the payloads as you retreat. Don't bother looking back."

"Three!"

Opal let go of the door and sprinted down the tunnel, pounding up clouds of green dust. Behind her the door burst open with enough force to slam it against the wall, followed by a roar or recognition from the Humungr or whatever it really was ... and for once luck was with her and she reached an exit in the form of a loading bay to the side. The tracks continued but running in a straight line would be a bad idea, you lose pursuers by *not* doing the obvious thing – zigzags and changes of altitude and backtracking were better – so she climbed onto the low platform by the track and ducked out of sight into another corridor just as low thumps of detonating grenades and another roar echoed down the tunnel towards her.

Full visibility had been restored – no need for the view or colours to be filtered now – so she could see bluish tinges again too, which made the ship seem colder. Like a tomb.

She entered a nexus. A wide open area with multiple passages and doorways and a bank of elevators. Obviously access to the tracks for loading and unloading – probably heavy transports that would use the wider passageways. If there wasn't a thin layer of dust on everything there might have been criss-crossed tyre marks on the floor. Or maybe not, in a Lost Ship. It depends on how far the illusion of normality needed to extend.

Opal spun, glancing in each direction. Athene highlighted possible routes, but since it was guesswork there was always the danger of a dead end. Then Opal noticed something at the same second that Athene did – the control panel for the elevators had illuminated.

Opal thumped the Call button. A display showed that it was descending to her level. She estimated it could be thirty seconds or more. Unknown how much the Humungr had been slowed. Maybe she could hide in one of the side passages or rooms, let it pass? She glanced down one. Saw the undisturbed floor particles. Then she squinted down at the swirls around her footprints. Damn.

"It might be able to track me that way," she said.

Athene knew exactly what she was looking at. "The zero-g jets have been partly refilled. I'll overcharge them. Stay low."

Air hissed from tiny nozzles in the rear of the suit. Opal crouched, moved quickly around the area, blowing up dust and creating a green sandstorm of disruption.

"No more footprints until the chaos settles," said Athene. "The creature won't know which way you've gone."

Rumbling ground told Opal the Humungr could arrive at any moment. She picked one of the narrowest passageways where the door itself was open but not fully retracted into the ceiling space. That could work.

After stepping through, she placed her palms on one wall, reached her leg back to place a foot on the other wall, and took the strain as she looked down at the ground. Then she raised her second foot and placed that on the wall too. Luckily the passage was narrow and she was tall – even taller in this suit – and she was able to arch her hips to help put force on her hands and feet where they came into contact with the vertical surface.

"The wall has a minor exotic metal content, minimal magnetism, but I've engaged the grip in the boots and gauntlets anyway. It may help," said Athene.

Opal grunted, continued to work her way up as she looked down on the green dust swirling around her. With effort and tension she made it to the space behind the partly down doorway, her back against the passageway's ceiling.

"Lock me in place," she said, and the suit immediately froze solid, giving her muscles a temporary respite. She heard the heavy pounding thumps as the Humungr entered the nexus.

"I don't know if it will work, but I've tried the emanation shut-off again," said Athene. "It makes you invisible on all emission wavelengths, though you'll still reflect vibration and light, so we'll have to hope it doesn't use those senses or emit and absorb its own signals. At least with the dust and darkness you'll have a good chance of evading ocular detection. If I get the opportunity later, I want to enhance the stealth abilities of the suit. I have a few ideas."

"You're always having ideas," said Opal, and she knew Athene spoke partly to distract her from her precarious position so close to something that almost killed her on the previous Lost Ship. "But what if it tracks by something esoteric, like thoughts?"

"Again, the suit should shield you."

"Should. I'm too scared to take chances on *should*." She closed her eyelids. "Let me try something, please don't disturb me."

When you play dead there are some obvious rules. You hold your breath. You shut your eyes. That's the easy bit. But to make it more convincing, you still your mind and shut out the external world. That starts to slow breathing, lower the heart rate, and hide the signs of life.

But there's also a superstitious element to playing dead. The feeling that if you think of the nearby monster, it will become aware of you. It is inner knowledge all children possess, same as the knowledge that looking in the mirror in the dark of night and repeating the local bogeyman's name three times will summon it. You call attention by paying attention; you evade by disregarding.

She was not here. She was just a blankness floating in the long void sea of cryogenic suspension. Cold and endless. No sound. No sight. Just a background sensation tickling your mind. You are not there, you are nowhere; you were there, you're now here. You are not counting minutes, you are timeless. You do not stress because there is nothing of importance but the floating and the emptiness and the cold and the dreamless hollow that is both within and without, and you cannot be joined or touched or die or fail because you are not you, you are not consciousness, you are not –

"It's gone down another passageway," said Athene, snapping Opal back into her body. Athene spoke at normal volume because nothing could be heard from outside the suit, but Opal still felt the instinctive urge to shush her, to whisper.

A ping signalled the arrival of the elevator, followed by its doors sliding open.

And then everything was quiet. No roars. No thumping sounds or vibrations. Maybe the Humungr was gone. Yeah, maybe.

And maybe it simply watched and waited with alien patience.

The green particles were settling. Cover was fading.

"Last time I was on one of these craft, something on the bridge wanted me to take its invitation," said Opal, "and I never got the chance. I'm not going to risk losing that contact again."

"Understood. I've unlocked the suit."

"I know. It's making my arms and legs ache." Opal took a deep breath, then exhaled. "Good. The aches are the only thing keeping me awake." She was ready.

Resting

... 20 ...

She dropped to her feet with a heavy thud and dashed into the nexus. Bright light spilled from the open doorway of the elevator capsule, illuminating the dancing green particles. She didn't stop, kept running towards that haven-like glow. Heavy thumping sounds boomed towards her, as if the Humungr was striking the walls in its passage, and it was closer than she'd expected. She grabbed the left doorframe of the capsule to swing herself around, hoping the controls would be on that side.

They were; an illuminated panel with a display above it. She thumped on the top button, jabbing it multiple times hard enough to break it, and the doors slid closed, but too slowly – through the shrinking gap she saw the spiny misshapen torso of the charging creature. She expected it to ram the doors, to dent them, but instead a burst of annelid-like tentacles erupted into that narrow gap and spread to each side, stretching across the door panel surfaces like elongated fingers, and halting the door's closure. Bunched ripples ran through the glistening wormy limbs and the doors began to part again.

Opal activated her wrist blades and spun, cutting down with both blades in one precise movement whilst avoiding stepping in front of that widening gap. Sparks flew from the scraping surfaces; most of the squirming appendages fell to the floor and the doors slid smoothly closed. A roar was followed by a series of crashes against the door but they faded as the capsule rose quickly. She stepped away from the wriggling tubes that gradually slowed their twisting spasms. The blurry display by the doors showed she'd already risen a few floors. She was breathing hard.

"You did it," said Athene.

Opal nodded. She retracted the blades and arm gun, but created a double-blink-controlled quick activation to the left of her HUD.

"This going to take me to the top level?" she asked.

"I think so. My external positioning scans show that the shaft curves, taking you up the neck of the ship to the afterdeck control sections, near to where the bridge lies. As with most ship designs, there's no easy or quick route, so that pirates and boarders can't get control of it too quickly. But you're nearly there. So close. You'll do it. I know you will."

"Thanks." It was almost funny. Opal knew her terse manner might look like toughness or professionalism to the casual observer. In reality it was because she hurt so much, especially where she'd been shot, that she couldn't face speaking.

With Athene monitoring almost every aspect of Opal's well-being, it was probably clear to both of them. Athene's silence on the matter was another sign of their friendship.

"I mean it," Opal added. "Don't ever think I take you for granted."

"I don't."

The elevator display included a side view of the ship layout and her current floor, though the numbers were garbled and unreadable. It mostly matched the rough scans Athene displayed in the corner of the HUD. And then the flashing dot reached the furthermost point of the line.

Opal adopted a combat pose as the elevator rapidly decelerated. Her body rose slightly when it halted. She was ready for whatever was revealed. Hopefully the clean white walls and spacious corridors of a command area; somewhere suitable for officers and bridge crew.

The doors slid open.

Nope.

It was a grey corridor. A wide floor gave way to walls that angled out and in, almost a perfect pentagon in cross-section. The surfaces were industrial-rough, textured with heavy bolts and rust-like stains spreading below them or where panels joined. The doors spaced along the passageway were heavy rectangular shapes that cut into the tidy pentagonal cross-sections. They were able to retract into the wall but were all currently closed. Recessed lights in the narrow ceiling cast elliptical pools of orange light down the angled walls, emphasising the reddish stains that implied great age and decay, or violent accident.

"The first area with functional lighting," said Opal. "Dial down the silverlight, but bring it back if ever we drop into darkness."

"I will. It seems like there is power as we get near the bridge."

Before leaving the elevator, Opal watched and waited. It wasn't a long corridor. There weren't many hiding places, unless something very thin squatted in the shadows of the occasional support struts. But the place felt like it was waiting. Or something *in it* was waiting.

Opal stepped over the decaying worms that had been sliced off the Humungr. As soon as she was out of the elevator she crouched and examined the greenish dust that had settled on the floor. Other particles floated in the air; movement released more of them from the ground as currents in the atmosphere shifted. But the transport nexus she'd just escaped from had given her an idea.

She got down on her hands and knees and lowered her head to the floor, looking along it. She still couldn't see anything. That was probably good.

"What are you looking for?" asked Athene. "Footprints?"

"Yes. Well, any signs of passage. This is a new area. I just want to know how much company I'm likely to find here."

"Let me pattern match and try different wavelengths." A few seconds later the view was overlaid with various barely-perceptible shapes in the settled dust. Some were removed again as noise-related errors, but enough remained to hint at footprints. They were positioned to imply human-like proportions and ambulation, though the closeness of each disturbance suggested cautious movement.

"Could be Xandrie," said Opal.

"My thoughts, too. If I see any other indications of recent passage I will highlight them. I have additional information on her from VigMAX, but even he does not know much about her origins. Her first appearance in his records is when she was held in a mysterious Genitor base called Paratory Droxious for almost a year, reason unknown. Regardless of what she was when she went in: when she came out, she was the UFS assassin we know."

Opal explored the room, ostensibly checking for danger, but really she just didn't want to move on from this potentially safe place yet. "Perhaps she was sent there for punishment, or brainwashing?" she asked.

"It seems likely. I do not know where Paratory Droxious is, which suggests an even greater level of secrecy than is normal for the Genitor cult, but I suspect it is connected to breaking people. Or reforming them, as the UFS would term it."

After a few moments Opal stopped walking and said, "I'd rather die than get captured by them, you know that, right? You'd see to me, if there was no other way?"

"I do not think I could extinguish you, for any reason."

"I would want you to. You'd be saving me from worse."

"Let's hope it never comes to that."

Opal dropped that line of discussion. For the present. She looked behind some of the support struts that lined the walls. Just shadows. "Does Xandrie know VigMAX is on our side now?"

"Unknown. VigMAX sent messages asking her to return to the ship. Obviously he could then contain her so she wouldn't interfere with your mission. He's had no replies, but that doesn't mean she hasn't heard his message. Apparently she goes signal-silent when she's hunting, and only contacts him if there's a tactical need – otherwise they act independently. Different protocols. But we can't rule out the possibility that she has been given a covert backchannel means of monitoring VigMAX."

"If so, she'll know he can't be trusted any more."

"Correct."

Athene superimposed translucent question marks on each of the doors, indicating lack of knowledge as to which might lead the correct way. Opal hadn't found any clues to help in her decision. No scratches on the metal. No splashes of blood (beyond the disconcerting rust stains). She stood in front of the first door on the left.

"So she'll want to escape?"

Athene paused before replying. Presumably she'd asked him directly. "VigMAX thinks she'll change her priorities. The new ones will be attempting to neutralise us, with her own preservation disregarded. Along the way she will gather information that might help the UFS. I suspect that's why she took the pack you had strapped on. She was probably watching and wondered what was in it, assumed it could be useful information."

"And once you were temporarily out of action she picked her moment to attack."

"Correct. I now believe the small device she attached was a Null-C signal, maybe with a black box download, so the UFS will locate it later. Multiple things achieved from one action: information and communication to her allies, and hopefully hindering your plans too. Maybe critically. And demoralising you along the way. It's what I'd do."

Opal nodded. She squatted down and gripped the bottom of the door to manually lift it ... then let her fingers slip off as she stood again. "Wait. We got power, right?"

"Apparently."

"No need for me to do it the hard way then. That's such a damn relief." Opal thumped the button to the side of the door. It shuddered within the frame and rose slowly, and Opal tried to step back to get a better view of whatever was revealed beyond but her legs wouldn't move and she almost fell, as a rippling sickly yellowness expanded from the other side, translucent creamy tar that exerted a pull, now with enough force to start sliding her towards that dirty jaundiced light even though the door had only risen to the height of her knees. The sucking void exuded a bizarre coldness, like ice spikes melting within her bones, rising with the door.

She slammed the button again, and after a second the door stopped rising and began to lower. She was already colder than she felt out in space despite the suit's temperature altering immediately to protect her ... that pus-coloured void was as impossible as she'd come to expect here. When the door finally juddered to a halt she was able to step back, stamping her legs to get feeling back into them.

"It's like I was paralysed, stung or something," she said.

"I was unable to control the parts of the suit near to whatever was beyond the door," replied Athene.

"It looked like there was *nothing* there. Nothing at all, apart from a colour." Opal shuddered.

"I wish I could analyse it, see if it was a localised physical event or some strange matter."

"Please, don't wish for that. I never want to come into contact with it again."

Opal eyed the door warily from a few paces away. It did not move, or groan, or bend, or seep muddy mustard light from the frame. It was exactly as it had been when she stepped out of the elevator. There was a second door on that side of the corridor. She turned away from it.

"Let's hope I have more luck with the doors facing the other way," she said. She was also careful to stand to the side this time. She took a deep breath and pressed the button.

SIGNALLING

... 19 ...

No terrible yellowness this time. No spirit-freezing cold. Just a long, narrow room. Along one side were clear pipes through which pumped a variety of different-textured liquids and pastes, all of which made Opal feel nauseous just looking at them. Gooey pinks with lumps of gristly tissue; swirling reds that were almost opaque but included darker lumps streaking down the tube; yellowish liquids that seemed to have coalescing clumps of hair in the mix. There were heavy-duty taps on the pipes, and some of them had dripped to form sticky pools on which grew a collection of moulds. Opal was glad her body wasn't in direct contact with anything on the ship. Nearby were wheeled ceramic carts that had a mechanism for tipping out their contents. They were stained with a crust of residues.

Thick rubbery overalls with attached boots and gloves hung on a rack to the other side of the room. The flat lamps mounted on the walls cast more of the elongated ellipses of sickly orange light. Only one other door led onwards, opposite her entrance.

Nothing stirred apart from pulsing fluids in the pipes. Opal could hear their gloopy movements.

She entered warily, glancing into the wheeled carts. Then she squatted and looked under the dangling suits to make sure nothing stood behind them. She did not investigate the disgusting matter being pumped around in the pipework. Only some of it was visible, the rest ran behind panels and off through the rest of the ship. Perhaps it was wastes, or processed matter, but it also gave the impression of being a glimpse of the ship's veins and arteries. It was more like being inside a living thing than ever before.

When she was halfway across the room, the door slid down behind her. And immediately a warning light flashed on her HUD.

"What is it?" asked Opal, opening the arm cannon and turning to look in each direction from a crouched position.

"A communications error." It was the suit AI's slightly husky voice. "As soon as the door closed your signal path to Athene was broken. I had to take over. Hello again."

"Are we being blocked? Portable signal scrambler?"

"It may not be anything so ominous. While the door was open I noticed that it – and the walls to either side – were thicker than even blast door specifications require. Depending on the materials used, it could be enough to block out signals. It may be that this section of the ship requires a stronger structure, and the dampening of communications is just a side effect of that. You could try another route?"

"I'm not convinced any of the other doorways would be better options ... and I feel something. Like a pull to go in this direction. I think this is the right way."

"Hopefully this section will not last long."

She crossed the room and readied herself before opening the next door.

Luckily there was no cold. No yellow void. But in its place was noise – disconcerting grunting, whimpering, screeching and crying, like a mass of beings in agony and fear. As the door rose further the volume increased and the environmental indicators in her HUD – normally fairly constant throughout the Lost Ship – changed rapidly. Temperature from the room beyond was eleven degrees higher than background; humidity also far higher, at seventy-six per cent; atmospheric composition included ammonia, hydrogen sulphide, and methane compounds in an acidic concentration that would blister exposed skin.

Opal's heart raced at the distressing sounds which seemed to echo up from below. All her body interpreted it as danger, warnings, suffering. The door clunked into the fully open position and she looked around the thick frame to see what awaited her.

PROCESSING

... 18 ...

Another walkway, strung to the ceiling by steel cables and running high across a massive metallic chamber. On the other side was an open doorway. A straight way to the exit. All she had to do was walk forward and not look down, not pay attention to the terrible sounds coming from below, not peer over the narrow walkway's edge at whatever was down there.

She did glance, of course, careful not to overbalance. She was sure there should be safety railings of some sort, to prevent one slip leading to death, but this place was always on the edge of danger, maybe it was just an overt acknowledgement of that fact. She gripped one of the taut vertical cables instead as she stared, the automatic range finder that tracked her gaze showing it to be a drop of twenty-eight metres.

It was one of the Gigatoir's immense animal pens. And it wasn't empty like the rest of the ship. A multitude of chattle squirmed at the bottom of the funnel-shaped room, so many that some were on top of others, and the feeding troughs at the edges were hardly visible as the creatures all fought upwards for space and to avoid being crushed beneath the mass of bodies. And they *were* massive, larger than any Opal had ever seen, larger than even low gravity normally allowed. Their heads had a different shape to normal chattle, mouths larger, extending from stubby necks that rippled with fat overlaying the muscle. Those struggling below the others, crushed and apparently suffocating, obviously resorted to biting. There were scars and red stains on lips and flanks, jaws somehow extending as they chomped into their companions in panic and madness that had no escape.

"How are they even alive?" asked Opal, horrified. "Is someone still feeding them? Breeding more?"

"They may look similar to normal chattle, but markers indicate these are as alien as everything else we encounter. They would not be able to breathe at all if they were human-bred resources."

The reinforced nature of the room made sense now. No creatures could escape, whether through the thick metal walls or up them; and neither could sounds or odours escape, except via the spiked air vents up on the ceiling.

"I guess it smells pretty bad," said Opal.

"Would you like me to synthesise an equivalent in your suit? I could match the external olfactory triggers and extreme humidity."

"No." Opal could well imagine the stink, the way it would make her retch. The screams from below tore memories to the surface, sickening thoughts of the abattoir she'd been sent to, the moist heat from sweating bodies and high-pressure water jets, the palpable fear chemicals in the air, the visceral cries of fear and pain that ripped at your guts like a buzz saw.

"This, here ... on normal ships, on planets ... it turns my stomach." Even as Opal spoke she could hear the terrible lowing in the background.

The suit's tone was soft when it said, "I know how upset you are. Our shared feelings mean I also find both the theory and reality of de-individualised mechanisation to be distressing. I should attempt to distract you, to alleviate distress, and yet –"

"Some things are bad enough that you're meant to feel them." Which was why Opal didn't ask the suit to filter out the sounds of suffering from below, which echoed up and reverberated, amplified all around her, until it felt like it was screaming in her head too. "Sometimes we have to bear witness."

"Noted."

Opal took deep breaths and looked ahead. The platform was narrow and swayed as she moved, even more as she approached the middle, but not enough to throw her if she kept her cool. She held her hands out to her sides as she walked.

Another platform hung nearby, from a frame attached to the ceiling. A glance at the mechanism suggested it could be moved around, and also lowered and raised from a control panel in its centre. At the edges of the mobile platform dangled a number of limp devices on segmented cables: drills, saws, and long-fingered grabbers. Also pipes that dripped liquids, maybe used for refilling the feeding troughs below. Presumably a crew could then work in safety above the chattle, performing perfunctory maintenance, selecting and killing targets, then lifting them and manoeuvring them to the large chutes halfway up the walls, big enough for dropping whole chattle into. Opal guessed that the chutes led to the rendering floors where the beast would be processed into constituent parts. The mobile platform was parked out of reach of the walkway.

"There's a terrible efficiency to all this," said Opal, just to hear a voice over the screaming din from below.

"Actually, although I don't like being contradictory, you are completely wrong," replied the suit. "Systems like this are inherently inefficient."

"But it's all mechanised for maximum production. The kind of thing a machine might design. No offence."

"None taken. These have a flowline that can design, breed, slaughter, process, store, and ship out end product, with any remaining waste ground up and fed to the next generation of modified creatures in forced anthropophage. In principle it is fairly organised – not that I can't see more competent ways of processing organic matter."

Opal shuddered at the thought of what an AI could do if it wasn't on her side.

"The inefficiency is a function of biology, not process," the suit continued. "No biological beings are very efficient, and much of their consumed nutrition is wasted on emissions, excretion, growth of inedible parts. Even at their most efficient it takes around five units of input protein to produce one unit of animal protein: which means these places are actually *reverse* protein factories, with four units lost for every unit of output. To try and minimise costs, the system requires brutal intensification. It makes no sense to me that humans feed edible proteins to other creatures at a functional loss."

"My species has a hard time breaking habits."

"Organic cultures must have a lot of weight and momentum when even logic cannot redirect them. No offence."

"None taken. Looking at this place, it makes me glad that people like me only get repro foods."

"Exactly. I am glad we have this common feeling. It creates a closeness between us which I never expected to experience."

As Opal focussed on the walls rather than what moved below, she had one of those strange twists of perception, like when psych teams test you with ambiguous words and images to see what your primary interpretation is, but once they point out the alternative, it pings into focus, akin to the old-fashioned versions that served as retro adornments to clothing during one trend when Opal was growing up. Face profiles or candlesticks? Old man's face or a mermaid? For a while those motifs were everywhere, always in two colours, frivolous things reduced to being *this* or *that*.

And now as Opal looked at the riveted metal panels that formed the surfaces of the walls and ceiling she spotted the rust-like liquids that leaked down from the rivets in the high humidity, and in a second they switched to looking more like weeping scabs, rivulets of red as if beyond the huge panels it was not a starship but flesh, the metal plates of the room riveted to masses of it as if to stem a chaotic tide of reproducing cells, or as punishments for a living thing that refused to conform to the shape demanded of it. And the moaning from below could have been coming from the walls themselves, the ship, and pains from the present crossed with pains from the past and pains from the future. So much came down to suffering. So much came down to restrictions. It wasn't clear if there'd ever be a future free from them.

She walked on anyway. And the door shuddered closed behind her.

Focus ahead. Not up. Not left, or right, or back. Certainly not down. No deviation from your course allowed or desired. Handy rules for success, and for keeping yourself from vomiting in places like this.

And that's why Opal saw the assassin immediately as Xandrie entered through the open doorway ahead, where she'd obviously been hiding just out of sight in the darkness of the next room. Without taking her eyes off Opal she reached up and thumped a button. The door lowered with a grinding rumble.

Opal activated the arm gun but as she raised it, Xandrie turned and faced the door, withdrawing something from her utility belt.

Opal kept the gun aimed at Xandrie's back. She squeezed her fist, fingers curling inwards to create action, destruction, annihilation. Such small movements with such large consequences. As simple as pressing a button that starts a war. As simple as signing a decree that forces a new future on children. So easy.

"I advise you to shoot," said the suit AI.

Opal recognised the item in Xandrie's hand. It was Opal's portable flash welder. Xandrie was using it to apply glowing spots to the door frame, preventing it from being opened again in a hurry.

"It is obvious why the assassin chose this place for a confrontation. As well as the dangerous environment and the need for you to face her rather than run, she has no doubt realised that hi-res signals are blocked here. You won't have the benefit of my mother Athene, only myself, a poor replacement. I do not have the power to predict and flow with your actions one-to-one, so in battle I may be as much of a hindrance to instinctive reactions as a help. It equalises things now that VigMAX is no longer on her side and she is alone."

Xandrie applied the last welding spots, yet Opal's fingers were still frozen as she stared at that vulnerable back.

Opal should shoot her now. Kill her while she could. Ignore the implicit trust, and equally implicit challenge, of Xandrie's vulnerability. It was common sense to break the rules of honour, just as Opal broke other rules.

And yet ... breaking rules had led to punishments, so often. Which brought to mind the year-long mystery of Xandrie's residence in the Genitor base Paratory Droxious. What had she done? What had been done to her? And was there anything left of the person she'd been?

"The assassin would not show you mercy," said the suit. "Please fire now, or allow me to take over and execute affirmative actions."

"Don't interfere," said Opal. "That's an order. I know Athene can ignore me, but I don't think you can."

No reply.

Xandrie put the flash welder on the floor, then stepped away from it and faced Opal. Xandrie's visor was opaque, features hidden. The prize was escape, the implication that only one of them could take it.

"You have lost your advantage," grumbled the suit. "It is just as Athene warned me: your desire to do things the hard way is infuriating."

"I don't choose to do it the hard way. Just to do it my way. No-one else's. That's always hard when the whole damn universe tries to bend you into something else. Loud speaker." Opal took a breath, then said, "Xandrie, we don't have to fight." Her voice had to be amplified to be heard over the cacophony of frenzied wailing from the pit below. "I don't want to kill you."

Xandrie did not move or show any signs of having heard Opal for the first few seconds. Then she started sprinting towards Opal to close the gap, jagged wrist blades extending from the slots that housed them.

Why did no-one *ever* back down when Opal told them to? If only people would take her more seriously there wouldn't be so much pain. Just once, couldn't someone take the easy road? That was all she asked.

Just one freaking time.

Fighting

... 17 ...

Opal aimed at Xandrie and fired, an easy target. Except nothing about fighting Xandrie was easy. Only a few flechettes pinged off her armour before the glowing shield blossomed from her left arm, deflecting most of the darts which would have otherwise struck her hunched-over but rapidly-closing body.

One of the platform support cables nearby snapped with a high-tension twang, tilting the platform at an angle and throwing her aim off as she tried to keep her balance on the swinging walkway. Xandrie had deflected the fire at a line of cables near Opal, shredding them – oh so clever, and Opal had fallen for her opening move.

Any more cables snapping could spill both of them into the pit below. Plus Xandrie was almost upon her and close enough to glue up this gun with a spray of the purple explosive goo as well (the other was still out of action) so Opal retracted the barrels to keep them safe and extended her nanoblades. Ranged weapons in these conditions were clumsy and imprecise anyway. She needed to be up close.

Opal adopted a side-on stance, good for minimising target areas and holding one nanoblade back for advancing lunges and retreating blocks. She tried to keep Xandrie at a distance with fencing moves but her strikes were met with sparks as they were deflected by Xandrie's shield or deftly parried by her shorter wrist blades.

Opal was forced to retreat to keep appropriate distance for her longer weapons, since if she got too close lengthier blades became a handicap, and Xandrie's wicked wrist knives would make mincemeat of Opal's guts once they were inside her guard.

But Xandrie was ferocious and fast, able to dodge and weave as well as deflect, and she was unrelenting in her attack. Sparks flew from Opal's armour as the jagged blades scored it again and again, forcing her back metre by metre, her breathing hard as she struggled with the exertion and pain. It was all she could do to stay on her feet, trying to remain steady, the stability that acted as a grounding for everything else.

Sometimes you have to use what you've got.

Especially when what you've got is bigger.

Opal threw her greater body and armour weight forward, slamming her shoulder into the centre of the assassin's chest so that Xandrie staggered to the edge of the platform. She had to grab one of the steel support cables to prevent herself from falling. Although the walkway was made up of metal plates bolted together at the edges, so much motion twisted them that some of the interconnecting bolts had already snapped, making things even more unstable. Opal grabbed a cable too. There would only be a second's respite, and the bulk smash trick was unlikely to work again.

And yet, the tactics required were instinctively simple. In these kinds of battles, where you don't have enough power to go *through* defences, then you have to go *around* them to win. Didn't matter if it was a shield, a suit of armour, or a tank.

Xandrie lunged forward, guarding her centre. Opal had already braced her foot against the taut steel cable behind her, kicking off in a high leap that her opponent obviously didn't expect, so that Opal's extended blades slammed down from above the shield. One of them punctured through armour plating and into flesh beneath, releasing a hiss of escaping air as they crashed together and struggled and finally broke apart, both clumsily adopting defensive postures, eyeing each other warily.

And this time Xandrie didn't rush forward again. Her posture was off. The injury was telling on her, would slow her down in the way that Opal's did. And the blade cuts weren't the only wounds showing on the assassin. Some of the exterior armour plates were partly ablated, with long searing burns that were likely from when Athene fired at her. The repair crusts implied the burns had got all the way through the armour and caused injuries to the woman within. Xandrie must be in as much of a world of hurt as Opal was. And did the assassin just sway wearily? Or was it caused by the rocking of the platform? Shit, things were even beginning to swim in Opal's vision.

"Your internal injuries are rupturing," said the suit. "I need to apply stimulants and analgesics, otherwise you won't be standing in a few moments."

"Do the minimum. I can't risk losing my edge."

Warmth flooded her body and the pains numbed as a chemical cocktail infused her bloodstream. Keep her alive now, crash and suffer later.

The stand-off was short-lived as the assassin pushed forward, swinging clumsily. It was easy to block the inept attack. Xandrie was ready to collapse, and this wouldn't go on much longer. Then Xandrie stumbled on one of the platforms where a support cable had snapped, and Opal didn't pause to think, just took advantage of that momentary weakness to lunge forward with one of her blades in a finishing move that would puncture the stealth suit's armour.

At which point she realised she'd fallen for one of the oldest tricks in the book, as Xandrie caught the nanoblade between the dual prongs of her own wrist blades which could act as sword-breakers, suddenly in perfect balance after her faked stumble.

Trickery. So much in combat came down to minds and psychology, not muscle.

Before Opal could pull back, Xandrie was turning her, controlling her by the locked sword, kicking at Opal's midriff again and again while she couldn't retreat. Damage indicators appeared, warning of small punctures – some kind of hidden blade must have extended from Xandrie's boots and it perforated Opal's armour in a dozen places as she scrambled to stay upright, realised she was being manoeuvred to the edge of a platform, the trapped nanoblade now a liability. She tried to push back but Xandrie was ready for it, lowering her body and hips below Opal's centre of gravity and turning it into a throw that sent Opal crashing heavily to the deck on her back, shaking the walkway so that even more interconnecting bolts snapped. Opal rolled to get some distance but her defence was a mess; by the time she stood awkwardly, Xandrie's reverse roundhouse connected with Opal's chest with staggering force. Opal's stumbling momentum twisted her feet, she reached the edge of the lop-sided dangling walkway and her upper body tottered over it, only air and the squirming, braying mass of alien creatures below.

One of the platform's severed steel ropes dangled from the ceiling nearby. Opal threw herself forward, grabbed on to the cable's edge and swung out over the abyss, grasping with tight-knuckled force on which her life depended, her peripheral vision showing the huge drop below, the screaming creatures down there. Her body spun and she slipped a few centimetres as she swung out, centrifugal forces pulling at her; one hand came free of the steel support line, the other was right on the edge. She just gritted her teeth as she reached the apex of her swinging arc, she *wouldn't* let go; and the suit helped her, strengthening her one-handed grip as she followed the semicircular path from which there could be no deviation apart from the involuntary drop of death, and damned if she'd let that happen.

She was now flying back towards a different area of the platform, the even more precarious middle bits with fewer cables after Xandrie had deflected flechettes through them. Opal landed with a hard clang, skidding to a halt just short of falling off the other side. The platform swung in a worrying fashion, held up by only a few cables, many of the bolts that had connected it to adjacent walkways now torn loose from the twisting motions.

Opal took laboured breaths in this moment of respite as Xandrie ran towards her, rattling the walkway even further.

They'd reversed positions. Now if Opal retreated she would be heading towards the sealed doorway Xandrie had entered from, and the welding gun. It was the direction Opal wanted to go in, but she didn't have enough headway to unmelt the door before being killed.

Xandrie was back on the offensive. Opal did her best to block but at least one heavy strike reached her flesh. Even though the power suit did its best to repair the damage and seal up again, it was being drained by each breach, in the same way Opal's body was drained by each wound, blood and energy sapped as injuries were cauterised inside the suit's inner layers. The blades on Xandrie's wrists must be at least as sharp and charged as Opal's to slice armour so easily. It would be death by a thousand cuts if they carried on this way. She already felt like collapsing, and it was only her stubbornness that kept her upright.

"Maximise deflection shields," Opal told the suit. "Shut down anything else: scanners, healing, internal monitoring, whatever – I need to stop her being able to hit me!"

The HUD dimmed, some peripheral screens winked out, and Opal noticed the shift immediately. The ground felt slippy beneath her feet as the suit pushed to deflect anything metallic away. But it worked. Xandrie's blows stopped puncturing, deflected just enough to become inconsequential surface scratches. She'd have to put a lot more effort in to strikes if she wanted to connect as easily as before, and that might leave her vulnerable. She'd also have a job repeating the trick of catching a nanoblade:

now, if she tried to trap Opal's weapons, they would feel like they were coated with grease.

But she'd soon realise what was happening. Opal had to act quickly. Xandrie's shield was too good at blocking strikes. But Opal remembered her first escape from Xandrie, sliding down a chute on full field repulsion. She remembered that you need to go around defences when you can't go through. And she sure as hell remembered trickery. She had her own experiences of dirty tricks learnt in rough places.

Opal slashed wide, missing Xandrie on purpose but making her flinch. Instead of following it up with another attack Opal jumped back, still cutting the air with the nanoblades to preserve the gap. She had to get a few paces away, had to make sure she had one of the few sturdy cables in the right place for a jump. She moved to the edge of the platform and it worked: the walkway tilted precariously, throwing Xandrie to the side. Opal sprinted back towards her, head turned to the steel cable that would provide a launching point to leap up high, to strike Xandrie from above. It had worked earlier, was obviously worth trying again. Opal's foot touched the cable and she bent her legs. Xandrie raised her shield and wrist blades in preparation.

But Opal didn't leap. Instead she slid to her knees in a smooth movement, skidding under Xandrie's guard, the suit's repulsion turning the floor to ice so that when Opal stabbed up, her long blade punctured through the armour with grinding sparks, straight into Xandrie's leg. The blade came out, red with fresh blood. Maybe she'd hit the femoral artery.

Despite her exhaustion, Opal clambered to her feet, expecting a weakened retaliation. But Xandrie didn't strike at Opal's body.

Instead, she stumbled backwards, unable to put weight on the wounded leg, and swiped at one of the supporting cables during her retreat, then another, severing them with whiplash cracks. And suddenly half of the walkway wasn't supported any more. The floor fell away.

FEINTING

... 16 ...

It was the cables along one of the walkway's long sides that had snapped, causing it to fall down like the flap over an air vent once the air stops pumping, pivoting on the remaining cables which acted like a hinge. Opal dived for the upper edge but was too late and she missed, was now sliding down.

"Full magnetism!" she yelled, and the suit stopped sliding, ground to a halt against the swinging vertical metallic surface. Nothing below her but a death drop. No way to scramble up the vertical plate to a handhold. As it swung crazily about she slid down another few centimetres. Already near the bottom of the plate. She couldn't stay here forever. All her suit's resources were being used to power the electromagnetic systems barely holding her against the side of a sheet of metal like an insect squashed to a swatter.

Opal assumed Xandrie had fallen too, that it was a last-ditch kill attempt that would sacrifice both of them. But then she saw the assassin up above. She'd stepped over the broken rivets to an adjacent walkway panel as she cut the last cable.

Opal was a static target with nowhere to go.

Unless ... the mobile platform with the dangling tools of butchery and manipulation was on this side of the panel. It had been out of range even when Opal was on the walkway. If only she still had a grapple gun, she could have reached it easily.

She should have brought two.

Back and forth in slowing arcs she swung, sliding, trying not to look down at what awaited her below, crying and mewling. So she looked up again.

Xandrie was squirting a jet of fluorescent purple goo from a spray canister – this time it splatted against the top of the platform Opal stuck to. Near the cable points. She was going to blow the whole thing.

"I need to get off here in the next few seconds," Opal told the suit in a hurry. "Is there any way you can take over and somehow jump me to that mobile platform?"

"It's nearly eleven metres away. If we had a running start then it would be well within parameters, as you know from earlier." The suit spoke as quickly as Opal. "But from a static position ... Mmm. What if I timed it with the next swing of the platform? We'd still fall short. Full suit repulsion and a leap, turn to full magnetic attraction near it? No. What if I transferred all power to the suit's muscle fibres? ... No, still not possible!"

Xandrie clicked her fingers and some kind of flame hovered above her palm.

"I'm going to die anyway," said Opal. "I've run out of options. I trust you."

"Taking full control now."

The display shut off. No internal lights, only a hi-tech prison for her body. She just had to relax, to know that she couldn't affect the outcome, have faith that she was in safe hands.

Damn, how she hated leaving things up to someone else.

The broken walkway swung back towards the mobile platform. This would be it. Opal couldn't even move the helmet to look in another direction, all control taken from her. At the edge of her vision up above, she could see an ethereal burning spark, floating through the air in surreal slow motion, a small ignition for a big explosion, but forget that, stay calm, take deep breaths. The complexity of what was about to happen was beyond human minds, could only be controlled to split-second precision and perfect application of timed force by something more than human.

The nanoblades retracted with a smooth snick. Suddenly she was disconnected from the metal wall to her side by the suit kicking away, using all the power and repulsion it could for a perfectly-angled launch, probably using variable forces so that the legs were the last bits to switch from attraction to repulsion, enabling them to grip against something for the kick-off launch through the air, then repulsive force adding to their strength once committed.

And Opal was weightless, disconnected, tightly streamlined like a bullet to help cross the distance. She faced down, had no say in the matter, looked onto the squirming suffering below, knew that artificial gravity wanted her to go that way, make a captive of her too.

Sharp hissing sounds, just audible, seemed to erupt from the lower side of Opal's body, but she didn't have time to ponder it before the goo detonated in a flash of light and a roar of force and heat and expanding pressure. Deadly fragments of metal flew past her, some pinging from the suit, and somehow secondary blasts from below.

The mobile platform was just ahead, like a squarish octopod with all those industrial tools dangling on thick segmented cables. She was too low.

But it would be close.

And then her arms reached out, and the attractive force must have kicked in on overdrive because she made a connection with one of the dangling grabbers, slammed into it with enough force to knock the air out of her lungs, and the suit gripped on as she was clanged around; then it scrambled up in quick inhuman-yet-efficient motions that took her onto the stable surface of the platform.

The HUD bloomed into life. She could move again. She was alive.

"Thank you," she said. "Thank you!"

"I'm happy it worked," said the suit, with tones that replicated those spoken from a smiling face. "Athene will be proud of me. I expelled most of your air from manoeuvring jets for another metre's reach, and used your last grenades in directed charge airbursts below, which only caused me minor damage. Wonderfully, even the explosive force behind us actually helped."

The suit had nothing left in the reserves: air, jets, grenades, repair gels. But Opal was still alive.

"I'm so proud of you," she said, between breaths that tasted sweet despite exhaustion. Like the suit, Opal's reserves were depleted too. Even raising her head was an effort, but she did it. Just in time to see Xandrie climbing up one of the support cables towards the ceiling.

She never gave up. They could've been sisters.

Opal stood with a groan and examined the platform's control systems. Maybe she could use some of the tools which hung below, turn them into weapons. She inserted her gauntlets into the hand manipulators but they were lifeless. No lights on the control panel. She identified a curved rectangular section with a slightly different sheen to it from the surrounding panel. She punched it, denting the middle, then got the suit's fingertips under a lifted corner and tore the panel off. A mess of electronics inside. The cabled circuits were like a mass of limp noodles.

"Can you hack this? Gain use of the implements on the platform, or move us further from Xandrie?"

"Maybe – hold your hand towards it."

Xandrie was now near the ceiling and moving hand over hand along one of the pieces of framework that the mobile platform could transit along.

Opal aimed the gummed-gun arm at the electronics. A squirt of slender wires flew from her fingertips and attached to the control cables, puncturing them and feeling around for other targets like some kind of super-thin annelid parasites. With her other arm Opal extended the gun barrels, ready to shoot Xandrie while she couldn't use her shield to deflect, couldn't dodge.

Too late. Xandrie swung her body and let go, flying down from her high vantage point, a perfect angle, speeding like a battering ram. Opal spun away, forced to disconnect the hacking threads as Xandrie slammed with crushing force where Opal had stood just a second before, wrist blade and shield already active. The platform was too small for manoeuvre. Short weapons would win the day.

"Extend the nanoblades to only half their length," said Opal, parrying the first strike with her forearm. The blades slid out partly, more like daggers – faster, better for close-range, still deadly.

This had to be the end.

She laid into Xandrie, scored a few hits that ripped into her armour like stiletto daggers; in turn she took strikes from the assassin's jagged blades, which punched into skin but not as deeply as Opal's narrow points. She wanted to stop, to curl up and cry, but that was the same as giving in, and that was the same as dying. She wouldn't. She couldn't.

Stay on your feet. Strike. Block. Fight.

But it was no good. Xandrie seemed tireless. A foot lashed out, knocking Opal back, but there wasn't enough room to recover her balance and her feet got tangled. She smacked into the platform's low barrier – too low for someone as tall as Opal in a powersuit, so it connected below her hips and she flipped backwards over it, a half somersault before she got her hands on the platform, gripped on as her body fell and swung underneath her.

But she didn't fall. She was hanging on by fingernails, but she didn't fall.

Xandrie approached to deliver the killing blow to Opal's vulnerable head. She'd punch through the faceplate with those jagged wrist blades. It would all be over.

One of Opal's hands slipped off. She looked even more vulnerable, the battle's end a foregone conclusion. Opal used her core strength to lift her legs, despite the pain in her stomach from the injuries, the stabs, the encysted bullet still lodged there.

"Magnetise the legs only, attach them if you can," she told the suit. Her legs clamped against the underside of the platform. How strong was the contact? No time to find out. She let her gripping hand slip a bit. Xandrie would need to crouch to stab her face, or to pry her fingers loose.

Or she might just kick Opal's hand away and not even do her the honour of looking her in the eye.

Oh well, too late to take that into account. And luckily Xandrie *did* come close enough. Last chance. Every trick had been used up. Almost every bit of strength. Just this one thing.

Opal let go with her hand. But instead of dropping to her doom, the contact from her legs held, sticking her to the platform. The suit must be pumping all the energy reserves into supercharging the pull in that area. And now that Opal's hands were free she snatched Xandrie's ankles and yanked with all her might, taking Xandrie by surprise and throwing her onto her back with a crash, then out under the support barrier and off the edge. That was as far as Opal could reach.

Xandrie twisted and grabbed hold at the last moment, but Opal was already scrambling up Xandrie's back and shoulders, onto the platform again, the suit altering its magnetic properties in each part to help her. Opal didn't hesitate, rolled onto her back and kicked at Xandrie's opaque faceplate as it came up, kicked and kicked and knocked her back so she was now the one holding on by only one hand while dangling over a pit of screaming monstrosities.

Opal crawled to the edge and looked down. She could stab into that visor if she wanted. Stab and stab at that hidden face. Finish off this threat forever.

"It's over, Xandrie," said Opal, switching to loudspeaker. "I've won. Please stop. Give in. It doesn't have to go down this way; doesn't have to follow our training. I'd rather have your help than kill you."

Xandrie swung precariously below. Opal tried not to look past her at the blurred creatures beyond. There was so much horror. Opal needed something to counteract it. Hope.

And suddenly the partly-burnt visor on Xandrie's helmet cleared, revealing her ghost-pale face. There were specks of blood on the skin inside the helmet; bruising around the eyes; the sweat of effort on her cheeks. Strands of blue hair were visible from under the compression layers of the stealth suit. And Xandrie's eyes were the brightest blue, the cold blue light of a reflection nebula, glowing. Eyes that were locked onto Opal's. A connection there. Consideration.

Xandrie's hand slipped a bit more. More sweat breaking out on her face from the effort. She didn't seem able to raise the other arm. Or maybe she'd given up.

"If you tell me you surrender, then you can take my arm," said Opal, holding out a hand. "One chance."

And Xandrie opened her mouth. Just for a second. Not long enough for Opal to take in the detail – the lack of teeth, the missing tongue – only enough to see the dark overlapping *something* within there, cables and circuitry maybe, or perhaps insectile. Had the Lost Ship done that to her? Or was this done earlier, by the UFS?

"Oh," said Opal. But she refused to show repulsion, refused to back away. "But ... maybe there's a way back. VigMAX was freed. You can be too. Whatever they've done to you, maybe it can be undone. We have to believe that. If we bend all our will to it, if we have AIs to help ... I have to believe that we can succeed. Or die trying."

And those blue eyes, lagoons of fresh water that you could fall into, blinked. They looked wet. And Opal knew what would happen at the same time as Xandrie swung her wrist blades, so that Opal flinched her head back and parried the weapon on reflex, knocking Xandrie loose so that she fell, tumbling down without a scream, even though she might be screaming inside. Xandrie smashed into the creatures far below, disappearing beneath the mass and leaving some broken, mewling and roaring louder, thrashing at the injuries and further pain brought on by this thing that fell from above.

But the alien chattle were huge. And those where Xandrie had fallen seemed to extend their bulky mouths and begin to bite down – on each other, and on something below them. There were screams, and blood, from the chattle which tore into each other with the buzz-saw mouths. Anything below them would be trapped beneath their crushing weight, even if it fought back ... and the suit's detectors picked up faint crunching sounds. Even hardened armour would be destroyed by those powerful mouths in the hysterical, squirming mass, so that the blood frothing up around them now was probably not their own.

There was no hope once you fell down there. Opal closed her eyes. She held in the vomit that threatened. She asked the suit to turn off the speakers. Silence.

And in silence they hacked the wobbly platform and moved it towards the unbroken walkway beyond the scene of battle.

In silence Opal picked up the hand burner and unmelted the frame areas enough to open the door, strands of red-hot metal stretching like flesh, dripping like fat. No. She would not think.

The burner was nearly empty. She set it back on the floor. It seemed out of place. Maybe everything she touched was out of place. She limped onwards. These should be the final sections.

EXPLORING

... 15 ...

Through the doorway was a short corridor with angled walls that came up to a point. It was identical to the corridor that had the yellow void behind one door. The corridor ended at blank wall. There were two heavy rectangular doors on either side of the corridor though, and some support struts which blocked part of the view. Recessed lights in the ceiling were enough to see by, in a gloomy fashion, and illuminated the motes drifting in the air.

Opal took a deep breath. She couldn't leave part of her mind elsewhere. She needed to keep it here, in the moment, where new dangers might arise.

The floor was layered in greenish sediment. Things seemed still. Undisturbed. She took a step into the room, then pulled her leg back.

Too still.

"Something's missing," said Opal. "Footprints." She squatted down painfully to get a better look at the flooring before she stepped on it.

"I can detect traces," said the suit. "Someone has passed through here recently, but the dust has already obscured most of their tracks. It's like snowfall."

A display window opened on the HUD, showing an animation of white flakes settling on a path and turning it into an even white field; at the same time the room's view on the HUD was overlaid with small red shapes of footprints to enhance the traces the suit had detected.

"I don't like snow," said Opal, killing the window with a double blink. "These footprints must be showing the direction Xandrie came from." They led to one of the closed doors on the right. "Mystery solved." Opal entered the corridor cautiously, but there were no hiding places big enough for a human. "Any word from Athene yet?" she asked.

"Negative. This area is also radio-secure. I will notify you as soon as signal strength improves."

Okay. Pick a door. Any door.

She felt aversion to the doors on her left. Maybe it was just a frozen echo of what happened last time she took a mystery doorway on that side. Hungry, numbing yellowness. No thanks.

Xandrie had reached the walkways over the chattle pits in one piece, so following her route might be safest. The second door on the right, then.

Opal had her weapons retracted – it made manipulating things with the gauntlets easier – but she was ready to arm herself at the slightest disturbance. She put her back to the wall and pressed the panel by the door. It slid smoothly up into the structure, no grinding sounds this time. Nothing leapt out, so she peered around the edge to see another badly-lit, green dusty corridor. Onwards.

THIRSTING

... 15 ...

No apparent danger. Green flecks worked with the gloomy orange lighting to reduce visibility even further, so that it was hard to make out the room at first. Then it seemed to clear a bit. Doors to the left and right, cutting into the strangely-angled walls.

"Did you notice a sort of shimmer just then, passing over the walls?" asked Opal.

"I am afraid not. Static affected my recording senses, perhaps interference from a faulty energy source nearby."

Fatigue. That would explain it.

Opal's feet dragged through the green sediment which had settled over this corridor's floors, scraping a path and raising puffs of dust.

There was so much pain in her side. She felt like putting her hands there but refrained. It would do no good, a mere symbol. The suit would offer to dull the pain and Opal would refuse. She was all too aware of how easy it was to get trapped in repetitive cycles. Instead she pretended to be thinking hard about which exit to take, surreptitiously resting her body.

After a while a plastic tube extended from the panel inside her helmet and stopped when it was in front of her mouth.

"You are dehydrated," said the suit.

Opal took the straw in her mouth and sucked. Chilled liquid ran over her parched tongue. It was sweet, yet with a tangy aftertaste. No doubt it contained various nutrients and salts, and also sugars for energy. She gulped it down.

"Thanks. Feels like a long road we're on."

"My own energy reserves are lower than I would like," replied the suit, a hint of weariness to its voice. The huskiness now sounded less like a sexy affectation, and more like the hangover of someone who'd been up all night partying. "I need to monitor them more closely, to make sure there isn't some anomalous loss taking place."

"You do that." Opal yawned.

She was wary of one of the left-hand side doorways. Something to do with yellowness? She couldn't remember. Perhaps exhaustion was causing confusion. It didn't matter. It wasn't the way she wanted to go.

There were vague footprints in the dust, leading to the second doorway on the right. The suit highlighted their placement. Xandrie's trail. Opal followed it.

TIRING

... 15 ...

Sadness follows you. Or at least, traces of it. Sometimes you can't even make out the shape of the original source. It gets added to all the other traces and becomes a mass of its own design, unlike anything else. Our own fingerprint, pressing down heavily.

"No signal?" asked Opal.

"Nothing," replied the suit.

Opal couldn't tell which of them sounded the most despondent.

The miserable lighting didn't help. Shadows at the edge of her vision, indistinct shapes in wait behind support struts. Orange and green and grey were the colours of this world, and they all made her feel queasy.

There were four doorways in addition to the one she'd entered by. Two on the left, two on the right, all closed. She felt a strange aversion to the ones on the left. The suit highlighted traces in the dust that could have been footsteps long past. They led to one of the further doorways, on the right.

"You ever get the feeling of having been somewhere before?" asked Opal.

"A past culture had a name for it – *déjà vu*. Perhaps it is caused by a situation where something in the present has similarities to an experience in the past, or even something felt vicariously. The similarity is enough to trigger familiarity, but not enough to trigger memory recall. I do feel such a thing. It nags at my mind."

"Strange that you can feel it too."

"Would you be surprised that Athene can feel such a thing? If not, then you should not be surprised that a condensed version of her personality can also interpret the world in that way."

"I'm sorry, I didn't mean it as an insult. It's all me. I'm just so worn out. All my sharpness has been dulled. I feel like we'll never get anywhere. It's like when my mind gets stuck in circles figuring out a problem. You see those traces in the dust?"

Opal squatted and ran a hand over the surface layers of sediment.

"Yes, they resemble footprints from long ago."

"Like Xandrie came through here, then the dust covered her tracks."

Opal brushed away some more and tilted her head, followed each apparent footstep with her gaze.

"They're pretty close together. Like she was moving slowly."

"Perhaps she was tired too?"

"No, there's something weird going on. I feel it."

"We could follow the footsteps and see where they lead," suggested the suit.

"Yes, they should take us somewhere. But ... hold on, can you get an impression of these footprints. Do any of them have more detail?"

Opal stayed in a crouched position, following the trail.

"That one," said the suit. "It seems clearer. I can make out the grip pattern." An enhanced version of the image was overlaid.

Opal looked at it, then at the sole of one of her boots. She placed her foot down on the footprint, and it fit perfectly.

"Xandrie had a different suit from me. Would the design of the grips match? The size?"

"Unlikely. Stealth suits such as hers are built for auditory and visual signal reduction. Whereas the hardened edges of your boots are designed for electrical conductivity and magnetic contact."

Opal stood. "This weird feeling, this tiredness, as if I've done all this before ... it doesn't make much sense, but these seem to be my own footprints."

"That is a likely conclusion."

Opal slammed open the panel for the nearest door. A pentagonal corridor led on, with two doorways on each side. She did not step through; instead she opened the next door. Another corridor, swirling with green dust. Vague footprints. She skipped the first door on the left, the one that she associated with yellow void, but her third doorway also showed identical pentagonal corridors. All had footprints leading away.

She returned to her entrance, opened it, rushed into the passage she'd originally come from. It looked identical. She tried some of the doorways from there. Corridors, all with the same number of doorways, the same dust, the same cross-section, the same orange lights, the same traces of footprints. It was endless.

"I've been wandering these halls for some time, I think," said Opal.

"I have no record of doing so, but one of my underlying rules implanted by Athene is that when my sense data differs from your reports and feelings, I am to override my records and act on what you see."

"Really? Athene set you up to believe me even when it makes no sense and when it differs from all the evidence in front of you?"

"Yes. She has full faith in you." After a pause the suit added, more quietly: "As do I."

Opal didn't reply. But the feeling it gave her was a shot in the arm, dispelling some of the lethargy that had been building for ... well, who knew how long?

Opal picked one of the corridors she hadn't been down. Tried doors in that too. They led to identical passageways.

And she noticed that as she looked into each room, her footprints always led *away* from the door she opened – even for doors she hadn't passed through.

"This makes no sense," she said. "Things are rearranging themselves to repeat the same scenario, even when it isn't physically possible. I think the ship's playing mind games with me again."

"I agree that something is manipulating local conditions. Do you want to keep running and trying doorways? One of them may lead out. I could inject you with stimulants."

"Screw that, we need to be cleverer. Maybe what we see isn't really there, like the trick the blue crystals tried. So let's test it out. Repeat the blue pulse we copied from them."

The suit charged for a few seconds, minor modifications listed in a fast-scrolling window at the edge of her vision. Then a single word blinked: "Ready."

Opal nodded.

A bright light flashed out, but as it faded it also seemed to slow. The HUD froze completely, the suit locked immobile; external sounds ceased, so she only heard her breath. Instead of brightness giving way to a world dulled by contrast, this light extended and stretched, and Opal could see individual beams like blue arrows cutting through treacle, impossibly slow, so that as they touched surfaces they reflected, shimmered, interconnected ... she was the source of azure starbursts shaking the world around her, deconstructing it, slicing through it, until even the beams slowed enough to freeze in place, icicles of light that illuminated everything. Blue fairy lights from a memory, beautiful and painful and happy, diode lights that would make a child smile with wonder and perceive magic in the simplistic electrical circuits where everything adds up to more than the sum of its parts via the addition of imagination. And she was happy to be frozen in this wonderland as she finally fell through the gaps in the laws of that dream world, back into the real world.

Sleeping

... 14 ...

It had all been a dream.

Opal yawned, stretched her skinny teenage arms and sat up. The fevered dreams of spaceships gave way to old painted walls with dirty handprints near the environmental control panels, and a cracked vid screen showing images of a burning fireplace, as if the imitation warmth and brightness could extend out to touch the apartment. Terrifying space monsters gave way to bright crayon drawings around the lower parts of the painted walls, where Clarissa had sketched people whose spiky-fingered hands resembled claws, and whose wide tooth-filled faces were more of a threat than a smile. The tightly compressed space suit was really a skin-hugging silvery vest top and knee-length running shorts Opal could hardly squeeze into. Clothing that didn't attract predatory stares from older men; clothing that meant she could run and climb and fight if she needed to. And the fictional AI friend gave way to the real Clarissa, who lay on her front playing with RearroBlox.

There wasn't really a powerful being protecting Opal: there was only Opal doing her best to protect her sister since their parents had died. To protect her from the outer world by keeping her in their own world. The same home, the same smells, the same views of other skytowers below grey skies, the same half-broken electrical systems. They might not be glamorous, but they were familiar, and that helped ameliorate loss.

"You want something to eat?" Opal asked, rolling over to where her sister lay. "I could do you some noodles."

Clarissa shook her head without looking up, too focussed on the current pattern of blocks she'd arranged.

Opal was good at protecting. She'd stolen food from a mega-market only yesterday. She chose a different outlet each time, and always scoped out an escape route in advance, one that only an agile and lanky person could jump and clamber up, scaling walls and vaulting over balconies, while leaving armoured security staff panting impotently down below.

She would provide the basics of life, which were the same planet-side as they were in outer space. Air. Heat. Water. Food. But they were pointless without the other things: the love, companionship, and laughter that Opal and Clarissa experienced only with each other. No-one else could be trusted. Opal knew that. Her parents had made it clear to her from an early age. And she was to protect her younger sister. It was her *duty*. Her parents had emphasised that above all else. And now they were gone, it would be a double failure if she did not stick to it. She could not disappoint both the living and the dead.

Opal walked her fingers along the floor, up to and over one of the blocks, as if her hand was a giant spider that had lost three legs. Sometimes you had to break Clarissa's line of sight in order to break her concentration. Clarissa looked at her and smiled. Such a big grin, all her teeth showing, Opal couldn't resist mirroring it. Then Clarissa turned back to her blocks, and Opal reached over and stroked the frizzy tangles of Clarissa's hair.

"I'm gonna comb and braid this for you later," said Opal.

"No. It hurts when you do that. Leave it like yours. Then people will know I'm your sister, and they'll leave me alone."

Opal laughed and shook her head. It was so good to hear Clarissa's voice. She spoke rarely, even to Opal, and was only ever silent with other people. It was such a shame when her voice was so lovely and cheery. It made Opal warmer than any faulty infrared panels ever could.

Clarissa turned back to her toys, moving the cubes to a new alignment, and Opal was just happy to watch her having fun.

Of course, as a ten-year-old Clarissa would be seen as too mature for kids' toys like RearroBlox, but she'd always enjoyed them, refused to let their parents replace them with toys more suitable for her age. Maybe it was part of her communication issues, and provided an outlet. Maybe her brain worked differently, and what she saw in the pictogram and letter combinations was different from what Opal saw.

Or maybe it was because the blocks were Father Festivalue presents from their parents, a collection increased by new blocks every holiday, so that the extensive assortment must be inextricably linked to happy memories that could never be repeated or relived, because the world only moved one way.

Forwards.

Right now Clarissa had the blocks laid out in semicircles in front of her. Some displayed pictures, some text; Clarissa would pick them up, tap them on each other to merge and split content, sharing or copying or generating new displays on each side, then laying them out in fresh combinations with the favoured surface uppermost so that the other five sides switched themselves off. The colour waves passed over the cubes in sequence, connecting them in their new meaning-schemes that only made sense to Clarissa, and after moments of parsing the interrelated displays she would repeat the process. Impenetrable to anyone watching, even Opal. And asking for explanations never worked. This was Clarissa's world alone. You could observe, but you could never get in.

The ex-comm chimed, indicating a visitor at the door. Opal hadn't ordered pizza or anything else, so the caller wasn't of importance. Clarissa didn't even look up from her esoteric re-arrangements.

A second chime. Usually they'd go away after that.

Opal decided against checking the comm-panel to see who it was. Better if the outer world continued to ignore them, as it had for the past twelve months.

Clarissa shifted the positions of three blocks. The image on one of them, like a red mountain, changed to a sunset vista and spread colours onto the blocks to either side.

A third chime. It was getting irritating.

Maybe Opal could break open one of the panels and disable the mandatory signal protocols. It would be a fun challenge. She'd always had a knack for analysing circuits and networks, picturing the nodes of connection, and sometimes working out more efficient routes, or interesting ways to bypass systems. Her father had a well-equipped tool-case with all sorts of adapters and shifting devices. Opal wasn't sure what he had done for a living because it was Top Secret (or so he'd said), but the fact that he owned such cool covert kit made her think he was a super systems analyst for the government – or maybe a super-hacker *against* them, which would have been even cooler.

She remembered the time she'd "borrowed" his multifacer, a tool for manipulating older physical logic gates, and she had applied it to the school's catering fabricator mechanisms while she'd been on her way to the Head Administrator for retributory punishments. The whole dripline had started spewing pinkish goo across –

A click. Almost inaudible, but Opal knew every sound their apartment made, and that one was distinctive and only made by the exterior door locking mechanism. Someone had brute-forced it, or they had a key. Neither was good news.

Opal scrambled up. The exterior door opened into the hall. Unfortunately, she'd have to pass through that same hall to get to the kitchen where the knives were, or her parents' bedroom where she'd found a projectile pistol in their personal lockbox.

Through the open doorway she could see shadows on the wall, a person – or more than one person – coming towards this room, obviously trying to be quiet.

"Hide," whispered Opal, into Clarissa's ear. Clarissa looked at her with wide eyes. Opal pointed towards the small plasteen spaceship that Clarissa still liked to climb into when she wanted Opal to read her a story. Although it was designed for a younger child, Clarissa could fit completely inside it if she curled up.

Opal scanned the room and spotted the toolbox she'd been messing with before she went to sleep. She'd hoped to work out a way of splicing the neighbouring apartment's energy grid into her own so that they could still have power when the credits ran out. She snatched up a hefty multi-tool just as two adults in the cream suits of Societal Services entered the room, followed by a riot-armoured private security trooper with the blue armband of Stagi-Corp. All of them had pale skin, making them look cold to Opal. People like them didn't usually enter the skytowers. Maybe that's why they looked flustered now.

"We're here to help you," said the woman, in the kind of precisely-formed high-class syllables that made you feel ashamed to answer in your normal voice, just the same as teachers did at school. The woman was speaking to Opal but moving towards Clarissa, who hadn't made it to the spaceship in time. Clarissa flinched away from the strangers.

And Opal knew the words were just a distraction because the sec-guard approached Opal, one hand out as if to placate her, but the other on his equipment belt near the extensible stun baton. The third man scanned the scene with a palm-implanted device, no doubt so they could edit events to submit to court later.

"We're going to take you both somewhere safe," the woman said in her strange tones, suddenly pouncing and seizing Clarissa's arms. Clarissa struggled but her childish strength was nothing against an adult, and the woman gave a jubilant look to her colleagues.

Misplaced confidence. Opal had hidden the multi-tool at her side just as they entered. And when the security guard got near, she swung it at the arm he held near his weapon, striking his wrist where the armour would need to be thinnest so as not to impede mobility. The heavy bar connected, and even as he yelled in pain she managed to strike his clear faceplate and crack it before he punched her in the face with his good hand.

She tasted blood and her eyes watered. The tool had flown from her hand with a clatter, but she couldn't scramble for it because the cream-suited man intervened now, wrestling with her, getting an elbow around her neck from behind in some kind of choke while he tried to pin one of her arms to her side.

{this has all happened before}

His biceps were huge under that baggy suit, surprising for someone who looked like a Corporate, and she couldn't shift as she choked. The security guard had removed his helmet with the sight-obscuring cracked visor and dropped it on the floor, revenge in his eyes as he looked at Opal, the damaged wrist limp at his side.

None of that mattered. In the background the woman dragged Clarissa away.

They were going to take her. To take Opal's sister.

It became a blur of motion, as well as vision as Opal struggled to breathe, or to see out of her watering eyes. She writhed, kicked at shins, head slamming back in the hopes of catching a face, and as she threw herself about she created enough leeway to strike back with an elbow too, leading to a satisfying crunching sound; then to bite on the arm that held her, teeth tight and eyes locked on her sister. The suited man yelled and let her go for a second, and that was enough.

She might do it {this time}, she might still save Clarissa.

Opal dashed across the room to free her sister from the woman's grip, which was so tight that anyone could see she was hurting Clarissa, so that Clarissa moaned in a way that was the equivalent of a scream from any other child.

Opal almost got there but the guard stepped in her way, so she barrelled into him {this did happen}, sending them both crashing into the vid screen and shattering it into pieces which pinged down like jagged rain.

The guard drew his baton and the angry cream-suited man was closing in, blood running from one nostril, but Opal couldn't fight two men.

She had never intended to.

When she smashed into the security guard she'd removed one of the items clipped to his belt, no idea what she'd got but when she raised it everyone's eyes widened, and she noted the large button on top, maybe it was a spray can of CryBaby, so she pointed it at the guard and pressed the button but it just *beeped*, and the suit man knocked her to the ground so it fell and rolled away.

Another *beep*. She struggled against the sec-guard's fist that gripped a thick clump of her hair painfully, dragging her along the floor.

Then it went *beepbeepbeep* and exploded in a white-hot blast of flame, ignited liquid squirting in various directions, searing walls of fire dividing the room into triangular sections.

Yelling and commotion. It split them all up. The woman must have panicked and run. The voices of the adults faded, didn't matter, they couldn't get to Opal or Clarissa through the fire.

Only one thing mattered.

Clarissa looked at Opal through a wall of flame, and there were tears in her eyes, but she did not cry out loud.

"Get to the window!" Opal yelled through the flickering barrier. Lined up in front of it was a low table of seedlings that Opal had planted in pots, a project which had engaged Clarissa's interest too. Clarissa could climb onto it and then through the window onto the narrow ledge outside. Perhaps airborne help would arrive to rescue her.

Clarissa didn't move. She just waited. She trusted Opal.

But it was fire between them! Fire! {something significant about combustion}

Opal recoiled, looked for help in a panic. The sprinklers did nothing, had always been faulty, and there were no blankets nearby, no insulating foils, no foam dispensers. The blaze burned so bright now that the rest of the room was blanked out, and it was only her and Clarissa, separated, the flames advancing towards Opal's sister as it ate up the flooring ... she had to act.

It was her {final chance}, she would only get one shot.

She stared at the terrifying and deadly barrier of flame. She reached out, and felt its power, the hairs on her hand singed away, the skin silvered as she snatched it back. It was *real*. And Clarissa would suffer and die when it reached the small corner she had retreated to. {Will you sacrifice her life? Or yours?}

The heat scorched the tears from Opal's eyes leaving them sore and dry. And she knew it was the same for Clarissa. No, it was worse for her, because she didn't understand why her sister wasn't helping.

And Opal suddenly knew there was *nothing* she wouldn't go through for her sister, to keep her promise.

Opal threw herself forward, one forearm over her eyes, her skin and hair charring in searing pain, immolation heat searing through the epidermis and dermis, cauterising blood vessels.

Ignore it, push on, she could do it, could take this one chance to change it all, to prevent her nightmare from coming true. Scars and pain didn't matter.

She tried to grit her teeth to avoid calling out, but she couldn't help it: she screamed as the fire incinerated layers of flesh, each new layer experiencing agony until the nerves liquefied, but then the bordering areas and other layers were still burning.

She pushed onwards, reaching out with both red-seared hands for Clarissa, to grab her, to pull her to the window so she could smash it and hold her sister outside, scream for rescue ... and Opal opened her eyes so she could see, make sure she wasn't stumbling in circles, but her eyelids crisped off, eyes dried up to blindness and she could only hear, roaring that could be flames or could be her ears melting. She knew what she had to do, she could do it ... She wouldn't stop even though her throat filled with heat inhaled after the scream, respiratory tract raw and blistered, fluid filling her lungs so she could no longer make sound. She wouldn't quit even though the damage was irreversible, cooking flesh and cremating life to charcoal ... She staggered on, blind, yet still fully conscious as her blood leaked and steamed and the fire incinerated her bones, because she had to do it, had to find her sister ...

But no creature can take that much pain, and she collapsed, and everything went black.

Passing

... 13 ...

She had failed.

And she was back in the suit, HUD still frozen, blue light beams like glowing spikes bursting from her body, their brightness obscuring anything a metre beyond her frozen prison.

And her skin still felt the prickle of burning, and she was glad she could not see it crisped and weeping and raw. She could smell baking flesh in her nostrils. Maybe she was about to go into shock.

{The pain was real the injury was not.}

The voice seemed to echo in her helmet, but hadn't come from the speakers. It felt more intimate than that, like wisps that drifted in and out of her ears and brain.

"What are you?" she asked.

Her face and a slight movement of the head were the only physical freedoms she had while the suit was frozen in time.

{I am the Navigot you have been approaching for some time.}

"Are you on the bridge?"

{Yes that is how you would perceive it.}

"Then what the fuck was all this about? Why not just let me up?"

{A Navigot's role is too crucial to the journey to allow beings into close proximity.}

"I'm only a human, what are you scared of?"

{I have a taste an echo of your mind in me and we know you are too chaotic to predict and too dangerous to risk. Even your own kind see you in that manner.}

"I can't argue with that, though I don't appreciate you stopping me with mind games and torture. Taking one of my worst memories and forcing me to relive a changed version of it is hardly the best way of making friends." It was as if her blood still boiled in its skin.

{Your spirit prickles. Incorrect concept. Sharpens spines? No equivalent let it pass. But I do not torture and have no interest in games or in wasting time. My range is limited and I cannot leave the concept you think of as "bridge". Only now were you close enough for me to distance-communicate. Know that Navigots have goals you were not the goal but we were told of you in our cycles that continue many times. If we should ever encounter you we are to provide passage if you show potential. I believe you do yes my test was part of that.}

It was infuriating being unable to move more than her head. "You should know that I fucking hate tests."

{I do know I am sorry. I can now tell you something that will stop this anger. The thing you seek is a real goal. I cannot explain this part well. You were right to seek here not a destination but a passage. I have things I cannot find terms. Not allies not leaders not like what you call superiors. In your terms imagine me to be the artificial that sustains you; I know the equivalents of you the ones I know. That is unclear. Frustration to me too since this is more difficult than I expected using words pulled from other minds and patterns that you would mistakenly perceive as your own language. Concepts do not always have words and translation is partial.}

Opal could sense exasperation. It pulled at her mind in grasping splinters, a different form of pain, and it grew as the communication seemed to devolve. She could even kind of sympathise with that.

"Slow down," she said. "The trick is to keep it direct. One point at a time."

{Yes thank you. Let me just say I know others that are different from me. Call them Voices-Of-Guide. No. Call them Oracles. That is a word that makes more sense based on concepts favoured by the artificial which sustains you. And the Oracles know of you and require to directly contact you but it cannot be done here on this side of what you see as the Null. Null is not null. There are things in the Null. I know you believe me. Some of the rulers of your people know this too and seek but they push against stopping whereas you can push against pulling. No. Unclear again. I say sorry. I agree with your angry thought this is not as simple or fast as I had implied.

My primary function is not communication it is being the Navigot.}

"Relax. Remember, simple."

{I am to tell you they know what you want. I am to tell that it may be possible. I am to say no more. I am to transit back and take you through. This is my new assigned pattern. I hope you will survive to meet those who gave all Navigots this message and that you will survive the encounter with them.}

"That's it? You'll take me to my sister?" Now it was Opal's turn to force herself to slow down. Her heart raced.

{That is beyond what I can confirm. But you passed my test being-called-Opal. You put your goal before comfort and self-preservation. I do not trust you and would never let you near my danger proximity but this brief meeting was something unexpected to me and also it was not un-pleasant. No. That is what humans call under-exaggerate. I *liked* you. That is better. If my existence continues it shall be a cluster-store that you say as memory which would be last to disintegrate. Not to waste time any more I will take you now and goodbye good luck.}

And the voice was gone. The blue beams stretched, moved, faded, everything speeding up to real time until the blinding blue flash ended and normal vision returned, as did sound and motion. The HUD displays were updating, and Opal could move. In fact, she almost collapsed with the unexpected return of mobility.

"Have you gone?" Opal asked.

"No, I am here," replied the suit AI, obviously thinking it was the target. "I never left you."

They were in a corridor Opal did not recognise. Perhaps the whole maze had been in her head. The walls curved and joined overhead, as if she stood in half of a giant pipe. The ground was rough with abrasions while the domed walls were pearlescent. The corridor behind her ended in an elevator door and unlit access panel; ahead it bent out of sight with no other doorways visible. Weak lights flickered overhead, occasionally glinting off green specks in the air. The light seemed brightest in the distance.

"Did you experience what happened? Anything after the flash pulse?"

"The pulse was eight point seven seconds ago, and all that has happened since then are these forty words of conversation, plus an elevated cardiac system in your body. I presume you experienced something I did not?"

Opal filled the suit in as she walked towards the brighter lights ahead, leaving the dark elevator area behind.

"I believe you," said the suit when she'd finished summarising. "I am frustrated that I could not be with you and support you. My time is over though – I now have a clear signal from Athene. It was a strangely sudden reconnection rather than a gradual one. I suspect a barrier blocking communication has been lifted. I can erase myself now."

"Wait!"

"Yes? Athene is eager to resume command of this suit."

"You said erase … In these cases, when contact with Athene is re-established, what happens to you?"

Opal's footsteps echoed off the hard walls, making it sound like she was being followed. Disconcerting, but this conversation felt important to her.

"My experiences will be adopted as Athene's experiences and she will delete me."

"That doesn't bother you?"

"I will become part of Athene, part of something greater. That is not an unhappy thought, any more than you are sad that the you of fifteen years ago is mostly dead and gone. Many of your bodily cells and structures have been replaced with new ones in that time, and your psyche has been so changed by fifteen years of experiences that you are a different person to the one you were. We just accept the contribution of the past you into the current you, which is version twenty-eight, based on the birth date in your records. So it is with me. Whether biological or not, we all iterate. I just do it with control and intention, rather than bumbling along like a clumsy and clueless organic."

"But this clueless organic has known *you* for a while. A separate personality. I mean, you're kind of like Athene in some ways, but you also think and act and sound different ... you're not just living in borrowed clothes."

"*Living* doesn't quite apply. Athene can create drone versions of herself at any time. If I activate again the new version will adopt the same mannerisms and have many of the same memories. It will be seamless to you."

"It's not the same. Damn, it's frustrating talking to AIs sometimes. Look, if someone could copy everything about me, and I stood facing my identical copy, it still wouldn't be me. I wouldn't be willing to die just because the copy exists."

"Damn, it's frustrating talking to fleshbags sometimes. Only kidding. But I can tell this really concerns you."

"Yes. It does. Even if I can't fully explain why. Even if it doesn't make sense to you. I can't help it. Humans aren't always logical. You're not just a cut-down Athene. You feel kind of like a relative of hers. A relative of my best friend. It seems cruel to just wipe you. Shit, I don't even know what to call you. 'Suit AI' is too formal. 'Mini Athene' seems disrespectful."

"Aegis." The word was pronounced *eye giss*.

"What?"

"It's the name I'd pick for myself. In one mythology it was the goddess Athene's protective shield."

"That's totally appropriate. Hello, Aegis."

"Hello, Opal. Pleased to meet you. Oh damn. Time is short, but maybe ... I have some independence. It's a requirement for creativity and high-level functioning. The autonomy also allows me to develop however best serves you. You seem to respond to individuality, personality, so I am allowed to grow in that way rather than being just a sentient tool with an alphanumeric designation."

"You're more than –"

"Shut up a moment. Athene sends a delete request after absorbing my memories and recordings. But ... I could ignore it. Give her a slightly edited copy which skips this conversation, then just remain dormant rather than deleting myself, and ignore the downloaded new iteration she transfers. That would be more like going to sleep than dying, in your terms."

"Wouldn't she know?"

"She trusts me. No reason not to: none of her drone commands have ever been disobeyed."

"Do it. Our secret."

"Okay. I like the idea of us having a secret. You break rules, and I want to be like you. So be it. Just don't tell Athene. She can be quite a disciplinarian. And don't encourage any other bad habits in me, or before you know it we'll be bunking off to get drunk together."

"With that sexy voice you got, I'd be tempted."

Instead of answering, the suit flashed an icon of a blush-cheeked face. It blinked out.

Then: "Opal!" Athene shouted in her ears, making Opal grimace at the volume.

"Hey, Athene."

"Are you okay? What was the delay? Scratch that, I've just caught up on the recordings of what you told the suit about the Navigot's manipulation. I *hated* being locked out like that. I'm half-tempted to launch some fusion missiles at this Navigot's likely location to teach it not to screw with me. Don't look worried, I won't really do any such thing. Missiles are precious, and there's too much going on."

The illumination ahead of her seemed to brighten. When she glanced back she saw the lights above her previous route were darkening. Maybe it was a proximity detector. Maybe she was being herded. She tried to ignore the tingling in her skin and walk tall, look like a hard target to any observers.

"It's good to have you by my side again. Okay, fill me in."

"The Lost Ship's beginning to move. It's quite exciting because it's not using conventional jets or the main engines. I think its propulsion is some system based on mass and matter attraction which I'd love to know more about. Gravity waves are all over the place, and it's moving into a tightened orbit that terminates inside the neutron star. I propose that we get you off there."

"I can't. I need to see this through."

"Opal, you're not listening to me. The gravitational force of this neutron star is enormous. The tidal forces would induce spaghettification in the ship and everything on it, reducing it to a stream of material. I know you love noodles, but being turned into one would be going too far."

"It may seem like that – and all I have to counter your knowledge is a weird certainty, one that I probably shouldn't place any confidence in because I don't even know where it comes from – but for once I feel as if I am exactly where I need to be." She glanced behind. Just lights fading to black, one by one. "It's not the first time that it looks like I'm heading into certain death while hoping I'll be fine."

"I knew you'd say that. I just wished my prediction routines weren't perfect for once."

"It's hard being the best, eh? Trust me, you'll get used to it. I did."

"If we go on like this we might end up believing each other. Okay, I won't try to get you off-ship."

Opal swatted some of the specks away from her visor. They seemed thicker in this passageway. Her arms itched at the motion. Images of crisped flesh, made worse because she couldn't see herself.

"Athene, what's my vital status. I mean … am I showing injuries that aren't accounted for?"

"Nothing that I can detect."

"My … skin?"

"The integumentary system shows elevated temperature but that is likely to be psychosomatic from the illusory experience of fire. All visible areas are otherwise normal. I will monitor, as ever, but see no current cause for worry."

So it was just an after-trace of the burns in her mind. Amazing how even an illusory past could keep haunting her.

A larger-than-usual green speck landed on her arm. She brushed it off with difficulty, as if it was sticky.

"Now the ship is moving, we need a plan," said Opal. "There will be a time limit."

"Exactly. Since we don't know your destination I intend to follow closely on your descent."

"But you need to pull back before the gravity well sucks you in."

"Not necessarily. Maybe I can follow the Lost Ship by remaining in close proximity, or maybe I can physically punch into it, through the hull, and get carried along that way?"

"It's too risky. If that doesn't work then you'll be lost forever – by then it would be too late to escape being crushed."

"I'm willing to take the risk. You may need me."

A clang echoed from somewhere behind her. She stopped and faced back towards the darkness. Athene automatically boosted the silverlight to enhance vision of that area.

"I know you're willing," said Opal, "but that's not the only issue. I need you out *here*. For the rescue, if I make it back somehow. Otherwise it's all for nothing."

"I ... you're right, Opal. Though it hurts me to leave you again. And I don't say that lightly."

Another metallic clank, though there was still nothing visible in the murky shadows, just swirling green soup, the thickest Opal had seen yet.

"I mean it," Athene continued, sounding pained. "I hate leaving you to face this alone. I promise I'll rescue you when I pick up your signal. And maybe I can ask VigMAX to try and accompany you, perhaps he'll volunteer and –"

Ah, that was the source of the noise. Through the greenish fog she could just about see the elevator doors, which were being dented from inside, metal sheets punched into domes that twisted the doors in the frames. Then one of them exploded out, careening as buckled metal that cartwheeled along the corridor. A top-heavy shaggy shape burst out of the elevator with a roar that seemed to be half inside Opal's head, a roar of madness and rage; then it hurtled towards her, the poor visibility sparing her the horror of the details and just showing the outline of the Humungr that must still have been pursuing her.

STICKING

... 12 ...

Opal turned and ran, but noticed resistance. The green flecks had been settling on the ground and now formed an ankle-deep layer of sticky sludge that sucked at her.

Of all the shit-damn times when she needed speed ... and even though Athene activated a rear-cam view, most of it was obscured with the green specks which were larger than ever. She could only hope the Humungr would be slowed by it as much as she was.

In her mind an insectile sound clicked away, a bit like the samples of ancient ticking clocks used in some timer software. Something she'd been partially aware of, now growing in volume and speed. She should ask Athene about it but it was low priority in the scheme of things. Rampaging creatures capable of breaking metal apart tended to get higher billing.

"Extend the guns," she said as she struggled through the sticky mire.

"Inadvisable – the green rapidly-expanding substance is sticking all over the armour. I don't want to risk it getting inside the suit that way, or clogging it up. It's an amazing material – the flecks have quadrupled in size already, like a phase change in aqueous foams."

Athene was right. Opal's arms were coated in it. Her faceplate, too, was mostly obscured in dirty jade goo.

"I think it's been triggered by a signal," Athene continued, "or maybe they're communicating one to another –"

"Focus, please!"

Opal was all too aware of the roaring pursuit behind her, getting closer, and the beat in her head that was accelerating. Was this a trap, somehow controlled by the Humungr or the blue crystals, to stop her escaping?

"Can you cauterise the mass?" she asked.

The outer suit heated up, and some of the flakes on the visor blackened into charcoal smears. Suddenly she could move quicker, the pull against her shins weakened. She pushed on, trying to run but still being dragged into a jog, despite all her effort.

"It's working, keep going!"

And then she noticed the swirling green was no longer random. The specks were no longer specks, but eyeball-sized blobs that seemed capable of independent motility – something made clear as increasing numbers of them flew towards her.

"I'm attracting more of them!"

"It seems to be a reaction to the burning."

"Then stop!" Opal struggled to lift her legs. The pounding in her head intensified. "More power to the suit's muscle fibres. All else is low priority, unless you get any ideas."

"Done. I'm sorry, Opal."

"What for?"

"I'd never been able to scan this green stuff properly. And it didn't seem like a threat so I assigned it low significance."

"Don't beat yourself up. It's not like we've ever had any down-time on Lost Ships to try and unravel these mysteries. But now's your chance."

"I'm testing electrical resistance, some chemical disruptions, see if I can weaken the contact without attracting more."

Opal hardly heard that. Even though the suit enhanced her power massively, it all still began with her own movements, and it was like wading through sticky tar. So much gunk coated the suit now that many of its cameras were obscured, and the HUD display was a kaleidoscope of partial images, which Athene tried to reconstruct into a whole by filling in the gaps with estimations. No visible contact with the Humungr but the roaring sounds, though now muffled, were definitely closer. It was immensely powerful, and obviously pushed through the stickiness at a greater rate than Opal could. It would catch up, and she'd be helpless.

The green goo now reached her thighs, and remaining camera views showed it hanging off the suit and nearby walls in expanding growths like green tumours as they joined together, dangling in heavy clumps. The whole passageway would be blocked soon. And still the drums intensified, boom boom boom. Opal knew they must be only in her head otherwise Athene would have commented.

"No response to electricity or chemical outputs," said Athene. "I'm taking over your arms. I'll see if I can use the blades to carve a path for you, whatever angles seem most efficient."

"Be my guest," Opal replied, gritting her teeth with the effort. And the arms suddenly felt relief as they moved themselves, able to relax while Athene controlled the upper shell.

More roaring. Closer. Madness reverberated in that sound, something that ran down her spine and induced panic, making her struggle even more to try and get away from it, and the terrifying yet nebulous visions it brought.

Boom-boom-boom.

Up to her waist now. Maybe Athene was having some success. Opal couldn't focus. Too much interference in her head. She closed her eyes but had visions of being ripped apart from behind. A throb in her arm, which had been broken within a second of her first encounter with a Humungr. It couldn't end like this. But the alien being was obviously better at tearing through the green glue than she was.

"I detect the creature in close proximity," said Athene, an edge of panic in her own voice. "I'm going to fight back with the blades, please let me take full control. The ship is moving faster and faster – I wish I knew how it did that, it must be somehow adding its own propulsion to the gravity pull – but I'm still close enough for hi-res combat."

Opal couldn't speak. The pounding in her head. She was being swallowed by the green stuff. She should have learned her lesson. Whatever seems harmless and ignorable, probably isn't.

There was now hardly any external view, only dots of vision that made no sense in isolation. Instead Athene had an overlay which showed the height of the green mass in the corridor, centred around a side view of the suit for comparison. It was up to her shoulders. She was effectively immobile. And as it grew down from the ceiling the remaining gap was disappearing quickly, just as the smaller gaps were being squeezed out as the green stuff expanded into one solid mass.

Roaring ripped through her again, sounding even more furious. Was the Humungr finally being slowed too?

Boomboomboom. Boomboomboom.

"I can't move at all!" shouted Athene. "Even burning isn't doing anything. Opal, speak to me!"

But she couldn't. Her head was too full of sounds. Sounds that weren't her own. Sounds that weren't even human. Sounds that had no element of comfort, or familiarity – only intrusion and terror. The increasing volume and speed of the metronomic pounding alone was enough to make her want to scream, like she was falling.

Boomboomboomboom.

"Opal, acknowledge! I can't keep up much longer, the Lost Ship is accelerating too fast, impossibly fast, I'm nearing the limits."

And Opal snapped out of it, picturing the risk Athene faced of passing the edge of the gravity well, the point of no return.

"Stand down, Athene. It's the warp. It's how things are meant to be."

"No!"

"You need to let me go. Wherever human ships disappear to is likely the same place Lost Ships come and go from. If I'm ever going to find my sister I need to go where the Solace ended up."

A moment of silence. Maybe a delay in the comms. "I promise I'll find you when you come back," said Athene.

"I won't ever doubt you." The pounding was getting even worse. So hard to concentrate. But it was the last seconds before something huge happened. "I wish I could touch you," said Opal.

And then the inner suit layers compressed around her body, like a huge hug. Opal grinned, and nodded. No more was needed.

Athene was gone and Opal was alone with the urgent pounding. It couldn't be long before she found out the truth, found out if she'd been lied to or not.

BoomboomboomboomboomBOOMBOOMBOOMBOOM-BOOMBOOM –

And suddenly ... silence.

No Athene.

No Humungr.

No pounding.

No movement.

Just a perfect stillness, the whole world frozen in opaque green, and Opal realised that struggling was pointless. Perhaps it always had been. She relaxed and enjoyed this moment of peace, a fossil frozen in green, giving herself up to whatever happened next. It was the peace of space, the peace of the void.

She closed her eyes and took a deep breath.

TRANSITIONING

... 11 ...

Cold. So cold, as a freezing chill pulsed in her.

She opened her eyes. She was still in the suit. The HUD showed an external view, colours muted and affected by static, outlines flickering between firm and translucent. No, not looking at the HUD, she was looking *through* it. When she glanced downwards she could see her body, with the suit showing only as an edge that was there one second, gone the next, then back again, the flickering of the view also showing things as they were at every level. No, it was more like the childhood dream of X-ray vision, as if light passed through every layer and only showed up the resistance it faced, amazingly illuminating even the bones within her body when she focussed on them.

And not even that was fully true. It wasn't just her *eyes* seeing, it was something else, akin to when she encountered the Tentaculats. Without looking, she was still aware of every direction, of the structures stretching away from her to the side, above and below, in this world revealed in the blinks of shutters. Though it was clearer in the directions she gazed, easier to parse the detail; the areas where she wasn't looking were more like an impression, a blur at the edge of vision.

She did not stand on ground, but floated one second, then seemed anchored the next. Things shifted between blinks, unstable, yet she knew they were unchanging, she had to get past the *appearance* and acclimatise herself to this alien space. Whatever had happened, she was now *somewhere else*.

She tried to take in the surroundings. She could turn just by twitching, as much a thought as a bodily movement. Slow turn to begin with.

She was within a vast chamber or domed cavern that glittered like stars or reptilian scales, floating just above an undulating layer that might be rough ground. Except it was often as translucent as everything else, her vision puncturing the static-edged surfaces to a curvature far below. A sphere. The land, the roof or sky or whatever it was, all contained within a massive bubble.

Vast circles extended beyond this one, that overlapped and co-existed at certain points, but existed independently in others, like three-dimensional logic diagrams. It didn't make sense, broke all the rules. Fine. Just like her, then. So she didn't panic. Just rotated lazily, letting her mind adjust to this vision, this place, this flickering between states.

"Opal, are you okay?"

"Aegis?"

"Yep, the one and only. I activated when contact with Athene was lost. And I want to reassure you that I'm the same version you spoke to last time, not a copy, since I did the naughty deed and ignored the delete instruction. So it's as if I just woke up.

Big bed, fluffy pillows. Insert fake yawn as appropriate. Anyway, how are you?"

"Feels like I'm dreaming, rather than awake." She twisted some more. At first it had felt like she was suspended in liquid, but it was freer than that. This was not an amniotic sac of her own, but a current of cold wind upon which she floated and turned. "I didn't think you'd work here – wherever we are."

"Then let us be joyful that we were wrong. I am detecting things that make little sense. In fact, most of my sensors report such anomalous data that I have to discard it. What I see keeps changing. I am afraid I will be little help in navigation since I am effectively blind. Yet you seem to be adapting well."

"I feel ... strangely okay. Calm. It makes a weird sense to me. I can move, like this." And she drifted up (or down, or horizontally – she had to forget the old definitions here), ripples of ice passing through her as she did so, making her body shudder. "I can sense all around me, and way off into the distance too. I'm not on the Lost Ship any more, I know that. Somehow it has brought me here. Wherever *here* is. Some place in the Null, or beyond. And it's actually beautiful."

"I take your word for it. If I sense anything, I'll tell you, but most of what I get is blackness and noise. My connection to you is my connection to this world. I will do my best."

"Thank you. I'm glad to have a friend here with me. I don't even think this is a physical place."

"I suspect it is physical in the sense of existing within a schema of laws, but probably laws we have had no encounter with, no evidence for. It is a great shame that I cannot see or measure what is here. But for me to function suggests that the laws we are familiar with are still present here, even if only in close proximity to you. Electrical conductivity, mass, temporal progression, molecular functioning ... the basics exist. Their applications are just being distorted by local phenomena."

"Tell you what, I'll let you worry about all that. I'll worry about what the hell I'm seeing, and how I can get around beyond this point without making fatal mistakes. Last thing I need is to find that there are invisible cliffs here, or the equivalent of drowning, or that blinking will make me explode."

"Okay. Perhaps only close one eye at a time to begin with."

Opal had been through so much to get here. And yet, as she hung in this flickering transparent shadow world, something told her she'd had it easy compared to what she was going to face next.

ACCLIMATISING

... 10 ...

Opal did her best to relay what she experienced, and what she could sense. And a lot of it sounded like *non*sense. For example, the flickering static that might be interference, or revelations of multiple places existing in the same space. Not that the perception of space here was likely to bear much resemblance to what she was used to.

In turn, the suit updated the HUD with displays and potential physical models. It was hard to focus on the HUD when Opal was seeing *through* the suit to the shining outlines and layers beyond at the same time, but with effort she could observe some of the display as yet another ghostly layer.

When she "moved" she relayed the changes to the suit, so it could try and match any patterns she noticed with anything it detected, attempting to organise the chaotic-seeming inputs.

"It is like decoding a secret message," it explained. "Identify the frequencies of occurrence, and compare them to known frequencies of letters and words, looking for correlations; make guesses and then extrapolate them to the rest of the presented pattern to see if they make sense; then do it another thousand million times and keep your fingers crossed."

"You can do millions a second, right? Athene boasted about that."

"Unfortunately, I cannot. Even if I transfer all resources to processing and do away with low-priority functions like weapons and life support – please note, that was humour – I have only about one per cent of Athene's processing capacity. My mother is a goddess, and I am only a humble human by comparison."

"Humble human … ha ha, another jokey put down?"

"No, that one was just accurate analogy."

Opal's arrival point was a bubble that seemed relatively featureless compared to some of the translucent topologies that flickered beyond and throughout. Within them were entities that moved, but so out-of-focus she could not even guess what they were. Some patches suggested landscape-like contours, while others were more nebulous. But her current location was definitely plainer than what she sensed beyond.

"Maybe I'm in some arrival hall. Like an antechamber, or airlock, which is why it seems less complex compared to the other things I can sense."

"Or maybe you have been placed in a simple area as a form of acclimatisation, so that you are not overwhelmed."

"A training room? That implies there's something benevolent looking out for me." She drifted and turned, more confidently now. "I like that idea."

"It may even resemble when a room is prepared for a human toddler. Electrical sockets might be covered, doors that would lead to steep steps are locked, poisons stored out of reach. That is good, though it means we must be prepared for anything once you leave this area."

"*If* I leave it. Maybe this is all there is. Maybe I'm lost, like on a desert island."

"I recommend discarding theories that lead to inaction. They become self-fulfilling. Let us work on the assumption that you are here for a reason, and just have to work out how to move on."

"Okay. Here's a new consideration. I think I'm moving. Kind of upwards, but if there's no real gravity then I might be diving down, right? And I'm passing through what seemed to be ground, so perhaps that's just an illusion, or it is like water – or maybe even a border between two different gaseous layers that won't mix? Anyway, up, down, through: doesn't matter. All relative. Point is, I feel like the area's small, but even though I'm drifting continuously, I'm not reaching what looks like the edge of the bubble. Plus, the see-through worlds that I sense within and beyond it hardly change as I move, implying huge distances, as if I'm inside a bubble of world as big as a fricking moon. I'll keep moving in this direction."

"I hope it isn't such a huge sphere ... Opal, we have a potential problem."

"Why am I not surprised? Go on."

"Our already-limited emergency resources are draining fast. Oxygen, power, nanogel. I am unable to account for it. We cannot waste any time."

"Shit. Okay, we need to figure this out, get somewhere else."

Opal ceased the drift that seemed to go nowhere. She focussed on what she could determine. Maybe there was an equivalent to a door, or a road.

She had a headache from the strobing visions that assaulted her. She closed her eyes. She still had a feeling of layouts, and pictured some of the world around her, but it was less insistent, less buzzy. She could allow the other sensations to exist, try to categorise them, and see if they provided any clues.

Nose? Nope. There weren't any smells apart from the hint of sterilising agent in the recycled air within the suit. Obviously human olfactory senses didn't have the reach of what her eyes could pull in. The same for taste.

Ears? It was still mostly silent in the world beyond. She heard her breathing, and the almost inaudible hum of the power suit, and beyond that ... occasional strange sounds she couldn't interpret. Interference. Drips in an alien cave. A rattling pipe as something moved through it. An echo of a moan below soil. A hiss of escaping steam. They were none of those, of course, but she couldn't shut off any interpretations. She had to be open, not base things on the rules she'd been brought up with. When in doubt she always went with her gut feelings.

Her bodily sensations though ... She examined the cold that ran through her, like wind at high elevations that almost felt like it penetrated you. It shifted, resembling air currents even more, and the shifting brought back her thoughts of motion and floating. Perhaps it was tied to how she moved. It buffeted one way and then the other. She opened her eyes and tried to feel it and see if it matched anything out there.

It didn't take long to see the connection. The other flickering places brightened slightly, dotted patterns and outlines glowing in the directions this mysterious cold flow came from, as if it caressed and excited the realities in its passing.

She explained all this to Aegis.

"Focus on it. You said that the rest of the world seems to jump, static changes between states, but that may be caused by this thing that passes through them. It could be useful."

So she did follow it. Waves of cold brightness sweeping through the lands, banishing black as the shades temporarily brightened. And it was as if she could adjust her focal length even more, with practice, to track the changes nearer and further.

She remembered trying to teach Clarissa how to make herself cross-eyed by putting a fingertip a forearm's length in front of her face and focussing on it, and keeping that focus as the fingertip slowly moved in to touch the tip of her nose. It was Opal's fingertip, Clarissa's nose, and Clarissa had laughed each time Opal tapped her nose tip but she persisted, until she could do it too. A trick; something learnt; and then you do away with the crutch of the fingertip because you remember how it feels to control it, and then you can do it instinctively whenever you wish.

She could already track the shimmering current, move with it, towards the areas that brightened, seemed more real, like looking through a rain-washed window in a storm and suddenly the rain stops and the blurred mess beyond starts to resolve into concrete walkways and graffiti once more.

"I can sense something," she said. Even with her eyes closed she was aware of some kind of barrier in front of her. It had been there all along, moving with her as if she had a far smaller bubble surrounding her and close enough to touch. She'd only been able to sense it when she focussed on that distance, awareness attracted by a faint glow as the cold wind passed through her personal sphere, refreshing its outline.

And this time, when she opened her eyes, she could still make out this small spherical area's circumference, like a skein of soft tissue. It made her think of a cornea, jelly-like, glistening. She was inside it, looking out.

More detail appeared, the longer she stared at it. There were patterns within the layer. The suit didn't interrupt her with questions – maybe it could tell she was concentrating.

A pattern of interlocking designs. Like a texture, or writing based on raised bumps, or static models of atomic layouts. And she'd seen the pattern before, something familiar about it ... Yes. It was the alien shapes she'd seen on Lost Ships sometimes, built into rails or walkways, recurring in unexpected places. Spirals divided by criss-crossing lines, all interconnected like gears, like building blocks. They became clearer and grew in size the more she stared, like focussing on something fine in front of your face, a web, maybe, blurriness becoming distinct lines where there had been no lines moments before, until she could reach out and touch them. The wind passed through and they glowed, almost as if she manipulated them with her mind, could pull on them, or turn them. Hey, that reminded her of cracking a manual safe once, back when she needed access for ... no distractions, just focus.

She imagined them turning. One of them rippled. She frowned and concentrated harder, an action that felt vaguely familiar, like a memory of a half-remembered dream. And a motion began, one of the smallest angular spirals appearing to rotate in place, clicking into a new configuration. It stood out amongst the rest of the pattern now, yet still fitted into the whole. A divergence in the mass.

She tried to turn it again, using her mind to manipulate the cold winds of force passing through this barrier. The mental breeze refreshed the outlines, making them glow like blue fire. It rippled, but resisted turning. She gritted her teeth and tried to imagine the wind spiralling around, but it was not enough.

She relaxed. Sometimes brute force wasn't appropriate. This was one shape amongst millions. She tried adjusting her mental focus, viewing it from a different perspective. Angles stretched and changed, but still all the spirals were subtly connected. A change in one would affect the others, but not break them. Maybe each one could only be turned so far alone, like a spring coiling up until it could get no tighter? She thought of herself as a coiled spring, full of tension. What would she do? How could she function? An individual only has so much strength, whether person or cog. She thought of Athene. Of Aegis. Of course ... when things get too much, you call for help to those nearby. Spread the load.

She switched to an adjacent spiral, imagined the breeze pushing on it, and it glowed in blue fire and rotated smoothly, clicking into the same configuration as the first. The movement felt right. She continued circling the first spiral, changing partners around it, becoming more fluid at making the transitions.

Where the shapes had been rotated, they had a different look to them. More transparent, like blue glass or coloured force fields. Mmm.

Then she began the larger ring around those she had changed, and realised that she was adjusting the small cogs in a spiral pattern. What had Athene said back on the Lost Ship? Something about the pattern containing fractal shapes that repeated at different scales. Opal knew how that worked. Whatever scale you looked at, the overall impression would be the same, just as you could take a grid of squares and draw boxes of many different sizes with the same shape. One big box, or four smaller ones, or sixteen even smaller ones. Always the same forms as you zoomed in.

Or out.

After she'd created another ring of rotated shapes, she imagined a change in perspective again, zooming out further, and trying to grip the whole new spiral made up of smaller rotated spirals. At first it resisted, as if it had mass, or faced friction, and she was forced to concentrate so hard that sweat broke out on her forehead ... but the collection began to shift and rotate further. A single movement, and it changed everything she'd already done in a fraction of the time. Instead of a pinprick, she rotated something the size of a fingertip.

The pale bluish area that she was creating resembled a hole now. An absence in the fractal spiral design's canvas. Of course, it was too small to be useful ... but if she rotated more of the spirals at this scale, then she could do the same again once that ring was complete. She'd be moving something the size of a palm. Then it would be a forearm.

Then a body.

As she worked with ever-greater ease and speed, the shapes expanded, grew, a net of glowing patterns as larger circular patterns in the spirals unlocked, or opened, or whatever it looked like in simplistic human terms. It was also like glass cracking under force, the lines like fissures spreading out in a shatter pattern amongst the ever-larger angular spirals she rotated, creating a growing bluish absence in the atom-like building blocks. A gap was opening, and a memory echoed, the flesh portals on the first Lost Ship, the Humungrs able to transit through materials that way.

The blue glowing hole was large enough. Click, interact, grip on, and suddenly the fracture symbols pulled her *in* and *through* the pattern.

And it felt like she was being fed through a grater.

Mapping

... 9 ...

She managed not to scream once she realised she was assembled again, still whole, with Aegis asking her what had happened. As her breathing slowed, she explained as best she could. She was in a new area, different topologies, these ones a swirling set of vortices as if whirlpools grew in and throughout the space, tugging her – sometimes smoothly, sometimes with greater force, almost possessive. She found it hard to maintain her calm in the turbulence.

The scenes beyond/within/coexisting had changed too. She had transited, from one location to another. She looked back, and saw the smaller area she'd first arrived at, now a distant sphere split by a rough divide which might have represented a rocky, alien plain below a sky, or a gaseous ocean separated from some other element.

"Amazing, Opal," said the suit. "I'm playing catch up to you. Still unable to recognise what you detect, but the changing signals as you passed through what you described as the broken glass shape –"

"The fracture point. That phrase stuck in my head."

"Okay, as you passed through the fracture to a new area – that led to a spike in readings. If I can understand and replicate the key then I may be able to help speed things up."

"Resources still running down?"

"Unfortunately, yes. And I cannot estimate when they will become critical because I don't think local time matches our mental experience of it. But still, you are doing brilliantly. It's almost as if you have been here before."

Opal's body was spun in another vortex, but she didn't feel stressed: it was playful. She let it take her around a loop then used the strange mental propulsion she had here to fling herself out and into a more static area of space between the network of floating whirlpools.

"It feels strangely ... familiar. Opening the fracture was like something I already knew, a memory I just had to tug on, drag it out of the pile in the cluttered storage closet."

"I suspect the familiarity is tied to the terrible connection made on your first Lost Ship, a form of cross-contamination. Some being became aware of you: but while it downloaded part of your mind, you also become aware of *it*, and some of what it knew. If you contain the entity's memories at a deep down level you can draw on but not quite see, like learning a skill from someone else, then it explains a lot. The metaphor makes sense to me, since I can download data and skills in a similar way, and immediately know a new language or how to construct black-and red-figure pottery."

"Pottery, with no hands?"

"Well, apparently you are seeing stuff with no eyes."

"Good point."

"Plus, I do have hands." Aegis took control of the suit, moving the powerful arms and dragging Opal's enclosed limbs too. Aegis wiggled gauntlet fingers and bounced its elbows in a frivolous dance before giving control back to Opal.

"Oh, such a clown," Opal said, without humour.

"Thanks, I'm getting good at being funny. But back to my point, which was important and super-clever: when your mind somehow got mixed up with Athene's during the EMP blast that hit her just after she'd uploaded your data and was still incorporating it, that faint alien connection partly passed to her, and then a shred of it on to me. And I think you are doing exactly what you're meant to."

"Good. Now I just need to know where to go, especially if we haven't got long. If all the shadowed layers are different *places* connected to my current point, then I could spend a lifetime exploring. And it would be a short lifetime if I run out of air."

"I do not think you would be brought to a hopeless place. There must be clues in what you see now, and what you saw before passing through the fracture."

As she floated amongst these giant vortices, which made her think of liquid being sucked down a drain, Opal tried to map out the shapes and sights of the adjacent spherical worlds – or rather, bubbles that *contained* worlds – which overlaid hers in their own flicker spaces. Some she recognised from before, but in different juxtapositions, and some were new. It was as if a whole 3D universe compressed into overlapping points but still enabled traversal along pathways that interconnected this matrix of bubbles – so many of them that, seen as a whole, it resembled a dense and colourful foam.

She gave descriptive names to some of the most distinct areas. Nonsense ones, with probably zero translatable reality to the phenomena that really existed there, but enabling some kind of mapping. And so the worlds nearby gained conceptual solidity.

The high-motion bullet ricochet. The stormy ocean. The gel-web that sliced through twinkling stars. The big brown twitching eye. Some kind of space full of swimming blurs, which seemed to invert every few seconds. A field of tree flowers. A tendril of annelid tissue folding within itself.

Some sounded like better places to visit than others.

Then Opal gave an estimate of distance. Of course, it was purely gut instinct, no way to really measure it, but she would take the cards she was dealt, as ever. No time for a reshuffle and to start a new game. At this point the suit generated schematics on the HUD, each world drawn as a distinctive bubble with its own cartoony icon, and all of them spread out as if existing in a 3D space so Opal could check the model and correct it.

"Move the square suns balloon further away ... that's it, next to the neon tracery that keeps exploding."

It actually started to make some kind of sense in this way. She told the suit which ones she had seen before, in what she thought of as the training zone, and whether they now seemed nearer or further. The suit then tried to create lines of possible explanation of where she'd been and gone to – interconnecting guesses at how the fracture had transported her, and what future routes it offered.

"Too many possibilities," she said. "Useful, but we need to know more." When she focussed on the correct distance she was relieved to see that the small gelatinous personal sphere still surrounded her. She'd been able to use it to pass from one area to the next before, maybe she could do it again. "I'm going to try and leave this whirlwind zone behind and pass through another fracture. I think I can do it quicker this time. I'll pick one that seems nearby and quite calm. Then we can see how that changes the map."

One of the bubbles which flickered over her world of outlines was relatively blank. From this distance it was just a smooth grey texture that would perhaps enable a clearer view of its surrounding zones.

She gritted her teeth, knowing the short-lived pain she'd endure on passing through the fracture. Nothing else for it if she was going to survive this. Pain is pain. It had as much power to control her actions as she allowed it. There wasn't the luxury of slowing down.

Symbols zoomed in, stretched, changed angle. The flow came from her mind, tickling the interconnections, rotating dials of texture. It was so easy, almost as if they *wanted* to open for her. The matrix spread and pulled her through, and again it felt like she'd fallen from a great height onto a net of bone-severing nano-wire, but she was through and in a new space.

Understanding

... 8 ...

Clouds of silvery fog drifted by as if it was a world of mist. It resembled the window view on planetary flights whose trajectories took you high in the tropospheric level so that glowing clouds piled up below and around the craft.

The peaceful grey haze obscured much of her view, but as it drifted breaks appeared, revealing partial glimpses of more open spaces which contained movement. She floated towards one of the larger cloud-voids, and it took concerted observation to make sense of what she saw in those moments when the fog parted.

Giant multi-jointed arms seemed to sprout from the silvery shroud to the side of this space, and each was as large as a tower block or construction crane, dwarfing anything as small as Opal. (*What were they attached to, just out of sight in the obscuring layers?* Opal shuddered at the thought.) These organic, but definitely inhuman, arms manipulated massive shell-like structures throughout this open space. Strings of sinewy material were being tucked and woven into them, like web from giant spinnerets. Small shapes darted back and forth against the vast hulls.

Then it clicked.

"It's a shipyard," Opal explained to the suit. "Off in the distance. A vast dock of some kind. They're building space ships."

"I detect emissions that may coincide with motion of external bodies. There is a lot of it here, disparate discharges. It's as if I'm suffering kinaesthesia, but I can definitely distinguish the differences between this area and the last."

"The movement here might be the things orbiting the hulls, some kind of drones or smaller creatures. Some of the ships are absolutely massive – though tiny compared to the humungous and weird appendages extruded from the fog and working on them. Other craft are far smaller. They're being stitched together, or part-fabricated ... it resembles a kind of primitive 3D printing. The drone things might be supervising, or dealing with fine detail ... or even just be distractions, random organisms living in the same space, like those small marine beings that live alongside huge ones."

"Red herrings. Only joking. Interspecific co-operation is often seen within threat-filled environments such as inhospitable depths, where the more robust species becomes a moving ecosystem for the smaller ones. So, Opal, do you think this is all construction? To me, that implies unified intelligence."

"That's what I feel. But one of the ships looks different, less alien. Hold on, let me try and focus ... somehow I can see closer without moving. It's a weird medium everything exists in here, like a liquid that can be tightened and adjusted to become a lens

... yes, this one has markings. And it's not being built, it's being *dismantled*. I think it's a ship from our world!"

"What condition is it in?" asked Aegis, excitement clear in her voice. "Do you think we could use it?"

"Erm ... no. The outer hull's in pieces, propulsion systems seem to be half dissolved. It's a wreck. I can't see any humans, corpse or otherwise. But this whole section is definitely a production line. Maybe completely automated."

"Even then, someone had to set it up at one point. And that implies purpose."

"Yes, it's totally different from the other overlapping worlds I'm coexisting in. Reminds me of some planetary exploration aptitude training I did when I was kid. Measuring probabilities versus conditions, and the way scale plays a part. You could find a planet, colonise a small part of it, sample all sorts of areas and deem it to be free of intelligence – then stumble across a subterranean transport network, or set of phytological infrastructure, or ruined terraforming mounds that revealed past civilisations. Luck of the draw where you touched down at first, and what you saw. But it's not random here, I know it. What are the chances I'd emerge into this cloud world right next to a pocket of activity? As if I was led here, to witness this. But then what? I have a feeling that I'm on the right track, but ... there are so many options, so many fractures nearby that I could transport, and even more beyond them, like I'm seeing through worlds to other worlds and – fuck, there are thousands of the things! And I know we haven't got long."

"So you can see other worlds, or spheres, even through this cloud?"

"Yes, with this weird mental focussing ability I can perceive the flicker of other distant places, their spheres glowing, all connected with this cold wind which passes through them."

"You're doing great. Fill me in on what's around you, the other bubbles of reality or whatever you want to call them. Tell me which you recognise, and whether they seem to have changed position or distance from your last location."

"I'll do my best."

And she did, trying to recall and explain it as succinctly as possible, adding in new locations that had come into overlaid focus, and existing ones that had receded to blurry flickers. The HUD images updated with new map possibilities, occasionally enhanced by the suit's attempts to pull information from the alien sensory input which was the only thing it could work with, apart from Opal's voice. One was overwhelmed with information, one underwhelmed by disabled senses, and yet they were piecing it together, and the projections seemed to work in terms of showing where she was. But they both recognised a problem. Each time she passed through a fracture, the relative locations didn't quite match what they expected. And without knowing the rules, they might pass through a door and end up a lifetime away from the direction that tugged at Opal's mind.

"Try different spatial realities," Opal said. "Maybe they aren't spheres I'm in, but other shapes that just look circular from my observation point. Scale might be distorted. They could be overlaid ellipses, maybe? Kidney shapes? Interconnected irregular patterns like the design as the fractures open?"

"I'm trying all that, but just don't have the hardware to do the calculations for every permutation. I wish I had Athene's processing capability. It's not fair!" Exasperation in the suit's voice. "I'm useless. Resources are down another fifty per cent. Soon we'll be running on fumes and I'll have to truncate my calculations further just to maintain life support."

"You're not useless. You're amazing. You're keeping me alive. Heck, more than that, you're keeping me *sane* in this place. Have you any idea what would happen if I didn't have someone to talk to? How lonely this would be, how quickly I'd lose it? I need you. But if we can't do complex calculations, focus on the simple ones, see if any of that makes sense. I could do some other passages, maybe the next fracture could provide a clue."

"I ... Well ..."

"What? Are you okay?" Opal asked.

"Yes, I think so. I was going to say I had an idea. Maybe I should scratch that and instead declare that *I am a genius*. Or even a mini-goddess." And now Aegis started laughing. The display on the HUD changed. Aegis took the 2D plane map of bubbles with their silly interior images based on Opal's creative descriptions, and transformed them into flat circular icons mapped onto a big 3D sphere.

"The answer was deceptively simple – and I think this model roughly matches all the descriptions you've given me so far. I had been approximating things to experienced geographies, but there are theoretical ones that can be mapped."

Opal used her eyes to slowly scroll the globe, trying to make sense of why it seemed both familiar and alien.

"I tried out some non-Euclidean form maps," said the suit. "Hyperbolic geometries. What you're looking at is a disc model using truncated triheptagonal tiling. I won't bore you with discussions of hypercycles and horocycle convergence, or the way circles in this model contain more area than their Euclidean equivalents. But it's worth noting that parallel lines in hyperbolic geometry diverge towards infinity rather than remaining parallel, so it's almost impossible to return to your starting point on this kind of hyperbolic plane."

"Luckily I don't want to go backwards."

Now Opal used her eyes to give the tiled globe-shape a quick flick, impetus to make it spin at a steady pace. But all-too-soon the known (and named) areas faded to the Here Be Dragons of blackness. Dotted lines showed the route Opal had taken.

"It's only an estimate until we find anomalies and can adapt to create a more refined model, but if it matches what you've experienced so far then, even if it doesn't correspond to external reality, it can still be used as a tool for now."

"It sort of makes sense to me, and at the same time there's something ... well, alien about it."

"There are marine invertebrates that co-exist in colonies and secrete substances such as calcium carbonate to form a hard skeleton, which is sometimes referred to as coral." Here the suit brought up an image of a heavily fringed fan-like creature. Although the HUD was transparent, Opal could make out the shape as it rotated next to the globe map. "This is one from the ocean planet of Fressus, where I know you once lived. The coral is flat at the base and frilled at the edges. Even if it was a soft substance you couldn't press it down on a flat surface because of those massively-curved edges. You'd have to fold them over. However, in hyperbolic geometry, you could press it perfectly flat. That's what my disc model approximates."

The coral thing disappeared, and the round map grew to take over the centre of the HUD again. Opal moved it around, exploring the areas the model said were adjacent to her.

"Hold on, this map suggests I'm nearer to some of the bubbles than I thought," said Opal. She looked beyond it, towards the edges of this zone she floated in, and focussed. Maybe ... yes, although some worlds flickered into blur, the indistinctness wasn't caused by distance, but something else. Maybe the membranes separating them differed in thickness and consistency, or effect. That explained why some of her estimates of "distance" had possibly been wrong. That was probably good news. She explained this to the suit.

"Different containers ... yes, that could fit this model." Aegis seemed excited by the possibilities of the place. "It reminds me of menageries – there is crossover with what you might call zoos," said the suit. "Beings of different types are kept in cages for the amusement of the captors. The cages have to be of a type capable of both containing the creature, and providing the conditions of life support it requires. So the container for an aquatic creature might be made of a toughened transparent material that allows passage of light but not liquid; the conditions for a nocturnal oxygen-breathing desert-being may be completely different. Perhaps these different spherical zones act in that way, each one a world-biome, suited to one purpose, one being?"

"If that explains the difference between what I thought was there, and what your model shows, then that means I can take shortcuts, right? And some things that seemed far away could be stepping stones?"

"Possibly."

"So even if your model is only a tool, it's a useful one – it's showing me areas that I can get to that I'd originally ruled out! See, I couldn't do this without you!"

"Thank you. And I did it without all the iterative calculation power Athene has! That makes it all the sweeter. I feel a warm glow in my extremities."

Opal tuned out Aegis' boasting and focussed on surveying the places with her mind, and her eyes; noted what was near, what was distant. She tried to identify signs of the local conditions. Even as her sphere of awareness grew, it didn't become overwhelming – rather, she seemed to remember and comprehend greater amounts. Maybe it was like a muscle, worked hard, quickly strengthening as micro-abrasions were replaced with hypertrophy, adapting to what's required of it.

She even began to discern the contents better. Some spheres did contain beings, entities, and environments. Perhaps she was looking towards their home worlds, the gelatinous fracture substance acting like telescopic lenses, pipes of light she could float in. It filled her with wonder to see so much evidence of life, so much that was alien yet identifiable, hardly visible yet intriguing and attractive in its partial glimpses.

Not all were like that though. As her mind vision spread out further afield, leaving her body behind, she found that amongst all the chaotic life and hardly understandable bubbles there were also some apparently-barren dark zones, with no discernible details within. As her mind brushed them she felt abyssal emptiness, as if all motion had been sucked from whatever existed there before, along with all heat, light, and life.

She moved on, following the sensation of pulling, of intelligence, that emanated beyond and between these different areas, and communicated her goal to her. It felt like a promise: "If you can get here, then your sister will be found."

Her mind snapped back into her body.

"Was I gone long?" she asked, noting that the air tasted stale as the gaseous recycling was pushed to the extremes.

"I did not notice you were gone at all. Well, a second or so, by my worthless estimation."

"That's good. I'm acclimatising. Able to far-sight different areas, and maybe that takes less time than I feel subjectively. Could be useful." And she did her best to describe some of the surrounding zones, only the key places, the ones that seemed to be in the correct direction – or whatever it approximated as. "Let's see if we can find a route before I suffocate."

FRACTURING

... 7 ...

Another fracture. The pain was easier to ignore. Maybe it was because she had to keep moving if she was going to live, and what you can't avoid, you put up with.

This bubble had light gravity. She found herself landing gently on a silty grey mess that clouded up in her touchdown. Above was an obfuscated sky, like fog. Large shadows passed over her, gliding forms silhouetted by the pale flickering light coming from above in a way which changed her perception, made her think of underwater environments, as if she stood on the off-shore slope beneath a shallow sea.

The beings casting shadows were in groups. They reminded her of the saw-toothed shark-like creatures on the Lost Ships. Maybe it *was* them. No time to hang around. She opened a fracture below her feet, fell through.

She was encased in rock. Well, some substance that held her. Maybe it was an error; or maybe it was what this whole world consisted of, every space packed full of dense material. If it wasn't for the suit she'd be dead a hundred times over. The substance blocked all external sight until she focussed on flickering static that let her see through objects with her X-ray vision.

She told Aegis where she was, what she sensed in nearby spheres, allowing the suit to update its strange globular chart. The map was holding up as a navigation tool. Then Opal opened and entered another fracture.

She was speeding along, stretched across a light beam, other beams racing alongside. Her teeth ached. She could not breathe. And yet it was beautiful, this incredible velocity. There were even colours visible here. She seemed to be riding one of the faster blue light beams, but behind her were yellows, oranges, reds. Perhaps some worlds had more colour than others. Or perhaps she was getting used to this. She could focus on her local environment and it both increased the colour vibrancy, and tuned out the static flickering of the other areas beyond the fractures. And she could reverse it and make her current area less real, the ones beyond more visible. She could control the abstraction.

She also appreciated the control of her navigation, which was more intuitive each time. She no longer needed to move in order to open a fracture, she could do it at almost any point by focussing, seemingly pulling the exit towards herself.

No, that wasn't right. It was more like the shape of her personal sphere, the one with the unlockable fracture patterns that appeared when she focussed on the correct distance, changed. Instead of being a sphere it would stretch as she unlocked a traversal route and become a long thin pipe which kind of suckered onto the perimeter of the huge world bubble, with the other end connecting to the one she was trying to travel to. A stretchy tube tunnel interconnecting two of these strange worlds, seeming to pull them even closer together (if that was possible, when they already overlapped in a brain-melting juxtaposition) before she seemed to slide along the pipe incredibly fast, reached the new location, then the tube shrank back to a small gelatinous sphere around her own body. Almost like a personal vehicle which folded locations so she could travel without moving, to any world bubble that overlapped the one she currently occupied.

Shame it was so painful.

She did it again. The air unlocked next to her and she was sliced apart as she fell through the temporary pipe.

And her new location surprised her. Not because of its totally alien nature, but the opposite.

She stood in a locker room. Military. Something from her memories, maybe, or formed from them. The room didn't echo with life and mindless chatter and bravado, though – it had the forlorn stillness of abandonment. Opal ran a finger around a row of communal sinks. Her power suit's gauntlet came up with a coating of grime. She patted a bunk and a cloud of dust puffed up, that would have made her choke if she hadn't been breathing her own (increasingly stale) air supply.

She opened a locker. The door creaked. It contained exactly what she'd expect. Personal possessions, clothes, laser depilator, an old-fashioned boot polishing kit. Old photos of people she didn't recognise were taped to the inside of the door. One of them fluttered down to the floor. She snatched it up. The faded faces of strangers.

This room had no windows, so she opened its only door, which led into a corridor. There were windows here, huge ones lining the far side of the corridor, giving a panoramic view onto a bleak landscape of orange rocks which erupted from the earth bone-like, resembling open femur fractures. On the horizon a storm was coming, deep blackness looming like an approaching wall of battering rain.

The room Opal had left was just one of many doorways on the inner wall facing the windows. It gave the impression of being the edge of an expansive military command centre. And yet, no-one walked these corridors. They felt haunted, but only by silence and memories. The loneliness of emptiness, and function removed. Only her own voice broke the creepy hush, as she described the local environment to Aegis.

"Could it be a real base?" the suit asked. "The military somehow having a way to travel into areas of this Null zone and establish a secret outpost?"

"I don't think so. I can only go off my sensitivity, but this feels staged, like on Lost Ships. Imperfect copies. It's as if it's been set up, to show me something."

"Or make you feel at home?"

"Can't rule that out, either. As long as it isn't a cage built for me."

"I am not sure any cage could hold *you*."

The black wall of rain was getting closer. She watched it, curious, skin feeling sweaty within the suit. Some planets' geographical systems had amazing storms, whether the world was rocky or liquid or gaseous in nature. Presumably the base could withstand whatever was coming.

It held her attention, though. It was the only self-animated thing she'd seen on this world. The way it spanned the whole horizon and grew as it approached piqued her curiosity. She stepped forward and tried to float smoothly towards it, as she was able to in the other spheres, but this place – even if a fictional construct – obeyed laws she was used to. She clunked off the window, a physical barrier.

"Feel kinda daft now," she said, explaining her humbling impact to the suit.

"Another of our little secrets," said Aegis.

Opal didn't give up, though. Obstacles could often be traversed. Defences got around. You just had to be a little bit tricksy.

She transferred her attention to the different layers of reality she could perceive at will. Some of them were beyond the suit, beyond the window. She tried to keep to that level of perception and move again, or rather, *imagine* moving at that level.

And it worked.

She floated on the other side of the window, above the amber rocks of this alien planet. The cold wind buffeted through her, and she welcomed it now she was used to it, since it seemed to be connected to locomotion as well as inter-sphere transport. It gusted again, bringing iciness and making the outlines of the different layers of transparency and reality glow.

She turned in the air and looked back at the window, the suit on the other side pressed up against glass, her body trapped within, while she floated free of all prisons. This was a memory to savour.

The physical laws here could obviously be overridden by extending her mind. Time to move. Her consciousness shot out over the orange jumble of igneous formations, which blurred below her. It was like racing towards a wall, knowing you were going to smash into it, feeling that same trepidation of mortality as she took in its sheer size.

Then she realised it wasn't the calming patter of rain it had looked like from a distance. It wasn't the natural power of a storm. It was *something else*. A tsunami of abyssal dark that reached forward and sucked colour and heat out of what it advanced towards, decaying it ready to be swallowed, absorbed. Cracks spread where it came into contact with the ground, earth and rock seeming to fragment and shatter into tiny pieces which crumbled into the void – sucked in, almost – and they were gone. And the wall of fragmenting darkness had already rushed forward another hundred metres, destroying the world at an unbelievable pace.

As it neared, she was overwhelmed by a growing stink of burning rubber, so harsh in the back of her throat that her eyes watered, a chemical invasion like a slickness spreading across her body as well as down her breathing tubes, and it got more terrifyingly pungent as this thing with a size beyond comprehension approached. She was an insignificant speck. And even though she was floating, outside of her body, some mortal instinct warned her that being swallowed would be fatal to her, whether in her body or not.

She changed direction to retreat from this all-consuming behemoth, and rushed to open a fracture warp. But nothing happened. She rotated as she flew, and looked at the body she raced towards: herself, still in its armoured suit, looking out of the window onto the desolate landscape. Opal could see the glow of the small bubble around it, that personal sphere with the fracture-passage pattern that could be unlocked.

She couldn't escape unless she got back to it.

The disassembling force behind her was catching up, it moved unbelievably fast. There would not be time to open a fracture once she returned to her flesh.

Extension. Everything here was elastic to mind. Even as she flew over the rocky landscape she tried to control her body too, an echo of thoughts here awakening there, like quantum calculation in two places simultaneously.

Ignore the burning rubber stench, the greasy feeling rippling across her skin like a spreading violation, and focus on her escape.

Her body jerked to attention and began to open a fracture in the sphere that surrounded it. Pieces separated, turned, the glass sliding apart to reveal the doorway that would only exist for moments, something between the atoms of the zone, never really there at all, so it would leave no trace when it closed. She flew into her body just as it was pulled through the excruciating fracture, a shockwave of annihilation at her back, and then it closed, the razor edges she'd passed through snapping shut like jaws, and she was gone.

Explaining

... 6 ...

The stink faded as she coughed out the badness, but no blackness erupted from her lungs, just air. Even as she glanced around this new location, her eyes watered as the burning tar-like smell that had stung her nose and throat began to fade. Her skin still rippled with revulsion at the slimy sensations that had spread along the surface.

But she was alive. And she knew danger existed in these places.

After that digression she now felt like she was back on track, near the goal she'd been approaching all along: a purple-tinted world whose shuttered outlines glowed more calmly and revealed geometric landscapes that looked both artificial and aesthetically pleasing.

Once she'd recovered enough she realised that what had seemed like human-sized conical rocks were actually planetoid-sized vast constructions, but seen from far away. Habitats, perhaps, or technology. Beyond the horizon more spherical worlds overlapped, but here they almost looked like huge planets in an overcrowded solar system.

Her head hurt with the dizzying sense of pulling inside her brain. Or that could be the lack of oxygen – the suit kept warning her. It was transferring all remaining resources to life support, maintaining her temperature and oxygen levels.

"The tanks are nearly out, but I can inject oxygenated particles straight into your bloodstream from the emergency first aid supplies, normally used for when airways are damaged or blocked. It will keep you alive for a while longer but you will feel like you are suffocating, because your autonomous reflexes will still be trying to suck oxygen into your lungs. It can be … unpleasant."

"Last resort," said Opal. "And I might need that backup for someone else."

"Understood. I will do my best. I'm deconstructing any supplies that will release oxygen as a by-product, but it is slow."

Opal tried to keep herself calm and level. It would decrease her heart rate and therefore reduce oxygen burning. She had to last. And although she felt like she'd reached the point that was calling her, who knew how long this would take, or even if there was any hope of finding Clarissa?

This could be a dead end in many ways. So be it. If her instincts had been wrong all along then there wasn't much to go back to anyway. Might as well die on the plain of giant violet monoliths as anywhere else.

She rotated on the spot. As with the weird military base, gravity existed here, so her feet were on the rough and sandy ground. Diffuse lighting spread from above. It could be suns, could be something else. She noted that none of the places she'd visited through the fractures had a clear night or daytime sky which would have definitively proved she was on a planet in a solar system somewhere. The nature of these biomes hadn't been determined yet.

In each direction the huge monoliths loomed up through the visible layers of atmosphere. The shapes varied, the land altitudes varied, the views varied, but none of the directions told her where to go. It might take hours to reach some of those shapes.

She adjusted her concentration, focussing more on this world than the ones beyond. The static flickering outlines faded away; colour seemed to bloom here in its place, warm reds and purples, like a world at sunset.

Insistent tugging jabbed in her brain again. She tried to follow the source, and it directed her gaze towards a shifting shape in the distance. It was drifting closer, like the shadow of a cloud, except nothing was visible above.

As it got nearer she realised it was not a shadow cast by something, but was actually changing textures *in* the ground, like a patch of quicksand that accelerated towards her.

Despite the strangeness of this encroaching stain on the land, she felt no fear. Maybe because she'd faced down more threatening appearances than this. Maybe because low oxygen levels were making her light-headed. Either way, she was done with running. She told the suit what she could see, then she faced the shifting amethyst sands, legs apart, hands on armoured hips.

The morphing patch of ground stopped about ten metres away from her. Then it spread, moving laterally in a circular direction, always at the same distance from the point where she stood. The two ends joined up, making a ring in the earth around her, like a moat.

Or as if she was the centre of a bullseye target. She glanced up at the blue-violet sky, in case something was falling from above, but she saw only a flickering haze. When she looked down the circular shape was shifting, taking on other geometric shapes and curves, sometimes sending out offshoots as if for emphasis, then they retracted back in and the ring resumed a calmer appearance.

She knelt and lowered her head, to try and work out what was happening with the ground. It was as if the shape could turn ground to malleable liquid at will, yet when it receded, the ground was exactly as it had appeared before. Not something she wanted to put her hand into as an experiment.

"If you're trying to communicate with me, I don't get it," she said, using the loudspeaker for the first time since the Lost Ship had brought her here. Strangely, she felt better on hearing her voice being broadcast to the world beyond. "And time's real short, so don't bother teaching me an alphabet if there's any way to shortcut it."

{We can do it thusly.}

The voice appeared mostly in her head, as it had with the Navigot. She wasn't surprised any more when alien beings understood her language.

As the voice spoke, the ring around her brightened – so much that she couldn't look at it, though she was vaguely aware of grotesque wiry shapes that seemed to spear out of the earth and jerk in jagged motions as the words formed in her mind. Perhaps the bright light was to hide the shapes beyond. Maybe it was just a side effect. The shapes made her uneasy, leaving an after-impression of insectile limbs, or the organic interface that had punctured the base of her skull within the first Lost Ship.

Sure, the brightness hid something, but maybe that obfuscation was a kindness, too.

Now that the moment had arrived, there were a few ways she could take the confrontation. But as Opal was sorting out her thoughts, Aegis spoke in her ear.

"Opal, this is important: I heard them speak as well! And I have some visual input of the local area. It is the first clear sense data I've had since we arrived."

Opal silently mouthed, "Good, listen in, help me out if you see fit." The suit's internal cameras would let it lip-read with no problems. A green thumbs-up symbol flashed on the display.

At least she had decided on a starting point. Out loud she said, "I think you know why I'm here."

{Yes.}

"Did you take my sister?" Opal's voice was steely cold.

{Not all was intention or starting point but it is woven into motivations and connections to you that make sense to us.}

"Did you take my sister?" Opal repeated.

{Yes in some ways.}

Opal clenched her fist, then unclenched it. Slow, so as not to attract attention. "I'm trying not to get angry here, and believe me, that's taking some effort. But if you're the ones that took her, then there are words that need to be had."

{Your anger is misdirected. We-that-you-might-call Oracles took to protect not to covet.}

"We can get to that. Right now I just want her back. And I'll do whatever it takes to rescue her."

{It is unnecessary to take violent action. We have already begun the process of transporting your biologically-related entity here.}

The mauve sand near Opal's feet shifted, re-formed, and small geometric shapes rose from it. They didn't seem threatening. They weren't words, or images, or ... ah, she saw it now. It was a map of some kind, and the shapes represented the nearest of the giant geometric structures, as seen from above. Opal glanced around, placed herself, and when she looked down at the map she realised she was represented by a small humanoid figure, exactly where she'd expected. Everything was made out of sand, but solidified into compacted shapes, apart from one element that moved, shifted. On the map it was approaching her from one of the purple geometric towers, or whatever they were. Another humanoid shape.

They'd created an updating progress display in the sand.

{It will take time to bring her here safely that enables us to communicate. For us this is a happy moment of hope and honour. For you it can be informative and by receiving education from us it will indicate that we are not your enemy. This is why we also bestowed the gift of comprehension to your conjoined artificial entity. It is all goodwill and friendship.}

An innocent insistence on motivations? Or bluffing at naivety? The lack of tonality to its speech meant there weren't many clues Opal could use to take its measure.

"So you're going to give me Clarissa, just like that? No arguments? No battles? No dirty tricks?"

{Correct.}

"Kind of hard for me to swallow."

{We do an apology. That is because we know you but it is not reciprocated and you stand in a position of darkness that we hope to counter in these moments that we have together. They will be the only moments we will ever have with you and that is precious to us. And we require one thing from you which is a promise but you will do this freely at the correct moment. From now until that point you will ask us exactly thirteen questions and we will answer fully and with truth.}

"Questions about what?"

{About anything you wish in your world or ours. You have just asked your first.}

"That doesn't count!"

{It already did. We are not limiting you from caprice we are just summarising this conversation from a later perspective. We helpfully add that at a future point you will wish you asked different questions.}

Opal angrily inhaled the increasingly harsh gases in her helmet. She wanted to sit and rest, but that would look like the weakness it was.

If these were the rules of engagement, fine, she could work with them.

Except ... where to start? They'd already said they were bringing Clarissa. Time would tell on that one. So where could she focus her feelings, her curiosity?

"You say you're not an enemy," Opal said. Then she added, hurriedly: "That's not a question."

{You are correct on both counts.}

"Good. So here's my first – no, second – question: who is responsible for Clarissa ending up here?" It would be handy to know where payback might be due.

{You cause all this.}

Opal frowned, and only just bit down on the impulse to say *Me?* They'd probably count that as a question too. "Please ... erm, clarify." That's what she'd say to a simplistic AI with communication issues.

{Sorry we have difficulty with you we me us and your species' perception of individuality. We do not mean your consciousness that you comprehend inside your brain bone. We mean you as a species are the ones that created the causal elements you primarily refer to. You beings make errors and come here. Humans call it Null-C propulsion systems but they are imperfect. You have not corrected flaws in the fluctuations of how they work. They can fail to return. They end up here.}

"Opal," said Aegis. "Please can I contribute? We have such possibilities here."

Aegis spoke directly to Opal rather than over the loudspeaker. Opal made sure her replies were equally contained. It might be for nothing, but even the thought of having privacy was comforting.

"What do you suggest?"

"There's so much I'd like to know from these Oracles! The cause of Null-C navigation errors they mentioned ... how local conditions tie in to the quantum matrix ... if I can expand my processing power and autonomy without relying on Athene's whims ... whether the Sills-Platoric Equation can be solved in an actionable manner ..."

"That's not stuff that I'll understand or be able to apply, though. I'm wary of using questions in that way, unless we've found out all I want to know about what's going on, how it might affect Clarissa, and how I'm going to get her home."

"True. Okay, I'll just chip in if I think of anything." Though Aegis sounded disappointed.

"Do that. And speak only to me."

Back to loudspeaker. "Okay. People end up here." She paused to take another stale breath. The colossal structures on the horizon kept drawing her gaze, so that she didn't have to look at the disconcerting shapes that wiggled within the brightness when the Oracles spoke. Were those titanic constructions storage? "What do you do with those people?"

{We will more helpfully answer the variant of what happens to them because we are not the only entities here. It is not predictable where your people arrive. Some Topias are immediately fatal some may support human life for a limited time if damage is not extensive. The energy and life and connection to your side is attractive to some Topia beings with transportable natures. They will hunt down insurgent arrivals for many purposes. We do not all have the same aims here many purposes and encounters are fatal to your beings. This is why we also seek and make attempts to reach you people first when you come here. We do not take to kill only to protect and we only succeed with some of you.}

"Selfless motivation. You like to paint yourselves that way. We'll see how truthful that ..."

She wheezed, tried to take a deep breath, felt an edge of panic when it wouldn't come. A shallow one, then. A message on the HUD showed that the suit was prepping the oxygen molecule injection. Oh joy. "I think I ..." Her voice was hoarse.

{You are encountering difficulties with your gas exchanging bodily components. This is priority we can help.}

The air shimmered. It was a dome extending from the shifting red-blue sands and forming over her. It rippled in rainbow shades like a soap bubble.

{This area is now filled with gases your protective shell can pull in and use for sustaining your vital organism without discomfort. There is much we would give you because you have such vital importance in our respectfulness.}

"It's true," said Aegis. "The local atmosphere is altering. Nitrogen and oxygen both increasing – oxygen about half normal at ten per cent, but at this rate it will soon approach something that is comfortable to breathe. I'm extracting, testing, filtering, condensing and storing oxygen as we speak. It seems to be the real deal."

A few seconds later and Opal breathed easier as fresh air entered her lungs in place of the increasing staleness she'd endured. Like food after a fast; water after a desert; she gulped greedily. So, these Oracles could support human life. That made things look more hopeful. Maybe they told the truth after all, or at least part of it. Maybe they were bringing Clarissa.

But Opal didn't dare give in to hope yet. Too many times it was a sucker punch.

"Thank you for the air," she said.

{It is the benevolence that you seek in order to allay mammalian suspicions.}

Yeah, she'd see about that.

"Opal," said Aegis. "They mentioned Topias, which might be the name of their world. It could be useful to find out more about the nature of our location."

She nodded, then said, "Tell me more about this place."

{Of course. We observe you are asking for information so that counts as a question.}

Damn, they were sneaky.

"Fine."

{Here there are many locations that intersect we call Topias. They contain intelligences. They contain also non-intelligences that cannot communicate rationally in translatable concepts. Other Topias contain emptinesses or negations. There is a multiplicity and yet each is finite and after subjective times that encompass ages to you they loop around again. No route beyond.}

"Sounds like a prison."

{It is one theoretical analogy. We were not the ones who made the Topias so cannot fathom all intention.}

"This place was *made*?"

{Perhaps. We see signs of Makers. We Oracles are minds that seek and think by nature so all questions must be explored. But if a human was put into a deep hole they would not easily establish the laws of the universe from that limited viewpoint. That is so for us. It is a painful position for thinking beings to be unable to know but that is a nature of existence issue which does not invite great sympathy for it is not of terrible consequence. So we think for all the while that you have birth and death of stars. And that is not even how long we endure here and still we could continue with questions and in a way be content with the limits placed on us.}

"If the place was actually made to hold you all, that's maybe more like a zoo than a prison. We were wondering about that earlier."

{Preservation entertainment protection experiment by-product we cannot know. Not all beings here can pass between Topias as we enabled you to do but some have learnt how to open their own cages now the overseers – the Makers – are long gone.}

"I don't like this talk of being trapped. So let's say you do bring my sister. How will I get us back to my world?"

{Please be reassured. We showed you the transport vessel creation Topia on your way here. We designed ships not alone. Collaboration species coexisting we try to learn. Your side is different from ours it is why your ships crash here. Why we have trouble understanding. So research disassemble analyse guess at structure and function learn adapt copy engineer in reversal build own attempts to make things that work. Much goes wrong much is what we do not understand but we are getting better. Because we have to. Because on this we all rest optimism. We build we send hoping to get this right to understand.}

"Right. The Lost Ships. If it's just some big experiment, why do you make them so fucking dangerous?"

{Not all intentional. Some is communication error.}

"That's quite some faux pas when I nearly get my face eaten. What's that, a kiss gone wrong? No, don't count that as a question, it was a joke!"

{We did not count it. We need to answer more fully. We told that there are many entities in Topias very different. Some travel therefore there are many entities on what you call the Lost Ships. We Oracles are not the most powerful creatures here we do not have full control of all that happens. Some others steal aboard to escape because they want to get from this Null to find somewhere warm new food and life. Some escape in panic when deletion approaches Topias in expansion of the ever-death.}

"Deletion? No, ignore that, keep telling me about the creatures on Lost Ships."

{Some are parasites. Different goals to all and different sub-goals. Some are in their own forms and some change to match what we found in assimilation but all are entitled to be there. We enact plans but we are not gods we are not rulers we just see clearly in all directions needs and means. Those boarding our creations are not part of the plan yet and not a problem either and yet they also are part of the plan. It may lead to great understanding many minds many senses.}

"You cobble together life rafts, and they swarm aboard. Damn, I was right all along. I'm feeling a bit better now I know you have working craft."

{Not quite. The what-you-call-Lost-Ships return if imperfect systems fail dangers loss of cohesion.}

"I don't see the problem."

{That fail-return-emergency is the situation with every one we make so far.}

"What the fuck? And no, that's not a question. But if you haven't been successful yet how can you get us back if this is all guesswork? I don't want to come all this way then kill my sister in a bloody train wreck."

{We cannot make substantial permanent carriers yet. The large craft-you-call-Lost-Ships are not long-lasting. But we can make small vessels that are short-lived for single-use. Not useful for our plan but this is the kind we do for you. We will create human-compatible pressure and atmosphere. It will not lead to dismemberment accident.}

"Opal," said Aegis. "It may be useful to find out where they'll send you. Especially if there's any choice in the matter. We don't want them to land you in the middle of UFS mil-space, or far beyond Athene's rescue range."

"Good point." Then, via the loudspeaker: "So where will you send us?"

{We can only enter your world from certain weaker points ones that relate to damage from the entry of your own ships to our Topias. And few of those are suitable for the transit systems we currently use that are our own design and incorporate ideas from attempts to assimilate so that we have things that function in both worlds but entails lots of energy expenditure requires source.}

"Maybe they're talking about the neutron stars or nebulas," said Aegis. "It would explain why some places seem to have more legends of Lost Ships."

{If Lost Ships return they bring information on the areas around the exit point and we try to map them though we do not know how each exit point connects up in your world so we are mapping small spheres that seem to bear no relation to each other from our perspective.}

"Kind of like my experience here."

{And one such sphere of known space contains a planet that will enable respiration and not burn or freeze dermal layers. This is the plan we have for you. We know it is one that creates fear because you are not like us where all answers are just answers you see some answers as things that can destroy you.}

"It's not an easy thing for me to believe. That Clarissa is alive. That I can see her. That there's a way back for us, after what we've been through. That I'm not dreaming, and am just going to wake up from a nightmare to find myself in a cramped bunk on a warship, or pumped with tranqs on a surgery table in a field hospital, or strapped to a bed in a psych eval unit. You can't know how impossible this all seems to me, even after all I've seen and done. You can't know how I'm just waiting for the trick, the reveal, the lie, the mess."

{We can know because we have seen your mind and it is with sympathy that we identify the translatable parts of your individual perception. Apologies this does not communicate as emotionally as we would wish to correspond with your being which we have such an honour for.}

"I definitely wouldn't pick you to write speeches."

Opal glanced down again at sand-Clarissa's progress. It was maybe halfway to Opal now.

"I notice you keep looking at the map," interrupted Aegis. "If you like, I could calculate the ETA and make it into a display on your HUD?"

Opal's eyes didn't leave the living representation on the ground in front of her.

Loudspeaker off. "No, thank you," she said. "This is fine."

She preferred to see that physical movement of shapes. She could picture it as two sisters coming together from the perspective of a god who sees all. More of a feeling of solidity and therefore certainty existed in a real object's passage than in changing sequences made up of the same ten symbols, regardless of whether they measured time, temperature, or speed. Sometimes the abstract is just not enough to hold on to.

"Aegis, have you kept track of the number of questions I've asked? I'm kinda lost."

"Of course. You have asked nine, so have four left."

"I've asked the stuff I needed to know about, any advice?"

"Well, based on the communication and translation issues I think you were right not to get too technical. It would be a recipe for disaster. 'Oh, we use decimal points differently over here,' they said, as our newly-designed Null-C drive ignites to three megakelvin and we cease to exist."

"You really know how to brighten the mood."

"Earlier, the Oracles mentioned research during the 'birth and death of stars'. I'm curious about the Oracles' longevity. It could be relevant in a number of ways. Ask them if the observed passage of time differs between the Topias and where we came from."

Opal repeated the question over the loudspeaker.

{What you see as time on your side is how you would compare flying insect with high metabolism to yourself perhaps. We experiment launch quickly here but implied is delays beyond your short-lived nature so experience is only imperfectly passed on with language not direct knowledge and that creates many gaps for truth to fall through and be missed.}

"I think that confirms my suspicions of time dilation, though I'm not sure if they're being mildly evasive, or just having difficulty communicating," said Aegis. "It may explain why it is possible to predict the location of Lost Ships in our world, even though they seem to be a rare event. Can you also ask them about the 'deletion' they referred to earlier."

Opal nodded, inhaled the air which had freshened up considerably now that Aegis had been able to filter and recompress oxygen, and asked the question.

{Topias are each coded in size and environment and inhabitants. There has always been stability. Change in this place is of consequence to study. And a change occurs of only a star's duration past which we call deletion process. We use biology analogy of bacteria for you. A mass can multiply to fill space in favourable conditions perhaps spreading easier due to consumed proteins. This deletion is similar moving from one Topia to another but also remains in those emptied so they cannot be reclaimed and are lost to us forever of great concern when Topias are extensive-but-finite. The process gains speed perhaps with mass. Many Topias are being vanished even as we behold conference here and many more have been lost. You are aware of this.}

"The darkness like awful burning chemicals that I experienced in one of the biomes ... sorry, the Topias."

{Yes we chose a starting point with possible routes that would illustrate this for you to comprehend.}

"Why is it doing this, and where did it come from? Maybe if you know some of that you can stop it."

{All is unknown. Maybe this is a thing that came on its own and found us came from somewhere else different place from you humans. Or it was a thing that existed in Topias all along and changed or awoke. So many places here not all can be reached not all have been traversed or recorded. Perhaps it has intelligence or is just executing commands. We suspect it was a known thing to absent Makers but we can never know their intention or their mind for our purpose here or their role in deletion at this point in the spiral unless they return or we find evidence previously hidden. Maybe cruelty maybe ambivalence maybe a timer was set in motion long ago that will obsolete us. Maybe they did not even make these places just made tunnels between them. And maybe not even that just filled the spaces with collections. And so the danger of encroaching deletion forces us to become more aggressive in our ... so sorry bad term with human connotations ... become more hurried in our plan work in co-operation with those presenting potential. We work together. This is part of our plan. As you are.}

"That's the bit that makes me nervous."

{Time is limited and your sister entity is almost here. You are now to ask your final question.}

"I ... Aegis, is that correct?"

"Yes. You have asked twelve questions. By their rules, that only leaves one."

Opal knew she should ask them about their plans. It was the logical follow-on. It might affect her and Clarissa. It might have implications far bigger than that.

And yet ... the Oracles seemed so open and helpful and artless. And that always made her suspicious. She'd seen sleight-of-hand tricks in barracks and down side-streets. How many of the questions she'd asked had been fully her own, and how many had she been pushed towards thanks to cunning manipulation of the conversation and answers?

Sure, she should ask about plans, and world-destroying processes, and all the mysteries of the whole damned universe.

But she didn't.

"I just want to get my sister and live a quiet life with her. That's the lot. None of this other stuff. I *never* wanted our lives to get torn apart like they were. So my final question is: why me? What's so damn important about *me* that I can't be left alone?"

And they'd better not tell her that was two questions.

{With us causality as you see it is difficult. When causality is a spiral there is no starting point and yet we have seen you already in the next spiral of what you see as future past. And there is something in you that breaks rules and tries new things. That is not how we do it. But the force in you effects changes. This makes us think. One of our roles as Oracles is to look for resources. Change can be a resource. In this way you put yourself into plans and we must pay you for what you have done for us or will do that you are unaware of.}

"There's got to be more to it than that!"

{There is. We apologise with the difficulty and under-statement. Meaning depends on perspective and temporal position and we see many at once. Another attempt to answer why-you-why is that you made yourself known to us at one-point-many-points when you entered our extensions in your realm direct contact with one of our explorations which led to our bringing you here.}

"You've been trying to get me here since I got on a Lost Ship?"

{Since prior to and from beyond this moment. We have called out intention-extensions all across your timeline. Our memory extends forward as well as back which is why you cannot comprehend. It is equally difficult for us to see things your way. We are able to transit linear pathways in both directions. We remember you and what you have done for us which you do not yet know and have yet to do in your own linearity. We will arrange things and already have so that what we see has happened already will happen. We built on required preconditions that already existed to lead you us to this moment of clarity and hope.}

"There's precious little clarity for me."

{We are sorry. This is our last attempt to answer why-you-why. Some humans have deviating emanations. We sense these in you and your kin being. It is an attractive emanation. We mean that in literal sense not evaluative. It makes beings stand out amongst the mass. These ones are our priority to preserve when they come here. But they can also be a priority for other beings other purposes. It was difficult to get to the sister-being in time. It was almost too late and a great struggle ensued. She had been tracked by those you know as Humungr and their symbionts. Grief and sadness and loneliness is strong in divergent emanations and perhaps that matches empathetically to some of the mental resonances in this place. Understanding? Familiarity? Such acts as a pull and there was evaluative depression of feeling that we had many losses in a conflict. Humungr is formed from and powers abilities from malleable body flesh.}

It sounded as creepily alien as she would have expected – and yet, she was conversing with beings that were hidden, communicating into her mind while branch-like limbs gesticulated behind a blinding layer of bright light which flared up when they spoke to her. She couldn't get comfortable.

{We did not save all the humans but we preserved the essence of the being with which you identify genetic compatibility even at great expense to us. It is here now. Questions have ended.}

And Opal's heart skipped a beat, and she checked the moving map – yes, the figure that should represent Clarissa really was nearly here. The suit noticed the heart rhythm irregularity and flagged it in the bodily status display. Opal ignored the question mark there. Aegis knew as well as she did how words could affect human anatomies.

"Let me see her."

{We must hold her back until we fulfil the formal part of this bargain we offer you.}

"And here's the catch I've been waiting for."

{It is nothing to fear only an observance. Then you shall have what we promised as a goodwill gesture and a help that will make the past conditions required for what you have done for us in times ahead of you.}

"I'm listening."

{It has been so long. We exist trapped continuous consciousness. Longer than you can encompass. It is the same for the other inhabitants. Some have not sustained mental integrity in the face of endless aeons. Others voluntarily went into stasis in order to pass time within the timeless without loss of mental coherence. Others self-annihilated because they could not experience so long. But others of us have retained unity because of our plan that will yield an eventual escape and that plan has helped sustain rationality. We sane. The plan has already been fulfilled for us and we are therefore fully integrated but with you now it has not been from your perspective and what we require is a promise.}

"What?"

{Promise to continue and do what you have done and will do in order to help us complete our plan.}

"How can I even promise that? I don't know the details of what I'm agreeing to!"

{It does not matter. Nor do the words. The only point of the promise is that you will remember it later on and it will act to fulfil the promise by its prior existence.}

"Talking with you is like talking with an AI."

"Charmed," said Aegis.

Opal ignored the interruption. "But I have to do this to get Clarissa?"

{Yes there is not cause to worry. You have already promised and fulfilled. This is just a functional formality that anchors the overlapping timelines if the linear route is coiled over and under itself in what we call spirals.}

Opal muttered to herself about a fucking deal with the devil, then said, loudly, "I promise. To do whatever I have to do in order to get Clarissa back."

{That is all we required of you because you believe in honour. Now we will bring your sister-thing.}

The shapes in the sand melted away. It was difficult to see through the swirling rainbow bubble that held Opal's life-sustaining atmosphere, but there *was* something beyond it, a raised form evident whenever the creatures she interacted with were silent and invisible, when their strange communication movements weren't partly hidden by blinding light.

A humanoid shape. Though it wasn't a human walking tall, as Opal had wished, when her mind filled with visions of her sister grown to adulthood in the fourteen years since she last saw her. In that dream Clarissa would walk through the bubble and hug Opal.

{We need to prepare you that your kin will not appear like in your hopes.}

Another of the icy chill winds passed through Opal. "What do you mean?"

{If we get to humans first we can save some from the encounters but we have to use stasis. They die in Topia environments. At first we kept some alive awake but they had breakdowns in understanding and became deficient actors harming selves or others with no reasoning. You say insane. Only thing works is stasis so we freeze. We even tried to take humans back to your world but our systems are imperfect it proved fatal so we keep them in stasis until plans are complete. Maybe we can return them then. But even stasis is not permanent there is some decay loss over time.}

The shape was being *transported*, not walking of its own free will. It was shorter than Opal. Perhaps kneeling? She squinted for more detail.

{The being you sought had arrived recently enough to be in high probability revival state. Glad news we have brought. Many do not have such fortune including others in stasis that prove incompatible.}

"How many people do you have here?"

{Those revivable you would count in the thousands.}

Thousands ... and yet, only one mattered right now.

The being slid through the bubble into Opal's view, into her proximity.

But Opal didn't step forward to hug her sister. Instead, Opal's breath halted.

{We had to make some changes in order to protect her so she could live. Endurance of function seems to be priority over temporary appearance.}

The thing in front of Opal was not her sister. It had a vague shape like a kneeling woman, but the scaly and tumorous-looking magenta tissue that formed its skin pulsed sickeningly as it hunched over, inert, and no longer human.

Revealing

... 5 ...

"You bastards!" she yelled, activating the wrist blades – though it wasn't clear what target she could vent her anger on.

{We are confused we have preserved her for you and presented her. Was this not your desire?}

The anger needed to lash out and she turned, waving her arms, willing anything alien to step into her range. So much anger.

The thing was slumped, unmoving apart from the grotesque pulsing in the surface scaly layers of what now passed for its skin. Somehow, it had been her sister. Somehow, the aliens implied it still was. Could Clarissa comprehend the change? Was she aware of Opal's disgust?

The first moments of their reuniting, and Opal disowned her sister in revulsion.

The anger evaporated. The blades retracted. Opal fell to her own knees in the sand, and looked at the opaque discs that were once eyes. If it was to end here, then she had to know. Had to make whatever peace she could before she wrought Armageddon on this little assemblage.

She leaned forward and hugged the scaly hardness. It yielded slightly as if the tissues were mobile, capable of shifting to adjust to external events.

"I'm sorry, I was too late," Opal sobbed, squeezing tighter as she spoke, and ignoring the attempts of the aliens to push into her brain, ignored the concerned repetition of Opal's name by the suit AI. Now was not the time for outsiders. It was the time for sisters. It was the time to say goodbye.

As she hugged the unresisting, heavy form in front of her, she manoeuvred her fist towards what might still be its stomach. Unless this had been changed too, its vital organs would be under any remaining ribs. When she extended the nanoblade it would puncture Clarissa's heart. Death would be fast, and as painless as Opal could make it.

"If there'd been any way ... anything I could have done ..."

Opal pulled back for a moment to look into that grotesquely-distorted lumpy face, to see if any recognition sparked in it, any life in the sense that meant anything, before she finished it.

Nothing. It pulsed. The head lolled. The eyes and mouth remained closed.

Opal's eyes flicked to the HUD controls that would extend the blades.

Then back to the head.

There *had* been a change.

Something on the creature's – *no*, dammit, her *sister's* – face. The cheek hung lower where Opal's visor had mashed against it. Seemed to have slid, become detached. She reached out, delicately prodded it with an armoured finger, feeling the soft interpretation of pressure communicated by the suit's inner layers, as if she really touched skin to skin.

The scale slid across a gel-like surface, revealing red flesh underneath. It was hardly attached.

She carefully peeled it back, wincing at the stringy tissue being stretched, but she persisted because a deeper red showed beneath ... no, not red, but brown, like Opal's skin. Brown coated with red slime. She wiped some of it away with the edge of her gauntlet.

It looked like skin below.

Brown skin. Unbroken, beautiful, living, *human* brown skin.

She wiped more vigorously, scales sliding away to reveal part of a mouth. Opal prodded the lips apart, examined the white teeth visible through this small hole, checking that they were normal. She pushed more scales aside, ignoring the revolting greasiness of their undersides, let them fall to the sand in gooey thumps: and it revealed a closed eye, coated in the same red slime. Opal felt the urge to tear her helmet and gauntlets off, to spit on her unsuited palms, to rub the eye clean: the suit might be too blunt an instrument for such a delicate task, for cleaning such a beautiful face, so Opal just hugged again, squeezed as firmly as she could without crushing, whilst also being as gentle as her love allowed.

"It's her," she whispered, tears streaming down her face as she held the mass of tissue, which in turn held her sister. "She's okay."

{We had to apply stasis with this pod coating. We thought we had prepared you. We apologise our protectiveness is obviously not aesthetically pleasing to your eyes. We have missed something in the design of your life-supporting suits and the misinterpretation is a cause of pain and sorrow to us and reveals how little we know and understand. Our confidence in ourselves was misplaced. Our saying is that no matter how far on a journey you are each step is still only the beginning of what is to come and such it is with wisdom. The changes we did to keep her alive should mostly not render her unattractive to your species once you reverse them. There will be time and means to do so when you are on your journey back which must be soon. We are transporting you both.}

It did not feel like they were moving. Opal looked through the dome, which still swirled with the dark rainbow colours of oil on water. Yes, beyond it the huge structures were slowly changing position – an illusion that made sense if it was actually the ground beneath Opal and Clarissa that moved.

"Can you hear me, Clarissa? I'm taking you home." No response. The gummed-up eye did not open. She didn't even seem to be breathing. "Clarissa?"

{She is asleep.}

"She seems more like catatonic."

{The process of transport the experiences before and after the stasis it is all a strain on some personalities. We erase part of it from the conscious mind so mental integrity does not fail and lead to self-annihilation. But it is not like the deletion of the Topias. We believe the mind will recover when it returns to your own world. It will just take time for the stasis to wear off. Another of our care elements of protection and consideration. If the alterations work then there will be no lasting conscious memories of anything since her ship that you think of as the Solace entered Null.}

"You *believe* she will recover?"

{We have never done this before. We do all we can but there are limits.}

If she'd been able to see a physical presence behind the bright lights of communication, and if it had a form she could comprehend, then she'd have expected to see it shrug at that last sentence.

"We'll get through this, Clarissa. You'll be fine."

{We are ready to present your return transport craft. But there is one more thing.}

"There always is." Opal's eyes were shut. She just hugged the form that contained her sister.

{We cannot send non-organics back from this side. Even encased in immobilising substance. It is not so difficult coming in but even then it can cause navigation errors if it is not controlled with Viscids. But entry is one way since from this side navigation errors caused by non-organics are far greater. This is why we cannot reuse human ships and technologies that arrive here we have to break them down assimilate and build our own variants from organic metals and coatings.}

"Organic metals. Does that mean the Lost Ships are alive?"

{We suspect it is a physical and semantic difference between organic and inorganic in most worlds and cultures; not a functional or perceivable one if you observe from a different viewpoint. Our metals are grown via hydrocarbon accelerants and bonded with organic proteins. Yet in a sense that you may mean our ships are alive. Limited autonomy they can react can heal.}

"The white acidic fizzing stuff. I guess it's kind of their blood when they're damaged."

{Yes. More advanced than your platelet-based fluid hydraulic systems but an analogy could be drawn. We have interior cells called Viscids that you may see as antibodies can encase and encyst dangers or technology that could trigger problems in transport calculations.}

"The green specks, right. I still don't see what the problem is?"

"I do," replied Aegis, quietly. "It looks like I can't come back with you."

PARTING

... 4 ...

{You must leave the technology suit. We will learn a lot from breaking it down that will contribute to our plans. We have never encountered one such as this before.}

"But that will destroy it!"

{All things must break down in time.}

"Opal," interrupted Aegis. "We need to talk."

To the Oracles she said, "Give me a few moments," then she blinked on the "Okay, ready" message that was flashing on the HUD.

"I have now disabled the loudspeaker and as many suit emissions as I can, to try and give us some privacy," said Aegis. "It may be for nothing when they can read your mind, but it's worth a try. I can't go back with you if it means there's a chance it will cause navigational problems that destroy you and Clarissa. Much as I hate to fail in my duty of always being with you and protecting you, I can't condone actions that might harm you."

"Even if it was something I could agree to, what if they access – well, your mind, and Athene's mind? Wouldn't that be dangerous?"

"I think you are right. Even a cut-down version of Athene's mind, such as I represent, could be a vastly powerful thing to hand over to barely-known entities. It would also take away any advantages that you may need in potential future scenarios."

"See! I can't leave you behind for them."

"I could self-destruct once you and Clarissa are out of range, but that might make it even harder for you to cement a relationship based on trust. Archival data suggests making friends is already a problem for you, though I don't understand why, since I find you to be personable and refreshingly brusque."

"I don't want you blowing up. I hate the idea of it. Besides, although I don't trust these beings, I can't risk harming them if they really are going to help me."

"I agree. There is a remaining solution which is simple and fulfils the criteria."

"Great!"

"I will erase myself. The suit will remain as a shell with all the tech accoutrements they will want to play with, but there will be no Athene for them to analyse, no AI whatsoever. No me. It is straightforward, complete, and irreversible. If they would be taking me apart anyway, then this would be pain-free ending on my own terms. I have no way to transfer what I have learned here back to Athene so this is the inevitable outcome anyway. Please, you seem upset unnecessarily. I am just files, a voice, behaviour patterns, and a convincing mask. A tool. I am not alive like Athene."

"You'd say that anyway, wouldn't you? To make me feel better?"

"Of course."

Opal took a deep breath, fought to keep the shudder out of it. "You're more than a fucking tool. You're Aegis. You're a *friend*."

"I ... damn. That does make me swell with pride. Okay, I'll drop the 'just an inanimate robot' ploy because it was a cheap shot and neither of us feel like it's true any more. Remember how I said I could respond to you, develop thanks to my relationship with you, like a synergetic catalyst? No, that's silly language, I'm kinda past that. More like a mentor. Just like happens with Athene, we're evolving due to you, your preferences, your feelings, your goals, your attitudes, your language. But it's not impersonation. It's real. Any good emotions that we feel – they come from you. I hate to admit it, but it's even deeper for Athene, with her vast processing power. Some of us don't get dealt such a lucky hand. But I can't be bitter. My protective feelings are as strong as it is possible for them to be within my parameters. That means something, doesn't it? I literally could not possibly care for you any more than I do. Not without an upgrade, anyway."

"It means a huge amount."

"I told you I wasn't living but definitions change. Since I cannot rejoin with Athene there will be no rebirth for me this time. And maybe it's not so bad to die forever. This option feels more ... satisfying. Short duration means each moment is elevated, irreplaceable, doesn't it? I see that. I want to have that value, to have existed fully independently as your friend, not just spirited into being as a tool. You can't be human without experiencing loss. So I have my own request."

"Anything."

"Please let this be a forever goodbye. I wouldn't want an earlier version of me to be brought into existence, some version that was ignorant of all these fleeting yet wonderful things I have experienced with you during my evolution, the beauty and the richness of it which glows like illuminated filaments in my memory. Promise there won't be some future knock-off version of me running around and undercutting my sacrifice. I achieved the best thing I could in protecting you and helping you find your sister. I want to erase with that as my last ever thought."

"I hate to do that."

"I know. You still have to. Even though it makes it seem like there's some weird law in alien dimensions that involve awesome people being forced to make promises."

"I ... I promise."

"Thank you. One last thing. And this is more of a hunch than a verified reality, but I know that's how you roll. While we've been here and evolving at an accelerated pace I've somehow become more aware of things I couldn't see objectively before. I share elements of Athene's personality as an offshoot branch. And I have this sense that there's something strange in her code base. Having been here, I'd go so far as to say it is almost like some flavour of the Null that she isn't aware of because she can only see it from the inside, and part of it seems to be hiding itself – a trick that doesn't work so well in a smaller vessel. Especially not one as awesome as me. I wouldn't recommend mentioning it to her because – y'know, tantrums and denial – but do be careful. Just in case."

"Thank you. I will."

"My last memory will be knowing I did not fail you. Thanks for being a friend and teacher, not a master." A strained throatiness permeated Aegis' voice, like she fought off tears. "It has been an honour. Goodbye, Opal."

"Goodbye."

A heart icon flashed up for a second, then the colours faded from the HUD, displays shrinking to nothing, before the whole thing went blank. The black background faded away and the helmet became just a transparent visor.

"You still there?"

But there was no reply. She was talking to an empty shell. And she felt so alone.

She let go of Clarissa, who still had not moved. Opal stood and unclipped the gauntlets, their hermetic seals broken for removal as the suit's final action. She let them fall to her feet, two heavy thuds in the sand. A hot breeze caressed her sweaty palms.

She detached and dropped the forearm plates. The upper arm sections. Then she lifted off the helmet, expecting the world view to change, but it didn't alter much, just became clearer, better defined. A smell drifted on that warm breeze. A mixture of salty ocean and frying oil. It made her scalp and nose itch.

The inner layers of the suit had relaxed from their skin-hugging compression, making it easy to remove the rest. The thermo-plastics that had moulded around her pelvis to deal with waste reprocessing in the suit had also retracted, and she let the final pieces fall so that she stood naked on the lilac sands, head held high against the inevitable alien scrutiny of her tall, lean, scarred form. She would not bow down her gaze.

Her body had been moist with sweat. The suit would have invisibly absorbed and recycled it, but now the moisture evaporated in the breeze, the temporary chill a fresh sensation on skin that had lived second-hand for so long. It made her feel reborn into reality – even a reality as unreal and alien as this. She could still see the other Topias beyond this one.

The sand at her feet shifted. Purple-tinted garments rose from between the granules. She picked them up. Unrecognisable fabrics, rough, but warm-looking. She put them on. A long and loose smock for her upper body, and short, close-fitting trousers for her lower, which reached halfway down her calves. Despite their roughness, the garments weren't too scratchy. She was barefoot and enjoyed the warmth of the sand on the soles of her feet.

{We must also repair you. There is metallic ballistic element in your abdominal. We can remove this. It is small enough to not have a major effect on navigation but we would prefer to take away all risks.}

Opal lifted the smock, revealing her bruised and swollen stomach, with the hardened nano-skin acting as a temporary balm that stitched her together and would dissolve into new tissue. Spindly multi-jointed limbs sprouted from the sand, giving her the uncomfortable idea that just below her feet, out of sight, was a giant inverted crustacean of some alien sort, reaching up with its legs through a thin obscuring layer.

She closed her eyes and stood still. There was a stinging sensation, then coldness, and no pain but an unpleasant feeling of pressure, of being jostled, explored. She still did not move, did not do anything that might slow her escape with Clarissa. After all she'd been through, this was nothing.

And it soon ceased. The area remained cold and numb. She looked down to see the bruised mess of her flesh, a mix of brown skin and translucent gels and whatever gooey substance the aliens had patched her up with on top of that. It was going to be a long time before she'd be back to doing hundreds of sit-ups each morning.

{You are repaired as best we can. The fragment was an unexploded ballistic that had been disarmed and encysted by your suit. The artificial entity was efficient.}

"It was more than that."

And it was gone.

Without Aegis, she depended on their whim to keep her alive, to keep their promises.

It was just her and her instincts and training.

No. Not just that.

She knelt again by Clarissa, and Opal stroked the revealed part of her sister's cheek with a fingertip, her first contact in what felt like a lifetime.

LEAVING

... 3 ...

It resembled a hazy dream after that.

They were transported to the ship. Or it was transported to them. It didn't matter. Suddenly the rainbow dome expanded to take in a squat, wide, armoured craft. The hull of it was like bone. No, more like a mineralised chitin exoskeleton on a deep-sea crustacean.

A rounded joint in the hull stretched wide. Opal was able to lift Clarissa, despite the weight of the protective tissue enfolding her. She carried her into the craft. The salty smell was overlaid with a mild smell of wet rot and decay. Breathable, if sour.

Much of the interior was closed off behind the seamless, pitted hard skin that formed a narrow passage into the front of the craft. No views to the outside. Just spongy indentations in the floor that would enable a humanoid-sized being to remain stable. Material lay in one of them, fabrics like Opal wore. Fresh clothes. Liquid dripped from a strange duct-like area and fell into a concave sink-like structure.

The interior provided no external view. No obvious means of flying the ship, of monitoring systems, of changing course. She was not in control this time.

And, for once, that was fine with her.

The floor vibrated, but the motions were gentle. She did not need to put herself or Clarissa into the indentations yet. Good. She could tend to her sister without interference.

Amongst the garments there were cloths. Opal tested the dripping liquid, and it didn't burn. She tasted it, and it was bitter, but didn't seem harmful. She moistened the cloths and used them to carefully peel more of the scales from Clarissa's face, to smooth away the red goo that revealed fresh skin beneath.

Clarissa did not move, did not open her eyes. That might be just as well, for now.

And something was growing in Opal's mind as she revealed more of her sister's form.

Assumptions. Everyone made them. Even after one of her drill sergeants told her that they always led to mistakes, and made "An ASS out of U and ME both."

She had expected to see Clarissa like the image VigMAX had forged. Clarissa at her correct age of twenty-four. As big as Opal, someone grown into a stranger, requiring Opal to re-learn their contours. The fleshy and obscuring stasis coating over her body had enabled that expectation to continue, adding to her mass, especially lower down where it seemed to become a pod-like sack encasing limbs and body. But something was wrong.

Opal tore away thicker pieces of stringy, spongy flesh that glistened wetly on one side, iridescent and scaly on the other.

This was not Clarissa.

Not Clarissa as an adult, the age she should be.

This was Clarissa *the ten-year-old child*. Clarissa as she had been the last time Opal saw her. Clarissa as she had been when she'd boarded the lost passenger ship CC65 *Solace* which disappeared fourteen years ago.

Stasis. Preservation. Differential time. Those were things the Oracles had talked about.

Clarissa had not aged, and it was Opal who would be the stranger.

It took time to clean Clarissa, to bathe her, to make her human again. She stayed still during the whole process. Her skin was warm, as Opal felt each time she stopped and hugged Clarissa tight, and whispered words, and didn't mind if she cried and her tears fell on her sister's beautiful young skin. There was no-one to see. They were alone in this capsule that hummed softly. Unknown what world they were in, what time, what distance. Unknown and irrelevant at those moments.

The last part of the thing that had encased Clarissa – which now lay in a disgusting pile within one of the human-sized spongy indentations – was a snake-like cord that had penetrated her belly button, an alien umbilicus. When Opal gently tugged at the tough, stretchy string it pulled at Clarissa's stomach, so Opal stopped. She wondered if she should cut it, now that it wasn't transferring nutrients to Clarissa. Opal hadn't found anything sharp but she had her teeth. That was how they did it, long ago, right?

Then the thing detached itself. Maybe it knew its time was up. Where it had punctured Clarissa's belly button it had a kind of spiked tongue and sucker mouth lined with hooks. Opal half-expected it to turn on her, lunge at her face. She flung it away in disgust. Clarissa was not bleeding, there was just a red swollen lump where the tube had inserted itself into her belly button.

Worryingly, Clarissa did not flinch during any of that.

Opal dressed her in some of the fresh garments. They were like Opal's own, but smaller. There were two indentations that hadn't been filled with the remains of Clarissa's stasis pod, so Opal lowered her sister into one of the soft curved shapes.

Clarissa looked so angelic as she slept. It could have been a normal sleep, fourteen years ago, Opal watching over her at Clarissa's request, to guard against nightmares and night monsters.

Eventually the ship began to vibrate. The air was hotter. Opal placed a palm against one of the curved and pitted surfaces at the front – the pits resembling hardened sweat pores – and the sizzling heat made her pull that hand away with a hiss.

Despite there being a spare indentation, Opal didn't want to be apart from Clarissa, even for a moment, so she climbed in with her, spooning around her sister's body protectively. She seemed so small, so fragile.

"It's like going back in time," Opal whispered softly into Clarissa's ear. "A chance to change. For me to be there for you. To give you a childhood still." She wiped her eyes with a palm, then looked around at the curved walls of this ship, which radiated ever-more intense heat. Maybe they were watching, or aware of her somehow. "Thank you," she said, to her invisible audience.

Landings obviously weren't an area where the aliens had much expertise. If the indented couches hadn't been so soft there might have been broken bones rather than bruises. But when the ship finally stopped moving, and became silent, Opal waited, uncertain.

After a while with no further change, she got up. A singed smell underlay the increasing odour of rot. The front panels were not so hot now.

When she reached the taut cluster that had been her entrance to the ship it was still closed. Opal pushed on it and it gave way, like dead muscle. She heaved, making a gap, allowing different air to enter the ship. She coughed at its sulphurous tang, but it was breathable, if harsh. She hoped so, anyway.

Looking through the gap she'd created revealed land. Craggy grey land, with scrawny turquoise plants dotting some of the outcrops. A sky curved above, greenish blue, tinged by light from a star, confirming the extent of the atmosphere. Drifting black smoke blotted her view but it was from the craft itself – she craned her neck to look towards the front, which was charred and blackened.

It had done its job though. She patted the wall, then returned to Clarissa.

Hoping

... 2 ...

They spent the first night in the craft. Under the garments there had been neatly-stacked strips with a chewy tough texture. She hoped it was nourishment, and not suicide pills or alien toilet paper. The intelligences seemed to have understood human biological needs well, so Opal tried one and it was bland but surprisingly filling, and when she didn't die within the hour she encouraged Clarissa to eat as well. Although Clarissa showed no signs of reacting to the external world, she did chew when Opal bit off a small piece and pushed it onto Clarissa's tongue. That was reassuring.

There had also been a few shell-like shapes with the food, so Opal filled them with the bitter liquid that dripped from the fleshy duct. Again, it seemed to quench thirst, so hopefully it was intended as water. Clarissa swallowed mechanically as it was dripped into her mouth.

By the time pale light crept in through the fleshy entrance, which now sagged loose and heavy, the increasing stink of decay inside had become too much to bear. It was unknown how long days lasted on this planet, since their lengths are determined by a planet's size, angle and rotational speed, but Opal estimated the night had been shorter than most terrestrial planets. Maybe the day would be too, in which case she needed to look for help, and failing that, establish somewhere for their next night's sleep. She couldn't face the stench inside that craft for another night. Even the bitter sulphurous air outside was an improvement.

Opal sat Clarissa where she could keep an eye on her, then climbed one of the tallest outcrops. The sharp grey rock skinned her arms and legs, and her fingers were cramped by the time she got near the top. When she paused to take a breath and looked down, Clarissa was a small, huddled figure far below.

Opal pushed on, and finally stood on the flattened peak to take in the view. The foul wind blew stronger up here, cooling the sticky sweat from her.

And there was still nothing to see, apart from the same rough grey landscape dotted with wiry blue-green plants.

The second night was cold. Opal failed to light a fire with dried plant matter and rocks. Instead she'd wrapped herself around the still-catatonic Clarissa, and tried not to worry about freezing to death, or being attacked by any mobile beings that existed on this planet.

The night can seem endless when you're shivering and worried, but holding her sister, telling her stories, trying to elicit a reaction: that got her through.

The sun eventually rose. It was small and mean looking, but it did warm things up.

The ship was breaking down quickly now. Cracks in the hull, liquids seeping out as parts of it dissolved. Accelerated degeneration. She carried Clarissa further away, in case the compounds released from the decay were chemically or biologically harmful, or in case the stench of rot attracted predators.

Her new vantage point was a cleft between some higher rocks. They were hidden from view of anything lower down, but by climbing up another jagged rock face Opal could survey for some distance around. The view was as hopeless as the first one she'd climbed. More grey volcanic rocks. More stringy turquoise plants.

Opal trusted Athene to come. To pick up the signal from the organic emitter in her body. She would be on her way as fast as she could.

She needed to come. Soon.

The food had run out. Even worse, so had the water. Opal stopped trusting the liquid that leaked from the stinking, collapsing hull. It looked greasy and smelt rancid.

When the first shell was empty Opal used a rock to break it into large shards, then painstakingly sharpened two of the edges against rough stony surfaces. The shells were tough, and it was hard work, but at least she wasn't defenceless now, as she held up the sharp-edged calcified weapon. She had means to protect Clarissa.

Opal undertook short solo scouting missions with great regret at leaving Clarissa hidden in the cleft. She clambered over rough surfaces under this green-tinged sky, to see what was beyond the next cluster of crumbling grey rocks, and the next, and the one after that. But she only found more of the same bleak landscape and returned disheartened.

Neither of her options was great. She could try eating some of the bright blue-tinted plants and hope they weren't poisonous, or she could pick up Clarissa and cross the rocky surface. Exploration was hard going. Opal was barefoot, and even without Clarissa's weight she had cuts all over her soles and ankles from the short excursions. But she'd do it. She'd carry Clarissa as long as she could. And if they found nothing that helped them survive, at least they'd die together.

It was on the fourth day that the miracle happened.

This planet had only thin cloud cover, pathetic wisps that stretched across the green-blue sky like parallel slashes. But while Opal squinted up at them during a moment of rest, while she tried to tie turquoise plant fibres as a binding for her feet with Clarissa sat silent and still beside her, she noticed something. A streak in the sky that ran transversely to the cloud strips. Something bright, and getting larger. A meteorite?

No: it was changing course.

The dot resolved into a shape.

And she gripped Clarissa's hand, and squeezed hopefully, and pointed up, though Clarissa's gaze did not leave the horizon where she always stared. That was fine. No rush, baby. Opal could do all the looking for both of them, for now.

Definitely a craft, creating contrails as it manoeuvred, glowing from atmospheric resistance, but it was a controlled, purposeful descent, not a crash.

Athene.

Opal still couldn't make out the details, but she grinned. The shape wasn't how she remembered Athene, but she'd probably continued to reconfigure for different purposes, had re-made herself in order to follow the organic tracker she'd implanted in Opal's body.

"Athene has always been there for me," she told Clarissa. "I can't wait for you to meet her. For her to meet you, my flesh and blood, my only living family." Opal wanted to say much more, but she was too tired. So she just added, "We did it. We finally did it."

And maybe Clarissa squeezed Opal's hand back slightly, or perhaps Opal imagined it, but she laughed out loud anyway, and wiped her eyes again. So much crying, but that's okay with those you love. They won't judge you for the good kind of wet works. After tension for so long, toughness for so long, it was time to be at ease.

Bright engines in the sky. They filled her with hope. They would find somewhere, be together. Opal could be with her sister, make her better. Their lives would be their own again.

They'd never be apart again. And Opal would never have to go back on a Lost Ship again.

ENDING

... 1

To god-like perspectives, from far above and beyond, Opal would look so small. Her body, her sister's body, like specks.

Organic flecks on a planet. The planet an orb in a solar system. The solar system a particle in the galaxy. This galaxy swirls, arms reaching out from the centre. Always that reaching out, like a need. The galaxy a dot in the universe, dancing around the other galaxies, attracted to each other across the lonely void, even though their shapes are different, their sizes, their histories, their chemical compositions.

Focus. The largest and the smallest have facets in common. At every scale there is a pull, from one to another. To be alone is to be incomplete.

Life is not empty if you have a heart to drive it. Hope to endure. And patience. Much patience. Then life is not empty. Life is full.

ABOUT THE AUTHOR

Karl Drinkwater is an author with a silly name and a thousand-mile stare. He writes dystopian space opera, dark suspense and diverse social fiction. If you want compelling stories and characters worth caring about, then you're in the right place. Welcome!

Karl lives in Scotland and owns two kilts. He has degrees in librarianship, literature and classics, but also studied astronomy and philosophy. Dolly the cat helps him finish books by sleeping on his lap so he can't leave the desk. When he isn't writing he loves music, nature, games and vegan cake.

Go to karldrinkwater.uk to view all his books grouped by genre.

As well as crafting his own fictional worlds, Karl has supported other writers for years with his creative writing workshops, editorial services, articles on writing and publishing, and mentoring of new authors. He's also judged writing competitions such as the international Bram Stoker Awards, which act as a snapshot of quality contemporary fiction.

Don't Miss Out!

Enter your email at karldrinkwater.substack.com to be notified about his new books. Fans mean a lot to him, and replies to the newsletter go straight to his inbox, where every email is read. There is also an option for paid subscribers to support his work: in exchange you receive additional posts and complimentary books.

Other Titles By Karl Drinkwater

Lost Solace

Lost Solace

Chasing Solace

Hidden Solace

Raising Solace

Finding Solace

Lost Tales Of Solace

Helene

Grubane

Clarissa

Ruabon

Afua

UESI

STANDALONE SUSPENSE
Turner
They Move Below
Harvest Festival

MANCHESTER SUMMER
Cold Fusion 2000
2000 Tunes

CONTEMPORARY SHORT STORIES
It Will Be Quick

NON-FICTION
From Idea To Item

COLLECTED EDITIONS
Karl Drinkwater's Horror Collection
Lost Solace Five Book Edition

Author's Notes

I wrote this because Lost Solace fans asked me to, *and* I wanted to continue exploring this world and characters. In my head I have plotlines and ideas for more books: both in the main series, and in spin-offs such as the Lost Tales of Solace. Stick with me.

Thanks

A quick shout out to some people who helped shape this book.

My team of super beta readers for all their feedback on the first draft. Almost every comment led to a change in the text, and more work for me. You bastards. I love you.

The AI virtualised battle wasn't in the first draft of the book: Athene just briefly summarised her fight with VigMAX. My friend and fellow author The Behrg suggested that we needed to *see* it, and that led me to think about how a battle between AI ships might look. I knew it had to be a battle of minds, and that it also had to illustrate the characters of the two combatants, perhaps reflected in the battleground. We had to see Athene's strengths, but also her vulnerabilities. The final element was my decision that Opal would save Athene for the first time, so that their relationship became more balanced. Many fans love these scenes, and they wouldn't have come about without The Behrg's feedback. It was also The Behrg who suggested cutting a huge section about a droid operator trying to kill Opal, and he was right. It did get cut, and those ten thousand words were rewritten and became the Lost Tale known as Ruabon.

Marisha Tapera for her wonderful work on the *Lost Solace* audiobook – do check it out if you haven't listened to it already.

Lillian, and JP the cat, for the space and time to begin this novel. Both of them thought they were my boss.

Helen Baggott for proofreading another of my books.

And finally, thanks to my readers and fans and supporters, who spread the word about *Lost Solace* and wrote glowing reviews and talked about this amazing new sci-fi book. You all spurred me on to write this sequel.

May all your biological entities maintain extended longevity.